I0762531

THE MIDNIGHT SHOW

THE MIDNIGHT SHOW

A NOVEL

LEE KELLY AND
JENNIFER THORNE

CROWN
NEW YORK

CROWN
An imprint of the Crown Publishing Group
A division of Penguin Random House LLC
1745 Broadway
New York, NY 10019
crownpublishing.com
penguinrandomhouse.com

Library of Congress Cataloging-in-Publication Data
Names: Kelly, Lee author | Thorne, Jennifer, 1980– author
Title: The midnight show : a novel / Lee Kelly and Jennifer Thorne.
Description: First edition. | New York City : Crown, 2026. |
Identifiers: LCCN 2025022248 (print) | LCCN 2025022249 (ebook) |
ISBN 9798217086672 hardcover | ISBN 9798217086696 trade paperback |
ISBN 9798217086689 ebook
Subjects: LCGFT: Humorous fiction | Novels | Fiction
Classification: LCC PS3611.E4498 M53 2026 (print) | LCC PS3611.E4498 (ebook)
LC record available at https://lccn.loc.gov/2025022248
LC ebook record available at https://lccn.loc.gov/2025022249

Hardcover ISBN 979-8-217-08667-2
Ebook ISBN 979-8-217-08668-9

Editor: Amy Einhorn | Assistant editor: Austin Parks |
Production editor: Liana Parry Faughnan | Text designer: Aubrey Khan |
Production: Heather Williamson | Copy editor: Sibylle Kazeroid |
Proofreader: Robin Slutzky | Publicist: Lindsay Cook | Marketer: Kimberly Lew

Manufactured in the United States of America

1st Printing

First Edition

For Jon and for Pam
You'd both have liked this one

Why are women, who have the whole male world at their mercy, not funny? Please do not pretend not to know what I am talking about. All right—try it the other way (as the bishop said to the barmaid). Why are men, taken on average and as a whole, funnier than women?

—Christopher Hitchens,
Vanity Fair

THE MIDNIGHT SHOW

To: DL Walker—Director of Features
From: Madeline Cohen
Date: April 12, 2023 9:47 AM
Subject: Pitch—What Really Happened to Lillian Martin

DL,

I've got a longer feature pitch for you—maybe even a cover story (?).

This year marks the 40th anniversary of *Midnight Show* breakout star Lillian Martin's death. She was the gold standard in sketch comedy, a guiding light for entire generations of female comedians, and yet nearly every *TMS* history/documentary/op-ed out there casts Martin's story in shadow, reducing her legacy to her tragic demise instead of her obvious talent. Consider the primary source on this subject:

> Perhaps the greatest contribution Lillian Martin made to *The Midnight Show* (however taboo it may be to suggest) is the air of danger and mystique her shatteringly short stint lent to the institution early on: a coupling of cutting-edge comedy with a sense of living on the edge.
>
> —Philip Horton,
> *It Started at Midnight: A TMS History*

As a conflicted *TMS* fan, I hope to tell a more complicated story. This piece would consider Lillian's life and legacy in the context of an industry that categorizes, commodifies, dismisses, and discards funny women—both at that time and pervasively today—and ultimately, how the comedy world contributed to her fall.

Feels like it could be timely. Let me know what you think.

All best,
Madeline
Culture Writer
Rolling Stone

To: Madeline Cohen
From: DL Walker—Director of Features
Date: April 12, 2023 10:23 AM
Subject: Re: Pitch—What Really Happened to Lillian Martin

I dig it, M, love *The Midnight Show,* but can't promise anything placementwise. Hate to be crass, but a cover story about a long-dead celeb is gonna have to have a scoop.

Now, if you can find new dirt about the night she died and work that into your angle, that's a different story (as in cover story of the year).

Keep me in the loop.

Dave
DL Walker
Features Director
Rolling Stone

PROJECT FILES

I.
BREAKING IN

The [Not So] Aspirational Comic
[1958–1980]

COMPILED TRANSCRIPTS— LILLIAN'S CHILDHOOD

(Transcribing and chronologically arranging project interviews as I have them)

First up: Glenn Martin— May 5, 4:00 P.M. ET—Zoom call

BACKGROUND: Martin is Lillian's older brother—nine years Lillian's senior, he still lives in Canada, about ten miles from their childhood home (both parents have died).

MADELINE: Thanks so much for taking the time, Glenn. As I mentioned in my email, I'm hoping to get a holistic sense of your sister, who she was before joining *The Midnight Show*. Do you want to just start from the early days? As far back as you can remember would be great.

GLENN MARTIN: Okay, sure. Well, Lillian and I grew up in Bradville, small town here in Ontario. Rural Canada—we're not talking Toronto. Our dad had been the local doctor for a long time. Our mom was a homemaker. She had a master's in poetry, so she was no slouch brainwise, but she gave all that up when she got married. And I was a good deal older than Lillie, nine years. I think she was a bit of a happy surprise. Mom was already, I think, gosh, forty-two when she had her, so they were older parents for sure by the time Lillian came around. I don't know if that affected her in a negative way. If that was what made her kind of . . . how do I put this?

Lillie was *funny*. And by funny, I don't mean in the sense of comedy, although clearly she was quite a funny lady later on. But, you know, as a child, she was an odd duck. She spent a lot of time by herself. *A lot*. She had this big old walk-in closet in her bedroom, which used to be a storage pantry. We used to find her in there with the door shut, paperback books stacked all around, and sort of . . . talking to herself.

I don't mean to make it sound like she was crazy or anything like that. I think she just enjoyed her own company more than anybody else's. And growing up, truth be told, she didn't have a whole lot of friends. It was never a worry—she wasn't unpopular, did after-school activities like chess club. I think she did that through high school, actually. Competitions and everything. And then there was 4-H.

Madeline: 4-H, the farming club? Was she an animal lover?

Glenn Martin: Absolutely. We weren't allowed to have pets—our parents weren't up for that—so there you go. Yeah, so she was active enough, sociable to some extent, but I don't think she ever had a boyfriend or anything like that. She'd go to the dances with a date, but you never got the sense it was anything serious, just sort of a friend of a friend.

I don't think Lillie even kept in touch with anybody from home after she left for college. By the time she was old enough for me to get to know her, I wasn't home a whole lot, living in Ottawa, you know, so we never formed much of a bond. And she wasn't real close with our parents either. As long as she was doing all right, getting good grades, keeping out of trouble, then they were happy to let her do what she wanted to do and not ask a lot of questions.

Madeline: Would you say she was someone who kept secrets?

[*He shifts, pausing for a while before answering.*]

Glenn Martin: She must have been. From the very beginning. And, I mean, gosh, it was all secrets in the end, wasn't it?

NOTES

Sam Petrosian—
May 12, 2:00 P.M. ET—Zoom call

BACKGROUND: Sam met Lillian in college and starred alongside her on *The Midnight Show* before moving on, in typical '80s funny guy fashion, to write or act in nearly every major comedy blockbuster for the next two decades. *Neighborhood Cops, Parent Pains I* and *II,* all five of the Demon Squad movies.

Now he's almost seventy—a little less aw-shucks "boy next door," more "Get off my lawn." The trademark floppy hair is pure gray, the dimples deepened by wrinkles, but he still has residual charm. Unlike some of the noted womanizers in the *TMS* first class (see: Kent Romero), Sam always came across as remarkably grounded despite his good looks. Of course, that could just be the image he's best at selling.

MADELINE: You and Lillian were close long before *TMS*. Did you two ever talk about her childhood?

SAM PETROSIAN (*TMS* CAST MEMBER, 1980–1983): Not often, but, you know, over the years, Lillian did tell me enough to paint the most charmingly eccentric picture. She had a pantry, her own personal cubby, and she'd store herself in there as if it were an imagination chamber. She used to go on all the time about how much she missed that pantry, wished she had one in New York. I always pictured Canadian kitsch, Anne of Green Gables surrounded by jars of preserves, heavens to Betsy, gingham ribbons in her hair. Lillie was as stubborn as Anne Shirley, I'll tell you that much. There were moments she'd have broken a slate or two over my head.

I know she held on to a lot of guilt about her parents. She was distant from them and blamed herself for it, like she needed to make more of an effort to pretend to be the sort of human being they would prefer to have as a daughter. Never a question of whether they could have been warmer human beings to her, but I never pressed her on it. We didn't have that kind of relationship. I absorbed every word she said as holy writ and nodded along comfortingly. I suppose the more charitable description of that dynamic is that I gave her space. Maybe I should have questioned Lillian more over the years, now that I look back on everything. I don't know.

I think despite not being particularly, let's say, cherished by her family, Lillian did grow up sheltered. Wide-eyed, but not in some Christian Coalition way. She was more like a being from an alternate dimension who'd accidentally slipped into our world, and every single thing was new to her. The good and the bad. I'm not sure she was ever fully able to tell the difference between the two. But then it's not exactly my strong suit either.

GLENN MARTIN: By the time college rolled around, Lillie was raring to get out of Bradville and never look back. I mean, she left the durn country, so that tells you something. She went to Boston University. I don't think our folks necessarily knew that she'd even applied there, but she got a scholarship and went off to study French—that's what she told us, anyway. She'd won a bunch of awards for her French in high school, didn't do drama or anything like that. So when she's down in Massachusetts for college and, you know, we find out that she's in these comedy shows, it came a bit out of left field. We thought, "What? No. You're talking about a different Lillian Martin!"

There was a big old disconnect, no doubt about it. We thought she wanted to become a professor. You know, after everything that happened, all the press about her lifestyle, the partying or what have you, Mom really beat herself up. She kept rehashing Lillian's whole life over and over again, saying, "Was she lying to us, starting from when she was a kid?" Not just the acting but, you know, doing drugs, drinking? I don't think that was the case back home, I really don't, but . . . there was obviously this hidden side to her all along.

There's a lot we're never really gonna understand about Lillie. No chance of figuring it out now. Or maybe there is, if you're writing this article. Who knows.

COMPILED TRANSCRIPTS—LILLIAN'S "TOWNIES" ERA

MADELINE: So how did the Townies first start? Was Lillian there from the very beginning?

SAM PETROSIAN: No, not at all. It started with me and Stevie Doyle, who I assume you've spoken to as well?

MADELINE: I wrote him a few times, but he hasn't responded.

SAM PETROSIAN: I could see Stevie being a little wary of talking about Lillian.

MADELINE: I'm sensitive to that. I know it's a difficult subject.

SAM PETROSIAN: It's not that, it's . . . Stevie carries around so much baggage these days, he's practically a bellhop. I'll get him to write you back.

But you asked about the Townies! Without boring you with too many personal details, I grew up outside Boston, went to middle school and high school with Stevie. At first, we were more what the kids call "frenemies." We competed to be the preeminent class clown, which our teachers did not appreciate at the time. Later, we worked on the school paper together, and very quickly grew bored, so on the weekends, we put together a satirical alternate newspaper lampooning the teachers and administration. We nearly got expelled over that one.

Stevie was the better student of the two of us, but I was the one who could actually get a date, believe it or not. Now, Kent [Romero] likes to paint me and Stevie as working-class heroes, just so he can seem more "of the people" by association, but the truth is, we're both from middle-class households. We went to college with minimal financial aid, let's put it that way. We just weren't international jet-setter children like Kent "We're Not Rich, We're Comfortable" Romero.

Anyway, Stevie got into Harvard. I didn't even apply—you kidding? It was a big win for me to get into BU. But we kept palling around. We'd go to a bar midway between our campuses, drink cheap beer, and scheme. At first we talked about doing a wider version of our newspaper, but then Stevie met this older kid in his dorm freshman year, wouldn't stop talking about how hip he was, how brilliant. I got pretty sick of hearing about this guy, to be honest, suggested Stevie invite him out with us just so he'd finally shut up about him, and one night, in through the door walks this absolute mannequin, just white teeth, bronze skin, thick dark hair, jawline of a god, so tall he nearly beans his head on the bar light. Kent's first-generation Venezuelan American, obviously, but I didn't know that at the time. I just thought he was from Olympus. As in Mount.

So now I'm thinking, "Gosh, this is it, Stevie's gonna come out of the closet and this is his boyfriend and damn, good for you, Stevie, what a score!" I was wrong about that, just to be clear.

Madeline: Duly noted.

Sam Petrosian: You know, Kent always had an almost toxic level of charisma. You could see girls turning to look at him, just about falling off their barstools to gawk at this, what, nineteen-year-old kid. And Kent walks up to me, slings an arm around my shoulder like he's known me all my life, and goes, "So, what are the townies drinking tonight?" Meaning us.

I wasn't sure whether to smack him in his stupid pretty face at that point, but then he started buying us rounds, so I figured he could hang out with us again. And that, by the way, is how we wound up coming up with the name of our little improv group.

And it *was* improv. People say "sketch" about the Townies, even though to this day, they still teach improv, not sketch, all over the country.

MADELINE: I was briefly a Townie before I moved to New York. I took classes at the Hollywood branch, on Sunset.

SAM PETROSIAN: Oh wow, look at that! Gosh, I hope you got something out of it. I've heard mixed things over the years.

MADELINE: Mixed is fair. I mean, it's definitely expensive. And it's tough to move up the levels and actually get a place in any shows. For me, anyway. I was trying to get staffed as a comedy writer at the time, and I thought improv might help. I think if I learned anything, honestly, it was that I am not a performer.

SAM PETROSIAN: That can happen! And hey, now you're at *Rolling Stone,* so that's nothing to sneeze at. Anyway, we sold the rights a long time ago. Me, Kent, and Stevie. We do still own a share in the franchise, but when we founded it, it was . . .

[*He laughs, recollecting.*]

It was literally in Kent's living room, with random chairs and sofas lined up like rows of seats in a theater. Like we were little kids performing for their parents. We were way too broke to rent a space, so that was our solution.

MADELINE: Including Kent? I thought his family came from money.

SAM PETROSIAN: Well, Kent was given a very rudimentary spending allowance by his parents—that Latin American immigrant-made-good heritage, trying to give him a strong backbone, which is a terrifying prospect if you've ever met Kent. Have you met him?

MADELINE: Not yet.

SAM PETROSIAN: He's a battering ram with arms and legs. Anyway, for all practical purposes, we were beyond broke. Stevie worked at a pizza place far enough off campus to avoid it having a ripple effect on his Harvard reputation. Kent and I used to sneak in the back during his shifts and eat the slices nobody wanted with ancient oil puddles on top. We were the human equivalent of wharf rats. But when we weren't scrounging for survival, attending the bare minimum of college classes, waking up still wasted from dorm parties, we'd meet up at one of our places—usually Kent's, because he had a room in an actual townhouse—and we'd talk about comedy. What we liked, what we were sick of, what we thought was the next wave, what was exciting, and to us, that was improv, not sketch. Obviously, we got less snooty about it all when *The Midnight Show* came calling, but at the time, we were *artistes*. We talked it all to death before ever stepping onstage—and still, *still,* we were leagues behind somebody like Lillian Martin, who understood improv at her core, despite having had no experience with it prior to joining us.

MADELINE: So when did Lillian enter the picture?

SAM PETROSIAN: You know, it's hard for me to pinpoint when and where I first saw Lillian. She was there in my subconscious for a long time, like I'd hallucinated her before we ever formally met. It must have been on the Boston University campus or thereabouts. I was majoring in business, at my father's insistence. Thanks, Dad. She was studying something delightfully random—French Arthurian romance, something like that?—but she took the core curriculum like the rest of us mere mortals. There was an elective drama class for those of us who either hadn't passed the auditions for the fancy BU drama program or didn't want to immediately commit to a life of penury and struggle at the age of eighteen. She was in that class her freshman year, but I don't think she showed up more than twice. It wasn't her bag.

She seemed to just drift in and out of classes. Out of parties more than into them. I remember seeing her in the student union on St. Paddy's Day, sitting on a sofa, looking around like she'd been teleported there—just deeply, deeply confused. As if the party had coagulated around her and she wasn't sure how to escape. Sure enough, before I could go up and introduce myself, she was out the door and poof, gone. And whenever you'd ask someone, in the dining hall, wherever, *Hey, who is that girl over there, the one who looks like one of the fairies in those fake Victorian photos, the one with the crazy long wavy hair and huge eyes?*, nobody ever knew!

I'd pretty much convinced myself she was a ghost when one day, I was out distributing flyers for the Townies—this would be senior year, by which point we'd graduated to a regular weekly gig at a dive bar on Commonwealth, but I still, you know, had to hand out flyers on the street corner like a busker—and I saw her and crossed traffic to hand her a flyer. I said something insanely intense, I'm sure, like, "The Townies, tomorrow night, you won't regret it, you'll never be the same!" And she said, "Okay." Which I figured was a brush-off, and fair enough. But then Friday night rolled around and there she was in the audience. I couldn't believe it. She might have thought we were a cult, or some political extremist group, not sure what it says about either of us that she turned up, but there you go. We won her over. And vice versa.

NOTES

Kent Romero—
May 15, 5:15 P.M. ET—Google Meet

BACKGROUND: Another lauded member of *The Midnight Show*'s first class, Kent Romero has mined his "bad boy" image for an impressively long run: his '80s John Landis era, as irreverent host of *The Late Hour,* his recent "Goldenrager" flicks, in which he nails the role of a suave retirement community gigolo. He might be past seventy now—salt-and-pepper hair, deep fans around his eyes—but he's still wildly charismatic, and he seems to delight in knowing it.

Behind Kent, there's a minimalist white-timbered living room with floor-to-ceiling windows showcasing a rosy desert panorama in the distance. His ranch.

KENT ROMERO (*TMS* CAST MEMBER, 1980–1983): So. Madeline, is it? I know there's a lot out there about me already, and this is about Lillian, which I'm very glad for, because she was an exceptionally awesome person. But I'll give you a little background.

Grew up in Westport, Connecticut. Family all from Venezuela back in the day, sugar money. My parents saw the socialist writing on the wall, sold up, moved to the US, and went into real estate. This was presumably my destiny. Much discussed over many dinners. Marry a good Catholic girl, sire five or more children, take over the business. But I have never been much interested in fulfilling expectations. My mom was particularly enamored with the American ideal of forging your own path, and she helped me wear my dad down over the course of several years. Though she's ninety years old now, and she's still pressuring me to marry a nice Venezuelan girl. "*¿Por qué no haces feliz a tu madre?*"

[*His voice changes completely with the imitation of his mother.*]

I attended Harvard, as you probably know. Had an early interest in comedy, almost an academic interest, though I abhorred everybody writing on the subject, all these stuffy academics—Goldstein, McGhee, Chapman, and Foot.

MADELINE: Foot?

KENT ROMERO: The name suits him. They all annoyed the crap out of me. That's what got me to nudge Stevie and Sam into doing something on our own. Young, smart, different. Current plus incisive, that's what I was after. And I was someone who could make things happen. I'm not sure that's true anymore, but it was at the time. People liked me; they'd bend over for me. Metaphorically, not literally. Well, probably literally, but I never tested the theory.

MADELINE: Did you set out with a specific comedy ethos in mind?

KENT ROMERO: Not a specific one, and that was intentional. We wanted to do improv, but not *old* improv. And bear in mind, by old, I mean like Second City, troupes that were active and cutting-edge, sure, and predated us by a few years, tops. But you know, we were Harvard kids, or close enough, arrogant as fuck, and, it turns out, with good reason. I'd studied Viola Spolin, old commedia dell'arte, ancient Greek theatrical traditions. And when I'd go back to Venezuela for visits as a teenager, I'd hang out with my cousins and watch these legends—Cantinflas, *Radio Rochela*. So fucking funny. Nobody knows them over here. So I had a rich and varied grounding, but as far as actual comedy performance experience went, I was a blank slate. In the end, I think that made us fresh.

Now, Sam and Stevie were such a pair, growing up together, close as testicles and just as adorable, and then me coming in to join them in the middle—well, I won't belabor that analogy, but let's just say it made for an interesting dynamic for the first few years we were doing our shows. Uneven, I'd say. Stevie in particular was, ah . . . he was not exactly a natural up there onstage. Too rigid a personality for true improv, and in terms of physical capability, he just wasn't a performer. He thought he was, but he wasn't. He was a writer. A really fucking good one, let me say that. Even then, I felt like, Stevie, my pal, maybe your future lies behind the scenes? But fat chance of any of us telling him that.

Madeline: I've been having trouble tracking Stevie down, actually, but I'm getting the sense he's somewhat . . . prickly.

Kent Romero: A human cactus. Can you see behind me? See that, on the hill?

[*He leans over so the computer screen fully shows his ranch's desert landscape behind him.*]

That saguaro right there, that's Stevie Doyle. Spiky from birth. You'd give him the smallest note, like "Turn to face the audience more," and he'd react like you'd said you were planning to fuck his mother onstage next week. So there was never any question of me and Sammy kicking Stevie off the team; he'd have come back with Molotov cocktails and burned down my house. Which was where we did performances, by the way, in those heady early days—in the living room of my townhouse, with my pothead roommates rambling around in the background in their underwear.

But even once we got our regular spot at the bar, the trio thing wasn't working. I think with me up there, all that virile masculine energy pouring out of me, it never fully allowed the spotlight to fall on Sam. But the entire dynamic shifted and in fact finally worked when Lillian joined us.

She just turned up in the audience. We were doing our one-night-a-week gig at this dingy cabaret at that point. Beacon Bar. I didn't know she was there, who the hell she was, I just noticed halfway through the show that something had happened to Sam. He'd looked out into the crowd and it was like someone had stuck a cattle prod up his ass. The funny thing was, he was great after that, post-prod. He'd seen Lillian, I now know, but instead of getting flop sweats, he cranked up the dial. Why he hadn't, you know, made a full effort up to that point is a mystery. You'll have to ask Sam about that. But simply having Lillian in the room made him funnier.

After the show, we're running on adrenaline, we're going to this Chinese restaurant we liked to hit up because the owners thought we were cute and gave us extra food to take home with us when they were closing up. So Sam invites Lillian along. And Stevie and I exchange a look, I remember, like, "Is our widdle Sammy finawwy going to get waid?" He wasn't, but we didn't realize that at the time. She was at BU with him, but they didn't know each other. She'd seen a sign for the show or something and popped in, pure coincidence.

Anyway, she was a pretty girl. Not head-turning, but she had a certain beauty. Looked like a silent film star: big blue doe eyes, long brown hair down past her ass. I started calling her Rapunzel before I could keep the name Lillian in my head, and the nickname stuck. It was the summer, so that night, she was in a loose tank top, camp counselor shorts. I saw the way Sam was looking at her with his stupid puppy eyes, so I backed off, but I couldn't resist a little flirtation. It's just my core operating system. I leaned against the table with my sleeves rolled up just so and said, "So, what did you think of the show?"

She was eating noodles. I remember that. She took two entire minutes to chew and swallow—or at least it felt that way—and then she said, "It doesn't really work, does it?" I got all puffed up, whatever. Said, "Care to enlighten us?" She took me at face value, listed all the beats that could have been made funnier, where we'd cut the scene off too soon, or watered down the joke, or winked too much at the audience. She closed with, "And it's boring only seeing boys onstage." I remember that—she called us boys, not men, like we were all still in middle school. And of course we *were* boys, we were so young; we just didn't realize it at the time.

So I, completely eviscerated by this exchange, came back at her with a tossed-off challenge: "You think a woman can make us funny? Seems like you know everything about improv, so hey, come join us onstage at next week's show, see how easy it is." And she said, "Okay." Paid for her meal, left.

I'll tell you, that night, I forgot to be scared of Stevie. I thought Sam was going to scale my townhouse trellis, break into my bedroom, and murder me in my sleep. Obviously, I hadn't meant it, that invitation.

I was flagrantly rude to Lillian, cockblocked poor Sammy, and that was that.

But she did turn up the next week, early for the show, dressed all in black like some mime, minus any makeup. She got onstage with us. And she was un-fucking-believable.

[**NOTES:** Sam Petrosian is a man of his word. Stevie Doyle finally wrote back, and we've got a FaceTime on the books for May 23. As soon as we're on, I get the distinct sense that Stevie is more anxious than I am. And that the years since he worked at *TMS* haven't treated him well. He's liver-spot bald, wearing a wrinkled mess of a Metallica T-shirt, swirling what looks to be the remnants of Metamucil (or maybe Tang and vodka?). He barely says hello, starts spouting off about four scripts he's writing on spec, his leads on new representation, how much the new "Reno pad" cost . . . It's all somewhat depressing.]

STEVIE DOYLE (*TMS* STAFF WRITER, 1980–1996): Okay. So. First impression of Lillian: "Why the hell is this fourteen-year-old coming to dinner with us?" I didn't want to get arrested. Second impression: "Why the hell is this little girl climbing up onstage with us?" I had missed that memo. Total news to me! Kent likes to say he knew she'd be great all along, saw it in her, that's why he invited her to join us, but that's bullshit. He was just as shocked as I was.

Third impression? Yeah. I mean, she was talented. Just this uncanny kind of savant, I don't even know, with off-the-wall commitment. Despite what happened down the road with *The Midnight Show,* I'm not too proud to admit that Lillian did make the Townies a lot better. That first night with her was a big turning point.

MADELINE: What do you think Lillian brought onstage that wasn't there before?

SAM PETROSIAN: That's something I've mulled a lot over the years. What was it exactly that made Lillian one of the greats of comedy—and I mean One of the Greats, with capital letters. [*He demonstrates the typeface with his fingers.*] Because she truly was. As a matter of fact, I mulled it a lot early on, trying to emulate it, or at least not derail what she was doing when we were sharing the stage. She came into her work with an unassailable belief in whatever the concept of the scene was. It didn't matter how wacky—in fact, the weirder, the better. You presented to her a setup that was, like, the deep end of the bizarreness pool, and she was cannonballing in before you could blink. I think part of the joy of it for her, the sense of home it gave her, was that it was pure imagination. Nothing else. No ego, not a glimmer of it, unlike with the rest of us.

MADELINE: Would you say she maintained that level of humility even after she became famous?

SAM PETROSIAN: Yes, absolutely.

STEVIE DOYLE: Fuck no. She changed completely. But hey, I guess we all did.

KENT ROMERO: There are different types of ego. I'm assuming you're not getting into actual Freudian terminology here, we're discussing ego in the framework of being self-interested, putting yourself first? I think her development as an adult was thwarted, and her "ego," if you prefer to call it that, was forced to emerge in oblique ways that were sometimes harmful to the people who cared about her. Does that answer your question?

SAM PETROSIAN: To me, it comes down to what your motivation is, as a performer. Lillian never craved approval from the audience. That didn't feed her sense of self—she never even knew they were there! The stage, the soundstage, wherever she was acting, it was her entire world. She had no formal training, no intellectual interest in the art form like Kent likes to hold forth about, but I'm telling you, if she'd lived longer, she'd have done what Bobby did: She'd have gone into dramatic roles and absolutely floored everybody all over again. She was a true actor.

Kent Romero: There was something childlike about Lillie. That sounds dismissive, like a pat on the head, but I don't mean it that way. I mean in the sense of play. Pure belief, faith, fantasia, a sense of impishness . . . and weirdness! God *damn*, was Lillian weird. Andy Kaufman had nothing on her. We had this setup once where we were in a school band, and about thirty seconds in, Lillian had us experimented on by the government. The CIA was controlling what we played.

The more bonkers moments were usually her, but there was also a give-and-take that's really rare, particularly among performers who are new to improvisation. She listened as well as she spoke. She ran with whatever ball we tossed her.

And so, yes, that first night, with the crowd falling down laughing around us, the energy she generated, I saw that she was right—though I don't know that it was female energy we'd needed per se, as in "anyone with tits."

Madeline: How would you define "female energy"?

Kent Romero: Ha! Nice try. I'm not falling into that trap. What I can define is Lillian's energy. Chaotic. Playful. Surprising. Sharp and versatile as a Swiss Army knife. And that's what we needed, completely.

After that first outing, we finally got our heads out of our asses and expanded the company for the first time, and it started to feel a hell of a lot less like a "no girls allowed" club we were running out of a tree house in my backyard.

Glenn Martin: Me and the folks came down for a visit one time during her senior year and we saw her Townies show. It was really something! She was pretty transformed. You know, she was playing these out-there characters, so it was almost like it wasn't her onstage. I'm not gonna claim I got all the jokes. I'm not a big comedy guy. It was a kind of off-the-wall humor, but everybody else seemed to really get along with it.

Sam Petrosian: Within a year of Lillian joining us, our shows were selling out. We'd grown into a company of ten to thirteen, depending on availability, bringing in guest performers who had enough of a name for me to be starstruck. Performing two nights a week.

Kent Romero: We were on people's radar far beyond Boston. Influential, you might say.

Madeline: Influential. How did Lillian react to that?

Kent Romero: [*He shrugs.*] I don't think she was aware of it. She had blinders on: school, studying, hanging out with us, shows, beauty sleep, repeat. She was contented. *La alegría,* my *papá* used to call it. A rare quality. I sure as fuck don't know what *la alegría* feels like. Even now, look at me, basking in sunlight, fresh air, hard-earned solitude, and you know what? I hate it. I've always had an exponential kind of greed. Lillian was the opposite.

Sam Petrosian: I think success felt intangible to Lillie, or at least unlikely. We'd be sitting around making wild plans for touring or moving the show to LA or whatever, and she'd walk by and squeeze our shoulders, like, *Aw, aren't you boys cute?* She never included herself in any of those pipe dreams, but I sure did. All my plans had Lillie in them.

Stevie Doyle: Of course Lillian didn't take our so-called fame seriously. She didn't want it. Not to mention that it did not exist! Kent likes to pretend we were Broadway-bound with the Townies, big-time from the start, that we didn't need Aaron [Adler] or *The Midnight Show,* we'd have made it anyway. Maybe he's right. He was certainly going to be successful, never mind who he ran over in the process, but who knows about the rest of us.

The truth is, that first year with Lillian in the troupe, taking it more seriously, we were still fitting it around day jobs. I was promoted to afternoon manager at the pizza place. Dream gig, let me tell you. Lillie worked between classes in the BU provost's office. Even Kent had a job in the family business despite all this "improv success" we were supposedly enjoying.

KENT ROMERO: So listen to this, Madeline—I had the sweetest racket going. I said, "Hey, Papá. I'm kind of a trusted local figure up here from my time at Harvard, so why don't you let me stay and check out some promising real estate opportunities?" Not only did he give me a title and a salary for a job that consisted of driving around and offering to buy things, but the very first investment I suggested was a fixer-upper Victorian in Charlestown. Four bedrooms, enough for me, Sammy, Stevie, and Lillie. Bam, done. We all piled in. Could have been a real powder keg situation, Sam and Lillian under one roof, but the thought didn't occur to me at the time. I just wanted to eliminate any excuse anybody might have to move out of town.

SAM PETROSIAN: Say what you want about Kent Romero, he never asked for a dime in rent. I mean, yes, he was loaded, but we, the "not loaded," very much appreciated it. And for a while there, we were an oddball little family. We'd take turns cooking—even Lillian, although my God, was she awful! She could turn spaghetti into red porridge. But we'd sit around the table on the nights we were all home and plan and laugh and everything felt like a big blurry "maybe" ahead of us. Or that could have been all the weed I was smoking. Don't tell my kids.

STEVIE DOYLE: "The Limbo House." That's what me and Lillian called it. For her, that was a good thing. She liked being "nowhere"—it took the pressure off somehow—but for me? I don't know. I wasn't a college kid anymore, not a functioning adult, just floating in the ether. Which, when you're extremely high, seems like an appropriate place to be, but then I'd wake up in the morning and think, "What the hell am I doing here, squatting in Kent Romero's investment property?"

What I'd *planned* to do after I graduated was go out to LA, get a waiter job and an agent, enjoy the weather, but Kent kept saying, "Stay a little longer. I've got a good feeling about this." And I guess he did. For him. Weird to think what might have happened if I'd taken off before Aaron came out to see us. I might have wound up being a guest host on *The Midnight Show* instead of whatever the hell I ever was. But I did stay, and, you know, it was a good time. Back then, I mean.

Sam and I were like brothers already. Still are. It took a while for us to find our way back to each other after everything that happened, but we're pretty close these days. And Kent was like a brother, too, an obnoxious bullying one, and that made Lillian our baby sister. I really cared about her. I don't know that anybody believes me about that, but it's the God's honest truth. I protected her. We'd go out, drag her along, try to inch her out of her cocoon a little, but if somebody tried to put the moves on her, we were her bodyguards, ushering them out the door. She didn't like that kind of attention. Didn't drink, smoke, nothing, not then. She was like . . . Snow White. And we were the dwarves.

[*He leans forward.*]

Not princes, mind you. She saw us as the *dwarves*. It took me a long time to realize that.

KENT ROMERO: I have younger brothers, no sisters. Lillian wasn't close with her family. Different species, I think, nothing traumatic, just awkward, but she needed family. So we gave her brothers, and me and Stevie got a sister.

Now, I'll say, for Sam it was different. There was a remove for me and Stevie; we did not/could not think of her in a romantic way, not once we got to know her. Lillie was untouchable. But Sam wanted more than friendship. He built her up into a golden ideal in his head, and I think that's part of what made her start squirming a little in his presence. Who wants to be held to that kind of standard?

Lillian was painfully, cripplingly innocent, is the truth, and it was going to take a lot for her to open herself up to intimacy at that level. She was virginal to the point of sainthood. Sam thought, "Well, hell, I'll wait. Weeks, months, years will pass, and she'll realize I'm the one."

When I talk about carrying a torch, Sam held it till it burned his fingernails black. He wasted a lot of time waiting for Lillian to love him back. I honestly think some part of him held out for her until the day she died.

GLENN MARTIN: My parents and I met Sam after the show that we came to in Boston, and it was a little bit awkward. It seemed like he wanted to go and have dinner with us. And I thought, "Well, if he's not her boyfriend, he wants to be." He was hanging on everything she said, hoping for that invitation, but she just glided on past and he got left in the dust. Seemed like a real nice guy, though. I tell people all the time, even now, "I met Sam Petrosian when he was in college!"

SAM PETROSIAN: Was I in love with Lillian? Sure. Of course. Everybody was, which got complicated down the road, but it wasn't a problem for me at that point. We were very good friends, and that was enough. But that's not why I fought for her to come with us to *The Midnight Show*. Absolutely not. It was all merit. She deserved to be there, and it took all of five minutes of the premiere episode for everybody to see I was right.

KENT ROMERO: We didn't know Aaron was coming to see our show the night he turned up, and if we *had* known he was coming, we wouldn't have known who the hell he was, so what's the difference? *The Midnight Show* was his first big TV deal after producing a handful of specials. He'd convinced the network to let him develop this different kind of sketch show, not *Carol Burnett*, not *Laugh-In*, something *chévere*, you know—something edgy, young, topical. Which, of course, was how we saw ourselves at the Townies. It was . . . must have been June of 1980.

SAM PETROSIAN: It was May. Lillian hadn't graduated yet. It was just an average Townies show he came to, good, not great. We had a few new company members and had slotted them in awkwardly in places they weren't quite ready for, if I remember correctly, but maybe that's why the three of us stood out so much to Aaron. Lillian was in all the sketches with the new kids, and that probably skewed her performance, being in the role of educator, as it were. But there were a few moments with me, Kent, and Stevie that brought the house down. After the show, Aaron came up, introduced himself, and asked to take the three of us out for drinks.

MADELINE: No Lillian?

SAM PETROSIAN: Not at first.

STEVIE DOYLE: Lillian was not invited. Sam tried to shoehorn her in, and I could tell Aaron was looking at him like, "Oh, I see; this is your side piece," getting wary of where Sam's focus was, so I jumped in with a very pointed: "Lillian, we'll catch up with you later, yeah?" She didn't give a shit. Looked happy to be getting out of it.

This is what I am always saying. She *never* wanted it. Just got dragged in.

SAM PETROSIAN: She had a French dissertation to write, so she didn't mind going home. Up to that point, she was still insisting she was going to stay in Boston and get her master's.

KENT ROMERO: Aaron took us to this corny lounge bar at the Copley Plaza hotel, trying to impress us, intimidate us, who knows. I'd stayed there before as a kid visiting colleges, but Sam and Stevie's eyes bugged out of their heads like cartoon characters seeing tits for the first time. "Yowsers!" So it had the desired effect.

Aaron was refreshingly direct. Said he'd enjoyed what he'd seen, liked our chemistry, wanted the three of us to come down to New York and test for this new show he was putting together. So I've got my business hat on, and I'm leaning back, assessing the situation, trying to get a feel for how real this was, the budget, that kind of thing, when Sam blurts out, "What about Lillian?" His voice practically cracked. "Gee whiz, mister, what about my girl?"

Stevie Doyle: Sam was ready to walk. *Aaron Adler,* who had a *national network deal,* had just said, very clearly, "I like the chemistry *you three guys* have onstage together, and I think it would work on my show." Us as a package. Not individually. And then Sam chucks Lillian into the mix as a make-or-break. If Aaron had said, "No thank you on the chick," I think Sam would have nuked the offer entirely. But Aaron, thank fuck, was in a good enough mood to simply wince like he had the mother of all migraines and say, "Sure, why not, she can audition too."

Sam Petrosian: I put my foot down because it was a mistake on Aaron's part to leave her out and I was not going to be a part of any team that made such a blatant unforced error in the first five minutes of the game.

And I think we can all now agree that I was right.

To: Madeline Cohen
From: Aaron Adler
Date: May 26, 2023 5:59 PM
Re: Re: Re: [EXTERNAL] Request for Interview—Lillian Martin Feature

Hello there, Madeline.

Thanks for following up. My apologies for the delay in responding. I've been up to my ears in contracts and paperwork post-finale.

To answer your initial question: Yes, I am very happy to talk about the late Lillian Martin. She was quite a special lady, a key member of that *Midnight Show* first class.

As for your second query: also yes. There is indeed a kernel of truth in the "lore" surrounding the show, as it were. At the time I drove up to Boston to see these kids I'd heard about doing improv at Beacon Bar, I already had offers out to two women to test for the show, both of whom were fairly big names at the time. That left one slot open for another female cast member, and immediately after seeing the Townies, it didn't occur to me to extend an offer to Lillian Martin.

She was fine, very cute, certainly presentable. But the Lillian you're thinking of—the Lillian you're writing your piece about—came later. She emerged as a result of the particular synergy of *The Midnight Show*. A product of her environment. She might have been good with Sam and Kent and Stevie, but it was with the full cast that she was great.

As for my take on what happened offstage, I'm not sure if I can be of much help there. I've tried very hard over the years to keep my relationships with cast members purely professional.

If you're looking for a window into the social heyday and whatnot of those days of yore, your efforts are better focused on Kent Romero and Gina Ross, Gina in particular. There is no story about the life and death of Lillian Martin without her perspective, although I will warn you—over the years, she seems to have become increasingly more resistant to sharing it.

Best of luck.

Aaron
Aaron Adler
Creator and Producer of *The Midnight Show*

POLICE DEPARTMENT CITY OF NEW YORK DETECTIVE BUREAU

TYPE ONE REPORT—MISSING PERSON

Det. Kyle Malone, February 23, 1983

Report on missing person Lillian Faye Martin (DOB 5/10/1958), last seen February 19, 1983, at 2:30 A.M. on East 6th Street and Avenue B, wearing a yellow cotton dress, brown shearling coat, cowboy boots.

Martin, 5'3", slight build, blue eyes, shoulder-length brown hair, was observed leaving Winthrop's, 130 West 44th Street, around 2:00 A.M. following an altercation with Mr. Bobby Everett and Mr. Kent Romero, after which time there are unconfirmed reports of Martin walking south on 6th Avenue, stumbling into the street. Multiple eyewitnesses report Martin exiting a taxi at 2:30 A.M. near Tompkins Square Park in lower Manhattan, then walking in the direction of the Williamsburg Bridge.

OTHER RELEVANT INFORMATION:

Mr. Everett, per statement, left Winthrop's at 2:15 A.M. and returned to the Plaza Hotel. Mr. Romero, per his account, left Winthrop's at 2:40 A.M. for Adam & Eve, 141 East 45th Street, where he remained until approximately 5:00 A.M. Both accounts corroborated by eyewitnesses.

By her own account, Ms. Gina Ross left Winthrop's in pursuit of Martin on foot at approximately 2:30 A.M. upon learning of Martin's departure. Various eyewitnesses corroborate Ms. Ross questioning onlookers near the Williamsburg Bridge as to whether they'd seen Martin, Ross appearing "teary-eyed" and "frantic."

Ms. Ross then went directly to Martin's apartment at 680 Park Avenue, arriving around 4:00 A.M., whereupon Ross spoke with doorman Robert Wiseman before going upstairs to Martin's unit, though she received no answer. Ross then returned to her apartment at 23 East 63rd Street alone around 5:00 A.M., at which point a distraught Ross asked building superintendent and acting doorman Carlos Ortega to phone police.

II.
THE BESTIE

Gina Ross and the LA Scene (1956–1980)

REDDIT

r/TMS4Life 3 mo. ago

Lillian Martin murdered: How come Gina got away with it?

Anyone else find it absolute garbage that Gina Ross is not only a free woman but also one of the most celebrated female comic voices of our time? Lillian's murder was obviously a cover-up by the Hollywood machine. Gina was there and pushed her. She should be wearing an orange jumpsuit to match her ugly-ass orange hair.

> Ellie_r 3mo ago
> Can you explain what you're basing this on? The police investigated this case for years–Gina didn't even leave the party with Lillian that night!
>
> Truecrimekitty95 3 mo ago
> How do you know it wasn't some psycho admirer? Or the Night Stalker? He was a *TMS* fan!
>
> Ellie_r 3mo ago
> I'd *maybe* be willing to accept that it was another cast member, but Gina was Lillian's bestie. Ride or die.
>
> comicpancake 3mo ago
> Bestie. Sure. In the way of Single White Female.
>
> Stacksofsharks 3mo ago
> I'd still bang her.
>
> Ellie_r 3mo ago
> Just Gina? Not Kent Romero, Bobby Everett?! Not any other cast member? Misogyny much?
>
> LillianFanGrl_r 2mo ago
> GIVE LILLIAN'S GHOST JUSTICE.

NOTES

Gina Ross—
May 31, 2:30 P.M. ET—Google Meet

BACKGROUND: Fringe conspiracy theories aside, Gina was never an official suspect—especially since Lillian's death was presumed to be a suicide—and her career, if anything, has only benefited from the associated intrigue. Award-winning screenplays, producing credits galore, along with select acting roles in comedy blockbusters throughout the years.

At 2:39, Ross finally appears on-screen, noticeably irritated. The big 1980s auburn hair that defined her look on *The Midnight Show* is long gone, as are the long waves of her *Drunk Wives* era. These days, Gina's red locks are clipped into a neat, shoulder-length bob. There's a hardness to her memorable features, a hollowness in her high cheekbones. Even at sixty-seven, though, Gina Ross is stunning.

MADELINE: I really appreciate your time today. I thought I'd start by giving you a little context for my focus with this piece—

GINA ROSS: Let's just cut to the chase, yeah? Both my kids are coming home this weekend, so I've gotta clear out their rooms, and I've got a virtual with Netflix in an hour that I should probably semi-prep for.

MADELINE: Two-second pitch, then: My working title is "What Really Happened to Lillian Martin."

GINA ROSS: Jesus. What an opening gun. My assistant told me you were a *TMS* groupie. Wanted a couple quick sound bites about the show's heyday. Emphasis on the *quick*.

MADELINE: Groupie, no, but I am a lifelong fan, which is exactly why—

Gina Ross: Listen, I've been over all this. Multiple times, with multiple authors and journalists. I've said everything I have to say about Lillian's death.

Madeline: I'm not focused on that night. This piece is different. It's about her life.

Gina Ross: Right. Sure. The forty-year-old cold case, unsolved to this day, not of interest. You're not touching that.

Madeline: I wouldn't go that far. But what I'm centrally interested in uncovering are the ways in which an industry that is and was often most toxic to women may have led to tragedy.

Gina Ross: Huh. So you're with the consensus. Lillian Martin, chased by her own demons straight off the Williamsburg Bridge.

Madeline: Not necessarily! I mean, yes, I want to talk about those final hours, but in the context of a more complex story. I mean, right before *The Midnight Show,* Martin was this Canadian naïf. A very talented one, but still. Wide-eyed. Three short years later, she's pushed to the brink, the quintessential Unhinged Young Woman. Fragile, drug-addicted, suicidal—

Gina Ross: Does your voice always quiver like this in interviews?

Madeline: I'm sorry?

Gina Ross: I'm starting to get the sense this is . . . I don't know, personal? Jesus, she's not your long-lost aunt or something—

Madeline: No. Like I said, I'm just a lifelong fan. I mean, there was a time I was fairly obsessed with comedy. I was a screenwriting major at USC. The goal was to get staffed on a comedy show. No dice. Tried improv. Dabbled in stand-up. And now . . .

Anyway. This isn't about me. Given how close you and Ms. Martin were, your personal and professional synergy, I'd really love to know what *you* think.

[*Gina leans in, voice hushed.*]

GINA ROSS: And what if I were to tell you . . . alien abduction.

MADELINE: I'd say if you've got proof, I might finally land a cover story.

[*Gina smiles.*]

GINA ROSS: You know, you remind me of somebody, Madeline. Am I pronouncing that right? Like the children's book, or—?

MADELINE: It's actually—

GINA ROSS: Think I'm partial to Cohen anyway. All right, where do you want to start? The beginning, I take it?

MADELINE: Yes! That'd be great. What was your very first take on Lillian, if you remember?

GINA ROSS: I . . . huh. As a matter of fact, I think it was *This woman must be from another planet*. Not literally; don't get excited.

MADELINE: Even before she performed, or—?

GINA ROSS: Immediately. We were *so* different. She was light. Airy. Fragile, like a paper doll. If she was the Fairy Princess of Funny, I was probably the bitchy troll that lived under the bridge. It was a rocky start, I'll say that much. I would not call Lillian and me simpatico to begin with, but then again, we came from two different realities.

MADELINE: Can you elaborate? Two different realities?

GINA ROSS: Listen, stand-up and improv are parallel but largely unconnected dimensions. You're a failed comedian, you know this. Lillian's world, the Kent-Stevie-Sam-and-Lillian world—the whole thing's very buddy-buddy.

Leaving aside that improv can be "cliquey," it's all about the *troupe*. It's a team sport, where jokes are sand and you're all kids playing in the sandbox. Who cares who designs the door or the turret, right? So long as you've made a castle by the end. Lillian came from a "no 'I' in comedy" school of thought, whereas I was 110 percent all "I." That's how the stand-up comedy world *is*, a sea of sharks. Somebody else's success—landing the stage, the best slot, Carson—means that you've lost out on that opportunity. Their good news is your bad news.

I came into *The Midnight Show* with that mentality, because of what I learned from Holly [Silver] and the guys at the Round, the club out in LA where I started. A stand-up comedian lives and dies alone.

MADELINE: Do you think that isolation is particularly common to female comedians? Because I'd love to hear—

GINA ROSS: Listen, Cohen, I'm not going to break down the patriarchal system of comedy in seven minutes. Gonna have to call it. Hit up my assistant for a follow-up.

Us Weekly

CELEBRITY NEWS

Stars—They're Just Like Us!

When Gina Ross needs her caffeine fix, she knows just where to JOE! The Astor Wild producer is frequently spotted at Payard Bistro on Manhattan's Upper East Side, ordering her favorite extra foam two-pump lavender matcha latte (yum)!

COMPILED TRANSCRIPTS— GINA'S ROAD TO LILLIAN

GINA ROSS: [*After we sit down at a front table*] All right, you've tracked me down, Cohen. Resourceful, aren't you? Tiny applause. Go ahead.

MADELINE: I really do appreciate your help with this. Last time, you had started to talk about improv versus stand-up, as it related to Lillian.

GINA ROSS: Right. So. We were oil and water, comedywise, at first. Lillian came from a school where a team builds a conceit together. A stand-up comedian, like I was, needs to *be* the conceit. For Lillian, I think comedy was an escape. A joyous experience. Whereas for me, going up onstage was like cutting my wrists and letting the jokes bleed out. It wasn't even like I *wanted* to write about my family—it was just that every time I cut, that's what sprung up.

MADELINE: I've seen some compilations from your early sets in LA. They're interesting.

GINA ROSS: What high praise. You humble me.

MADELINE: I meant from the perspective of someone studying women's sets to see what resonates with audiences. Which female archetype each comic slots herself into: bitchy, self-eviscerating, slutty—

GINA ROSS: Cool. So you could write a gender studies thesis on it. Starting to see why comedy didn't work out so well for you there, Cohen. Anyway, the clips you saw were probably from later on, in '82, the summer I was out there shooting a movie in between *Midnight Show* seasons, hopping up to do sets where I could. Trust me, there aren't any "compilations" from my early days in stand-up.

When I was starting out in the '70s, my material was . . . well, it was dark. Kind of fucked-up. A deep dive into growing up in a massive guilt-plagued Italian Catholic family in Burbank. It seemed to resonate, though. I think a lot of people felt trapped by circumstances and beliefs back then. I certainly did.

MADELINE: Were you and Gina close growing up?

KAREN ROSSI SMITH (GINA'S OLDER SISTER): [*via phone call*] Nope. We still aren't. My sister thinks she was the only one who wanted out of our house. The misunderstood artist, the tortured soul. Truth is, she was the only one who managed to break out.

GINA ROSS: Family defined so much of who I was, so of course it informed my material. I was one of five kids, last in the lineup. Thing is, my parents weren't the sort of people you'd expect to have a big brood—I don't think they particularly cared for any of us—but they held a special grudge toward me. *How the hell did this extra kid get here?* As if I'd just decided, on my birthday, to redirect the stork to their front stoop on a lark. Unhappy people, I tell you. My dad was quick to use the belt. My mom was quick to condemn us to hell. Nothing like eternal damnation to motivate you into washing the dishes.

KAREN ROSSI SMITH: I was a year ahead of Gina in school. I had the sense that she never knew who she wanted to be. She was always trying on different personas to see which one truly fit. It made it hard to get close to her. It made it hard to trust her, honestly.

GINA ROSS: I had a habit, growing up, of waffling between wanting to be accepted and not giving a fuck. First year of high school, I was the wallflower. Sophomore year, the mean-girl slut. That one was fun. Junior year, the anti-establishment hippie-dippie. By senior year, I came to the realization that I didn't know who I was because there was no "me" in Burbank. I didn't belong there.

My grades weren't good enough for me to get into college, though. And I had no real interest in becoming a stylist or makeup artist or whatever in LA. By that point, I'd caught some episodes of *The Comedians* and developed a serious Mel Brooks obsession, along with a nonsensical crush on Peter Boyle's Franken-monster. There was something about comedy that really appealed to me. About laughter being a livelihood. If there was an antithesis to Burbank in the late '70s, comedy might have been it.

KAREN ROSSI SMITH: Sometimes I wonder if our school had had organized sports for girls, like tennis or a track team or something, Gina would have become a professional athlete. People don't realize how few opportunities there were for girls to be competitive in the mid-'70s, and my sister—God, she was competitive. Still is. I think Gina's issues in high school were really about striving to be the smartest or edgiest or meanest person, whatever, in the room. I'm not at all surprised she became famous. There's no bigger competition than that, right?

MADELINE: Do you think Gina was competitive with her old co-star, Lillian Martin? What did Gina tell you about Lillian back then?

KAREN ROSSI SMITH: Honestly, the only time I ever heard Lillian Martin's name was from *The Midnight Show* announcer every week. Gina never talked about Lillian. I didn't even know they were friends. But then after I heard about everything . . . of course I wondered what happened. If Gina, you know, could have played a role in any of it, out of jealousy or whatever. Kind of a sad thing for a sister to say, but it didn't seem outside the bounds of possibility.

GINA ROSS: Burbank was close enough to Hollywood that everyone knew someone or knew *of* someone who was trying to make it in La-La Land. There was a guy from my high school who'd graduated two years earlier, Dominic Demoggio, who'd landed a gig as a stand-up comic at the Round. He'd become a kind of local legend. "Oh, you remember Dom. He was a riot!" Dom's legendary status in LA was very much oversold—he had a single weekly mic spot, if I recall, Thursday nights around midnight. But he lived with a few other guys in this West Hollywood shack, and they had an open couch. Dom told me I could crash. So after graduation, I packed a suitcase and headed up there, only to find out the bastard planned on charging me rent for the couch. Like ten bucks per cushion, the math worked out to be, which was a shitload in those days. "Fine," I told him. "But you've got to get me a job."

[**INTERVIEW NOTE:** Dominic Demoggio, who's now a senior pharmaceutical sales manager living in Pasadena, takes my call during his lunch hour on the road.]

DOMINIC DEMOGGIO (FORMER STAND-UP COMEDIAN AND THE ROUND REGULAR): Nobody's ever interviewed me about this. About anything, actually. Besides product surveys. But hey, I guess you could say I got Gina Rossi, aka Gina *Ross,* her start. My big claim to fame, ha, right? Once upon a time, I thought I was going to be the next Wally Winters, if you can believe it. Haven't thought about Gina in a while. She was a looker back in the day, my God. Long auburn hair, cat-like eyes. Plus, she really thought I was funny. Which, you know, was the quickest way to my heart.

GINA ROSS: Dom had a thing for me, but that was absolutely not happening. To me, wit is essential in a fuck buddy—sorry, I'll keep it clean for your precious cover story. Actually, fuck that, this is *Rolling Stone.* A sense of humor is sexier than anything else, and Dom was definitely . . . well, let's call him an "anti-performer," and not in a meta way. Bad stage presence, stock jokes, ticky-tacky delivery. But give the man credit, he did introduce me to Holly, like he promised. The Round had a waitress opening. I think I was the first and only person Holly interviewed for that job.

[**INTERVIEW NOTE:** I connect with Holly and Hal Silver over the phone. They're in their eighties now, so Holly's daughter made all the arrangements, but as soon as they're on, Holly takes the lead—it's immediately apparent that the lady is still as sharp as a prison shiv.]

Holly Silver (co-owner of the comedy club Round of Laughs): Gina Rossi, she went by back then. Big Italian hair, even bigger attitude. One of our regular comics introduced us. Dominic Demoggio, one of those guys who used to practice his jokes in the mirror. I could always tell; the pauses were all wrong. I gave him the second-to-last slot on the main stage—you know, the guy who gets some groans, the guy who sets up your finale to kill? That guy. He brought Gina in when one of my regular waitresses quit, said Gina had been living on Rice-A-Roni for a month and needed to make some cash, pay him rent to sleep on his floor or something.

Once I saw Gina, I knew the regulars would love her. She had a good look. A hard look, mind you, but it worked—sometimes you'd catch yourself staring, wondering how all those big features came together so well, like on a Mr. Potato Head. She didn't say much during the interview. I still remember that. "So what?" I thought. "That's good. Her job is to serve drinks." Boy, can first impressions be deceiving!

Madeline: Are you saying Gina Ross was a chameleon?

Holly Silver: A chameleon implies someone actually adaptable. Gina? She's just a woman with a lotta masks. Nothing's gonna change who she is deep down.

Gina Ross: Dom warned me before the interview that Holly was a piece of work. A control freak. Alpha woman, hear her roar. Used to be hard for me to keep my mouth shut, back in the day. I've worked on it over the years. But I knew the waitress gig was riding on it, so I zipped lip and showed Holly who she wanted to see. A docile little lamb.

Holly Silver: Whoo boy, Gina had a temper. Angry little thing, she was—ever see her early material? But she was cunning, too. She could play the game, all right. She'd cut my guys to pieces while slinging drinks behind the bar, use every moment she had to ingratiate herself. I still remember what she said to Jake Camato, my pretty boy headliner, when he asked if she could give him service with a smile. "You one of those guys who like teeth with their head, too?" These guys are all masochists, I swear. Jake fell for her then and there. They all liked her. They liked that instead of folding, Gina would raise the ante.

Madeline: So those early days serving drinks . . . did you know you wanted to be onstage yourself? Or did you fall into it?

Gina Ross: [*She smirks.*] I don't fall into anything, Cohen. Of course I was after the stage. That's why I wanted the gig in the first place. I'd work my bar shift, linger afterward and watch the talent, then I'd go out with the talent and study them some more. I'd try to figure out their cadence, how their stage voices differed from their real voices, how they put together their jokes—but not as, like, an academic exercise. I was learning on the ground and immediately applying it to my work. The Round was my crash course in comedy—very different comedy than what Lillian was doing on the other side of the country, mind you.

That's how I built out my first set, by learning from my competition. And all the successful comics—Jake, Pete McGillicuty to some extent—were borrowing from their own lives and experiences, and pushing that material to the brink of absurdity. The less successful guys, like Dom, would serve up the stock-photo equivalent of comedy, which just doesn't work. Comedy has to be intimate. Personal. The set as an extension of the self.

I get the sense you think female stand-up is defined or confined by the patriarchy or whatever the fuck, but comedy is about voice. I mean, maybe there's a system, but you can still say something honest and fresh that transcends that system.

Now, as for *using* my first set . . . that was trickier. Holly set the lineup, and she was ruthless about it. She wanted all her guys to pay their dues. Work slowly from the graveyard slots to weekdays before ever getting a prime-time slot onstage. She controlled everything, all of us. The Cult Guru of Comedy. And she didn't want to put me up. Too green. Too much estrogen. Not my time. *Stick to martinis,* that's what she'd say.

HAL SILVER (CO-OWNER OF THE COMEDY CLUB ROUND OF LAUGHS): Miss Ross was a pistol, all right. You could tell she was going places. What a party girl! A great presence to have behind the bar—the sort of gal who's willing to take the extra shot of tequila, do the line, up for anything.

You know, though, when I heard what happened to poor Lillian Martin years later, knowing those two were bosom buddies, out and about on the scene . . . I wasn't surprised. Hard for anyone to keep up with Miss Ross.

MADELINE: Would you say Gina Ross was a heavy drug user back then? What was the scene at the Round at that time?

DOMINIC DEMOGGIO: There was lots of booze, obviously, lots of grass. Harder stuff, too, floating around, but I never went there—thank God, because if I had gone down the same path as Jake, God rest his soul, I wouldn't be on the phone talking to you.

Gina was similar to me. Even when we met up a couple years later in LA, during her *Midnight Show* days, she had a line she wouldn't cross. I mean, she took to partying like a duck to water—I'd go home and she'd keep going strong with Jake and Pete, hitting the clubs on Sunset—but I never once saw her lose control. Jake might be falling out of his chair, but you could give Gina half a bottle of vodka and she'd still be standing somehow. She'd still be slinging digs.

MADELINE: When did you finally let Gina move from working the floor to the stage?

Holly Silver: When did I *let* her? Ha! I didn't. She took the stage, honey. All-out stole it.

I forget the exact night, but it was a Friday, I know that, big night at the Round. Lots of scouts were coming in hunting by then; the place would be alive even at one A.M. And one Friday, I think it was around the holidays in '78, if I had to guess, my guy due up—Christ, I forget his name now, this Irish comic, mainly dick and fart jokes—can't be found. Maybe he's in the bathroom taking a dump, shooting up, I don't know, but *whatever* he's doing, the stage is just dead. Jake Camato, my emcee, introduces him, and then it's crickets. For like a full minute, which is an eternity in stand-up. People were starting to leave.

Gina Ross: Pete McGillicuty had been pounding whiskey at the bar before his slot. I think his girlfriend had broken up with him, and it was like witnessing a slow train wreck, watching him devolve shot by shot. I mean, I kept serving him, but it wasn't like I was purposely sabotaging him—I'd seen guys on three-day benders get up to do their act. If you had a slot at the Round, you showed up, come hell, high water, a bout of consumption. Somebody had to do something.

Holly Silver: It was pure silence, so loud I heard it from my office. So I went out and hurried over to Jake and told him to do five minutes to stall, just till I could figure out how to recalibrate, and as we're talking, Gina walks onstage. Grabs the mic.

At first everybody's catcalling, shouting. "Hey baby, you take a wrong turn out of the bar?" "Where's my gin and tonic?" "Show us your tits." Gina stays stone-cold, no reaction. Then she just rocket-launches into this monologue, about her Italian family, her sadistic Catholic school where they made a sport of torturing the kids, I don't know, Our Lady of the Bleeding Stigmata or some shit, how the nuns looking for a little release invented a fun game called Scream-hut where they'd line up the whole fourth grade, call it a scoliosis check, and take turns whipping the kids with a belt in the janitor's closet. I remember it perfectly.

Looking back, it was clearly the warped inspiration for her debacle on Carson. Weird and pitch-dark, that was Gina back then. But hand to God, it *worked,* maybe 'cause what was coming out of her mouth didn't match the face. That's the thing: You can easily underestimate Gina. She always used that to her advantage. Catch 'em off guard and knock 'em over.

The laughs kept coming, even I can admit that. Regardless of the fact that I wanted to take Gina's head and plunge it into a toilet, I was so pissed off.

MADELINE: Would you say women have to be particularly ruthless in terms of taking advantage when an opportunity to get ahead presents itself?

GINA ROSS: Any comic should have done what I did.

MADELINE: Right, but what's the fallout for a woman? Isn't there a different kind of backlash?

GINA ROSS: Yeah, I mean, sure. Your generation, I swear, you can make anything about gender, even as you're on your soapboxes shouting, *Gender's just an illusion!* Obviously, there are realities you've gotta navigate. Onstage, women tend to tear themselves down to get laughs. *Off*stage, though, you've got to be your own fucking yes-man. True then, maybe even truer now. An opportunity presented itself, so I took it, I *seized* it, end of story. It just so happened that there was a scout in the audience for a show called *Two for the Money,* which was canceled like a year or two later. But the scout was big enough in Holly's world that he mattered to her. After that, Holly could no longer play her Jim Jones "Only I can sanctify you" routine with me. I was a cult victim no longer.

HOLLY SILVER: Lord, did I want to can Gina's ass so bad after that stunt she pulled! Problem was, Fred Dormsley from CBS came up to me after her set and said, "Who was that girl? Why didn't you tell me about her? Damn, Holly, she's got something, she really does." Now I'm in a pickle, 'cause Fred's telling his network people about Gina. If I say this was a fluke, then *I* look bad. That's Gina to a tee, though, isn't it? The balls. Act first, ask permission later. Not even *forgiveness.* Just permission in perpetuity throughout the universe.

GINA ROSS: It took a full six months until I was in the Round rotation as a regular, but immediately after that first set, I was at least a presence at Holly's. A draw, whether she liked it or not.

DOMINIC DEMOGGIO: No, I don't resent that Gina came into my backyard and took over. How can I, right? Stand-up is a zero-sum game. Everyone knows that before they decide to play. Besides, I wasn't the last comic Gina left in the dust, was I?

HOLLY SILVER: Intensity was not a good look for a woman back then, and yet somehow, Gina made it her comedy brand. She lit up the Round, sure. People loved her. She felt fresh. The mouthy hothead, the loose cannon, the shark. Bully for her, yeah? But somebody like that, you can't one hundred percent trust, that's for damn sure.

MADELINE: Okay. Let's get back to the timeline . . . after working at the Round for a year or two, 1979 into '80, did you go straight to New York for *The Midnight Show*?

GINA ROSS: Ah. Tell me, Cohen, have you ever watched my performance on *The Tonight Show*?

MADELINE: [*Silence*]

GINA ROSS: Go on, I can take it.

MADELINE: They showed it in my intro to comedy class at USC as an example of losing the crowd.

HOLLY SILVER: You have any doubts as to Gina Ross being a secret psychopath, see her hot mess on Carson.

GINA ROSS: I still remember the exact date I was told I was going on-air. January 28, a Monday, winter of 1980. I was shocked, even though, again, I was prepared. Carson's scouts were everywhere; it was a theoretical opportunity for every comic who graced the Round stage, or any hot stage in LA, really—you never knew exactly who was gonna show up, and when and where they might be in the audience. You had to be ready.

Holly broke the news, begrudgingly. It freaked me out. The guys at the club were supportive when they heard, but I could taste the envy like flop sweat in the air. Dom made a few snide remarks about Carson calling before I'd even unpacked my suitcase. And I get it: Pete had been working at the Round for a decade. Even Jake had been emcee for three years with no big break in sight. Here I was, newly minted, waving the golden ticket like Charlie winning a tour of the fucking chocolate factory, about to go on Carson *live,* maybe in front of millions. Yeah. I felt like an imposter.

HOLLY SILVER: I have no love for Gina, but it was hard to watch her sabotage herself. You've got to be a particular brand of masochist to take an opportunity like Carson and throw it in the trash.

LEW BICKLE (GINA ROSS'S MANAGER, 1982–2012): Everybody in the comedy world watched Carson. Everyone saw Gina swan dive off that cliff. I was all over the scene in both New York and LA and for about three days, all anyone could talk about was *What the hell happened?*

GINA ROSS: Carson gave you a lead time of three weeks before you went on-air. That was the problem. Too much time. I started aggressively reworking, rewriting my best material, then second-guessing, then *triple*-guessing. I was a mess. Drinking way too much—which would become a pattern for me—and Jake was all too happy to strap in as a passenger on my self-destructive joyride.

So yeah, I showed up to the studio that day pretty strung out. But I *did* have material. I'd gotten it together enough and planned on delivering. I did not want it to go the way it did.

LEW BICKLE: She still mentions it sometimes, if you can believe it, even after all these years. Even after *The Midnight Show, Fatigues, College Crush*. The *Drunk Wives* series. Her deals with Paramount and Netflix. She's still mortified. And at the time, you know, it made her stop trusting herself. She'd been handed the literal opportunity of a lifetime, and she did something dangerous with it.

GINA ROSS: I remember sitting in that *Tonight Show* dressing room chair staring at myself. All made-up, framed like a film star by those idiotic marquee mirror lights. A PA comes in and tells me I've got fifteen minutes. Somebody else comes in for a touch-up. The stylist offers me something to help me calm down—totally par for the course in those days, mind you. My mouth says, "No, I'm good." My hand takes it anyway.

Of course the joint was laced with PCP. Of-fucking-course. Blew up everything I'd worked for over the course of a year in three minutes and forty-eight seconds.

HOLLY SILVER: She told you someone slipped her *drugs*? [*Long pause*] What a convenient story.

DOMINIC DEMOGGIO: Holy shit. That Carson act! Spewing about Jesus's "cave detox," insulting Johnny and slapping herself in atonement, then threatening the audience with, like, some supposed off-screen machete? Utter shitshow. Classic Catholic sadomasochism. Classic Gina, really.

HOLLY SILVER: Gina Ross was *done* after Carson. Dead comic walking—we all said it. How she landed *The Midnight Show* after that detonation, I'll never know. A cat with nine lives. A cat with claws, too.

[*Holly's voice goes low, as if fearful of eavesdroppers. I'm sensing she's binged too many* CSI *episodes.*]

Holly Silver: I'm no detective, Miss Cohen, and I know she was never formally charged, blah blah blah, but you ask me plain who or what killed Lillian Martin? Gina Ross sure as shit had something to do with it.

Lew Bickle: Isn't all good comedy dangerous? Isn't the best humor risky? I think Aaron witnessed and *wanted* that danger. Just look at those first couple seasons, once Gina and Lillian found their groove. They were a roller-coaster ride without safety belts, momentum itself. There was no stopping either of them.

Though if hindsight's foresight, maybe someone should've tried.

Madeline: So after Carson aired your bit, that's when Aaron's people called? And you went to New York that winter?

[*Gina stands from the table, tosses her coffee cup in the trash.*]

Gina Ross: I've had enough caffeine for a week now, Cohen. Listen, just come to my place for our inevitable round three. Much more convenient for me. Here's my address. [*She winks.*] Dox me and I'll kill you.

NEW YORK POST

Friday, May 13, 1984

LAST LAUGH

Local Fishermen Discover Body of Missing Beloved Comedienne in East River

By Colin McCormick

The New York City Police Department confirmed that a woman's body was found in the East River on Wednesday by two fishermen seining in kayaks around 6:45 A.M.

Officials have yet to comment, but speculation continues to grow that the body is that of Lillian Martin, breakout star of the late-night variety show hit "The Midnight Show." In the early hours of February 19, 1983, after a night of celebrating professional and personal milestones with the show's cast and crew, Lillian Martin, 25, disappeared without a trace from the Williamsburg Bridge.

The discovery brings little closure to Martin's family, friends and fans who have held out hope, and only deepens the mystery of what happened the night of the comedy star's final performance. Was Martin a tragic victim of her own excesses, resulting in suicide or an unintentional overdose? Could she have slipped—a fatal accident? Was it murder by a stalker, as some claim, or a mugging gone wrong? Or was Martin killed by someone in her inner circle?

The police investigation continues, though with each passing day, it feels less and less likely that authorities will ever uncover the full story. Martin's death might haunt us forever, a cruel joke without a punchline . . .

III.
PRE-PRODUCTION

All Roads Lead to One Astor
(Spring–Summer 1980)

TRANSCRIPT OF INTERVIEW

One Astor Studios

June 6, 2023

For our in-person follow-up, Aaron Adler greets me at the front desk on the fifteenth floor and brings me to his cluttered office, where we meet *TMS*'s former head of production, Phil Ackerman. Maybe Phil's bored now that he's retired, excited to visit his old stomping grounds . . . although there's also the possibility that Aaron insisted Phil join us as a corporate buffer, indemnifying anything he tells me in our interview.

Aaron Adler (creator of *The Midnight Show*): My vision for the inaugural class. Let's see. You have to understand, Madeline, an intrinsic part of achieving that quote-unquote "vision" was the back-and-forth quid pro quo I had to maintain with the network. They handed me a prospective budget; I returned a more realistically expansive budget. They handed me a proposed cast list as a rider on that budget, and of course I had to gratefully accept at least two of the names on their list.

As for Lillian particularly . . . well. As I mentioned over email, I underestimated her talent when I saw her perform in Boston.

Madeline: You also indicated that there were only three spots for female performers in the cast. I'm curious, why did you have a set number?

[*Aaron looks confused by the question.*]

Aaron Adler: Why three? Well, it was a big cast, intentionally so. Carol Burnett had had four regular cast members, for example, but I wanted something more dynamic, with seven. Back then, I'm sad to say, if you had more women than men, it would become a women's program rather than something that appealed to all audiences. That said, times have changed, and I like to think we've been a part of that change.

PHIL ACKERMAN (*TMS* HEAD OF LATE-NIGHT PRODUCTION, 1980–1990): You bet he has. This guy right here. Did you know, Madeline, that Aaron was once named one of *Glamour* magazine's Women of the Year for the work he's done promoting women in entertainment?

AARON ADLER: I certainly don't deserve all the credit. But if you look at all the comedians who have graced the *Midnight Show* stage over the years, you will find there are more women than men on that list. And then there's our record on diversity—look at Nolan Young, look at Kent Romero, who a lot of people still don't realize is Latin American. Those are achievements that I'm very proud of.

[**NOTE:** I have, in fact, noticed the abundance of past female and BIPOC cast members—along with *TMS*'s pattern of firing said cast members after a single season while promoting their white male counterparts, which might account for that difference. Too early in the conversation for me to risk abbreviating it by bringing that up directly, though.]

MADELINE: I finally had a chance to connect with Gina Ross.

AARON ADLER: Excellent. Glad you persisted.

MADELINE: Gina intimated that her own spot on *TMS* almost didn't come to pass. Could you speak to that a bit?

AARON ADLER: She's correct. I for one was rooting for Gina, but the powers that be . . . Phil, really, at the time, was not a fan.

PHIL ACKERMAN: Come on, Aaron, you know I loved all those first class mischief-makers, some of them more than my own kids.

Aaron Adler: I recall his precise words were *Why the fuck are we bringing in Carson's disaster for an audition?*

Phil Ackerman: All right, all right. I confess. Aaron wanted a stand-up voice in the mix, and that was A-OK by me. That'd be a nice contrast to the Townies, I thought, who we really had our eyes on, and given that the network was insisting on Nolan [Young] and Brooke [Balsinger], who were gonna be costly, I knew we could save some change going with a newcomer. There were so many other choices, though, over two dozen other stage comics we were looking at from LA, New York, Vegas. Female comics who, you know, hadn't gone on live television and literally slapped themselves in the face!

Aaron Adler: Despite Phil's reservations, I pushed hard for Gina to screen-test. Watching her spot on Carson, I saw character work. Verve. Guts. Spontaneity, malleability. And a sense of danger I felt we needed to stand out. Casting a live ensemble show is night and day from casting a sitcom or drama. It's got to be nimble rather than consistent. Putting on *The Midnight Show* is like trying to make a thousand recipes using the same seven ingredients week after week. Those ingredients must be interesting enough, multifaceted enough, to keep things fresh. And say what you want about Gina's set on Carson, it put *The Tonight Show* on everybody's lips again for weeks. I wasn't going to say no to a boost like that.

COMPILED TRANSCRIPTS

GINA ROSS: I couldn't believe I got that call. I think *TMS*'s casting director rang up two weeks after Carson, and she told me I was the only stand-up talent they were looking at. I assumed it was a joke. She said, no, really, some guy from New York was putting a new ensemble show together, but, you know, edgier than Carol Burnett, skewing younger than everything out there, too. "Anarchic," that was the word she used.

I don't even think I caught Aaron's name at the time. Nobody back then was leading with "Aaron Adler"—it carried as much weight as "Joe Schmo." My immediate reaction was I don't do troupe work. I am a shark. I swim alone. But after Carson, I'd basically stopped swimming, is the truth. And when sharks stop swimming, they die.

AARON ADLER: The network wanted Nolan Young, who'd been one of those four cast members on Carol Burnett for two or three years. My assessment was that the material they were giving him was fairly one-note, that he'd been pigeonholed as the "Black cast member." They were underpaying him, too, and it was obvious Nolan had serious talent. Pitch-perfect delivery. A bottomless bag of impressions.

PHIL ACKERMAN: We flew out to LA to woo Nolan early on, if I recall. Maybe December of '79? Jack [Denson, network executive] and I met with him and his team and pitched *TMS*—a loose pitch at the time, but we knew we needed some known entities. We led with the money.

AARON ADLER: He didn't audition. He was gifted to us from on high, which dovetailed well with the rest of my plans. In fact, I do believe Nolan Young was the highest-paid cast member that season.

[**NOTE:** I've also included relevant excerpts from Nolan Young's last interview, published in June 1989 in *The Village Voice*.]

NOLAN YOUNG (*TMS* CAST MEMBER, 1980–1985), EXCERPT FROM "NOLAN'S FINAL BOW," *VILLAGE VOICE*: I was what you called "offer only." Those are good words in anybody's career. No audition. Make an offer, make me move. As it happens, I was sick of LA. I'm a New Yorker. I wanted to come home. I liked Carol Burnett, she really did right by me, but I liked the idea of starting something new. And I really liked how much *The Midnight Show* was offering to pay me.

They say I was a name. I wasn't, but I was "a face." Like, I'd be walking down the street, or in the airport, you know, and I'd see somebody glance over at me and recognize me with that look, like, *He's somebody, but I have no idea who.* They weren't sure if they'd seen me on TV or if I'd come and fixed their TV. But that right there was more famous than everybody else in that cast, except for Brooke [Balsinger]. She *was* a name; she was doing those magazine pinup photo shoots at the time. Not *Playboy,* but just on the line, if you know what I'm saying. So I was the highest paid, then Brooke, then everybody else. Might have been the first time in American history the white guys got paid the least.

AARON ADLER: Now, Brooke . . . that's the cast member I didn't understand at first. Of course she had charm—that sex appeal, if you will—but she was also pushing thirty and still playing a snarky teenager on *Settle Down*. Kind of a poor man's Suzanne Somers, I thought at the time. And when an actress becomes synonymous with a role, it's hard to see them as anyone else, let alone dozens of new characters. But the deal was inked; *Settle Down* was on its last run, Brooke's contract was ending, and the network wanted to keep her. Before the show aired, I had no real leverage, no real power to veto their list completely. But, you know, I'd say it worked out.

NOTES

Brooke Balsinger—
June 7, 1:00 P.M. ET—Phone Call

Brooke takes my call while she's driving through Topanga Canyon, her distinctive breathy voice coming in fits and starts over the line. Service is tough. I'll assume that's why she keeps getting my name wrong.

As a *TMS* fan, I do tend to be charitably inclined when it comes to Brooke. You never see a "Worst *TMS* Performers of All Time" list that doesn't include her name—usually accompanied by a photo of her in the notoriously revealing milkmaid costume from the sketch where Captain von Trapp cheats on Maria, implying that you can show either cleavage or talent, never both. She was hired for her sex appeal and then punished for it, an age-old story and one that I've always found infuriating.

Unfortunately, the more I talk to Brooke, the more I wonder how much of her reputation is actually of her own making.

BROOKE BALSINGER (*TMS* CAST MEMBER, 1980–1985): Aaron and I didn't start on fabulous terms. You have to understand, Maddie, I was lending so much cachet to the show. I was the only cast member with any name recognition whatsoever. Even Nolan's fame was, like, niche, right? Confined to select comedy circles. I accept, fly all the way to JFK. I had settled for a co-op apartment near Sutton Place while my manager's assistant took her sweet time finding me a house in Westchester County—trust me, nobody wanted to live in Manhattan at that time. It was all derelicts. But I didn't go to my apartment first. Oh no, from the airport, I take a two-hour ride into Midtown in a taxi—not a limo, mind you, not even a car service, a yellow cab, body odor and everything, bumper-to-bumper traffic—and finally step into the lobby of One Astor. And I am a professional. I am bright-eyed, ready for my close-up, right then and there. And Mr. Aaron Adler, who, again, is nobody at the time, does not even stop his mad pacing of the halls to greet me. He's like, "Hey," grunting over his shoulder, "we didn't expect you yet." Super accusatory. His henchwoman Sally [Schumacher] shoves me into this shared office smaller than a prison cell. Shared! And that was my hello. Welcome to *The Midnight Show.*

AARON ADLER: I think Brooke . . . How do I put this, Phil?

PHIL ACKERMAN: Brooke's agent may have oversold to her how eager we were to have her join the cast.

BROOKE BALSINGER: I'm hot off a hit TV show, multiple photo shoots—*Cosmo, Sports Illustrated* Swimsuit Issue—and now I'm being stored in an overpacked windowless cubicle?! I had standards, and this did not come close to meeting them. After a half hour of no one checking in, I am fuming, and restless, too, so I start walking the halls, conducting my own tour, and I run into some other people, screen-testing or what have you. I realize real fast that the rest of the actors are all about five years younger than me, minimum. Not the way you want to start the breakout chapter of your career, let me tell you! I should have walked at that point, honestly, but as you well know, Maggie, I did not do that.

NOTES

Sally Schumacher—
June 7, 4:30 P.M. ET—In-Person

I first meet with *The Midnight Show*'s head writer/"henchwoman" at a coffee shop near the set of her current show, a Hulu series shooting at Silvercup in Queens. Schumacher was affiliated with *TMS* for nearly a decade, finally hanging up her late-night reins in '89. She's over seventy now, with long gray hair, wide, playful eyes, and a soft Southern drawl at odds with her daunting clout as a producer.

SALLY SCHUMACHER (*TMS* HEAD WRITER, 1980–1989): The day of Lillian Martin's audition? First of all, Brooke was not meant to be there. We had negotiated the details of her arrival over the phone with her people in truly agonizing detail, but she showed up early for some unknown reason. This was our first audition day, remember. We didn't need her in the mix for that—no use running chemistry tests until we whittled down the possibilities—so we sent a page after her to kind of steer her away from the studio where we were doing our screen tests.

I was in charge of the process. Aaron had herded all the hopefuls into One Astor, and I got to try them out, say "Yes," "Maybe," or "I don't see it." There were five I-don't-see-its that day and I'm not going to tell you who they were, but let's just say, they wound up doing fine for themselves. Aaron trusted me with this, which, when I look back, is kind of amazing. I was twenty-seven, a college dropout with a thick north Georgia accent, semi-openly bisexual, a *woman*. I mean, how many strikes could you possibly have against you working in the big leagues in 1980?

MADELINE: From speaking to Aaron, I get the sense he sees himself as a champion of diversity.

[*I am trying hard not to sound dubious, but she laughs anyway.*]

SALLY SCHUMACHER: I wouldn't go that far. It's more that Aaron doesn't see demographics beyond how they'll affect the bottom line. He's a little bit context-blind that way. But we'd been friends for a good while, starting with the variety special we did for a New York charity soon after I moved to town, and what he saw when he looked at me was that I hustled. I worked late hours, delivered under pressure, and that's what he needed. I was not a "good enough is good enough" person. I never stopped punching jokes up, and over the years, that sometimes made me incredibly unpopular with other members of our writing rooms, who, you know, wanted a better home-life balance, or wished they could leave early and go party with the cast.

The accusations I've fielded over the years—I'm a power leech, a control freak who gets off on being too involved with personal matters between cast members, you name it. But I was running a war room. Nobody can deny that I ran it consistently and well.

Now, I wouldn't consider myself that funny a person—

MADELINE: *Central Park Patrol* is one of the funniest shows I've ever watched.

SALLY SCHUMACHER: Well. That's awfully kind. I obviously wasn't the only writer on that, but thank you. On season one of *The Midnight Show,* I didn't do a whole lotta writing. I was keeping the cast and writing team on task, helping pick the weekly hosts, booking the musical guests, handling the house band, gaffers, costumers, makeup artists—directing traffic, essentially. And defusing bombs. There was a lot of traffic to direct, starting from that very first screen test day. The bombs came later.

COMPILED TRANSCRIPTS

MADELINE: Do you remember the audition day for *The Midnight Show*?

SAM PETROSIAN: Vividly! I still have nightmares about it, the way other people will dream about taking a test they haven't studied for. The dreams are worse than the reality, I should note. There were jitters, for sure, but we managed them. We all drove in together that morning, a one-day quick turnaround thing. Lillian rode shotgun, looking out the window. Stevie and I were in the back, relentlessly mocking New York City the whole way, calling it a shithole, excuse my French, because one, you have to if you're from Boston, it's the law, and two, New York *was* a shithole. And us parking in Times Square, jeez Louise, it was apocalyptic. Peep shows open at ten in the morning, girls out front trying to get you to come in, strung-out junkies harassing you for change. We thought, hey, if this gig doesn't work out for us, at least we can get back to a decent city.

But then we went inside One Astor. It was a brand-new skyscraper, shiny as tinfoil. The network didn't own the whole thing—they do now, but back then it was about half ownership. Even so, it was branded as if these were the gates of heaven and heaven was the network. The desk, the security, the gleaming lobby, the enormous network sign, our footsteps echoing. Immaculate. Stevie and I shut right up. No more smack talk about New York, not in that sacred space.

That's when the nerves really hit. Whoo boy. Even Kent, who was doing his best to pretend his family owned the building, I could tell it affected him. This was the real deal. We'd been playing at being pros this whole time, thinking we had buzz, we were the avant-garde, everybody wanted to be us. [*He shoots goofy air guns in demonstration.*] And just by checking in at that security desk, we realized we'd been kids having a good time in our little after-school club up until now. This was adulthood. This was professional. This could change everything.

Now, the only one who wasn't cowed, not at all, was Lillian. She didn't really understand the Boston–New York dynamic, so the whole ride down, she'd been trying to reassure us in her very Canadian way, like, "Don't worry. I'm sure it isn't as bad as you think." And in that grand gray lobby, she turned to me and beamed and said, "See? This is nice! I told you!"

GINA ROSS: If you're craving an inferiority complex, a quick masochistic hit straight to the veins, take a stroll through One Astor's lobby. It's show business incarnate, marble columns and slick slate floors and gilded elevators. Walking in that summer, I would've bolted, I really think I would've, if not for the Carson debacle, which I know sounds counterintuitive, but put it this way: If I'd gone into my audition on top, I would've had everything to lose. As it happened, I was already swimming at the bottom of the world. Nowhere to go but up to the fifteenth floor.

STEVIE DOYLE: We rode in the elevator with Gina. I'd seen that kamikaze stunt she'd pulled on Carson, everybody had, but I didn't make the connection right away. I figured she was somebody's secretary. I probably sound like a jerk saying that, but . . . she had *really* big hair back then.

GINA ROSS: My first impression of the Townies? Bush-league Rat Pack. Kind of cute, but like . . . forgettable. I mean, Kent, of course, had star quality, this sort of unplaceable appeal—was he Latino? Italian? Persian? Wherever he was from, you wanted to say thank you for the donation, because my God, was he hot. And he knew it—I can still picture that shit-eating grin he sported the entire elevator ride. Which, of course, became his calling card. He's got a kiss-me-or-punch-me face, doesn't he? Even so, he was nervous that day, they all were, it was obvious. Stevie, in particular, looked like he was seconds from shitting his pants. Not sure if you've met Stevie yet, but he's set to a higher frequency than even your average neurotic comedy writer—anxious bugger, teeth always clenched—so maybe it's more accurate to say he looked like he was right in the *middle* of shitting his pants. I didn't even register Lillian until the doors finally opened and a few PAs accosted us in the fifteenth floor's elevator lobby, funneling us into a jam-packed waiting room, which had been filled for quite a while, judging from the scent of disgusted annoyance in the air.

MADELINE: What did you first think of Lillian when you did see her?

GINA ROSS: I dismissed her. She was such a waif of a thing, the antithesis of a presence, really. Long, long dark hair to her waist, totally barefaced, and wearing all black, an emo teen before it was in vogue. I can still picture her now, perched on the edge of her folding chair, leaning around Sam, hanging on Stevie and Kent's every word. And I think, okay, a chuckle fucker, yeah? A comedy troupe groupie—all she needs is a floppy hat and we've got late night's Yoko Ono. But then they call Kent's name, then Sam's, then Stevie's, and then "Lillian Martin," and this brunette Twiggy stands right up. Jumps up, really, like an eager student about to solve a quadratic equation on a blackboard.

STEVIE DOYLE: I can't remember if it was Kent then Sam, or Sam then Kent, but I went after the two of them. Had a little material from one of our shows that I'd worked into a sketch. It went great—from my perspective, anyway—and then it was Lillian's turn. Sally called her name, and Lillie went deer in the headlights. Looked like she was being called for a deposition.

I thought, "Oh shit. We didn't prep her. We didn't tell her anything." We were clueless, too, the three of us, but we'd assumed we were going to work on some bits to bring in, and never thought to tell Lillie, you know, you might want to prepare something. I mean, like, she hated wearing makeup, right? But this seemed like a moment for an exception. She hadn't spruced up at all. Nothing. She was about to fall flat on her face, and I wanted to strangle Sam for putting her in that position, to fail like that, which was bound to blow back on the rest of us. I paced around in that waiting room, clenching my jaw to keep from saying, *I fucking told you so.* Worst case, she was going to be so green, they'd rethink including the Townies altogether. Lillian was about to cost me my big break.

[*Not sure if Stevie's wincing or smiling.*]

I was right about that. Wrong about everything else.

Sally Schumacher: Lillian had done zero preparation for the audition and didn't seem to be particularly intellectual, but it was so obvious she was this live wire of talent—I mean, watch her tape, and you'll understand why I was not going to let this show go on the air without Lillian Martin—whereas Stevie Doyle, who Aaron had talked up to no end, was a nonentity on camera. His material was all right; I could see how on paper it would work. But if you watch the footage, he was a vacuum into which humor disappeared. You know that expression "all hat, no cattle"? He was all clever, no funny.

Madeline: And what about Bobby Everett? Do you remember the first time you met him?

Sam Petrosian: I don't think any of us actually spoke to Bobby that day. Not until our first actual day of work, when we all joined the writers' room for the first time. But that audition day, we saw him in the waiting area, this kind of bare-bones greenroom just off the studio. Like a hospital waiting room but with a fruit bowl, to make us feel fancy. Which worked, by the way. I did indeed feel fancy.

Bobby's turn to do his screen test was right after Lillian's. When Lillie came out, she ran up to me and gave me this big hug, and Bobby's eyes did not leave us, which obviously attracted my own attention. I remember he looked startled when they called his name, like he was waking up from a trance. I don't blame him. Lillian had that effect on everybody.

Kent Romero: I knew *of* Bobby Everett, tangentially. He did the talk show circuit in New York and LA, his literal song-and-dance routine, the *mamarracho*. He tap-danced, played the guitar, I can't fucking remember. He was older than me, but I thought he was a kid; that seemed to be the whole gag, like, look at this sweet little ultra-white ghost child singing outrageous things. Even for the audition, he'd brought in this miniscule twee piano. He was sitting in the waiting room holding it on his lap like a pet. Completely bizarre—so, of course, Lillian noticed. I saw the way she looked at Bobby and thought, "Uh-oh. Here we go."

Gina Ross: That stupid fucking piano. If he'd brought a bassoon, who knows, Cohen? Maybe Lillian would still be alive today.

Kent Romero: When Bobby went in to test, I got a pit in my stomach, thinking, "Huh. Maybe this show isn't going to be at the level I expected." But I don't give a shit what people say, this is the truth—I decided to reserve judgment about Bobby. Right then and there, I said to myself, give him a chance, get to know the guy and then see what you think. And I did. I got to know him.

[*Kent sits back, smiling tightly.*]

Madeline: Can I take that to mean . . . you did not grow to like him?

Kent Romero: You can take it to mean whatever you want. There are a lot of rumors out there. I want to make it clear that at that point in our relationship or whatever you want to call it, I was more than willing to befriend Bobby Everett.

Sally Schumacher: We needed Bobby. The show, in that first season, wouldn't have worked without him. He walked in very comfortable because I think he knew Aaron a little socially. They were both in this sort of New York oak-paneled-drawing-room scene that bridged . . . how shall I put this? Smart people and rich people? Like, the late '70s version of *salons*. Old ladies loved Aaron. Still do, actually, which is another thing he pretends not to notice.

Back then, Aaron was good at working all kinds of rooms, making the right friends. That's what got him up the ranks of the network so quickly. Don't get me wrong, he had killer ideas—he was a great producer and a solid guy—but he was also very good at becoming the darling of whoever held the power.

Bobby wasn't dissimilar. He was rich and smart, like Kent, but Bobby came from one of those Manhattan families that can trace their lineage back to specific Dutch merchant lords and—unlike Kent—he never really came across as arrogant. He was boyish. Again, nowhere near as handsome as Kent, or even Sam in his prime, but he sort of radiated wholesomeness, which in terms of comedy worked most effectively when he was being subversive.

Bobby was relaxed in that screen test, no doubt about that. He'd been in front of cameras, unlike our Townies kids. But it wasn't his experience we needed. It was the adorable factor. If we had Bobby *and* Lillian, we'd have "likable" kind of covered enough to be edgy and push the line in other ways with the rest of the cast. It's sort of funny to think about it now, because I don't know if they even met in the hallway or in the greenroom on that first day, but I was already saying "Bobby and Lillian." Like they went together.

Anyway, it was obvious to me after her audition that Lillian was a keeper. But she left the room and Aaron gave me this noncommittal, "Hmm. Maybe as a backup," and I swear, I considered violence right then and there. Chucking a boom mic at him or something.

Aaron Adler: Sally did fight for Lillian in the room. That's accurate. I would say what gave me pause that day was that I saw in that audition some of the vulnerability that would later haunt her. She was like a fledgling bird. Incredibly fresh. But of course, that was the same quality that Sally rightly recognized as brilliance.

[**INTERVIEW NOTE:** Aaron and Phil need to wrap up before Aaron's next meeting, but Phil kindly obliges my request for the first class's audition tapes. He sets me up with a private viewing room on the fourteenth floor and then goes one better, asking a PA to grant me access to *The Midnight Show* archives in case anything there may also be of use.]

TRANSCRIPT: LILLIAN MARTIN SCREEN TEST FOR *THE MIDNIGHT SHOW* (JUNE 25, 1980)

LILLIAN: Hello, all you strangers sitting around in the dark. My name is Lillian Faye Martin, and . . .

[*Off-screen voice unintelligible*]

[*Lillian drinks from a glass of water.*]

LILLIAN: Should I go? Is it—Are we on? Just talk? [*Giggling*] Tell me what to do.

OFF-SCREEN VOICE: Did you prepare—

LILLIAN: Hi, no, yes, just tell me anything. Call it out.

OFF-SCREEN VOICE: Do you mean character work?

LILLIAN: Sure! Yes.

SALLY SCHUMACHER (*off-screen*): An old Icelandic woman.

LILLIAN: How old?

SALLY (*off-screen*): Ancient.

[*Lillian bends at the waist, spine contorted into a lopsided hump, eyes squinting, chin jutted out, mouth curled with cartoonish delight.*]

LILLIAN: Come inside, sticka-sticka. I have shermalen cooking on the pit fire. You drink it, glug-glug, it will warm your bintas and make hair grow down on your bjernins!

[*Off-screen laughter*]

LILLIAN: You want to know how I keep my girly-girly figure at my age? You come close, I tell you my secret. My papa was that old rascal Odin. My mother did the hanky-panky with Odin, this is why I live to four hundred and seven. Now drink the shermalen, go on—

SALLY (*off-screen*): Have you ever met an Icelandic person?

LILLIAN: Absolutely not. Why do you ask?

AARON (*off-screen*): Seemed Icelandic to me.

SALLY (*off-screen*): There's a Nordic vibe, I'll buy it.

LILLIAN: Do you want another?

OFF-SCREEN VOICE: A Deep South . . . schoolteacher. Who's afraid of children.

AARON (*off-screen*): You know Deep South, Sally.

SALLY (*off-screen*): Sure do, all too well.

[*Lillian's body becomes upright, buoyant, kinetic with perky anxiety.*]

LILLIAN: Well, good mornin', sunshines. Ooh, not too close, not too close! Take your seats. Billy Steve, why are you approaching my desk?! I don't want that apple, Billy Steve, you've got your germs on that, you just take it right back with you, bless your lil' heart. Now, today, sweet babies, we're gonna do a duck and cover drill, because you know those

Russians are tryin' every day to steal our freedoms away with their nuclear bombs! So go on ahead and get under—that's right, under those desks, where I can't even see you. So much better. Good boys and girls. And I'll stand here and breathe real slow and try not to cry, 'cause that's part of the drill too—

Sally (*laughing, off-screen*): Accurate. Anybody else got . . . ?

Off-screen voice: Ronald Reagan.

Lillian: Just Ronald Reagan?

Off-screen voice: "Just" Ronald Reagan, she says—

Sally (*off-screen*): Reagan baking cupcakes.

[*Lillian stands rigidly, head wobbling, hands in two stiff lines. It's an uncanny imitation.*]

Lillian: My fellow Americans. I come to you today with a new proposition. We're gonna restore the greatness of our cakes. End the tyranny of Big Cake, and instead, do you see what I'm making here? Little cakes! Cake of the cup, bit of icing on top, red, white, and . . . yes, here we have a lovely vibrant blue. Gosh, I'm hungry, but I don't think—Nancy, am I allowed to eat? Nancy says no.

Off-screen voice: She sounds like him.

Sally (*off-screen*): The cakes are now drugged.

Lillian: Okay, folks, just going to take a little bite. Chef's rights: You make it, you eat it. No handouts. [*Mimes eating*] Whoo boy, have a nibble, Trigger. Giddyup, ol' boy. Who's a pretty, pretty pony? And the lights are shining all over America—

[*Off-screen laughter*]

Aaron: That's great, Lillian. Thanks.

[*Lillian leaves the studio.*]

Aaron: Definitely different.

Sally: Yeah. Her I like. Plenty to work with there.

TRANSCRIPT: BOBBY EVERETT SCREEN TEST FOR *THE MIDNIGHT SHOW* (JUNE 25, 1980)

[*Bobby perches on a stool holding a tiny piano on his lap.*]

BOBBY: Hello, hello, fine ladies and middling gentlemen.

AARON: Nice to see you again, Bobby. Have you prepared anything today, or—?

BOBBY: I have composed a song in your honor.

[*Off-screen laughter*]

SALLY (*off-screen*): In Aaron's honor or everybody's?

BOBBY: I'm afraid I only just met the rest of you ninety seconds ago, so you'll have to wait for your song. But feel free to hum along and invent your own lyrics. I'm not precious.

SALLY (*off-screen*): I can live with that.

[*Bobby loudly clears his throat. Plays a chord on the tiny piano.*]

BOBBY (*singing, folk-style*):
I've come here with a question for you, Aaron
There's a secret I hope you won't mind sharin'
See, this mystery's been playing on my mind
And I do hope you don't take this as unkind
But the thing I'm frankly desperate to know
How the hell did Adler land a network show?!

[*Laughter*]

Bobby (*singing*):
They're throwing money into an abyss
Forgive me if I say something's amiss
Sure, you've had a nice gig here and there
I'm a fan, as you are well aware
But hearing my acquaintance Aaron's got
Himself a shiny prime-time network slot—

Aaron (*off-screen*): It's not prime-time!

Bobby: No?

Aaron (*off-screen*): It's the midnight slot, Fridays.

Bobby: Middle of the night.

Aaron (*off-screen*): Pretty much.

Bobby: That's better! It is! No pressure at all. *The Midnight Show*. Of course. We can do whatever we want. Because nobody's watching.

Aaron (*off-screen*): I hope people will watch, but that's the idea. Do what we want.

Bobby: I like it. Exciting times. Keep me posted!

NOTES

My trip to the *Midnight Show* archives proves fruitful indeed. Amid the labyrinth of old costumes, prop pieces, and cast memorabilia, we find Lillian Martin's personal sketch journals (the PA confirms that yes, it's fine for me to take pictures).

The moment feels strangely sacred, almost as if I've picked up a telephone call from a ghost. Of course, these pages have already been examined by the police and the network's legal team. And yet these notebooks are buried, collecting dust, what's left of Lillian locked away in an archive. Did any of the previous writers and journalists consider these in their efforts to crack the famous cold case? Ever bother to even read them?

All these interviews and opinions I'm collecting on what really happened to Lillian . . . her own voice suddenly feels essential.

Listen carefully, she tells me. *Maybe you'll be smarter than the others.*

FROM LILLIAN MARTIN'S NOTEBOOK

Should I organize? Later. This is for quickness, rain to fill the well.

Put a wig on Stevie and have him show up as me. Or redo his audition. Time travel impossible, pull future Stevie in. First step, DO WELL ENOUGH. FULL WELL, DO WELL.

Sunflower war, classroom drunk teacher, child prayers, imaginary horses, the fridge thing

9/8/80

NEVER TAKE SUBWAY

Room very full, hard to focus

Drunk teacher might happen, ask Stevie? Driver's ed— everybody expects that, what if nice just crazy means well

A game, just like a big chessboard. Listen for rhythm and be ready to say the smart thing then ride that into the next move, know when to stop.

I can do this, I can do this

Breathe

The New York Times

VOL.CXXIX-No. 44,641
New York, Friday, July 11, 1980
25 Cents

New "Late-Night Comedy" Show to Debut in Fall

Joining the ranks of late-night television star Johnny Carson and variety show queenpin Carol Burnett, "The Midnight Show" will premiere this September, on Friday nights, in the midnight slot. The topical comedy sketch show will feature television veterans Nolan Young (of "Burnett" fame) and Brooke Balsinger, season regular on the hit sitcom "Settle Down." The cast will also include theater funnyman Bobby Everett, Boston improv comics Kent Romero, Sam Petrosian and Lillian Martin and LA stand-up Gina Ross.

The 90-minute program, which will air live each week from the network's studio in One Astor, will showcase a different guest host and musical number each week.

Created by New York comedy performer and writer Aaron Adler, the show promises to introduce a different and refreshing brand of comedy for the Vietnam generation . . .

IV.
GETTING STARTED

Lillian's First Day
(September 8, 1980)

To: The Office of Bobby Everett
From: Madeline Cohen
Date: June 10, 2023 12:54 PM
FW: FW: FW: Request for Interview—Lillian Martin Feature

Mr. Everett,

I thought I'd reach out once more in reference to the *Rolling Stone* feature I'm writing on the legacy of Lillian Martin. As my aim in this piece is actually to shine a light on Martin separate from the long shadows cast by the famous men she's been associated with, I'm not likely to require much of your time, but as I mentioned before, I did want to give you a chance to chime in, in lieu of a "Bobby Everett could not be reached for comment."

Best,

Madeline Cohen
Culture Writer
Rolling Stone

To: Madeline Cohen
From: The Office of Bobby Everett
Date: June 10, 2023 1:55 PM
Re: FW: FW: FW: Request for Interview—Lillian Martin Feature

Hi, Madeline.

I'm so sorry for the delay in responding; it's been quite a busy start to Mr. Everett's June!

Mr. Everett would love to speak with you about your project. It will have to be in person, as he's committed to a digital detox this summer. He has a week off from shooting starting on the 19th, so I'm sure we could make a pocket of time work within that frame, assuming you're in town?

Please provide some times that work from your end, and we'll get it scheduled!

Sincerely,

Alanna Ramon
Assistant to Bobby Everett

COMPILED TRANSCRIPTS—LILLIAN'S MOVE TO NYC

MADELINE: So when did you hear the Townies had landed *The Midnight Show*?

KENT ROMERO: We auditioned on a Wednesday, late June, drove back to Boston that night, wiped out, went straight to bed, no pre-celebration. We really had no idea what to expect. Received the call of destiny on the house phone the next morning and of all the people to answer the damn ring, it was Stevie. If you want to track the beginning of Stevie Doyle's downward spiral into the bitter little gnome he is today, it's right there in our living room at eleven o'clock in the morning. Stevie takes the call, writes all the info down. He says something suggesting passable enthusiasm, like "I will discuss with them and let you know," and hangs up before he tells me, "Oh yeah, that was Sally Schumacher, and Aaron wants us in New York by the end of the summer. We're hired."

STEVIE DOYLE: It was an awkward beginning to my writing career, leading into an uncomfortable middle, and eventually a really fucking anticlimactic ending. Sally was transparently disappointed when it was me who picked up the phone; she had some script she was working with and had to rearrange it on the spot. I heard *papers shuffling*. She said, "I'm so glad I've got you, Stevie." Bullshit. "We'd love to have you in the, *ahem ahem,* the *writers' room* for *The Midnight Show.*" Which I didn't even realize was on the table. I'm recalibrating the whole thing in my head when she adds, "And if you could let Kent, Sam, and Lillian know they've made it into the cast, that would be fantastic." Just offhand, like that wasn't as big a prize as getting to be a behind-the-scenes, off-camera nobody like me. That was Sally right there, smoothing all the ruffled feathers. You've heard of fluffers? She was the smoother. But I said yes. Of course I did. "Yes, thank you, how far should I bend over?"

MADELINE: And how did Lillian take the big news?

SAM PETROSIAN: We were all pretty beside ourselves. The offer was a thousand bucks an episode, more than we'd ever made in our lives, even Kent, as far as I know. We spent nearly that much going out to celebrate that night. Our victory parade. [*He mimes playing the trombone.*] I got Lillian her own bottle of champagne and she carried it around taking tiny sips, and every half hour or so, she'd panic. At a street corner, she grabbed my arm and said, "I'm getting a master's in French lit. I've already been accepted into the program!" I found an answer for everything. "You can defer enrollment, Lil!" "What if they change their minds about me?" "Then you come right back here and do your master's!" "Where will I live?" "You can live with us, same as now. We'll get an apartment together. A big one!"

But by the time we headed to New York, in late August, I think it was, she'd decided to get her own place. I'm still not sure why, but I saw it as a good sign, her feeling confident enough to be that independent.

KENT ROMERO: The night we got the *Midnight Show* offer, we went out carousing and Sam tried to kiss her. I saw it in slow motion from down the bar, like a train wreck, powerless to stop it, watching her go pale, turn her face, evade him, and excuse herself. Sam played it off like a pro. One hurt blink and back to the party. Lillian vanished for an hour and then came back to the bar and we continued on our merry way like nothing had happened. I don't know if they ever talked about it. Anyway, I wasn't all that surprised when she decided to create a little distance from us when we got to New York. I was, however, unbelievably surprised by the place she chose to live in. It was . . . masochistic.

STEVIE DOYLE: It's not like my own living situation was all that plush. Sam and Kent talked me into rooming with them in a two-bedroom near the park. *Two.* You do the math. Guess who wound up making a bedroom out of half the living room with a sheet as a divider, sleeping on a futon? Yep. But it was still a different category of shitty from where Lillian lived. I did not fear for my life, let's put it that way.

SAM PETROSIAN: You're young, Madeline, a New Yorker yourself, I take it. You think of Bryant Park today, you think Fashion Week, right? Luxury brownstones. Nicely tended flower beds. Well, allow me to give you a little history lesson. In 1980, it was called Needle Park. And Lillian is off in Lillian-land, pointing out the dusty window. "Look! Down there! I've got a view of trees." Yeah, four elms and a couple lovely junkies passed out under them. How scenic. But it was like she couldn't see the bad, anywhere. She decided, "This is nice; this is what I'll do," and there was no talking her out of it. At the end of the day, we had to let her live her life and trust that she knew what she was doing.

KENT ROMERO: She'd found this place in a classified ad and thought it was gee-whiz super-duper, because it was dirt cheap and it was, *ahem,* "furnished." We come up with her boxes and suitcases, helping her move, and oh yes, it's furnished. There is a mattress on the floor. A collapsing, stain-riddled puce sofa. A shag carpet with the distinct smell of Gouda emanating from its tendrils. A museum-piece television set. Best of all, topless pinups everywhere. From *Playboy,* not even vintage, literally pinned to the wall with tacks. Sam and I exchanged a look and started taking them down, but Lillian stopped us, said, "Oh no, Anthony said to keep them up. He was very particular about that."

SAM PETROSIAN: *Anthony,* the subletter–slash–potential serial killer. He popped in while we were still there, thank Christ almighty, giving me and Kent and Stevie the chance to form a protective triangle around Lillian and make clear that she was not in fact all alone in the world. But after we managed to scare the little perv off, bid good night to Lillian, and continued on to our own lodgings, Kent said, "We have got to get her out of there."

STEVIE DOYLE: She got more and more edgy those first few weeks, jumping at every car honk. Boston was one thing, but she was like a country mouse in Manhattan. It was August, then early September, a really hot summer, but she stayed covered up like a tiny elderly bag lady, and she still got wolf-whistled at and everything else. I thought, she's gonna move home before this show even hits the air.

GINA ROSS: I'd sprung for a place in the West Village, one of those bizarre shitholes so tiny the builder just plopped the shower in the living room, tucked the toilet bowl in the closet. Charming, right? But the outside was gorgeous, a brownstone with potted plants and a pristine stretch of sidewalk. It was a perfect metaphor, really, for my then state of mind: presentable exterior, barely functional interior.

I knew absolutely no one in New York, so I'd find myself just, like, wandering the streets that August, thinking about possible sketches, and suddenly I'd be at the doors of One Astor, as if all roads led to *The Midnight Show*. Every time I'd head up to fifteen, I assumed I'd have the place to myself, you know, like maybe I'd get an afternoon to sit in my office chair and just reflect, to revel in the serendipity of landing an opportunity like this, but the place was always bumping. The Boston crew wasn't in town yet, I don't think, but everyone else was there, hustling. This was weeks before our first official writing room, remember. And I thought, shit. This might be an ensemble show, but those old stand-up rules still apply. Everyone wants this as badly as I do. And there's only ninety minutes of airtime a week.

MADELINE: Would you call *The Midnight Show* environment more competitive or collaborative?

AARON ADLER: I think in order to answer that, I'd have to consider the two qualities mutually exclusive, which I don't. I've always been of the mind that the show would do best if it formulated its own tempo without undue interference on my part. There were lots of ideas, egos, different comedy styles coming in. I suppose my assumption was that the compressed, real-time nature of *The Midnight Show* might lend itself to a certain dynamism, a healthy competition from which collaboration would then ensue.

GINA ROSS: As our producer, Aaron of course exploited that—how shall we say?—cutthroat framework. Sketch comedy by way of *Squid Game*. He can be very manipulative. You've heard him tout how "hands-off" he is, yeah? How deferential he is to his talent? That's because he *designed* the show as kill-or-be-killed. As to whether it helped or hurt his cast in the long run . . . I think you know by now that's a very complicated answer, Cohen.

AARON ADLER: I launched every show week with a rapid-fire pitch meeting, Monday morning at ten A.M. We still keep the same schedule forty years later.

KENT ROMERO: Day one, September 8, 1980. That writers' room was like a kindergarten classroom filled with a bunch of feral children. Pure mayhem. Survival of the loudest. So, naturally, I came out in an extremely strong position. I grew up vying for my parents' attention amid chaotic family dinners. Interrupting is one of my many superpowers.

BROOKE BALSINGER: You can tell Aaron never had any friends as a kid, Margie. He set up his writers' meetings with these "tiers" of seats. Those in his favor would, like, sit right beside him at the actual conference room table. Then the people who were on the outs, like the writers and actors who'd maybe lost airtime for a few weeks because of crappy material or whatever, they'd be the *next* tier. And then the people Aaron found annoying were banished to the outer rim, with their backs against the windows. Some days, I swear, I worried someone might fall out of the building into Times Square!

Basically, it was all one big weekly birthday party for little friendless Aaron.

Now, Lillian . . . that girl could play his game. She never left Aaron's inner circle, no siree. She'd sit right next to him, week after week, whispering sweet nothings in his tiny goblin ear.

MADELINE: Where would you place Lillian on the strategic continuum?

GINA ROSS: Right alongside me. And Brooke. We had to be strategic. Not only were we players in a highly competitive field, we were women, trying to differentiate ourselves from Aaron's catch-all designation of Interchangeable Vagina. Lillian, Brooke, and I had been stuffed into one office together like a three-pack of gum. Pretty easy to get the sense that one or two of us were expendable. Three chairs, two desks, you do the math, while Kent, Bobby, Sam, Nolan, all the rest of them, even Sally, our head writer–slash–mother hen, got a nice spacious two-seater.

MADELINE: So Sally rose above Interchangeable Vagina status?

GINA ROSS: She was the Vagina to Rule Us All. Aaron's deputy. She shared an office with Stevie Doyle, so, yeah, okay, I didn't feel *that* jealous of her. But I noted the difference.

The ridiculous thing about it was that, yes, Lillian, Brooke, and I each had a pair of X chromosomes, but our comedy styles couldn't have been more different. I was edgy and dark. Lillian was whimsical, wacky, and weird. And Brooke—God, maybe you're onto something with your female archetypes. Her jokes, her style, her look, everything about her was just gaudy, so forcibly seductive. The comedy equivalent of Frederick's of Hollywood. She'd have done better in England, honestly, running around jiggling on *Benny Hill.*

MADELINE: And you don't see that as Brooke's own type of survival tactic? Her attempt to thrive within a sexist system?

GINA ROSS: I mean, sure, Cohen, but we can still admit her shit wasn't good. Anyway, I went into that first meeting ready to fight for myself.

I was pissed at Aaron and, while I am slightly embarrassed to admit this now, also pissed at the other vaginas just for existing.

NOLAN YOUNG, EXCERPT FROM "NOLAN'S FINAL BOW," *VILLAGE VOICE*: I knew from the first day working on *The Midnight Show* that I was going to be happy staying there awhile. What I did in that writing room that first week and all the weeks that followed was this: I kept my mouth shut. I leaned way back in my chair and listened to all the pitches. When I liked one, I would let out a big laugh and everybody'd turn and look at me, like "Ooh. Nolan likes it. That's going on the air." That's not to say I didn't have ideas. But I knew I couldn't pitch like everybody else. The Black guy had to have a team of writers behind him. I'd pass my stuff their way in a subtle manner. Collaborating, you see? But in that room, Monday mornings, pitchman was not my role. I was the tastemaker. I liked being the tastemaker. I also liked watching the circus around me without having to be one of the clowns.

STEVIE DOYLE: Day one was tense. Everybody was on edge. Lillian hadn't turned up. I didn't figure she was in any *danger*, like Sam did. I just assumed she'd choked. I knew even at that point that we'd made a mistake dragging her along with us onto the show. And yeah, that first morning of work, I guess part of me hoped she had moved home, re-enrolled at BU or whatever.

But then she walked in. Late. No explanation. Nobody said a word about it. She got a free pass, right away, where none of the rest of us did. I found that interesting.

KENT ROMERO: I tried to cut the tension, *taima, taima,* like my cousins used to say. I stood up and introduced myself, held on to my confidence, because why the fuck not, and had the room laughing by the time Lillie got settled in. There were hardly any seats left. She went straight for the far corner, where there was an empty chair next to, I don't know, some teenage page boy, but I was in a good spot right in the middle, so I said, "Shuffle down, everybody. She's fine-boned, we can make room." She wound up sitting next to the executive producer of the show. Which might have ruffled a few feathers, but I couldn't give two shits and still don't. She deserved to be there. And hey, white knight's a good look on me.

Stevie Doyle: It was a tough situation. I wasn't exactly ecstatic to be relegated to the wings, but I also knew I needed to have a backbone in that room and make the most of the melee situation or I wasn't even going to have *that* job for long. And it was warfare in there. Everybody one-upping each other, finding that tiny millisecond when the dominant player is breathing to interject their own idea. I did it too! You had to, to survive.

Lillian wasn't even trying. Just sitting there while the rest of us were jumping into the fray. I had this great idea about the Miracle on Ice, you know, the hockey team? Somebody mentioned sports, so there it was, my angle, an opportunity for me to pipe up, and then I hear, "I think Lillian's got an idea." *Fucking Sammy.* And everybody went silent and waited for Lillie to talk. So there went my first shot at making myself known. Poof, gone.

Sam Petrosian: It became a good way to sort of reset the game, get everybody to quiet down, whether she had an idea or not. Whenever cacophony reached fever pitch, one of us would say, "I think Lillian has an idea," and the room would go quiet. It was like a magic trick. And the best thing was, every damn time, Lillian *did* have an idea! And little by little, you could see Aaron paying her more respect. Fun to watch, as her friend.

Madeline: What were your feelings toward Lillian in those early meetings?

Gina Ross: God, this was so long ago, Cohen.

[*She glares, as if this is a loaded question.*]

Yeah, fine, detective. At the start, I didn't like Lillian, but with good reason. I'd been circling One Astor for weeks, remember, dreaming about sketches, practically camped out on the doorstep waiting for our first writers' meeting, while Lillian waltzed in a half hour late. All waif-fairy-princess energy, like she'd completely forgotten about this little obligation, she's just so busy, you know, getting lost in her art. "I was having tea with my squirrels and just *completely* lost track of time. Where *is* that white rabbit with the watch?" For the record, I told Lillian all this only three months later. Had a good laugh. Water under the troll bridge.

Brooke Balsinger: Lillian kept her first-tier seat next to Aaron *all season*. I still remember that first meeting when she came in over an hour late and plopped down right next to him! Gina looked at me and mouthed, "The f-ing nerve." Well, *she* said the real curse, but I'm not going to do that on the record, Margaret.

I'm sure you've heard the *Midnight Show* legend by now: Gina and Lillian put aside their differences, joined forces, took New York by storm, blah blah blah. Best friends forever. But that is bull-you-know-what.

Madeline: Were you ever jealous of Lillian?

Gina Ross: It was . . . complicated. I never considered myself the type of woman who begrudges another woman's charisma, but with Lillian? We were duking it out for airtime from that very first day, and it was like she'd stacked the room. All the guys in the cast were obsessed with her. The Townies favored her, for obvious reasons. They had a history. But God, Bobby . . . as soon as Lillian took her seat at the table, he just locked in on her. Like a tractor beam. Very first day, you could already tell they were going to fuck.

Sam Petrosian: Bobby? Gosh. I wouldn't say that he was the only one taken with Lillian, by any means. I also wouldn't say she was the sole center of attention for anyone that first Monday meeting. We were feeling out our fellow cast members, you know? Gina was quite a presence, for one. She had a great energy in the room, and she was always on. Even when we went out into the hallway to smoke, she was ready with the one-liners. That kind of person is always going to rise to the top in pitching. She was punching up her own ideas on the spot.

I was concerned for Lillie, that her energy might get buried in a room full of actual writers. She'd only ever done improv; that was her comfort zone. But she came in prepared, and I kicked myself for doubting her. She had a student's notebook, mottled black and white. This was like coming to class for her, and she'd done her homework. Of course she had.

Stevie Doyle: Soon as Lillian started pitching, her personal emcee Petrosian giving her intros, I realized she had *never* been as hapless and innocent as we'd wanted to believe. She probably turned up late to make everybody notice her. Wouldn't put it past her, knowing what I know now.

Sally Schumacher: Lillian was an easy person to discount, *so* young, but that first day, she demonstrated more maturity than a lot of the others. She came in prepared, pitches ready, took notes throughout, so that when she did speak up, it was with ideas on how to combine concepts or make them funnier. Here's an example. Do you remember those driving instructor sketches? I can't remember who brought that pitch in, but it was half-baked, just a middle-aged dude sexually harassing his teen driver. Like, sure. I wasn't wildly enthusiastic, and I could see my expression, my wince or whatever it was, mirrored across the table on Lillian's face.

Stevie Doyle: That was me, that was a pitch I finally got through, and then Lillian tore it to shreds in front of everybody. So much for Townies loyalty. First day, everybody out for themselves.

Sally Schumacher: Lillian shifted it to what it became, those ridiculous pieces of life advice the instructor gives, which is so much more unexpected and therefore funnier than the pervert everybody's expecting. And that became one of our longer-running sketches for Bobby. We used to swap out the student driver role and give it to the hosts sometimes. So for my money, just with that sketch alone, Lillian earned her place at the table.

But of course, it was onstage that she really came alive. Even in rehearsals during those next two weeks, you could see everybody nodding at each other, like oh, yep, this was a good call. And I was never too proud to say, "I told you so." [*She laughs.*] I said it *all* the time.

That wound up being the first Lillian and Bobby sketch. We had that adorable factor with them. And ultimately, more than I'd bargained for.

TRANSCRIPT OF INTERVIEW WITH BOBBY EVERETT

(*TMS* cast member, 1980–1982)

June 19, 2023

Bobby's gated estate boasts acres of manicured gardens, a pond, a pool, and tennis courts scattered around a sprawling white dictator-style megamansion.

His petite wife, Sunny, welcomes me with an explanation I struggle to translate. "Bobby's just stepped out of the float cabin. He'll be down any moment."

Bobby emerges in jeans, a T-shirt that looks like it costs more than my monthly salary, and a black *montsuki,* his shoulder-length hair still wet. Far cry from the clean-cut boy wonder look of his *TMS* days.

Bobby Everett never had the sex appeal of his old colleague Kent Romero, but there's always been something desirable about him—the same je ne sais quoi that allowed him to easily transition into Oscar-winning roles. He's a superstar who clearly cares about the world: attending red-carpet events for Equality Now, serving on the board of the Malala Fund . . . he even started his own scholarship fund for marginalized directors at the Sundance Institute. After a surprisingly lengthy round of small talk (mainly centering on Erewhon smoothies), Bobby and I head to the living room to delve into his life with Lillian.

MADELINE: Thanks for agreeing to chat with me. I know you're incredibly busy.

BOBBY EVERETT: Not at all. I'm so glad we could finally get it scheduled.

MADELINE: And I know this is, potentially, quite an emotional and fraught topic for you—

Bobby Everett: You know, it is. I won't lie. It's hard to talk about Lillian. But it's also a joy? Do you know what I mean? It hurts because it was beautiful. For all the pain, I would not take back a second of what we had together. From that very first day.

Madeline: Did you initially meet during screen tests?

Bobby Everett: No, not until the cast assembled with the writers on that first official Monday, two weeks before our premiere. I was just getting my footing on this rocking ship. A lot of big personalities were crammed into one room, and that was our introduction to each other. I sometimes wonder what might have been different if Aaron had thrown us a nice cocktail party to meet one another instead of shoving us together in a corner office, but hey. As Thich Nhat Hanh says, "The universe exists in this present moment," so that's where I prefer to stay.

Madeline: In that case, I apologize in advance for asking you to delve into the past.

Bobby Everett: Not at all. Go on.

Madeline: What was your first impression of Lillian?

Bobby Everett: My impression was that I was impressed. Ha—this is why I'm not a journalist. It is the right word, though. She was clearly somebody important, since we all moved over to make room for her at the central table. She was fashionably late, which my socialite mother, God rest her soul, would have approved of. And she quietly held space for herself in a way that I found incredibly magnetic. When she did speak, people listened. And then, my God, the things she said were so unbelievably strange.

Madeline: Strange in what way?

Bobby Everett: She had a truly unique sense of humor. Boy, she was funny. There really was only one Lillian Martin, and I sensed that from the day I met her.

[*His face breaks into a "you got me" smile, even though I've said nothing.*]

And yes, of course, I noticed how beautiful she was. I was across the round table from her. I had a good view. Impossibly delicate and glowing . . . she was wearing a peasant shirt that tied with a bow at the neck, and it gave her this look of having traveled to us through time. Unforgettable. As you can probably tell, I was a goner. At first sight. The other guys in that early cast, they'll tell you wild stories about the revolving door of girls they slept with, the friends with benefits and groupies and everything else, but my experience of *The Midnight Show* was an entirely monogamous one. It's all wrapped up in me and Lillian.

I had one thought when we took our first break that day, and that was her. I practically climbed across the table to get to her before anybody else. I didn't know if she was with Sam—I'm not sure if *Sam* knew whether she was with him or not at that point—but I needed to find out. Introduce myself. Or just . . . get closer. I felt like I was going to die if I didn't at least shake her hand. Literally. It was a physical desperation.

[*A ring sounds from the credenza. Bobby picks up the landline.*]

Just a moment, Madeline. My apologies.

[*He paces to the window, voice dropping to a murmur.*]

Hey, short notice, I know, but it's the downtime that . . . Yes, the mantras helped, but I thought . . . I believe she did get the new citrine. No, absolutely. Let me wrap something up, give me five.

[*He sits down again.*]

Sorry about that, Madeline. My shaman. Do you have a spiritual coach? Essential, especially in this business. Speaking of, I'm really sorry to have to cut our meeting short, but I do need to get back to her. My door is always open, I know we just scratched the surface. What about the same time next Monday?

Madeline: Oh, totally understand! Unfortunately, I'm only in town through the weekend. Maybe we can arrange a follow-up meeting via phone, or—?

BOBBY EVERETT: You know what . . . [*He consults a leather planner on the end table.*] I've got a window Wednesday afternoon. Two-thirty?

[*I nod, and he offers me a hand up from the sofa.*]

This is a priority. I'm so glad you're writing this retrospective, you have no idea, and I want to help. However I can. Where are you staying while you're in town?

MADELINE: West Hollywood. Melrose and San Vicente.

BOBBY EVERETT: Oh, fantastic. Stop by Yamamoto! Not *quite* Urasawa standards but still fabulous, really. Tell Yusuke I sent you. [*He winks before turning to go.*]

V.
PREMIERE

The Snake in the Office
(September 19, 1980)

COMPILED TRANSCRIPTS

SALLY SCHUMACHER: We needed a host for the first episode, and Aaron suggested, "Why don't we ask Redford?" As in Robert Redford. Sure, why not the Pope? So I came back with "I thnk we could land . . . Wally Winters?" Aaron was thrilled, thank the Lord. Wally was a get, actually. He was still big at the time, though rumored to be a little, shall we say, eccentric? But he had that Hollywood royalty sheen, he was selling out in Vegas, getting big cameo movie roles, which made him pricey. Still, we knew darn well we needed a draw for that first episode, so if everything else went tits up, at least we could say, hey, we're legit, we had Wally Winters on our show.

STEVIE DOYLE: Man, when I heard it was gonna be Wally Winters hosting the premiere, it got real. I idolized him. We'd listened to his comedy records on repeat back in college. It upped the ante for the material we were producing, no doubt about it. And if anything, I was even more pissed off I wouldn't get to be on camera with the guy.

GINA ROSS: Wally Winters. I know he's like ninety now, so I feel slightly bad saying this, but what a crude, cheesy motherfucker. First thing he says when he walks into the writers' room on Monday: "Hubba-hubba ding-dong, New York, behold Big Wally's schlong!" I mean.

MADELINE: He has not stood the test of time.

GINA ROSS: He hadn't stood the test of time back in '80. Just a totally different, and in my case unwelcome, energy to what we were doing. Our *TMS* crew had spent weeks building this perfect playhouse, constructing our sketches, stacking them up just so, and Wally stumbled in like a three-year-old hopped up on apple juice and sent the whole thing crashing down.

Brooke Balsinger: Wally Winters? Gross. Barely human. Wait, is he dead yet?

Gina Ross: I'd lobbied hard to get my stuff in, you know. I had this piece that week with Sam where I was a ventriloquist with this super mouthy dummy. Sam was the dummy, and he was supposed to pick a series of escalating fights with these guys who were hitting on me at a bar. Wally thought *he* should be the dummy, and cooked up this whole double-entendre monologue about *wood.* Another sketch I'd helped on featured Kent as Jack Torrance from *The Shining,* who's now teaching creative writing at a community college. Wally inserted himself in as this, like, sixteenth-semester senior who got most of the lines. It didn't work. None of it worked, but I felt like Brooke and I were the only ones who noticed. Maybe Lillian, too . . . but she never, ever talked shit in our office—at least during those early days. Later, it was all fair game.

That first season, those first few shows, we'd talk shit about Lillian, too, when she went to the bathroom or whatever. I'd heard Kent call her Rapunzel, endearing on his part, I suppose, but Brooke and I mocked her with it. *Rapunzel, Rapunzel, let down your hair!* I.e., loosen the hell up, princess, you're boring us. If anybody was going to summon my better angels, it wasn't gonna be Brooke Balsinger.

Sam Petrosian: Wally was game for everything, I'll say that for him. He would have played every single role in every sketch if we'd agreed to it. Hard to say no to a legend. The one bit he wanted but we managed to keep him out of was my John Wayne sketch. John Wayne and his nagging mother-in-law, played by Brooke, Lillian as the damsel in distress. I'd auditioned with my John Wayne impression [*he does the John Wayne impression while saying "John Wayne impression"*], so Wally had to keep his geriatric fingers off my sketch, thank you very much.

Brooke Balsinger: A mother-in-law, *me,* at twenty-eight! I mean, have you *seen* pictures of me at twenty-eight, Mary? You better believe my manager got a dozen calls that week. My last gig before *TMS* was playing Heather on *Settle Down,* who was eighteen, nineteen max. But since Lillian was prepubescent and Gina was already in half a dozen sketches, it fell to me to wear the curly gray wig and nag John Wayne. Ab-surd.

KENT ROMERO: I was on the desk, doing *Late-Breaking News,* and those jokes were written morning-of, so I had my hands full when I wasn't onstage, but I did have a chance to watch bits of the dress rehearsal. Live audience for the first time, four hundred strong. Hours to go until air. This was my first time on a production like this, with all the cameras, over a hundred lights, backdrop upon backdrop waiting in the wings to be shuffled onto the three stages. Sets, costumes, wigs, everything you could think of, thirty stagehands managing it all. Just a vertiginous amount of bustle in every direction, bordering on outright panic. I centered myself, as it were, by watching my fellow cast members.

Everybody was either coming alive or falling on their faces. Nolan was himself, relaxed; this was old hat for him. And Lillian was remarkably solid throughout—everybody else was a raw nerve, but she just kind of glided through as if she wasn't really sure what we were all so worked up about. To her, at that point, there was no pressure at all. It was just fun. Some of it was clearly not working, including the *Shining* sketch, so I wasn't surprised when Aaron took the hatchet to it. Lillian didn't get ruffled when some of her stuff got cut. Her driving instructor bit made it, and the John Wayne cold open, which absolutely killed in dress. Brooke was great, hand-to-heart, probably the best she ever played that role.

I have no idea what happened between then and the live taping.

STEVIE DOYLE: All my sketches, apart from the John Wayne sketch I'd worked on with Sammy, got cut between dress and live. All I had was that cold open. I thought well, shit, here we go, I'm the outcast of the show in week one, unless that first sketch kills, right? Everybody knew what my contributions were to that script. Which was what wound up *dooming* me. Brooke, too, both of us trampled under Lillian's so-called talent.

PHIL ACKERMAN: The network, in our infinite wisdom—please note the sarcasm here, Madeline!—was counting on Brooke and Nolan to carry the show. They were our known quantities, the names on the marquee, the highest-paid cast members, for goodness' sake. We'd expected them to light that stage on fire during the premiere, and while Nolan was the star we'd signed, Brooke's performance was shocking. And not in a "zeitgeist moment" way. She froze up. It was painful to watch, really. Infuriating! Although I felt for her. I am human, after all.

BROOKE BALSINGER: Of course I know I became a punchline that fall. Everyone blames me for ruining the premiere. "Brooke makes the most money; shouldn't she be perfect with that price tag?" Blah blah blah. You know I really don't appreciate reliving this, Molly, and have nothing to prove through this little project of yours. But for the record, that John Wayne sketch was not my fault, it was *Wally's*. And Lillian's! She was hell-bent on stealing the spotlight. The only thing I did wrong was give her the opportunity.

MADELINE: I'm . . . having a bit of a hard time picturing Lillian Martin as "hell-bent" on anything.

BROOKE BALSINGER: Don't believe me? Ask around. I am *not* the only one who saw her for who she really was.

TRANSCRIPT OF VIDEO INTERVIEW WITH GINA ROSS

[*TMS* cast member, 1980–1983]

June 20, 2023

MADELINE: Thanks so much for jumping on with me on such short notice.

GINA ROSS: At your disposal, my liege. Nothing to do over here but twiddle my thumbs and wait for your various and sundry questions. Wait, where are you now? What's that background?

MADELINE: It's West Hollywood. Through a window.

GINA ROSS: I assume the magazine's footing the bill?

MADELINE: It's not a hotel. I'm crashing with a friend from college.

GINA ROSS: That's reassuring. I was starting to worry I was your only friend. But I digress—you wanted to ask me something?

MADELINE: So, ah, last conversation, we covered up to prepping for the *Midnight Show* premiere. I've heard from others that the first episode was an eye-opener in terms of competition among the cast. That Lillian, in particular, was somewhat eager to steal the spotlight for herself, starting with the John Wayne—

GINA ROSS: The mother-in-law sketch? Stealing the . . . who said that? You know what, never mind, it was obviously Brooke.

MADELINE: She did not have a good night.

Gina Ross: For which she blames *Lillian*. Fucking typical.

[*Gina turns away from the camera for a second, jaw clenched.*]

Okay. I'm going to go out on a limb for you, Cohen. This is information I've never shared with anybody outside the *Midnight Show* circle. It's sure as shit not in *It Started at Midnight*. Picture the fifteenth floor, September 19, 1980. The night of the premiere. It's the hour between dress and the live show, and we've just run all the way upstairs from the studio—this was before the extra offices were built out around the lower stage. The clock is ticking, Aaron's pacing the halls, agonizing over scripts, shucking the pages he doesn't want while Sally and the writers follow him, birds trailing breadcrumbs, manically pecking, scrambling to reframe what's survived Aaron's cuts around the timed commercial slots. And the stuff that stays doesn't just *stay*. Aaron's barking *his* reactions to the *dress rehearsal audience's* reactions to every. Damn. Joke.

We're all gathered in the hall around him, hovering near our office doors, Wally Winters gleefully floating amid the chaos like a Macy's Thanksgiving Day Parade balloon, Lillian with that composition book at the ready. It felt like we'd been tasked as a group to dismantle a ticking bomb. Then Aaron finished his rant, and we all booked it back to our offices. Lillian, Brooke, and I—

Madeline: What time was this, approximately?

Gina Ross: What time? I don't know, Nancy Drew. I guess after the final sketch, we changed out of our costumes, then rounded up, and Aaron's meeting lasted maybe fifteen minutes . . . so eleven-twenty? Eleven-thirty? Eleven–who fucking cares? The relevant piece of information is that as the three of us hurry into our office, who ambles in after us but Wally Winters. And he shuts the door behind him.

Madeline: Wally Winters. In your office. Just the four of you.

Gina Ross: Correct. Our first live show is thirty, or whatever, thirty-*two,* minutes away. Write that down. Aaron had cut my *Shining* sketch, rearranged the ventriloquist number. I knew Sam and I were going to have to round up on it, but first, I had to punch up my Rogue Soprano bit—this was show numero uno, remember, before Lillian and I did those opera sketches together. Brooke and Lillian are at the other desk, with the pages of the John Wayne sketch splayed out in front of them like a road map. They'd been tasked with shaving off a minute. Stevie was too precious about his material, so they decided to do the cuts themselves. And Wally saunters over to them, unzips, and . . . lays his anaconda penis across their pages.

MADELINE: I'm sorry. What?

GINA ROSS: Gotta hand it to the guy, I never thought a man of his stature could be endowed like that. The potbelly, the rounded spine—what is he, five foot seven?

But I digress. I don't know if he was on something—the drugs weren't flowing on set yet like they would be a couple months later—but he's got this manic glint in his eye. He's wired. Dangerous. Clearly! I start sputtering, Lillian has gone stock-still, and Brooke, who's the closest to this snake-monster, just recoils. Her eyes go wide, her mouth falling open in a silent scream. Wally grins at her reaction. And the bastard says, "Even wider, doll, for a boy this big."

MADELINE: I feel like I should not be as shocked by this as I am.

GINA ROSS: Try to watch *Wizards of Whimsy* now, knowing what a pervert he is.

MADELINE: So what did you do?

GINA ROSS: He was advancing on Brooke like a dog attempting to mount, so I grabbed his collar. All I saw was blood red—and I shoved him, full force, into the hall.

He just kept cackling like the Mad Hatter, like this was all one big spoof, so I started screaming, "Aaron, Sally, get the hell in here!" But out in the hall, *everyone* was screaming for Aaron and Sally, and so Wally just took off, going "Tee-hee-hee," like little Georgie Porgie, incorrigible rascal, couldn't help his charming predisposition toward, you know, sexual assault.

MADELINE: And then?

GINA ROSS: And then what? With minutes to go before the show? I got back to work. What were my options? Call up the network brass? Blow up the boat and go down with it, shouting "*Vive la femme!*" as I drowned?

MADELINE: But what about after the show? Not a word? I mean, anyone who pulls a move like that is clearly a serial offender. Why do you think, over the years, no one has ever said anything? Why didn't Lillian?

GINA ROSS: Lillian's instinct was always to nurture. She was like a triage nurse. When I went back into the office, I found her rubbing Brooke's back, both of them bone white, still trapped in Wally's fun house, but Lillian turned that energy into helping somebody else, while Brooke kept muttering, "I can't do this. I can't do this."

MADELINE: No wonder Brooke was so shaky when she got onstage.

GINA ROSS: It happened to all of us, though, and not all of us fell apart. Lillian and I dug right back in. This was our first show, remember. We weren't about to let that fucker set the tone for it. And by the way, this shit still happens, Cohen; ask any female comedian working today. The industry's a cesspool of predators.

MADELINE: Okay, but I feel like you're arguing against yourself a little bit here. Wouldn't speaking out at least shine a light on—

GINA ROSS: You're assuming—huge assumption—that anyone would have cared. I will remind you once more that Wally Winters was a beloved star. We were three young women in 1980 who barely had our feet in the door, and the second you complain, that's all you are. *You* become the problem, not him. We were expendable, and we knew it. All we could do was put our heads down and . . .

You know, even in the chaos, I bill that as the first moment Lillian and I actually worked together. We had a literal show to put on, and Brooke was near comatose, so revising John Wayne fell to us. We made a ton of slashes, punch-ups. I remember this lightning-fast rat-a-tat, using shorthand for jokes, filling in each other's punchlines like we'd been working together for years. To this day, Cohen, I've never experienced that kind of madcap magical synergy again.

We headed down to the stage, handed the new pages to the cue card guys to write out on poster board. All the while, Lillian's stroking Brooke's hair, I'm muttering that I'm going to murder the son of a bitch as soon as the curtains close. But we had a job to do, a network and audience to woo, and all our futures rested on our ability to play the game and deliver.

I thought, with those sketch edits, that we'd done just that.

And then we went on-air.

TRANSCRIPT—
COLD OPEN SKETCH, LIVE PERFORMANCE,
SEPTEMBER 19, 1980

[*An Old West homestead. A farm girl (Lillian) churns butter. John Wayne (Sam) saunters up, bowlegged.*]

FARM GIRL: Oh, jeepers. Oh, fret and bother. That was the last of it!

JOHN WAYNE: What seems to be the trouble, little lady?

FARM GIRL: Bandits rode through not an hour ago. Mister, they cleaned out all our food, our money. We're bound to starve with winter coming on!

JOHN WAYNE: Not if I've got anything to do with it.

[*An old woman (Brooke) in present-day clothes walks up, clutching her handbag.*]

MOTHER-IN-LAW: What're you gonna . . .

[*Brooke stares past the scene, teeth clenched tight, silent. Very awkward beat, and then—*]

FARM GIRL: Oh, golly gosh, and they've stolen this poor old woman's voice as well! That's what they call them, you know. The Muteifying Banditos.

JOHN WAYNE: Muteifying, you say.

FARM GIRL: That's right, mister! Only reason they didn't steal my voice is because my mama told me never to sing in broad daylight or the Lord might confuse me for an angel and snatch me right up to heaven. But you said you could help?

JOHN WAYNE: You bet I can. Not only that, but I'm a'gonna.

FARM GIRL: But do you even know how to churn butter?

[*Laughter*]

FARM GIRL: Here, give it a try. There you go, just like that.

[*She teaches John Wayne to churn butter, somewhat suggestively.*]

FARM GIRL: And ma'am, don't you worry about your voice one bit. I bet it'll fly right back home like the souls of those baby pigs Pawpaw made me butcher.

JOHN WAYNE (CHURNING): Now listen, little lady, this here is women's work. What I'm a'gonna do is pull together a posse and round up those—

FARM GIRL: You want your wife to churn the butter?

JOHN WAYNE: My what now?

FARM GIRL: Your—

MOTHER-IN-LAW (*weakly*): I'm his mother-in-law.

FARM GIRL: Your voice, it flied back like I telled you! And just in time, thank golly, because . . .

FARM GIRL AND JOHN WAYNE (TO AUDIENCE): It's time for *The Midnight Show*!

COMPILED TRANSCRIPTS

Stevie Doyle: And boom. [*Makes an explosion noise.*] There goes my script.

Brooke Balsinger: Lillian gave me zero time to recover. She swooped in and stole my big premiere moment straight out from under me. She was conniving. Like *sooooo* conniving. And this was after she pretended to be all supportive when . . . well, there was some drama with Wally, but I'm not going to get into that.

Madeline: What was your reaction to Lillian's pivot in that sketch?

Gina Ross: While I was watching? Admiration. I'd never seen such on-the-fly thinking. Brooke had bombed in Oppenheimer proportions, and Lillian saved the day. Ad-libbed beautifully. Never been the strongest skill of mine, live improv—though you probably got that from my Carson set.

So along with admiration, there was . . . a certain degree of unease on my part. All the female cast members were fighting one another for airtime. Expendable, remember? The brighter one of us shined, the dimmer the rest of us appeared. That was reality.

Sam Petrosian: I loved it! You kidding? Lillian jumped on the moment of Brooke turning deer in the headlights and steered that sketch into absolute absurdity. She made the entire *Midnight Show* what it was, from that very first cold open. With Brooke going off the rails, it could have rendered us all catatonic. Instead, everybody came out electrified. And boy oh boy did it validate the presence of we mere improv comedians among the cast.

Kent Romero: The audience reacted with that kind of startled laughter you get with good improv shows, rather than canned yuks from

PAs holding up LAUGH NOW signs. We came out, made a huddle, embraced each other. Dragged Stevie over too, to celebrate. That was probably the last hurrah for the four of us, before the cracks started to show. But right then, it felt like a win for the Townies more than any of those other self-important fuckers in the cast. And yes, I do recognize the irony of me saying that, given my industry-wide reputation for . . .

[*He raises his eyebrows like he wants me to fill in the blank.*]

MADELINE: Arrogance?

KENT ROMERO: What can I say? I've always known my worth and never bothered with observing the niceties of pretending otherwise. Life's too damn short, Madeline. Wouldn't you agree?

AARON ADLER: We had a ten-episode order, a runway to take off from. Even so, of course there was pressure on that premiere, which, minus a few early hiccups, went as smoothly as I believe it could have . . . and yet the pressure didn't let up. I think everyone in the cast was aware that this was going to be a continually fluid situation. In a sense, everyone was constantly auditioning, week after week, which is still how I run things today. Along with a bit of celebration, which is essential for team-building.

SAM PETROSIAN: We could have said good night, everybody, gone to bed like good boys and girls and woken up in the morning to the reviews. But performing live for a national audience does something special to your adrenal system. There was too much blood pumping for us to go home, you know? [*He mimes a cartoon heartbeat.*]

NOLAN YOUNG, EXCERPT FROM "NOLAN'S FINAL BOW," *VILLAGE VOICE*: They were kids in a lot of ways. I was only five, ten years older than them, but I'd lived a lot more life than they had in that time. I felt like their good-time uncle. They looked up to me, kinda cheered every time I'd walk into the room, and I did enjoy that. Right there at that first after-party, following our premiere, I said to myself, "You're gonna need to be careful not to get swept up in this." I was four years clean and sober, but that bubble can burst in an instant, I was well aware. And I could only be their buddy to a certain extent, you get me? At least half my life needed to stay my own. Anyway, they were a fun bunch. I had the sense that we were gonna have a great time. Didn't see all the sadness that was on its way.

KENT ROMERO: Me and Gina went out to a bodega and brought back cases and cases of booze and we all got wildly intemperate, right there in our place of work, even Lillian. Nolan Young was several years sober, but he hung around so he could laugh at us. Only one who left was Wally Winters, thank Christ. Brooke stayed, which surprised me. She'd looked like she was planning to move to Tijuana and change her name after that performance.

BROOKE BALSINGER: I had no interest in spending extra time with those people, *especially* after what happened during the premiere, but being the team player that I am, of course I hung around for that first unofficial after-party. I'd also, like, had this epiphany about halfway through the show, and I needed to talk to Stevie stat.

He was about three drinks in when I cornered him. Lillian had done the nasty to *both* of us reworking that John Wayne sketch. I wanted Stevie to write for *me,* to create characters for *me,* Brooke Balsinger's own material, and in exchange . . . I'd scratch his back in the writers' room. Lend a little star power, right?

That lit him up like a Christmas tree, so I kept going, told him he was undervalued, invisible, when he should be leading those Monday meetings, blah blah blah. I mean, sure, Stevie Doyle was a good writer. But the main reason I went after him? He was the black sheep of that Townies crew. They were already starting to shut him out of their little clique.

From then on, me and Stevie were a duo. Not the way he wanted, *blech,* but professionally. And I was happy about that. I guess I thought he was nicer than the others, maybe a better person. But Stevie is messed up in all kinds of ways I did *not* see coming. Like . . . psycho messed up.

Don't ask me about that either, Marilyn. My apologies, but I really can't tell you any more than I already have.

The New York Times

VOL.CXXX-No. 44,713
New York, Sunday, September 21, 1980
25 Cents

REVIEW

How Many Laughs Equate to "Funny"?

Adler's "The Midnight Show" Bows with a Meow

By Elliot Huxley

In theory, "The Midnight Show" is a great idea: Take a bunch of energetic, decent-looking, young funny people, add an of-the-moment celebrity host and musical act and perform a variety sketch show live on late-night television.

Unfortunately, the success of any great idea rests squarely on execution, and if Aaron Adler's premiere accomplished anything, it was underscoring that fact.

Cast members Sam Petrosian, Bobby Everett, Gina Ross and veteran Nolan Young never seemed to find their stride as an ensemble, awkwardly transitioning from one improbable sketch to the next, while Boston comic Kent Romero, headlining a "Late-Breaking News" segment featuring bogus headlines, seemed more concerned with preening for the cameras than roasting politicians. Host Wally Winters was underutilized, while sitcom actress Brooke Balsinger notably struggled with the vehicle's format, lending the whole show the vague aura of a high school stage production.

One diamond amid the rough: newcomer Lillian Martin, an improv comedienne hailing from Canada with impeccable timing and flair for the absurd. Let's hope Adler is smart enough to realize he's got at least one gem on his hands, and that he adjusts his camera lens's focus accordingly . . .

VI.
THE RUNWAY

In with a Whimper
(October–December 1980)

Spontaneity became the show's core element from the very first episode. In that sense, Aaron Adler had achieved his first goal—but it took the steadying paternal gravitas of his now-legendary leadership to harness that youthful lightning and direct it into what it became: a major force in American pop culture.

—PHILIP HORTON,
It Started at Midnight: A TMS History

FROM LILLIAN MARTIN'S NOTEBOOK

All congratulations, all change. "Gem on his hands," blood on mine. Stevie hates me now. This city hates me. I leave work, curl up like a dead bug.

Cockroach sitcom—too gross. Moths?

Leave? Everyone will hate me.

Small town where everyone hates clueless woman running errands

Play on it, everyone hoping to be canceled, Sam lives w/ bears, Kent Playboy Mansion, I'm interviewing for jobs

Job interview w/ potato

COMPILED TRANSCRIPTS

Aaron Adler: As I said, it was a runway. I knew there would be an adjustment period.

Sam Petrosian: Lillian was embarrassed reading that first review. We went to our coffee shop, corner booth, usual Sunday-morning routine, but this time, we're hoping to read rapturous fawning nonsense about all of us. Some needy infant in your brain is always desperate for that; it's what makes you go into the fame game in the first place. But Lillian wasn't like that. She was more one to bury her head in the sand.

Kent's flipping through the Arts section. Lillie's trying to distract us, talking about anything she can. Finally, she says, "I've got this issue with Anthony," her stalker landlord, and whoo boy, that got our attention. "He's been popping by unannounced. I was in the shower one time and he let himself in . . ." Now, I'm not a murderous guy, but I'm ready to start cooking up harebrained schemes about how Lil and I might take the guy out—Acme anvil trap? rent check with ricin in the envelope?—when Kent shouts, "Here!"

He reads us the review. And it's fine. *Mid,* as my kids say. Lillian was singled out as the performer showing the most promise, and she just about crawled under the table hearing that. In the process of congratulating her, we cheered ourselves up and wound up going from the Three-Star Diner to a bar to celebrate.

By the end of the day, I think a little bit of our parade glitter had made its way onto Lillian, because Monday morning, walking into the writers' room for the second show's pitch meeting, she was on time, sitting next to Aaron. And there was a certain confidence there I hadn't seen before. I was glad to see it! But it marked a change. Good and bad.

Sally Schumacher: Monday morning, Lillian is there, punctual, one of her schoolgirl notebooks at the ready. She didn't give a hoot about the impression those made, and neither did I, because what was inside was serious business. She started speaking up for herself, nobody needing to shush the room like a few weeks prior. And the sketch she pitched that day was so dang strange. I laughed hearing it, in shock more than anything. It was . . . do you remember the potato?

MADELINE: The potato job interview? Of course, that's in all the Best Of videos. I always assumed it was Kent's pitch, given that he's, you know, the potato.

SALLY SCHUMACHER: As well you might, but nope, it was Lillian. She laid it out, potato in a job interview, interviewer trying not to point out that he's a potato because, you know, that would be rude. Everyone in the room is attempting to get their heads around this. Aaron's coming up with dialogue for the potato, and Lillian, dead serious, says, "No. The potato doesn't talk. It's a potato." "A small—" "No, it is a person in a potato suit, but it does nothing a potato wouldn't do." "So then you end with a button, like a handshake, 'I'll introduce you to your coworker, Gravy.'" And Lillian, "No puns. No punchline. And it will never be acknowledged that it's a potato."

Everybody was thrown. How do you end this, then? Lillian wasn't interested in endings; she said it should continue, even as a standalone, spin it as far as it could go. She laid it all out. And that's how we wound up with that montage of—

MADELINE: The potato getting married—

SALLY SCHUMACHER: Running for office, becoming president, then we end with that scene at the funeral, the interviewer laying flowers on the grave. All that was in her pitch.

AARON ADLER: The potato interview? I saw the potential right away, sure. And judging by the sketch's endurance, I'd say my instincts were spot-on.

PHIL ACKERMAN: Yeah, that was one of the jokes I just never got. And yet it's a classic, so there you go! I leave the comedy to the comedians.

SALLY SCHUMACHER: We're gettin' laughs around the table. I'm just taking notes and marveling at the absurd way we've somehow managed to start episode two of *The Midnight Show* when Aaron says, "I like Bobby for the interviewer. Who plays the potato?" Lillian says, "I do." I mean, obviously, it's her sketch, her role, right? But this chuckle goes round the table, and my hackles go up. I think it was Aaron who says, "We're already straining credulity having a potato as the president of the United States, let alone a female."

That room went cold. At least for me, it did. I looked around the table, met Lillian's eyes, Gina's, Brooke's. The men were unperturbed. And Kent, famously, played the potato.

GINA ROSS: Fucking bullshit is what it was. I mean really, the audience can buy a goddamn potato rolling itself down Fifth Avenue, pulling strings to land an interview, but whoa, whoa, a female carbohydrate in the White House? Now, that's too much!

I watched Lillian all-out deflate. She'd floated into the room like a birthday balloon, Cohen, shiny and starry-eyed, almost stream-of-consciousness laying out this brilliantly cuckoo sketch, beat-for-bonkers-beat, and with one line, one misogynistic, bullshit comment, she gets punctured. So I blurted out, "Are you fucking serious with this, Aaron?" Everyone just blinked at me, like a room full of possessed dolls. Or like I was a goddamn ghost.

AARON ADLER: I don't recall Gina shouting at me, no. In my recollection, we all came to a consensus in that meeting. It's odd that she told you that.

GINA ROSS: Of course it is. Aaron can't shatter his self-indulgent fantasy of being a great champion of women. He's such a sharp, observant guy, right? He'd never miss such glaring inadequacies, not him.

MADELINE: So then why did you pivot that sketch from Lillian, who'd pitched it, to Kent playing the potato?

AARON ADLER: It wasn't a question of male, female, if that's what you're . . . Gina's memory is not in line with reality, I'm afraid.

MADELINE: It was actually Sally Schumacher who quoted you.

AARON ADLER: I don't have notes on that day ready at hand, obviously, but as far as I recall, no, it was about size. What's funnier, a petite potato or a very large one?

KENT ROMERO: That was a great sketch Lillian came up with. She didn't wind up writing it in the end, that was me and Sally, my partner in crime at the time, but there's no way I would have come up with the concept. I did look good in the potato costume, though. That's one of the stills they like to use whenever there's an article about season one. So hey, we didn't get a woman president, but at least we got a Latin American one.

GINA ROSS: Lillian didn't say another word that entire meeting. What else was there to say? Aaron had basically confirmed that One Astor ascribed to the same gender hierarchy as everywhere else. She closed her notebook, I remember, as if locking herself up, shutting the door.

MADELINE: I'm assuming you appealed to Sally. Did she help at all?

GINA ROSS: So that's a tricky one. Kent had already suggested Sally team up with him on the potato sketch, and she'd seemed more than fine with that. Absolutely no mention of, you know, Lillian pitching this, so she should write it. Nothing. That was one of the reasons I distrusted Sally early on, actually. She seemed so "aw shucks pleased as punch" to just blend in, stay neutral, take shelter under Aaron and

Kent—she was *literally* under Kent by that time. I would've bet money that they were sleeping together.

You gotta understand, Cohen, before *TMS*, I'd always been the only woman in the room. Holly didn't count at the Round—I'm talking about the talent, the hustlers. It wasn't men and women, it was me and everyone else, and I could always defend myself, claim my space in the conversation. But this was a different game, with higher stakes, led by Aaron Adler, a fucking network ref who was sure as shit keeping track of female airtime, lest we become *a women's show*. I knew it was time for long-game strategy, an actual plan.

As soon as Aaron broke us for lunch, I steered Lillian and Brooke into our office—screw Sally, I thought. Let her keep pretending she's just one of the guys.

I shut the office door and laid it on them. We were obviously second-class citizens among the first class. And we needed to change that. Start, I don't know, not "teaming up" per se, but watching out for each other, Female Potato Society–style. Like we did after Wally Winters tried to get a triple blow job after dress.

Brooke Balsinger: I remember Gina's rant on smashing the patriarchy. I told her *no thanks*! Stevie had just pitched a Crack Addict Barbie sketch for me that Aaron seemed to dig. Things were already changing for me, you know? It wasn't the time to, like, burn my bra.

Gina Ross: Brooke goes, "Nah." Fucking typical. Fine, stick to *Cosmo* and pouty-lip shtick. She wasn't adding much to the equation anyway.

Madeline: So, okay. After Aaron steals Lillian's pitch and lobs it to Kent, your plan is partnering up to weather the sexism together?

Gina Ross: I'm sensing you have a retroactive suggestion?

Madeline: Couldn't you have gone to Aaron, lobbied for Lillian to get the sketch back?

[*Gina sits back, fingers steepled.*]

GINA ROSS: Okay, Cohen. Remind me, what generation are you? Millennial? Generation We Ran Out of Letters?

MADELINE: I'm twenty-eight. On the cusp—

GINA ROSS: You girls think you invented feminism. It's hilarious.

MADELINE: I wouldn't say invented. More . . . audited.

GINA ROSS: You know, that's an apt observation. An appropriate word. You're auditors, consultants nobody hired. You criticize without actually doing anything.

MADELINE: I would argue that speaking out is doing something.

GINA ROSS: Is it? I'll tell you what I've done for the cause. My job, really fucking well. I've kept going, for four decades. And yeah, I can hear your next rebuttal already: I did it for myself, to which I might reply that sometimes the most feminist thing you can do is what is necessary for yourself.

BROOKE BALSINGER: Was I the catalyst of Gina and Lillian's whole, whatever you want to call it, "feminism rise to fame," "dynamic female duo," "comic besties," blah blah blah? I mean, maybe? Looking back, Marley, maybe I should have played both sides. I'm just not that kind of calculating person.

STEVIE DOYLE: Brooke had approached me to propose a partnership after the Wally Winters show. Did I think she meant a platonic partnership? I mean, she had her shirt pulled low at that after-party, leaned on the office door with her hip stuck out, knew what she looked like—she kept waving that "Maybe I'll sleep with you" card for years. In any case, Brooke thought I was the funniest of the Townies contingent. She preferred my writing on the John Wayne sketch to the batshit direction Lillian took it in, so I knew we had similar sensibilities. It made sense to me to team up and write some pieces where she could have half a chance of shining. Brooke didn't have the greatest range. I did what I could, and if you look at our track records, we did wind up staying on the show longer than anybody else in that first group. Make of that what you will.

Gina Ross: You could sense the fracture in Monday meetings after that, all our little armies marching in with weapons drawn, our ideas and material, preparing to go to war, claim airtime.

There was the Brooke and Stevie faction—I still don't get what that was about. No way Brooke was fucking him, and they were an odd couple comedywise, apart from the general toxicity coursing through both their veins. But everything Stevie pitched had a part for Brooke, and everything Stevie suggested at the table—even if he announced he was going to take a piss—would get a giggle out of Brooke. A united, annoying front.

Then there was the Kent and Sally faction—this was season one, remember, when Kent was on the desk solo, before I coanchored. I told you Sally perpetually rubbed me the wrong way back then, so I guess I thought of Kent as an enemy by extension. And between the potato theft and the fake news, they were a cocky duo. They knew they were always guaranteed a few solid minutes of airtime every week. Top dogs.

Bobby had been friends with Aaron before *TMS*, so he had Aaron's ear by default. Even before Bobby would start tapping on that cheesy piano, belting out his next tune, Aaron would be clapping like a delighted little monkey. Nauseating for a variety of reasons. But yeah, Bobby was a force that season. Someone to watch out for in more ways than one.

Now, Sam and Nolan were free agents; they got along with everyone and didn't involve themselves in politics, which meant everybody wanted to add them to their club; they were both strong players who could elevate any sketch. Plus, they were both genuinely nice people.

And then there was me and Lillian. I'd known we had potential since the night of Wally's assault—er, show. We could cut through the bullshit that often kills collaborators, when people feel the need to explain and contextualize *everything*. Lillian got me; she was game. Besides, I loved that our female duo was a middle finger to Aaron. A perfect way to prove my point, in a way that felt *sustainable,* to use a word that makes sense to your generation, Cohen.

And then, to my delightful surprise, we were fire together.

BROOKE BALSINGER: I became the third wheel fast in that office, although I couldn't tell if the new Gina-Lillian thing was phony or real. What would have happened if *I'd* been willing to pretend I wanted to stand up to the Big Bad Boys' Club? Maybe I'd have won a dozen Emmys by now, ha, right, Mia? Or heck, knowing Gina, maybe you'd be writing a feature about *me* instead. I could be dead! Really could have gone all sorts of ways.

GINA ROSS: Looking back, working with Lillian that first season is some of the most exhilarating, bonkers stuff I've ever done. She pushed me out of my comfort zone, brought out my wacky side. I think I challenged her, too, to go edgier, add some bite. I'd been planning on Rogue Soprano being a recurring solo piece, but once I started working with Lillian, I realized the opera singers had to be a pair. One would be opera seria and one opera buffa, so every mad caper they'd find themselves in, one of those idiots would approach it glass half-empty, the other half-full, and they'd constantly one-up each other.

We cooked up the French teacher sketch series that season, too, the commercial spoofs for Vagisil "and other feminine unmentionables." That first year, man. We were prolific. We started meeting for coffee on Sunday mornings to throw around ideas before the big *TMS* Monday roundup, and those Sunday coffees led to Monday-night vent sessions, midweek walks around Times Square to clear our heads . . . even field trips, sometimes, if we had a seed for a sketch and needed inspiration.

I distinctly remember a random trip Lillian and I made to the Central Park Zoo. We spent fifteen minutes voice acting these two depressed sea lions. Ad-libbed a whole marriage therapy shtick, how their relationship had tanked, pun intended.

MADELINE: That sounds . . . wholesome. So when did that shift?

GINA ROSS: You mean when did we trade sea lions for speedballs? I assume that's what you're subtly getting at? We started partying fairly early on. Least I did. The first time I remember blatantly "using" on fifteen was maybe the third, fourth episode. The week Ray Sharkey was hosting. Remember him? *Wiseguy*? No? Anyway, our cast was not the most enthusiastic welcome party when he showed up that Monday. Just collectively wrecked from round-the-clock thinking and writing and revising and acting for weeks. None of us had gotten used to the schedule.

AARON ADLER: From the beginning, *The Midnight Show* has operated on a three weeks live, one week rerun schedule, September through May. So I'd say the Sharkey episode was a low point for all of us—our first week three. It's the most physically spent I've ever been. And I've run half-marathons.

GINA ROSS: Drugs weren't new to me. At the Round, there was a revolving door into Holly's backstage bathroom from like ten P.M. on, the guys going into the shitter nervous and downtrodden, only to reemerge like a parade of Supermen right before their sets. I'd smoke with them, yeah. During my years there, I downed more tequila shots than half the stand-up regulars put together. But I'd never done a line before *TMS*. Blame my Catholic guilt, but the idea of leaning over Holly's cracked sink and snorting a chemical substance into my nose felt irredeemable. It was different at One Astor. Sanctified, somehow.

Anyway, back to the Sharkey week. Aaron could see I was spent. Depressed, really. I staggered around the fifteenth-floor halls that week like a big-haired zombie. He finally pulled me aside and mentioned that Stan, the house band's drummer, had some blow he was more than willing to donate to the cause.

[**NOTE**: Stan Jacobs, drummer for the *Midnight Show* house band for twenty-two years, passed away in 2016.]

Gina Ross: Aaron had been running on Stan's stuff since the show's inception. The Townies guys were partaking just to get by. Sally, too, Aaron assured me. Something about Sally joining the party tipped me over the edge. Blame the game, my competitive streak, fuck, the cool-girl ideal, I don't care, but my desire to outparty Sally trumped any lingering Catholic guilt.

Madeline: Do you think there was a culture at the show that made people feel pressured to use drugs?

Brooke Balsinger: Um, *YES*? It was ludicrous! Gina had made it beyond clear that she thought Stan and the house band were a bunch of space cadets. I think the direct quote was "Like the Mamas and the Papas with twice the drugs and half the talent." Then halfway through the Sharkey week, she's suddenly their biggest fan, telling me and Lillian they're visionaries, we've just gotta try Stan's coke, it's a *miracle* substance. So yeah, Lillian's drug problems were all Gina's fault. One hundred percent. Write that in your official transcript, Mara, and go ahead and quote me. Gina Ross is a drug pusher, versus Brooke Balsinger, who has principles.

Kent Romero: Brooke was "Just Say No" before Nancy Reagan popularized it. Except she never had the chance to say no, because nobody ever offered her anything. We weren't going to waste our hard-earned drugs on Brooke Balsinger. *Ni de vaina.*

Gina Ross: You know what's adorable, when I reflect back on that time? This was before everything went so wrong, so take it in context, but . . . once, Lillian was *really* crashing—I want to say it was before the Halloween episode. We were trying to plot out our Slovenly Coven sketch, and she was falling asleep at the desk. I wanted to help, so I said, "Hey Lil, you want some of my coke? Pep you up a little?" She was clearly flattered that I was looking out for her well-being. But then she starts going on about the sugar and the carbonation aggravating her stomach and how it's probably smart to abstain.

Coca-Cola. She thought I was talking about Coca-Cola. Devastatingly ironic when I think about where things went—Lillian in the ground and me a model of sobriety, after God knows how many attempts.

Sally Schumacher: I'm not gonna claim to be a saint. I joined in, but not to the extent the boys or Gina did, or later, unfortunately, Lillian. As head writer, I was sometimes more like a babysitter, much to my dismay. The one grown-up in the darn room. *Any* room. And I'm including Aaron when I say "the boys," by the way, despite what he always claims in interviews. He was one of my kids, for sure.

Aaron Adler: There was drug use. It was 1980, it was a very different time, so I remained nonjudgmental, but I never touched drugs myself. It was always important that at least one of us stay compos mentis, steering the ship through the night. And that I remain separate, with a view over all of it, to make sure nothing got too out of hand. I've never been authoritative—that is not my style—but at the same time, there needed to be a calm remove to my leadership, which I have tried my best to maintain over the years.

Sally Schumacher: And I have a bridge in Brooklyn to sell you. Aaron did a whole lotta cocaine during those late-night work sessions. A worrying amount. Not sure if he still does. It was uppers, then downers, like a cook adding too much salt to the dish, then putting in some sugar to counteract it, and back and forth it went. Constantly.

PHIL ACKERMAN: I wasn't sure what my role should be back then. Was I just a network conduit? Was I supposed to stop the madness? Curtail it? Punish people? I settled on looking the other way. Denial ain't just a river in Egypt!

SALLY SCHUMACHER: It wasn't a smart playbook, but during that first season, I've gotta say, the drugs were effective. And it felt aboveboard because Aaron was at the center of all the bad behavior. Well . . . not *every* kind of bad behavior.

MADELINE: I was actually going to ask about that, too: the other bad behavior. The cast and crew sleeping with each other?

SALLY SCHUMACHER: Yeah, Aaron was way outside of all that. At the time, I thought he was good at maintaining boundaries or privacy or whatever, but knowing him this long and looking back, I think he's probably asexual, aromantic, a-everything but work. He's married to *The Midnight Show*. Has been for forty years. Now, as for the rest of us?

KENT ROMERO: Fuck, where to start? Sally and I started sleeping together early on, week two or thereabouts. Not exclusively. Obviously. It didn't feel scandalous, all of us being involved with everybody else. It was natural. There were a lot of hormones, egos, good-looking smart people trapped in an office together in the middle of the night, steam to blow off, and hey, it happens. No regrets.

SALLY SCHUMACHER: Kent's an asshole, but he was good in bed. You can even tell him I said that.

GINA ROSS: It was incestuous, but in a staggered way, which makes it slightly more palatable in hindsight.

Brooke Balsinger: It was gross. But don't ask me, ha, I was just a lowly professional with actual *workplace standards*.

Kent Romero: It wasn't everybody jumping into bed together. [*He squints, thinking hard.*] Not Brooke, despite her reputation coming in. Not Nolan; he kept his personal life well out of One Astor, as far as I know. Not sure how much play Stevie actually managed versus what he told us. And Lillian . . . even if Bobby hadn't preempted her, I can't imagine she'd have jumped into the Roman orgy feel of it all the way the rest of us did. And in "the rest of us," I'm including the crew, the band, the administrative assistants . . .

Sam Petrosian: I was more an amused observer of the soap opera of our cast's and crew's after-hours swingers scene at first, but, yes, there was a lot of sex from the start, even before we had a "following," as you might say.

Gina Ross: It was like those new reality dating shows, honestly. "Lock seven comics on an office floor, pump them with drugs, jack them up on adrenaline, see the sparks fly!"

Phil Ackerman: Another thing I shut my eyes to. Happily married fifty years, for the record.

Madeline: And did Lillian have other admirers by then? Die-hard fans?

Sam Petrosian: As a matter of fact, I remember the exact moment we weren't just anonymous funny people anymore. After our third episode, we had a week off and Lillian and I went for a walk in Central Park. It was one of those gorgeous, crisp autumn days that make New York City halfway livable. Lillian was bundled up in this huge woolen coat she always wore, like a kid playing in her mom's closet. We were talking about my little sister's birthday; I couldn't get back to Boston for her party, wanted to send her a nice gift. Lillian was giving me truly terrible ideas, one after another, like "How about mailing her a hamster?"—that level of bad—when this group of people walked by, girls in their twenties, and one of them let out a scream, pointing at us, and they sort of fell over each other laughing, and I'm thinking a pigeon must have defecated on me or something, but then one of them goes, "We know you! We saw you on TV!" I said, "Thank you!" Which made no sense—she hadn't said, "Love your work. Big fans." Just stated a fact. But it was still pretty darn thrilling. For me. I turned to Lillian, and all the color was gone from her face.

I know *now* that what was happening for Lillian was the first realization that she was no longer a private person enjoying her hobby and getting paid for it, that she was entering the realm of celebrity. Whereas I turned radioactive, energized with hope—you know, we're big shots, look at us. [*He mimics a strut, chest puffed out.*] She was extremely shaken.

Gina Ross: People caught on to us quick. Week one, we're niche, anonymous; week three or four, people are stopping us in the streets. Lillian was in large part to thank for that, but she struggled hard with the whiplash. Among other things.

Sam Petrosian: What I thought that day in Central Park was "Hey, maybe Lillian's upset because she thought those girls were flirting with me. Maybe they were. Maybe she's jealous!" That would have been great news for me, exactly the sign I was looking for. So I got home and I told Kent, "I'm gonna do it. It's time. I'm going to tell Lillian how I feel."

Madeline: Did you think there was any chance Lillian felt the same way about him?

Kent Romero: No! Absolutely not. I just didn't know how to tell him not to do it. Mechanically, I could have opened my mouth and said, "This is a bad idea," but I didn't want to break his little heart. And yes, I know that that qualifies me as a grade A chickenshit. I thought, "I'll let Lillian do it. This is between the two of them; she can be the bad guy."

Little did I know that I was setting our Sammy on the fast track to becoming a gigolo to the stars. I assume you've heard what happened with Tammy Fletcher?

VII.
TURNING POINT

Episode 8
(The Tammy Fletcher Incident)

COMPILED TRANSCRIPTS

Madeline: Some of your castmates have pointed to the eighth episode of the first season, the week that Tammy Fletcher hosted, as a particularly fraught one, at least behind the scenes.

Gina Ross: Oh God, yeah. Though if I remember right, the Sam and Lillian drama started the week before, show seven, when Martin Sheen was on. Lillian and I had found our footing by then. Brooke had started going out to the conference room to work, calling us annoying. To be fair, when we'd get excited, Lil and I would start shouting over one another, finishing each other's sentences, you know, anticipating what the other was going to say. Our first Rogue Sopranos bit had landed, to our delight—she and I were really gaining traction with the audience. So that Sunday, we'd taken a long walk around Belvedere Castle together, spitballing other two-handers.

We settled on this French teacher premise, where Lillian's a lush of a middle-school schoolmarm, and I'm the kid in the hot seat in front of the class, tasked with translating her bleak existential pop quiz into English.

Madeline: That's one of my favorites.

Gina Ross: Appreciate the casual flattery, Cohen.

Madeline: It was fairly premeditated flattery.

Gina Ross: I'll note the effort on your interrogation feedback card. Anyway, after Aaron gave us the green light, we started building that one out, and we both had Sam in mind for the principal.

Sam Petrosian: It was a good episode, that Martin Sheen week. Do you remember the French teacher sketch? Lillian with her wine bottle in a paper bag, Gina translating, "My worthless lover has fled to Provence," all that.

MADELINE: I love the moment where you come in and she falls off the desk.

SAM PETROSIAN: That was spontaneous! She didn't do it in rehearsal, and she wound up banging up her knee pretty badly. Now . . . here's where I should have wised up. Between sketches, before the second to last, something like that, Lillian's doing a costume change, limping a little, and I hurry over to see if she's all right. But then I see Bobby. He'd gone up to the office kitchen and gotten ice for her knee, and he was kneeling in front of her, applying pressure, and she was laughing. Maybe there was a glimmer of "Oh. Huh." But it wasn't until the after-party that the truth hit me. And it hit me very hard.

STEVIE DOYLE: Sam got unbelievably wasted at the after-party for episode seven, the Martin Sheen week. And I don't even mean the after-after-party, out at a club or bar or what have you; this was the *network* party. I grew up with Sam. I was there the first time he vomited up peach schnapps, age thirteen. But I'd never seen him like this, and honestly, it freaked me out.

SALLY SCHUMACHER: Sam Petrosian is a man of many talents. Holding his liquor is not one of them.

KENT ROMERO: Before we could actually go celebrate and blow off steam after an episode, we were obliged to pretend to celebrate and blow off steam in a dusty, leather-banquette, Tiffany-gas-lamp establishment called Winthrop's, which was a private club around the corner from One Astor.

Aaron was culturally old New York—he was a senior citizen in a youngish man's body, and so he thought a place like that gave us status. To me, it felt like some WASP heaven post-church brunch at the golf club. Deeply, deeply uncool. Bobby liked it. We had to turn up, sit in our assigned booths, greet well-wishers, and bow before our musical acts and the host and the network bigwigs before escaping as quickly and graciously as we could. It was not in our contracts, but it might as well have been.

We didn't drink much, not there. We sipped. And then we went to the real party, wherever the scene was on any given night, mutually agreed upon, usually after Nolan told us where he was going, because he was by far the most "in the scene" of all of us. Clean and sober by the time we met him, but still leagues hipper than the rest of us.

But remember, we stayed well-behaved at the company party, that was the deal. So imagine my surprise at seeing Sam stumbling over to that week's host—I think it was Michael Caine—spilling tequila all over his shoes.

SAM PETROSIAN: The host was Martin Sheen, and it was scotch. Winthrop's was not the kind of place that served tequila.

PHIL ACKERMAN: I bought Mr. Sheen a new pair of shoes and socks. Had them delivered to his house in California with an apology letter the next week.

SAM PETROSIAN: The tequila came later, when we went to Danceteria, or so they tell me. The rest of the night was a horrible blur.

What I remember is early on, just after the show, preparing my declaration of . . . whatever you want to call it. The case for me and Lillian. Running through it in the very short walk we used to take every week past peep shows and rent-by-the-hour hotels to our office party at Winthrop's, which was like a time warp to the fifties. The doorman sees me in, Lillian's already in the elevator with somebody, I'm about to join her when I see that it's Bobby. And they are holding hands. Fingers entwined.

It felt like I'd been stabbed. I blocked the door, I remember. There were people lining up behind me, total bottleneck, because I couldn't move. Lillian and Bobby were very obviously together, but it hadn't been obvious to me before that, even with the knee, the bag of ice.

There were other signs, too, that I could only pick out after the fact. The first several weeks of work, every Monday, Lillian had bought a black-and-white cookie from the network commissary, and she'd bring it to the meeting and split it with me. I'd take the white side, and she got the black side. But she hadn't done it for a few weeks. Seems like a tiny thing, but it should have tipped me off.

It didn't. Seeing her with Bobby was a complete shock, leading to instant heartbreak.

TRANSCRIPT OF FOLLOW-UP INTERVIEW WITH BOBBY EVERETT

June 21, 2023

BOBBY EVERETT: Gosh, I'm trying to remember the exact timeline. It was early, I'll tell you that much, after one of our Monday meetings in the writers' room. I was very formal about it. I said, "Lillian, please feel free to shoot me down, but I think you are an incredibly lovely person and I would like to take you out for a dinner date." She was formal right back, might have even curtsied, said she would like that very much. And I went into my office and did a full shamanic victory dance. Miracle I didn't break any of the furniture.

[*He grins.*] Here's a funny story. I got us a table at Elaine's. You've heard of it, I'm sure. I'd grown up going there plenty with my parents, so I knew Elaine Kaufman, could sort of say, "Is this a good night for dinner? Who else is going to be there?" And Elaine said, "Oh yes, yes, don't worry. We've got Norman and Saul and somebody else I can't tell you about because of security clearances, but she'll be impressed."

So that night, first of all, I'm already on the back foot because Lillian, when I collected her from this horrific squat where she was living, tiptoeing around the passed-out junkies, saying, "Excuse me, sir, pardon me, picking up my date," she looked pristine. She had a peach-colored dress on, under this giant fuzzy coat, which I later came to realize was like a stuffed animal for her, an emotional support coat. She had her hair pinned loosely at the nape of her neck, creating this wild halo, and I just thought how improbable it was that someone like her could emerge from a building that shitty. The whole taxi ride over, I was stunned into muteness, what I'd now consider a Zen state of *ashi,* but Lillian kept the conversation going. I think we talked about elevator design, of all things.

Well, we go into Elaine's, and first of all, it's clear right away that Lillian has never heard of it. This famed New York institution, ultra-exclusive, nope. She was peeking at the menu when we walked in, wondering what kind of food the restaurant served. She'd thought it was a Southern food joint, I think. And then I see men in suits, standing alert, obviously Secret Service. So Lillian and I sit at our table and I kind of nod over my shoulder. "That's Walter Mondale. We're dining with the vice president." And I feel like, okay, I've got my flow back, this is going well, and she just shrugs and says, "I'm Canadian."

[*Bobby laughs.*]

But it still went well! We ate and laughed, had a little bubbly, and honestly, I think we were in love by the time we finished dessert. It was that fast. For me, at least. My parents had already passed by that point, sadly, but if they hadn't, I would have gone straight home and called my mom and said, "I've met the one." And I had. I've been lucky in love over the course of my life. I am very happily married now; you've met Sunny.

[*Bobby lowers his voice, glancing over his shoulder.*]

But Lillian was the love of my life. What you saw on-screen, what people thought about us, this dream couple, it was true. It sounds cheesy, but it was authentic. Rare. And, it turned out, much too fleeting.

MADELINE: Did the rest of the cast know you were together so early on?

BOBBY EVERETT: Well, huh. Let me think. I guess they didn't, no. We decided to keep a low profile, relationshipwise. Our little secret. One, because it's nice to protect something that you have the strong inclination is going to wind up being quite special. And two, I didn't want the fact of the two of us to mess with Lillian's momentum at work. She was gaining respect in a way that I think was new for her, and I was not going to spoil that.

But of course, there's only so long two people can hide the fact that they're rapturously in love with each other.

COMPILED TRANSCRIPTS

Sam Petrosian: I moved on from Lillian after that night. There were a few ugly weeks there, moments I'm not proud of, stories I'm not about to regale my kids with anytime soon . . . but I did what I needed to do to move past her. And maybe this is just a product of old age, I don't know, but it's only recently that I've indulged in what-ifs. What would my life look like now if she'd chosen me? And would she still be here, or would I have wound up mourning her from an even more painful position? I don't know! At the end of the day, the only honest answer is that I don't know. And it doesn't solve anything to mull it over, to play "what-if," because she chose Bobby, and history played out the way it did. And that's that.

Sally Schumacher: I generally skipped the network after-party, which was my prerogative as a barely-above-the-line staff member, so I didn't witness firsthand the aftermath of Sam finding out about Bobby and Lillian. I only heard about it later—and by the way, it was news to me, too, that the two of them were dating. It was whispered about very quickly in the halls before the next Monday-morning meeting, that Sam had been a train wreck, that Kent and Stevie had had to leave Danceteria almost immediately to save him from public humiliation. To which my initial reaction was "That was fast." I'd assumed I'd have to deal with a Sam and Lillian breakup at some point in the show's life, but not this early, and not when they hadn't even been dating in the first place! So now I've got *Bobby* and Lillian breaking up to worry about.

I did not approve of cast members getting involved romantically.

Madeline: But . . . weren't you and Kent—?

Sally Schumacher: Writing partners with benefits? Yes, fairly ironic. Not to mention everything that's happened since. Be that as it may, I was judgy back then and majorly worried going into that morning session and then . . . in comes Tammy f'in' Fletcher.

MADELINE: So if I've got the timeline right . . . now we're up to episode eight?

SAM PETROSIAN: I was still desperately hung over that Monday morning. Utterly humorless, which is not very useful going into a comedy pitch meeting. I can't imagine I was at my best appearancewise either. [*He pulls at his cheeks, creating a gaunt effect.*] But . . . Tammy Fletcher did not seem to mind.

SALLY SCHUMACHER: I was ready to throw Tammy out the window almost immediately. She dragged me aside like we were best friends rather than people who'd just met a few hours prior and begged me for information about Sam's dating-slash-marital status. Not that a ring would have stopped her. She was like, "He's sooooo cute!" I reckon at least half the draw of coming on the show for her was hooking up with a cast member. And for whatever reason, she chose our Sammy.

GINA ROSS: Lillian and I *could not* stand her. Lillian for good reason and me by extension. Listen, you couldn't just show up at One Astor at ten A.M. Monday and start screwing a cast member by lunch.

Of course I recognize the hypocrisy; we were a crew of humping rabbits ourselves. But we were a *crew*. A troupe, and despite all the factions and drama, a true—albeit dysfunctional—family. Tammy was an outsider, and right after Monday's meeting, I swear, she had the gall to drape herself across Sam while he, Lillian, and I were sitting in the conference room building out a new installment of John Wayne's Mother-in-Law. Straddled him like an extra in *Boogie Nights*.

BROOKE BALSINGER: You'd have thought Tammy had pantsed Sam and started pulling on his pecker, the way Gina and Lillian reacted! She was flirting, that was all. And why shouldn't she? She and Sam were both single adults.

Gina Ross: Sam was irritatingly smug about it. All week, they'd disappear, giggling, and then two minutes later—or five, if I want to remember generously—they'd emerge from the costume room or solo bathroom in fifteen's back corridor or the editing room or wherever they'd had their latest fake-clandestine tryst, Sam all flushed cheeks and mussed hair and huge grin. It was flagrant. And very un-Sam. Sam-I-Am-Not.

Sam Petrosian: Tammy was the right person at the right time to help me move on. Could I have handled it more discreetly? Absolutely. Was I mature enough to resist the temptation to parade my sexual exploits directly in front of Lillian? Oh boy. Not a chance.

Kent Romero: Lillian didn't like it. Sam the lothario, Tammy Fletcher's cabana boy. None of us did. It was fucking weird.

Gina Ross: Listen, I respect Sam. I've always liked him. But he was acting desperate. You could smell the agony from the lobby. Eau de Friend Zone.

Stevie Doyle: Say what you want about Lillian and Bobby, at least they were discreet. Sam was . . . not. Of course Lillian reacted. I think he was still her best friend up to that point. Not after that.

Aaron Adler: There were notable tensions that week. I tried to stay above the fray with the more soap opera aspects of the team's relationships with each other. It was something I did not have any particular interest in, except insomuch as it affected performances. Sally came to me, said, "Aaron, you need to step in. This is going to go nuclear." But to me, that didn't necessarily sound like a negative. We had a few episodes left to prove ourselves to the network. We needed an injection of energy, because offbeat, different, young was still not quite adding up to cutting-edge. And I thought, let it play out. Let's see what happens.

Sally Schumacher: Aaron was in a complete tizzy about the interpersonal drama, but he wanted me to handle it, as everyone's apparent foster mom. I ignored the request, but then . . . it did start to annoy me. You know, I couldn't take our *movie star host* aside and ask her to stop dragging Sam off to fool around every time we had a smoke break. So I had a word with Sam. Incredibly awkward, direct as I could be. "Hey, glad you're having a good time, just maybe hold off on shoving your tongue down her throat until you're off the clock, because we're all trying to concentrate here." To which he immediately threw the fact that I was sleeping with Kent back in my face.

Sam Petrosian: She was my boss, and I should have recognized that, but I didn't. I was all rage and libido and hurt feelings that week, so I said something I shouldn't have, and honestly, it's a miracle I didn't get fired.

Gina Ross: She slapped Sam so hard he actually staggered, almost comically, like it was a stunt. At the time, I had no idea what had prompted it, beyond how irritating he and Tammy Fletcher had been all week, and I still thought, "Good for you." Hadn't really cared for Sally up till that point . . . but that was by far my favorite Schumacher moment of season one.

Sam Petrosian: It hurt like hell! She had an arm on her, could have pitched for the Mets. I deserved it. And anyway, what happened later that week hurt worse.

Sally Schumacher: We all pretended not to see it, but Sam and Lillian had been picking at each other throughout rehearsals. In the dress, Sam kept flinging these little unnecessary jibes, critiques for Lillian when there was really nothing to critique, and laughing way too loud at Tammy, who was very funny in the movies, not at all funny in the dress rehearsal. The final straw was when he tried to get one of Lillian's lines shifted to something for Tammy to do. Lillian very quietly walked away. Then right before we went live, they had it out. The audience was filing in, and I had to go out and tell the band to play something loud enough to cover the two of them hollering at each other.

BROOKE BALSINGER: I'd never heard Lillian scream before! Holy heck, it was, like, terrifying. Her voice went very deep, very dramatic, very ominous. But, if I'm honest? It felt staged.

PHIL ACKERMAN: I heard these god-awful cries while I was pacing behind the cameras with Aaron, running through the new lineup before air. Immediate thought: Everyone's doing blow and knocking boots and now someone is actually dying on my watch. Stressful!

SAM PETROSIAN: Lillian was well within her rights to lose it. Accused me of acting like someone else, of turning on her for no reason. She was upset. Said I'd been body snatched, which in a way I had been. I was, of course, very hurt too, and we said things to each other we needed to say but with the wrong intensity. And at the absolute worst time and place.

SALLY SCHUMACHER: I overheard it. I felt . . . it was part of my role to stand sentinel and stop it if it went too far. The gist? Lillian told Sam he wasn't acting like himself, and he said that she wasn't either, that maybe they didn't know each other at all. She got upset, said that wasn't true, that he knew her better than anybody in the world.

[*She pauses, emotional.*]

I'm sorry. Give me a sec, if you don't mind. It's just hard, given everything, remembering how vulnerable she was that night. Okay, so. She said how much she cared about him, and he pressed her on that. Asked why she hadn't chosen him. Accused her of toying with him. Said she was going to lose him forever if she didn't pick him now, that she was being selfish, wanting everyone to love her. That she was a "collector." Petty stuff. She said she did love him—to which Sam shot back, "Like a brother, got it"—but that she was with Bobby, and he needed to accept it and leave her alone. To which he snapped, "That's what I'm doing. Trust me, I don't think about you at all when I'm going down on Tammy." That was the line crossed right there. So I broke it up, we went live, and the rest is history, I suppose.

Bobby Everett: I was upset by the incident. It was obviously threatening to me, personally, to hear a deafening declaration of love from Sam Petrosian to my girlfriend right before I'm about to go onstage as a used-car salesman with a fish head. But as Lao Tzu says, "He who conquers himself is mighty." I've always lived by that. That day, I conquered my anger, let it play out, and then tried to console Lillian as best I could in the aftermath.

Stevie Doyle: I do think there was a part of Lillian that was jealous. Sam had succeeded in his own stupid way. He won't entertain the notion today—it's too hurtful—but Lillian had some degree of feelings for him. Of course she did. Bobby just got in there first.

Kent Romero: It was complicated between them. There was a lot of love there, in one form or another. And that night, there was a lot of screaming.

Sam Petrosian: No resolution, really. We just ran out of time to yell at each other because the show was starting. I went into the greenroom to mop the sweat off my forehead, unbelievably rattled, and thought, "This show's going to be a disaster, and I don't even care." I'd lost my best friend, maybe even the love of my life. So at that point, if I also lost my job, so be it.

The weird thing is, it wasn't a disaster. It turned out to be the episode everyone credits as our turning point. The one that made us all famous. Go figure!

Sally Schumacher: I'm not sure if there's a direct correlation here, but the breakout episode, the Tammy Fletcher episode, season one, when the energy really exploded for us, was not only the breakup moment for Sam and Lillian but also the episode that served as a sort of public coming-out—excuse the expression—for the Bobby-Lillian romance. They did this duet.

MADELINE: The piano concerto.

GINA ROSS: Bobby and the goddamn piano. Again. At least it was a big one this time.

SALLY SCHUMACHER: Yep, Bobby on the grand piano, Lillian in an evening gown, and you expect her to sing, like in the soprano sketches, but she just makes piano noises: *plinky plink plink.*

MADELINE: I still think that's one of the funniest things I've ever seen. I can't even explain why it's so hilarious.

SALLY SCHUMACHER: It was brilliant! That was another Lillian idea, though Bobby wrote the actual notes for the duet. What's wild is that it didn't sound terrible. It's ridiculous, but still music, you know? Anyhow, at the end, there's that moment when she's curtsying and Bobby kisses her hand, and it was very obvious from the way they looked at each other that something real was happening on-screen.

KENT ROMERO: That kiss on the hand, so chivalrous! Looked sweet, didn't it? *Sí Luis.* I just rolled my eyes from offstage. That was Bobby Everett marking Lillian Martin as his. Like a dog pissing on a hydrant.

I can't really complain, can I? America ate it up. And that benefited the rest of us. *Hugely.*

But for Lillian . . . that kiss marked the beginning of the end.

FROM LILLIAN MARTIN'S NOTEBOOK

Horrible, horrible. Once there's Sam, there's no one else, and I can't do it. Way too young for that. AND SELFISH.

"Collector sketch"—girl brings man home to parents, "This one's a keeper," they lock him in basement, next boyfriend comes in, string of victims

Stevie knows what I'm doing. Obvious heist sketch.

He's gone. Right there but gone now. Imaginary friend but real person.

Sketch where I just sleep. Sleep whole episode, corner of stage.

Salad bowl party—one veggie they hate and try to kill

Drunk teacher school trip to France airplane

VIII.
TMS SEASON ONE, PART DEUX

The Fame Game

(January–June 1981)

VANITY FAIR

FROM THE MAGAZINE

New Late-Night Comedy Crew Conquers the Small Screen (Along with All of New York)

The Midnight Show, produced by Aaron Adler, Introduces a Different Type of Laugh Troupe—Poster Kids for the New Generation

By Vanity Fair
December 1980

It's a happy holiday season indeed for Aaron Adler and his crew of merry misfits. Christmas has come early this year, and the gift under the tree? Impeccable timing.

Adler's *The Midnight Show,* a late-night-Friday live sketch show billed as edgy alternative comedy, premiered to middling effect this September, with mishaps ranging from wooden dialogue and missed marks to debut jitters. Still, the young, boundary-pushing cast keeps upping the ante week after week—and many would say they've now earned their seat at the late-night table, with some of their more absurd and memorable material ("Potato for President!") having already entered the cultural lexicon.

The cast—particularly breakouts Lillian Martin, Bobby Everett, Gina Ross, and Kent Romero—possess that ineffable "cool factor" that's eluded and frustrated network executives eager to air the Next Big Thing for the "baby boomer" generation, TV's largest demographic. The fact that the troupe can keep up with rock gods, movie stars, artists, and the avant-garde of course adds to the appeal.

[*Photo caption*] *Left: Kent Romero,* TMS*'s leading man and head of the comical* Late-Breaking News, *enjoys table service at the Mudd Club alongside Billy Idol, David Bowie, Tammy Fletcher, and co-star Gina Ross.*

[*Photo caption*] *Right: Lillian Martin and Bobby Everett, both in togas, partaking in Club 57's "bacchanal," a recent themed night of pagan merriment complete with a fake pig sacrifice and blood cocktails (Martin shown drinking O negative).*

Every Friday-night post-show can last until dawn, after which the crew of the hour crawls to the nearest diner for pancakes and a day of rest before the cycle of frantic writing, pitching, acting, and celebrating begins again.

The only change? Week by week, sketch by sketch, more and more Americans fall under *The Midnight Show*'s strange, enchanting spell.

COMPILED TRANSCRIPTS

Gina Ross: It was like one of those weird morning dreams where you're half asleep, half awake, able to choose your own adventure, steer the dream toward fantasy. That *Vanity Fair* feature, Cohen. One of the biggest turning points in my career. People started asking for my autograph in the West Fourth Street subway station. My mom, who at the time I spoke to every other month, called, gushing that her friends and their kids were crazy about me, loved and quoted my correspondent bits for the desk. All of a sudden, life was sparkly, rosy, everything we'd secretly wished for coming true.

Phil Ackerman: Start of 1981, we got the official greenlight from our, ah, corporate overlords. Full season one and season two a go. Off and running, like Clydesdales out of the gates!

Aaron Adler: Hmm. Clydesdales don't race, Phil. You want . . . quarter horses. Arabians.

Phil Ackerman: I'm sure Madeline knows what I mean.

Gina Ross: There was so much electricity on the fifteenth floor, we didn't know what to do with it. We had to channel it somehow—even after working on an episode round-the-clock Monday through Friday, then performing in front of the dress audience and again for the live show audience and the cameras, nothing tempered the motherfucking *lightning* running through our veins. We had to physically burn it off. Aaron's pathetic Winthrop's shindig wasn't cutting it, so we'd hit bars, clubs, burning all night long. And whenever you dipped or felt down, there was always a way to boost yourself up. Stan and the *Midnight Show* band, they were our walking pharmacy.

BROOKE BALSINGER: After the first season's winter break, I felt like I'd come back to a different show. Somehow, over Christmas, Stevie had decided he and I were no longer "gelling"? It was a PC, garbage way of saying our alliance was over. Probably because I wouldn't sleep with him. Well, sorry, Stevie, you're unattractive, and I don't take my romantic cues from an office of sleep- and love-deprived horndogs.

STEVIE DOYLE: I was coming in Monday mornings with killer pitches, and you could look around the table and see people laughing but also wincing, just waiting for the anvil to drop on their heads. They'd say, "And who do you see as this character?" And of course, I'd say "Brooke," and then, gosh, darn the luck, they wouldn't have room for it in this week's episode. Brooke was fine as the feed. She just wasn't funny enough to lead any sketches, no matter how good the writing was, and it was fucking good, I'm not just blowing my own horn here. The second I surprised everybody by going, "Oh, you know, I think Lillian for this one," hey bingo, suddenly I'm getting airtime again. Apologies to Brooke, but she was an albatross.

I learned real quick, though, that it's better to work with an albatross than a snake.

MADELINE: Are you referring to . . . ?

STEVIE DOYLE: Lillian. Yeah. I don't want to speak ill of the dead. I'm gonna leave it at that.

BROOKE BALSINGER: Stevie eventually came crawling back with all sorts of new ideas for sketches for me, and that was what made me say yes. It certainly wasn't his half-assed apology. Pardon my potty mouth. I was, let us say, armed with more *knowledge* at that point than I had been before. I was a little more *wised up*.

STEVIE DOYLE: Not sure what Brooke's referring to, but, uh, I had a bit of an epiphany later on, sure, which was that we were every single one of us in it for ourselves. Didn't matter that I couldn't stand Brooke.

We clocked in, did the job, and then I got a break from her after hours—unlike from Lillian, I might add. Brooke was not part of the social scene, not one bit. I appreciated that.

Brooke Balsinger: Performance, to me, was a job. What a wild concept, ha, right, Madison? All around me, everyone was going, like, gonzo with the sex, drugs, and rock 'n' roll. They'd all whine, "Come on, you've got to snort up and come to the Mudd Club!" "Everybody's blitzing out and racing to Danceteria." "Aw, one bump, one hit, one tab and you'll be right as rain . . ." The peer pressure they put on me was disgusting.

Meanwhile, I'd go to Winthrop's after each show, sip a Malibu Bay Breeze for fifteen minutes, then train home to Westchester—my manager's no-brains assistant had finally gotten me a permanent place by then. Bed before three, nice and cozy and civilized. FOMO is for children! Which is what they were.

Gina Ross: We were getting access to all these new places because of the nature of the show. Every week there was a new musician and actor coming in, each with their own favorite party place, and we'd ride their coattails straight out of Winthrop's.

It was Bowie who introduced us to the Mudd Club the night he performed—I think that was the show where I interpretive-danced beside him to "Let's Dance" as a Jane Fonda workout devotee, but I can't remember. He came back as a host the next year, so it could have been then. Whatever, back to the scene: The club spaces in New York, Jesus, they were indoor coliseums, modern-day Roman Forums—I'd never experienced anything like that in LA. My party days in Hollywood were mainly spent crowded around the bar at the Round, and if we did go anywhere else, it was to a bar just like it down to the layout.

But the Mudd Club was something else. First off, we all walk up to the velvet rope, trailing David fucking Bowie. God rest his soul, he was so *cool,* looked and acted like he came from another planet—a better planet, one of those alien civilizations that actually has their shit together.

The bouncer asks him, "How many, Mr. Bowie?" And David shrugs and says, silky smooth, "Who knows." The bouncer looks over Bowie's shoulder and sees the whole pack of us, nods to Nolan—everyone knew Nolan back then; he was a fixture. But it wasn't until this stone-faced heavy spied Lillian in the fray that his face lit up like a little kid's on Christmas and he waved us in. Her mere presence was universally delightful, Cohen. Coldhearted bouncer eunuchs included.

KENT ROMERO: There was a certain Lower East Side scene in 1980 that was in part the holdover from Studio 54, which had closed due to tax evasion, but there was something more intellectual than disco here—this indie rock, pop art, alternative everything culture, which we were only *barely* hip enough for but which appealed to me as a young, pretentious Ivy League grad. The Mudd Club, for example. I'm going to be totally frank here: I think we all swept in on the tide of weirdness that Lillian produced. She appealed to the artistes in an enormous way.

GINA ROSS: The noise in that place was deafening. Bass and drums ricocheting around the huge columned space, hundreds of people. The long bar trailing the back wall was three rows deep—and I still remember Kent sliding beside me with that self-satisfied, annoyingly gorgeous grin of his and purring into my ear, "We made it, Ross."

He was an arrogant prick, still is, but I swear I almost grabbed his face and made out with him then and there. This was waaaaay before we did *Late-Breaking News* together, the messing around, mind you. But I felt it, with everybody, this collective current running through us. All our futures linked and intertwined. At that moment . . . man. We were untouchable.

Kent took my hand, dragged me and Lillian to the bar for a drink. He and I did like a trio of lines on the back of his hand while we waited. Can't remember if Lillian did too. She'd definitely dabbled by that point. It was a slow slide into partying for her, followed by a very rapid one.

But that night, God. We mocked Kent mercilessly every time he pointed out some accomplished literary figure he was supposedly cultured enough to be able to identify. Allen Ginsberg, Bill Burroughs. "I'm Kent Romero. Did you know I went to *Harvard*?" Lillian and I were all-out hysterical by the time Fab Five Freddy took the mic.

Anyway. It was Disneyland. Disneyland for fucked-up comics.

This was before AIDS hit hard and things started turning scary. Those first-season days were, I don't know, innocent, in a weird way. Lillian and I were inseparable. We all were.

MADELINE: Was it hard for you, spending so much time with Lillian on and off the clock?

SAM PETROSIAN: At first, sure, a little. But Bobby was ever-present and we traveled in large packs, so we found ways to orbit each other but never collide. And I had a, shall we say, active romantic life of my own by that point.

Here's a funny story! You'll like this one, Madeline. I promise not to get too lurid, but . . . I took a cocktail waitress home from Danceteria one night. She was a fun girl, no strings, very energetic. Told me she was going to be a big star, and I had no response to that except, sure, yeah, I mean, if somebody like *me* can become famous this quickly, I don't see why not!

Our paths didn't cross again until the *Vanity Fair* party after the Oscars, 1992. I'm there with my wife and *Madonna* comes up and says, "Remember me?" And it is only right there and then, I kid you not, that I put two and two together. Susan figured it out too, but she was nice enough not to say anything until we got back home. Honestly, I think she was impressed I'd ever been attractive enough to seduce Madonna. Tammy Fletcher was one thing, but this was the biggest pop star in the world! I still can't quite believe it myself.

NOLAN YOUNG, EXCERPT FROM "NOLAN'S FINAL BOW," *VILLAGE VOICE*: People are gonna want to say, Nolan Young, he had two lives. Truth is, I had about twenty-seven different lives. You think about my personal life, well, I had the clubs I'd go to with my work friends, my *Midnight Show* people. There was a gay scene all over the place then, everybody all mixed together so you didn't know or care what was what, but I was not gay, not there. Not with photos being taken and gossip columnists and everything that came with being Nolan Young in public. So I'd spend the first part of those nights with my cast, and then I'd get "tired," right? I'm gonna call it a night, but what I'm really doing is going out to the other scene. To Better Days and Zanzibar and the Garage, where it was Black and it was queer and nobody was gonna tell a soul Nolan Young was there. No way. That was the code.

Now, that's not to say I wasn't having a great time in that first half of the night. Lillian was everybody's little baby doll, Sammy was having such a good time it was contagious, Kent was just so damn *pretty,* you know? And the artists, my boys Jean-Michel [Basquiat] and Keith [Haring], they knew who I really was. And they could put on a hell of a show for the straight kids.

Sam Petrosian: We went from delivering absurdist sketches on national television to being part of even more absurd scenarios at the after-party. One night, I can't remember where we were, but they'd filled the dance floor with a plastic swimming pool with cereal in it, gallons of milk. *Fake* milk, thank God. A huge foam bowl of Trix! That rabbit was right: They're not just for kids.

Gina Ross: Nowhere except the Lower East Side in 1981 could you be high off your ass, floating through a literal bowl of cereal.

Sally Schumacher: I was always chaperoning the others to some extent. Making sure the cast got into the right amount of trouble but never more than that. Bobby never got into any trouble. He was always completely in control of himself, which I found interesting, even then.

Gina Ross: My loathing for Sally as Just One of the Guys had dulled by the Mudd Club era, since she'd gotten Lillian's back and put Sam in his place—there's something refreshing about a girl with a strong right hook. Still, I kept my distance. I'd see her watching me and Kent shooting the shit at the bar, or Lillian and me dancing like idiots, and

I'd wonder if she felt jealous or left out. But that was the gig, right? Playing mother hen, even as she was snorting lines herself. It was a tough line to walk, I'll give her that.

Sally Schumacher: Now, don't get me wrong, I had a fine old time. Kent was someone I was involved with sporadically, but he slept with plenty of girls he met out on the scene, and so did I. Sometimes the same girl. Sometimes at the same time. It was a nice little blip of time where everything felt easy. We were on a ride, that was all.

Madeline: Was this around the time that Lillian started really throwing back? Getting into steady drug use?

Kent Romero: I cannot imagine a scenario in which she would not have gotten into drugs and alcohol during that period. Life was a candy shop, in every sense. We had access everywhere, to everything we wanted to drink, smoke, sniff, or otherwise ingest, and—for me, at least—a dizzying array of willing women every single night of my life.

Cría cuervos y te sacarán los ojos, as my aunties used to say. It all got exhausting. I started having to schedule nights off from sex, usually Thursdays, so that I could do my job on Friday night. Then we'd go out after the show, conquering heroes on parade, and I had my pick all over again. This sounds boastful, I know, and I know what my reputation is. Not that I give a shit, but maybe this will allay it a little: There was a considerable period of time in which Sam Petrosian was having more sex than I was. Multiple partners a night. And he didn't take days off.

Sam Petrosian: I mean, I do feel a little sheepish about it now, but what can I say? I was single. I had the sense that this was a once-in-a-lifetime blip of an opportunity before I settled down, and I was right. So I set out to enjoy myself. Sow my wild oats.

Brooke Balsinger: I found the whole Manhattan scene so stupid. Really, who the hell was Andy Warhol, this ugly dude who painted soup cans? Who cares? Everyone was splooging in their pants over the guy, who approached *me,* actually, not Lillian, on my way to the bathroom. He handed me this gold picture frame, expecting me to hold it around my face all night. The thing weighed ten pounds. "There," he said. "You're my Mona Lisa." And you know what I told him? "*No thanks!*"

AARON ADLER: I went out with the cast a few times, not often. Work was strange enough. That whole world felt vaguely hallucinatory. I wanted to keep my focus on the show and not drop off a cliff into . . . whatever that was.

SALLY SCHUMACHER: Aaron preferred to do his drugs at One Astor. He didn't see any value in the scene. But to me, at that time, going out, being visible and celebrated in that way, provided fuel for the work we did. We were cocky little shits, honestly, but that kind of confidence let us take more risks, be even bolder in our creativity, because people were eating it up. There was very little insecurity at that point. The shakiness, the unevenness people talk about a few years into *The Midnight Show* didn't come until around the time Lillian died. That first season, we were nothin' but golden. And I really do think it solidified the bond that the cast had with each other.

KENT ROMERO: There was one night, passing a roach around. I'd smoked a hazardous amount, Lillian a small amount, which was plenty for her, and she decided she was going to teach me some French. Not to be outdone, I declared that I would simultaneously teach her Spanish. We went back and forth, her in academic French, me in colloquial Spanish, for over an hour, and the incredible thing was, we could understand every single thing the other person was saying. Found out the next morning from Sally that in fact we weren't speaking any intelligible languages at all. Just complete gobbledygook. Lillian thought that was incredible, that we'd achieved a complete mind meld. And, ah, Bobby did not like that one bit. Left in a huff that night, as I recall.

MADELINE: So Bobby was a part of the party scene like the rest of you?

GINA ROSS: He was present in the *omni* sense. But not like the rest of us. It was work for him, not play. He knew exactly how valuable a photo of him with Lillian on the hottest dance floor in the city with Brooke Shields as a photobomb was. He was savvy. Everything was calculated for him.

STEVIE DOYLE: You kidding? There was no way he'd ever let Lillian go out on the town without him. He barely let her go to the office bathroom alone.

FROM LILLIAN MARTIN'S NOTEBOOK

Make myself do it. Life but wildlife. Topiary person in Central Park. Lifestyle choice.

Relay race, different existences (run to work, run to bar to dance floor to dawn and then we're lost when we sleep and if we're lucky we never even need to look at ourselves in the mirror)

Crazy ex grabs you, pretzel cart wrestling match, restraining order, going into courthouse in disguise. Which one of us is the villain?

Old landlord stalker, deranged fan letters—doorman with cape, secret society of doormen superheroes

Flower shop musical number, singing manure

I used to love in-betweens. How to make them safe again?

TRANSCRIPT OF PHONE INTERVIEW WITH BOBBY EVERETT

June 23, 2023

MADELINE: Thanks for all these follow-ups, Bobby. I know you're back to set on the Gerwig project, so I appreciate you making the time. I have nearly everything I need but would love more color on your time with Lillian, once *The Midnight Show* took off.

BOBBY EVERETT: Of course. It was a magical time for me personally, because I wasn't just having this very special creative experience with this amazingly brilliant group of comedians, I was falling in love with one of them. We were, by circumstance and choice, inseparable. There was no "Bye, honey, see you tonight; I've got to go to work" because we worked together, and, frankly, we pretty much lived at work.

I'd led a somewhat solitary life until I met Lillian, and her background wasn't dissimilar. Sure, there were obvious differences between us. She was this Canadian small-town girl and I'd spent my entire life on the Upper East Side, but the more we got to know each other, the more we could see some true parallels. I was lonely as a kid. My parents were . . . I feel guilty even saying it because I don't think it was their fault, necessarily, it was their own upbringing carrying on to the next generation, perhaps even a karmic residue from past iterations, but they were *cold*. There was a remove there. I was closer with my nanny than with my mother, and when my nanny died suddenly when I was eight, my parents just could not understand why I would go to bed crying. They called in an army of psychologists and psychiatrists, and ultimately upped me from day school tuition to boarding so they wouldn't have to deal with it, with me. I actually think I started in comedy by clowning around in school, deliberately getting into trouble so a note would be sent home to my folks, and I could see if maybe this time they would react.

Eventually, they registered the fact that I was funny and kind of propped me up as a party act for their friends on the weekends, and I was so desperate for their approval, I'd put on a bow tie and do a show in the living room, and then back I went, upstairs to my bedroom, out of sight, out of mind. It messes with you, that kind of existence. I've made my peace with it now, done serious self-excavation, some deep therapeutic work, but at that point, my mid-twenties? I don't think I'd begun to reconcile it. The fact that my parents had died a few years prior and I'd never really known them.

Lillian, more than anybody I'd met before, had so much empathy for that, because she understood it. She could not communicate with her family, who were deeply, unwaveringly conventional. Even her brother. I met him one time—he was the oldest thirty-something I'd ever seen in my life. Ready for brandy, bathrobe, and slippers by seven o'clock. Whereas me and Lillian were not just *on* the scene—for a little while there, we *were* the scene. Lillian didn't mind the photographers at first. She'd turn around and wave, say, "Hello!," and of course, they loved her for that, for these beautiful shots they got of her smiling at them like they were dear friends. As her mental state declined, her feelings toward all of it, including the press, soured quite dramatically, but if we're talking about season one, that winter through spring, none of that had happened yet.

MADELINE: But the creep into drug use had begun?

BOBBY EVERETT: I'll be honest: Yes. There were drugs around—they were rampant back then—and I did participate. We would smoke together, that sort of thing, and I think maybe I normalized cocaine use for her, along with everybody else on One Astor's fifteenth floor. I don't take responsibility for what came later because I never ventured into more serious substances—that was a line for me, excuse the pun—but do I wish I'd been as clean and sober as Nolan was? Do I wish I'd fully comprehended the road we were embarking on? Yes. Of course. I wish she'd never touched a thing. And the fact that the two of us took part in all that while we were together is a wound that will never heal for me.

But I'm getting into the dark times, and I don't mean to. We were so happy. We used to take these spontaneous trips—I loved showing her around the city, because she was wary of New York but I loved it; the city was my home. So I'd help her see past all the graffiti, the subways all chalked up and rancid, take her over the Hudson, up to the Cloisters, to the Met—museum *and* opera, although she preferred the ballet. In . . . I think it was March, I finally, finally convinced her to leave that hellhole of a sublet and move in with me. It was great, Madeline. Easy. Her old landlord was an issue. Kept pestering her for the forwarding address, and then thank God we had a doorman, because he kept turning up in the lobby. But other than him, we were able to just relax and enjoy spending time together, without a taxi ride between us.

MADELINE: Do you think she ever got over her fear of New York?

BOBBY EVERETT: That's an interesting way of putting it. Manhattaphobia, I suppose you'd call it. No, I don't suppose she did, not completely. She was determined to face it, not to hide from the city, but I do think she felt most safe at home with me. I wish I'd had the same understanding and respect for self-examination and healing that I do now. Maybe I could have helped her work through that intentionally. My God, Lillian would have seen such benefits from Reiki alone.

We used to entertain, though, a decent amount. *Midnight Show* people and other folks. She was not a cook, exactly, but I would make dinner and she would spruce it up and make it pretty for the guests. Good division of labor, we found. When she turned twenty-three in May, we had a birthday party for her at our place that got a little wild. Kent and Sam went up to the roof to smoke and wound up getting locked up there for a couple hours, so there were some ruffled feathers in rehearsal the next day, but nothing we couldn't get past. They just wanted Lillian to have a wonderful birthday, and she did. She felt valued, she felt loved, and for the first time, so did I.

When season one ended and we were on summer hiatus, I suppose a lot of the cast felt like they were at loose ends, not really knowing what to do with their free time, without the show holding it all together. That wasn't the case for me and Lil. We were the glue. The show was just a backdrop to it all.

TEXT CHAIN

Friday, June 23 at 5:16 PM

MADELINE
We haven't talked much about them as a couple, but through other interviews I'm hearing Bobby and Lillian were the "glue of the cast."

GINA ROSS
"The glue"?

GINA ROSS
Are you fucking serious? 💋

GINA ROSS
I assume that quote is Bobby's, because NO ONE ELSE would say that.

GINA ROSS
Bobby didn't also happen to mention he was married when he met Lillian, did he?

MADELINE
• • •

GINA ROSS
Yulia. Yolanda. Yayaya.

GINA ROSS
I can't remember the ex's name. Shit.

GINA ROSS
I will, though. It'll come to me.

GINA ROSS
You know what? Find the marriage cert in the meantime. xx

IX.
SEASON TWO

Trouble in Laughland
(Summer 1981—Spring 1982)

NOTES

June 24

Was Bobby Everett really married when he met Lillian? I've never seen that mentioned in prior interviews, memoirs, or anywhere else.

No luck finding Bobby's marriage certificate online. Certain documents aren't digitized, the website tells me, but they can be accessed in person at the appropriate courthouse.

Also need to follow up on the autopsy report with OCME and schedule a visit to Lillian's gravesite at Woodlawn.

COMPILED TRANSCRIPTS

MADELINE: What happened after the first season wrapped? Did you stay in contact with Lillian and the rest of the cast during the summer hiatus?

SALLY SCHUMACHER: I probably could have used more of a break from everybody than I got, to be honest.

AARON ADLER: Season one was fairly well received—we had some kinks to work out, but in general, it seemed we were on an upward trajectory and had earned the right to a couple months off. Most of the cast started asking in May what my plans were for the summer. I think it was Lillian who finally cornered me after our final Monday meeting and said, "Aaron, people don't want to say goodbye just yet." I don't know if they were expecting *Midnight Show* summer camp, but eventually I was strong-armed into hosting a postseason roundup at my vacation retreat in the Catskills. The place was nothing fancy, nothing like my parents' home in the Berkshires. I was only twenty-eight, after all. It was a four-bedroom bungalow in New Paltz, steps away from gorgeous woodland trails, with an in-ground pool that overlooked the peaks. Lo and behold, by week's end we had fifteen confirmed participants for the Aaron Adler Postseason Retreat. Two weeks in the mountains. I believe Sally even wrote up a little itinerary, which I thought was sweet.

SALLY SCHUMACHER: Aaron made me put together a detailed schedule for the summer trip. Just . . . beyond.

GINA ROSS: I can't think of any other job where you plan to vacation with your colleagues, because that's normal, and you actually want to go. Besides, "colleagues" is such a dry husk of a word. The cast and crew of *TMS* were not "colleagues." They were war buddies, confidantes, family, the only people who'd shared the whole damn wild ride of the past year and were just as grateful and in denial about it as I was.

The pockets of my life that didn't include them had taken on this black-and-white quality, like Dorothy before Oz . . . I'd be shopping at the supermarket and expect Kent to appear with some interjection about shitty American coffee. Or for Stevie to stick his head out and call down the hall, "Finally getting that gonorrhea checked out?" as I'm running late for a checkup. I'd hear the counter guy at my neighborhood coffee shop make some unintended double entendre about cream and turn around to laugh with Lillian, only to find myself alone. I was haunted by them. Consumed by them. My shark days were gone—these people were everything.

So yeah. No way I just wanted to say, "See you next season."

STEVIE DOYLE: I thought I needed a break from everybody that summer of '81, but eh, I got bored. Sammy and I went home to Massachusetts, visiting family, and we'd sneak out every night to the local bar, like when we were eighteen, except now people wanted autographs. From Sam, not me. Nobody had any idea who the fuck I was. To put it mildly, it got old fast. Love my family, God rest them, love my hometown, but it was a relief to get back to New York. My shitty bed in the living room felt like a life raft. Although at this point, I was starting to look around for my own place. It was time to upgrade to a modicum of self-respect.

SAM PETROSIAN: We were all very excited to go to Aaron's vacation house and wreck it. That's not what we told him, but it was the obvious subtext.

SALLY SCHUMACHER: Summer hiatus, I'm in my twenties, living in the city. I thought, hey, here's my chance to stop being everybody's mom for once, right? And yet there I was in the *Catskills* making back-to-back grocery runs to get all the snacks everybody likes. Fourth trip to the A&P, I said, "No more, this is insane," went back to Aaron's, opened a bottle of Wild Turkey, and rendered myself physically incapable of operating a motor vehicle.

Sam Petrosian: We drove up wondering, what is this? Is it a house, is it camping? It was both! Not enough room for all of us, so half of us slept on various floors. Hallway, living room, three to a bedroom, except Aaron's, which was decidedly off-limits. Bobby and Lillian had a hotel room nearby, which was what any sane grown-ups would have planned to do, but the rest of us thought, "Free lodging, woo-hoo!" First night, awkward. Second night, Kent and I went out in search of a local hotel. It was terrifying. Shades of *Deliverance*. Whatever direction we'd driven in, it was the wrong one. Day three, Gina revealed the psychedelics she'd bought from Stan, and suddenly, the entire situation felt a lot more normal. Fancy that!

Aaron Adler: I don't know what I was thinking. I spent a lot of time in my bedroom with a book, hoping nobody would notice I was gone.

Kent Romero: I dreaded it. Two weeks in the mountains. I've always had a complicated relationship with nature. In my teen years, I'd been dragged back to the Aragua Valley to see family every summer, after the fighting had cooled enough to make it safe to visit. Forced family treks, camping, wandering around the cane fields for hours on end—by the time I was in my twenties, my wariness of the great outdoors had grown into outright resentment. Which is funny, as you're speaking to me here on my working ranch, so obviously I have evolved as a human being.

But this two-week rustic adventure . . . it became infamous, didn't it? It's in the annals of *Midnight Show* lore, the time we invaded a small town in the Catskills. Pretty sure our pictures are still on the wall of some greasy spoon in Pine Bush. We were not well-behaved, but in a way, we felt like that was being well-behaved. Like it was in the contract for us to be Tasmanian devils, to be funny and memorable wherever we went. We certainly were that.

STEVIE DOYLE: Nolan turned up a couple of days in, and the cheer that went up from the pool when he arrived in his taxi was one of those warm fuzzy moments that stick with you over the years. His face lit up, seeing how happy we were that he'd joined us. He did this dance move with a spin. I remember it perfectly.

Bobby and Lillian were there, but they'd show up midday, then leave and do their own thing, except for a couple nights. Brooke came briefly and then left, and we might have also cheered to see her drive away.

BROOKE BALSINGER: Why would I spend two weeks unpaid in the Catskills hanging out with my boss? I *wouldn't*. I'm not stupid, Melanie! I went for a night, maybe two. Total obligation, kiss the ring. I turned up on that first Friday, had dinner, sat on a lawn chair beside Aaron's rinky-dink pool, then took off before Sunday traffic got bad. Kiss-kiss, bye-bye, barely a memory.

AARON ADLER: I had half a notion that we could do some work. Come together, do some visioning for season two, where we saw ourselves a few years down the road, how to evolve our comedy to stay fresh, but it quickly became clear that that was not going to be a possibility. It was a twenty-four-hour bar and pharmacy with occasional hiking trips.

SALLY SCHUMACHER: Every time someone would head out for a "nature walk," I would assign a less fucked-up person to go along as chaperone. I clocked a lot of steps on that vacation.

SAM PETROSIAN: I didn't wind up seeing much of Lillian. I was glad she and Bobby had come at all. But there was one day . . .

[*He grins, recollecting.*]

It was ungodly hot. Late afternoon. I'd dropped a tab that hadn't kicked in yet, was sitting at the edge of the pool, and Lillian came to join me. She was a little ahead of me with her trip, I could see. She was putting her hands out in front of her like she was trying to touch something, and when she caught me looking, she started laughing, and then I started laughing—and then I saw the reflection from the pool, strands of light suspended in the air between her fingers, and you know, we're like "Wooooow," we're seeing this deep truth of the universe. We start plucking the strands together, like it's this massive harp.

And then Kent comes running, *screaming,* from the house, jumps over our heads, and cannonballs into the pool. I swear, the shape of the splash hung in place like an ice sculpture for an hour! So of course, Lillian and I got in the pool too, fully dressed, experimenting with splashes, cracking up.

Bobby didn't love that, I remember. It was a bit much for him, and I think he got the wrong impression about me right then. I certainly wasn't putting the moves on his girl. It was just nice to have my friend back. Really nice.

Sally Schumacher: I think that day at the pool was the first time I really saw the *other* Bobby. It doesn't come out very often. He's got the reins pulled tight on it. But I saw his face when he looked out the kitchen window and saw Lillian in her sundress in the pool with Sam and Kent. He went stock-still. A muscle was twitching in his jaw. There was this cold fury radiating from him.

I honestly wasn't sure what he was going to do when he went outside to the pool. But he just coaxed Lillian out, which was probably wise, wrapped her up in a towel, and they went back to their hotel after that. It was not outside the bounds of normalcy, by any means. I remembered what I'd seen on Bobby's face from then on, though, that was for darn sure.

Kent Romero: Bobby had an issue peeling himself away from Lillian. There were a few people he deemed safe for her to hang out with.

Gina was one of them—at that point, anyway. I was not. Sam absolutely was not. But Gina, sure. So sometimes they'd go off and "explore nature" together while the rest of us got wasted by the pool.

Gina Ross: Lillian and I . . . we had a lot of fun. I'd wake up with these 9.2 Richter scale hangovers, but she'd somehow manage to cajole me into "adventures." I swear, we went hunting for frogs one day. Hopped up on mushrooms, imagining most of the frogs we caught, but still. Another time we walked all the way to the Springtown Bridge, which had to be over ten miles round trip. Lillian had been clamoring to see it. I don't know what the hell distinguishes one bridge from another, but she made it her mission to walk across each and every one she could—bit of a crackpot pastime, if you ask me, for someone so terrified of dying. I remember she walked right to the middle, put her hands on her hips, and declared herself "Nowhere." The exact spot between Here and There. The in-between.

Hard to forget something like that, you know. Considering.

Kent Romero: It was memorable. I wasn't exactly checking local real estate listings for my own weekend house while I was there, but it was decidedly not awful. It was nice to get back to the city and into my own bed, though, without two other men huddled around me, farting in their sleep.

Gina Ross: By the time we came back to the city, I considered Lillian my closest friend. I wouldn't have told her that. God, what the hell was this, *The Baby-Sitters Club*? But I'd never had a real female friend before her. Surprising, I know, Cohen, as I'm so darn lovable.

We kept on hanging out through the summer, those adventures and walks of ours becoming daily check-ins, stop-bys. "Hey, want to grab a drink or something?" Sometimes we'd catch a movie in Chelsea, you know, without the boys. *Little Darlings,* one of those flicks we knew they'd hate. Or we'd walk around the Village, spiked deli coffees in hand, talk about everything that had happened, everything we still wanted to happen. Listen, I was still a gloomy motherfucker, but if I was Eeyore, she was Tigger, yeah? Sparkly and kind and . . . we fit. Despite the odds.

Madeline: What about Bobby?

Gina Ross: What about him?

Madeline: Was he supportive of your friendship?

Gina Ross: Not really. I mean, Bobby was capital O obsessed. Honestly, Cohen, it felt like Lillian and I were sneaking around sometimes. She'd even justify why we'd gotten to hang out together. "Bobby's busy with Aaron tonight," or "Bobby's out of town visiting his carny cousins," or whatever—like that's what made it okay. "He's gone. Let's party!" Whatever was the friend equivalent of a mistress, the outcast you secretly make out with under the bleachers, that was me. Bobby was always there that summer, even when he wasn't.

And once the second season started? It got much worse.

Brooke Balsinger: The only thing more annoying than sharing an office with Gina and Lillian? Sharing an office with Gina, Lillian, and Bobby. Ugh, the PDA. Ohmigod, get a *room*. One that I am not in!

Gina Ross: Don't get me wrong, I didn't *not* like Bobby at the time . . . he was charming. It required effort not to like him. You've met him; you know that. I just didn't appreciate how possessive he was.

Madeline: Possessive. That's a strong word.

Gina Ross: That's why I used it. I think his investment in Lillian's career went beyond the normal confines of a healthy relationship. Yeah, I do. It got to the point where I couldn't even ask her opinion on a joke in the office without him jumping in and putting in his two cents first. I'd been a comic in Los Angeles, for God's sake, I was used to everyone thinking they were the funniest schmo in the room, but Bobby took it to another level. It was like he wanted Lillian's brand to be an extension of his own. He wanted them in lockstep in every respect. And quite honestly, Lillian was funnier than he was. I didn't particularly care for Bobby's take on lyrics for a Vagisil jingle. Like, fuck off, Bobby, this is our skit, you know? It was frustrating.

BROOKE BALSINGER: It was hard not to notice how ruffled Gina got about Bobby. She was *so* jealous of him, that was glaringly obvious! I think Gina was the possessive one, if you ask me. Like she was in love with Lillian or something.

MADELINE: How would you describe your impact on Lillian's career?

BOBBY EVERETT: I was a help, an ally, as much as I could be. I'll give you an example. When she first started *The Midnight Show,* she and Sam and Kent had a rather low-rent manager jump at the chance to sign them all. Kent moved on within a few months. I don't know if you've met him yet, Madeline, but Kent is very good at looking out for Kent. Lillian was a completely different kind of creature, loyal to her core. She stayed with this manager mainly because she didn't want to hurt his feelings. She had a contract, but it was a one-year deal, and it would have been unconscionable for me to let her sign that re-up. I can't even remember what his name was.

SAM PETROSIAN: Arnold Fleishman. Good old Arnie. He was my manager from that first year of *The Midnight Show* up until twelve years ago, when he passed away. I gave the eulogy at his funeral. Great guy. I owe my whole movie career to him.

BOBBY EVERETT: Lillian was an actual talent who needed actual representation. I was very happy with Mandy Druthers. Still am—she'll never retire! Mandy had signed me early on, when I was doing theater, and she introduced me to the talk show circuit, which is what led to *The Midnight Show* for me. She had a vision that dovetailed with mine, and that included getting me enough buzz to get movie offers. I could see her working well with Lillian, so I set the two of them up.

MANDY DRUTHERS (TALENT MANAGER): I liked Lillian. I mean, yes, woman-to-woman, it appealed to me to try to help boost her. I didn't totally connect with her type of comedy or her presence on-screen, but what I did see was that once-in-a-generation talent thing, that she was the type of comedienne who was going to be hugely influential decades from then, which is not the easiest thing to manage. Someone ahead of their time doesn't necessarily make bank in the present day, you know?

I'll admit, Bobby was much easier to get your head around as a leading man, somebody with a wide range who could carry a film. That said, I did get movie offers for Lillian. Small roles, but that's how you start out: You make a splash in a brief but memorable scene. That's the formula for comedy success, in the movies, anyway. But Bobby was protective of Lillian, bless him. He said to me, "Mandy, I worry about her. She'll burn herself out if she's running around doing the wrong roles. We've got to be selective." So it became a situation where nothing was ever good enough for Lillian, because the stress of being cast in a shitty part would be too much for her. I rolled my eyes about it at the time, I'll be honest, but in hindsight, yeah, she was clearly a very anxious and troubled person, so Bobby was right to intervene on her behalf. And in the meantime, I was able to keep that relationship with him going, which has been very good for us both throughout the years.

LEW BICKLE (GINA ROSS'S MANAGER, 1982–2012): I never particularly cared for Mandy Druthers. I'm retired, so I can admit that now. Just seemed like Lillian was an afterthought, more of a favor to Bobby than anything else. And that's not a way to advocate for somebody's career, for someone's best interests, especially since Lillian was a rising star, truly, by that point. I'd have been happy to rep her, but fat chance. She moved in lockstep with Bobby.

Bobby Everett: Part of it felt like bringing everything under our shared roof. Our manager, apartment, joint bank account. Everything we did was with the presumption of a whole life ahead of us. Together.

SCAN OF WEDDING CERTIFICATE

The City of New York
Office of the City Clerk
Marriage License Bureau

Certificate of Marriage Registration

This Is to Certify That
ROBERT WINCHESTER EVERETT

And
YUNA FREJA CLAASEN
New Surname: EVERETT

WERE MARRIED

On 05/12/1976 at The Office of the City Clerk

141 WORTH STREET
NEW YORK, NY 10013

Witnessed by Mrs. Emeline Loughlin and Mr. Aaron Adler

NOTES

June 25–26

Divorce records don't show the dissolution of Bobby's first marriage until 1982.

Yuna Claasen isn't a common name, but from a quick online search, there are still several possibilities.

Aaron's response comes in first, a curt one: Yes, he was present, small affair. Although he's still close with Bobby, he has long since lost touch with Yuna, afraid he can't be of help. But yes, he does have a few minutes tomorrow morning for some follow-up on the show.

Bobby takes a much longer time to answer.

To: Madeline Cohen
From: Bobby Everett
Date: June 27, 2023 9:39 PM
Re: Re: Re: Re: Quick Question

Hi there, Madeline.

I must say, I'm taken aback by your latest query. It feels intrusive, as well as far afield of your project as you represented it to me.

While I'm more than happy to assist you with this project about Lillian, I also want to stay within the scope of that endeavor.

Gina Ross was notorious for stirring up trouble back in the day. While it's nice to know that some things never change, it also feels like she's trying to manufacture drama where none exists.

You might want to consider why that is.

Looking forward to our follow-up call next week, assuming you're able to keep our conversation focused on the topic at hand.

All the best,

Bobby

COMPILED TRANSCRIPTS

Madeline: Thanks for meeting with me again, Aaron. I was hoping to pick your brain today about Lillian's and the rest of the cast's second season.

Aaron Adler: Season two! Wonderful. I would say the show had the feeling of a well-run factory at that point. I got more money from the network, offered everyone a raise. A smaller bump for Brooke and Nolan, who had started at a higher scale to begin with. Only pushback I got was from Kent's people, but I could see where they were coming from. He was a central figure for us and was considered a breakout star.

Sam Petrosian: That second season pay raise. We thought we were rolling in dough. It's sweet to think about now. But hey, no mortgages, no car bills, no kids' college tuition to save for—we did pretty well off that income at the time!

Stevie Doyle: I got my own place. One bedroom. So I could take girls home.

Sam Petrosian: Also sort of sweet was how we stuck together. Stevie had sprung for his own place by then, but most nights, he'd find an excuse to tag along back to our place. Usually ended up crashing on the couch.

Kent Romero: I don't think anybody necessarily knew that I was now making more money than them. I was rich to begin with. Family money. But it was important to me for it to be acknowledged that I was, at that point, the headliner of the cast. Even if it was only acknowledged privately.

Listen, I wasn't Desi Arnaz, playing up how Latin I was. "*¡Ay, caramba!*" Most people thought I was a tan white guy, probably still do. But for me, for my family, community, or whatever, it mattered. First-generation

Hispanic American, and at the tippy top of the pay scale on a major American TV show. My *abuela* would not have believed it.

Turned out being at the tippy top of the hierarchy was equally important to Bobby, but for completely different reasons. He didn't even see himself as a comedian, though. He was a *serious thespian*. I might have maybe possibly let it slip at some point that I was making more than him. Just to watch him fight hard not to react.

Gina Ross: Lots of things changed for me, second season. Season one was an uphill battle of earning my place, from flopping on Carson to proving myself as a worthy prime-time player, a voice that deserved to be heard in the room. And the "gals of the show" obviously had a particularly rough go at that, as we've talked about . . . but by season two, we'd entered an alternate reality.

By October 1981, Aaron's perspective on me had shifted: I was no longer clamoring for sketch time, Aaron was clamoring for *me*. So maybe I shouldn't have been shocked when he told me his plans for *Late-Breaking News*, but I was. Sure, I'd been a correspondent here and there for the desk, but this was *guaranteed* airtime every single week, not duking it out, sketch for sketch, to be seen. I think when Aaron asked me, I just let my mouth fall open. Kent and me, together, on the desk.

Hell yes, I was interested! I mean, it wasn't a female potato president, but it was a start.

Sam Petrosian: The fun thing about Gina doing the desk with Kent was one, watching them bicker on-screen every week, and two, I got to fill Gina's old role of "correspondent" with a whole slew of ridiculous titles. [*He adopts a dramatic Hollywood voice-over tone.*] "Tropical Produce Correspondent Sam Petrosian." "Women's Undergarments Correspondent Sam Petrosian." Those are still among my favorite bits I got to do on the show.

Stevie Doyle: Nice thing about having them both on *Late-Breaking News* is if I pitched one of them a joke and they went, "Meh," I'd go to the other one and odds are, they'd like it. So I got double the airtime without ever having to go to Lillian.

MADELINE: Were you still writing with Lillian in season two?

GINA ROSS: Mainly Kent. And not just because of the desk. That breakneck, creative collaborative energy Lillian and I channeled week after week in season one was effectively obliterated once Bobby started popping up in our office, the conference room, everywhere we went to write like a goddamn Whac-A-Mole. Any material I tried to float to Lillian was increasingly subject to the Bobby veto, so I gave up. Turned elsewhere. And before you ask, yeah, I missed her. I missed the work we'd been doing. But it seemed mighty clear that Lillian wanted to focus on that romantic relationship in lieu of continuing to explore any sort of professional collaboration with me, so I felt like I had to read the tea leaves and move on.

SALLY SCHUMACHER: The show was solid. Absolutely fine. Not necessarily the kind of reckless abandon comedy of season one, but it didn't seem to matter, because our ratings grew every week. And I felt like I had to do a smidge less refereeing, which was a very welcome reprieve.

PHIL ACKERMAN: Man, I dined out on *The Midnight Show* that year. I want to say three nights a week, when I wasn't at home with Linda and the kids. It was a cash cow, and I was the lucky cowboy who'd wrangled it.

AARON ADLER: That one was a nice analogy.

PHIL ACKERMAN: Why, thank you, Aaron.

SALLY SCHUMACHER: So professionally, we're fine and dandy. But when I think of that time socially, it's a murky mix. It felt like watching a beautiful fireworks display while in the back of your mind you're thinking, those aren't fireworks, they're bombs. The drugs were turning sour, and people were vanishing. Folks you used to meet up with every week wouldn't show for a while and when you'd ask about them, like, "Hey, where's Felix been?," you'd hear he was sick. And then he was dead. Nobody had a real word for it then; it was just starting to get whispered about. Nolan wasn't affected at that point, not healthwise, but his best friends and exes were starting to go. I think I was the only one of the bunch who even knew he was gay. Maybe because he knew I was queer, too, he trusted me with that information. I think Lillian, later, as well. Obviously, I did not tell a soul until he gave that interview, the week he died.

NOLAN YOUNG, EXCERPT FROM "NOLAN'S FINAL BOW," *VILLAGE VOICE*: My partner that was, Jackie Diaz. We'd split up the year before he got sick but stayed close. You know how it was, that brotherhood. Hard to explain. Special, though. I was working all week, big smiles, stage energy, keeping it going, joining my castmates out on the town so the cracks didn't show, and then going over to St. Vincent's to see Jackie. Watch him shrink down. Hey, you're looking at it now—this, me, this is what he looked like. But what could I say? Part of me wanted to grab the mic from the host on Friday night and say, "Wake up, America. We are dying right in front of you and you are doing nothing." But I kept the peace, kept my job, kept my secrets, and wound up right here. Talking to you.

SAM PETROSIAN: I didn't know about Nolan. I was young, naïve. [*His brow furrows.*] No. Let's call it what it was: I was a self-absorbed dumbass. My social life at that point was one long, very entertaining temper tantrum over having had my heart broken. I should have seen that Nolan wasn't just the cool guy, the smooth nondrinker who could still get down. He knew everybody—and he was losing them, one by one.

At the time, I was entirely focused on private booths and VIP lounges and photographers and beautiful women. On the fact that I finally had money but didn't even need it because when you're famous, you never have to pay for anything. It was juvenile hour.

Still, some things were starting to worry me. The crowds were growing. Wanting autographs, wanting to touch us. It got to the point before and after tapings where we needed to travel in limos with bodyguards to keep people from stampeding. Sounds fun in theory. In practice, it ranged from irritating to downright scary.

MADELINE: How did Lillian respond to the growing fan response after the show became popular?

GINA ROSS: Not well, Cohen! It was weird to me, too, and my skin was a whole lot thicker than Lillian's. We'd become public property without realizing it. One thing that was really new was the fan mail. I didn't bother reading through mine—anybody who took the time to handwrite and mail a note to One Astor was in all likelihood a creep—but Lillian, God love her, felt this personal obligation not only to open and read every letter but also to respond, as if her household-name status obligated her to become a pen pal to thousands. There was this lovely innocence about it, or so I thought, until she happened to leave one of these fan letters on her desk.

I swear I didn't open it; it was halfway folded, flapping open like a warning flag. I was walking into our office, and my eyes fell on a few snaggletoothed lines of this handwritten letter. "I watch you all the time. Not just on television, but as you sleep. And eat. And peepee in your toilet." I'm paraphrasing. "I love you, Lillian. I need you. Plans are already in motion to bring us together. Don't be afraid. It's meant to be. If you tell anyone, you'll regret it and everyone you know will bear the brunt of your selfishness." That type of shit.

BROOKE BALSINGER: The stalker letters? You're talking about the ones on the striped stationery? Oh, I knew about them. I knew *all* about them. But that's all I can say. Don't even ask; change the subject, Mira. I cannot tell you any more.

Gina Ross: I wasn't sure what to do. I sort of felt like I'd betrayed her by snooping. As if I'd walked in on Lillian changing or something and seen that she was cutting—she was punishing herself for some reason, clearly wanting to keep it a secret, but now that I knew, I couldn't unknow it. I finally brought the letters up to her a week or so later, before the Christmas break, a casual aside when I caught her sorting through the latest batch of envelopes: "You know, hon, you don't have to read your own mail. The network pages can help with that."

And Lillian's response was fucking weird. She was like, "Well, Bobby reads my mail. But if he found one of these"—*these,* plural, because apparently this same psycho had been writing to Lillian for months and always used the same pastel striped envelopes, like a wackadoo calling card—"it would really mess with him. He worries about me so much. Don't tell him, okay?" And that just felt . . . *so* beside the point? It's like, you're getting fan mail from an aggressive stalker and you're worried about how your boyfriend is going to react? It just seemed like she wasn't thinking straight.

Stevie Doyle: I knew she was getting fan mail, but, man, no, I didn't realize the extent of it. Wow.

Gina Ross: Fame, Cohen. It fucks people up. I'm serious, it isn't for the faint of heart. It can make you see things that aren't there, make you fixate on things that aren't a big deal, ignore things that really *are* a big deal . . . and I think Lillian had had a big old fame overdose by that point.

Forgive the tactless analogy. This was all before that awful summer in LA and the trouble she had with the harder stuff. Before I understood what was really going on. Before it was pretty much too late.

Kent Romero: Now I knew what I was going to be doing during our *next* summer hiatus, and it sure as fuck was not hanging out at Aaron's place in the Catskills. I would be on the West Coast, shooting a movie, and the only question for a while was which one. I was getting offers, mainly shitty ones. A couple of "Latin lover"–type roles, which was not happening. Stupid sex comedy bullshit, everything playing on my looks, which was boring. This wasn't unique to me, mind you. Everybody in the cast had Hollywood calling to some extent.

Sam Petrosian: *I* wasn't getting sent scripts! [*He laughs.*] I was getting *auditions*. And not booking them. Kent had me do script coverage for him. I was like his personal assistant. One thing he passed on looked good to me, so Arnie sent me in for it, I booked it, and then the whole film got canned! I tried not to take that personally.

Bobby Everett: I'd known Louis [Malle] for a while, same social circles. Paris and New York intersect more than you might think. Anyway, he was in the US at this point, we'd been talking about adapting something, and then he had this script for what became *The Blackboard*.

Gina Ross: Inspirational teacher porn. Bobby as the tragic English teacher. Gag me with a spoon. Or a chalk eraser.

Sally Schumacher: It was a smart, calculated move on Bobby's part. Completely in keeping with what I knew of him. He said, "I'm not only going to launch my movie career with a lead role, I'm going to get an Oscar nomination for it." And he was right.

Kent Romero: *Fatigues* popped up in early March. I did have to read for that one, but I was more than happy to. It was the exact right role to move me up the ranks. You've seen it, I assume? Corporal Sherman was a quieter role as written, more of a dry kind of wiseass, but it wound up being a lot more freewheeling than that. John [Landis] listened to my notes, smart man. And they eventually let me bring Gina on board in a supporting role, which was fun.

Lew Bickle (Gina Ross's manager, 1982–2012): If not for Kent Romero, Gina's career trajectory might have been . . . slower to mature, shall we say. I know Gina and Kent had this whole competitive friends/

rivals sort of thing going on and weren't always on the best of terms, so Gina might not admit this herself, but the spot Kent got her on his first picture opened up doors and fast-tracked her career. And the American public wondering if they were screwing did not hurt.

MADELINE: I have to say, there's this narrative of Kent Romero "launching your career" that's always rubbed me the wrong way. Does it bother you?

GINA ROSS: This goes back to the game. And semantics. Did Kent launch my career, or was I so good that he couldn't ignore me and was compelled to take me along? *Fatigues* started it all. End of story.

BROOKE BALSINGER: Are you catching some repeat themes here, Miley? Everyone's all "Thank you, *Midnight Show,* all hail Aaron the visionary," but do you know how many gigs I got after *TMS*? Three. Mom in a two-season sitcom. Stepmom in a movie. Spinster neighbor in a limited series. Oh, and gastro commercials! A regular Meryl Streep!

BOBBY EVERETT: At home, I downplayed signing on to *The Blackboard* because . . . you know, Lillian was sensitive. I didn't want her to feel like anything was going to change between us as a result of it, which was naïve on my part. And she wasn't getting the kind of offers I was, which was probably a good thing. She did not enjoy being famous.

STEVIE DOYLE: Lillian took to fame like a vampire takes to blood. Sure, it's distasteful at first, but once you try it, there's no going back. She craved it. It's part of what made her so dangerous.

BOBBY EVERETT: Her own celebrity made her highly uncomfortable, which was another reason I downplayed the fact that I'd be in LA filming all summer. I framed it as a vacation for us. But then in comes Kent—bless him, he's very different from me—the conquering hero, and it's an all-out party to celebrate his booking . . . what was it called? God, I'm blanking. That military comedy. Anyway. I figured we were the kind of cast where everybody was rooting for everybody else's success, and I thought that was pretty special. But it turned out I was wrong.

GINA ROSS: I think our greatest hope heading into *TMS* was that people would like us. Maybe we'd parlay the show into stand-up gigs, a cushy sitcom like Brooke's, or hell, get to keep doing sketch comedy for the rest of our lives. Instead, a year and a half in, the ceiling opens wide. *Vanity Fair*'s doing features on us, Bobby's tapped for a Louis Malle film, and Kent lands the lead in a John Landis movie? John fucking Landis!

I gave Kent a ton of grief about *Fatigues* when he got the offer, harmless poking. Told him army green was not his color, which was bullshit given that perfect olive complexion. And sure, there was some natural jealousy there, but I was also insanely proud of him. He didn't want to be typecast, and he wasn't. Every funny white guy in Hollywood was vying for this role, and he got it.

He felt like my partner, in a way, that season. We'd been doing great stuff on the desk together—we'd fallen into this ad-lib rapport. He'd quote a real-world headline, I'd riff on that, spin it ninety degrees, and then he'd spin *that,* and we'd basically just keep ad-libbing fake news headlines until one of us cracked and started laughing on camera. For whatever reason, people liked watching us play the comedic equivalent of chicken, so we kept it going. Sam came on as various correspondents, like I had in season one, but we also cooked up a bunch of fake guests. Bobby's Zombie Abraham Lincoln, you remember that one? One of his few bits that I actually found funny. Hard to keep a straight face.

MADELINE: Okay, so when, exactly, did Kent get this movie offer?

GINA ROSS: The timeline, the timeline—you're like a dog with a bone. Okay. Kent first found out about *Fatigues* in . . . I think it was March of '82, right around then—it was the week that Harrison Ford was hosting, and Olivia Newton-John was the musical guest. I remember we had "Physical" stuck in our heads all week. Kent's manager had called into One Astor that Friday, right before we started counting down to dress, and I remember Kent burst out of his office and shouted, "They want *ME* for the US Army!" None of us knew what the hell he was talking about—maybe he'd finally lost it and quit the biz to enlist? We all come out into the hall and he tells us John Landis is making a war comedy and he's the main recruit. The *lead*.

And, holy shit, our entire collective reality shifts in three seconds. We are big enough to do movies. We are big enough for John Landis. I mean, yes, we knew about Bobby's touching art film [*she mimes gagging*], but Bobby hadn't ever been one of us; it was different. Kent's new gig made the future bright and shiny for everyone—and yes, eventually for me, specifically. You call that a "narrative," I call it the reality of a very competitive industry, the whole game of riding coattails until you're fancy enough to get your own coat. No shame in owning up to that; it's mandatory in this business.

Anyway, we killed that show, probably because of all the dialed-up, communal bravado—Harrison, too, was phenomenal, just so perfectly wry. Great foil. He came on the desk as Han Solo and gave an exclusive interview on Luke Skywalker's secret Wookiee fetish—you can see how much fun we're having if you watch those old tapes. We could all anticipate the night of triumph ahead of us. That show was just our pregame.

Page Six

Issue 117
March 8, 1982

TROUBLE IN LAUGH LAND?

The cast of Aaron Adler's runaway hit "The Midnight Show" is suddenly everywhere this year, with many of its breakout stars penning deals for their silver screen debuts. Hunky "Late-Breaking News" anchor Kent Romero has been cast as lead funnyman in John Landis's army satire "Fatigues," with filming scheduled to commence in Los Angeles this summer. Meanwhile, cutie crooner Bobby Everett will lean into his serious side, captivating minds and hearts as a high school English teacher determined to make a difference in Louis Malle's upcoming "The Blackboard."

But sources close to the "Midnight Show" cast claim that not everyone is thrilled by these developments.

"There's a lot of jealousy, real resentment among the cast, given that 'TMS' is a team sport," Page Six has learned from a "TMS" writer, a source who has asked to remain anonymous. These recent movie developments have also, apparently, created a sizable rift between Romero and Everett. "Kent has always fancied himself a renaissance man—I think he assumed he'd be the first cast member to break new ground, and he's not taking Bobby's victory well," our source confesses. "The day-to-day tension at the studio is reaching a boiling point."

Sounds like the cast is pulling no punches on- *and* off-screen, with rumors abounding of actual physical altercations spilling out into the streets of Manhattan . . .

COMPILED TRANSCRIPTS

Gina Ross: That night put Lillian in an awkward position. She was with Bobby, obviously, but Kent was like a big brother to her. She was proud of both of them, which divided her focus.

Our celebration spot was Club 57. Picture the scene: the music's pounding, Harrison's buying Kent some fancy shot of Bruichladdich, saying, "Hey, man, that's great. Welcome to Hollywood." I drag Lillian into the bathroom, we do a line, then snare Kent and Sam and pull them out on the dance floor.

Side note, as I'm sure you've seen the pictures: I hadn't planned on making out with Kent that night. And before you ask, this was before he lined up a part for me in *Fatigues*. Our first kiss was spontaneous . . . I sort of attacked him as we were dancing to the B-52s.

Sam and Lillian went hysterical. They put on this fake baptism for us—"I christen you Children of the Church of Terrible Ideas!" Dowsing us with champagne, like a real christening. It's sweet to think about now. Sort of sad, too, considering the summer of shit we had looming, and us none the wiser.

Anyway, we're all falling into each other that night, drunk with happiness and potential, and needless to say, I'm bombed out of my mind. I grab Lillian and Sam and smoosh the two of them together, rambling, "I just love you. I love all of you." So not my style, but that's why I think they were acting so delighted, and then . . .

Bobby storms onto the dance floor. Pries us apart, like a parent chaperone at a dance. The preacher dad in *Footloose*. "We're leaving, Lil. Let's go!" And I don't know, something snaps. I pull her back fast like she's a rag doll. "Stay with us. This is our night." And Lillian's face. She was obviously torn. But she said, "It's fine, I get it. He's tired. This is a big week for him too!" So she and Bobby left . . . but I could tell things weren't right, so I asked Kent to go after her.

I can still hear her. [*Gina shakes her head.*] "It's fine, it's fine. He's exhausted. We're gonna go. It's no big deal." She was getting adamant in her insistence, which was bullshit. She wanted to be part of it all, not cut it short. It didn't feel right without her there. Bobby was this anchor dragging her down, down, down.

BROOKE BALSINGER: Of course Gina hated Bobby! She was *jealous.* If anybody was gonna control Lillian, she wanted it to be *her.*

BOBBY EVERETT: I really don't like to speak ill of anyone. It's a part of neither my character nor my journey. Kent has faced a great deal of anger-management issues over the years; I believe he's been open about his struggles with them. I wish him well in his own journey of self-evolution.

KENT ROMERO: I'm not going to comment on what happened outside Club 57. People are going to believe what they want to believe. [*He hesitates, then grins.*] Aw, screw it, I'll get into it. Did I throw the first punch? You're damn right I did. Did I do it again at Lillian's memorial service? Of course! Will I punch Bobby Everett in the face again in the future? Never say never. Hope that's clear enough?

SALLY SCHUMACHER: Yeah, I'll chime in, why not? I saw it happen. I was late arriving that night and, what luck, my taxi rolls up right as Bobby and Lillian are leaving and Kent's coming out. Bobby has his hand on Lillian's upper arm in a way I did not much like. Kent said something to the effect of "You okay, Lil?," at which point Bobby jumped in, telling him to mind his own business, and Kent said, I don't remember *exactly,* but it was something like, "You want to see my business?" and socked him hard on the upper cheek.

It wasn't about the movie roles, despite what the gossip columns said. How could Kent know that Bobby would get an Oscar nomination? We all thought he was doing some weird little art movie, which was just like him. *Fatigues* was the kind of gig they all wanted. And it wasn't jealousy over Lillian either. Kent just didn't like how Bobby controlled her every move. And neither did I. Difference was, I wasn't a six-foot-three alpha male, and also, my job was to keep *all* of them happy. So that's what I kept doing. If that meant turning a willfully blind eye to whatever was happening with Lillian, so be it.

MADELINE: You must feel some guilt over that.

SALLY SCHUMACHER: Yep. [*Pause*] Yes. You'd better believe I do.

GINA ROSS: That Monday, Lillian walked into the writers' room and it took me a good five seconds of staring to recognize her. Prior to that morning, her hair had been long, down to her waist. I don't even think she had cut it once, for superstitious reasons, during the entire tenure of the show, like those baseball players who never shave their beard or wash their hair for fear of bad juju. And why would she cut it? It was gorgeous, dark and wavy—her calling card, part of the whole Lillian Martin package.

She tiptoes into the morning meeting with this super short bob, eyes rimmed with liner, lipstick, miniskirt. It wasn't bad. She looked like a brunette Twiggy. Thinner, if you can believe it, hipper, older. Just a totally different person.

The audience loved it, in a different way. And it worked for her, publicitywise; people go so apeshit over celebrity makeovers. But on a personal level? It was out of character. She hadn't said a word about it to me in advance, and we were at the level where I would have thought she would have if she was planning a change that big. So it surprised me. Not in a good way.

PHIL ACKERMAN: The haircut? Well, Lillian probably should have run it past the network before getting the chop, but it worked for her and it seemed to coincide with better ratings, so what the heck, right? Bob it is! Bob's your uncle!

[*He chuckles at his own joke. There's no response from Aaron on this one.*]

BROOKE BALSINGER: All anyone could talk about that entire week after Lillian chopped her locks was her "new look." In One Astor and in, like, those god-awful gossip columns, like Page Six. "Funny Girl Gets Serious Makeover!" "Lillian Martin Is Hot in More Ways Than One!" "New Look, New Midnight!" It's hair, people. That tells you everything you need to know about the show, doesn't it? We'd jumped the shark by season two, if Lillian's *hair* was a hot topic.

Sally Schumacher: I found it . . . [*She considers.*] This is going to sound hyperbolic, but I mean this: I found it chilling. I got cold looking at her. Even as she was surrounded by compliments. And I looked at Bobby, quiet in the doorway, overseeing the reactions. He had this placid steeliness in his smile, like he was orchestrating everything going on around him. Like he'd scripted it. I found it very off-putting. Lillian turned to me and I sort of cupped her hair and said how fab she looked, but inside I'm going, "Red flag, big old red flag." I did take her aside later that day and very gently, carefully pried as to whose idea that haircut had been, whether it was what she'd really wanted, but she made it clear she had no interest in continuing that conversation.

Sam Petrosian: It worried me because it wasn't her. Back in Boston, we used to call Lillian Rapunzel. Kent would search through her hair for squirrels. [*He demonstrates.*] Not because she was unkempt, far from it. She kept it clean and brushed and took a certain pride in it. In letting it be what it was, I think that was how she put it: "I just want to look how I really look." She didn't go for makeup except onstage, jewelry, anything like that; she just wanted to be herself and let the world deal with it. But here she came with a new hairstyle and a new outfit and a full face of makeup—not an evolution, a reinvention, which she didn't need! And I thought, "All right, Sam. There, she's gone now, you can really and truly move on. The Lillian you loved has left the building."

Kent Romero: I have two theories on the hair. One is Bobby made her do it. I'd heard him butt in that he preferred shorter styles on women when the girls were complimenting Lillian's long hair, which made me want to pick the guy up and drop him out of one of the fifteenth-floor windows. Who says that to their girlfriend? It was little cutting comments like that, constantly undermining her.

My second theory lets Bobby off the hook a little, which, whatever. I'll tell you anyway. I think that by changing her style, maybe Lillian was trying to hide to some extent. Not put so much of who she really was out there in the open. She was getting jumpier by the day, I remember that. The rest of us were happy fish swimming around in the fame pond, but it was not her natural habitat and she wanted out. Didn't help that she was being watched—stalked, really—left and right. And not just by her old landlord, who was still trying to stay in touch. It was coming from multiple angles.

Lillian used to talk all the time about John Lennon being killed. She was fixated on the Dakota, had this morbid fascination with the spot where he'd died, the fact that it was a fan who'd done it. Reagan getting shot also shook her more than the rest of us, and at first I thought it was because she was playing him in sketches, but it wasn't that. She was afraid of dying. Of being murdered by a fan. Isn't that awful to think about now? I'd try to reason with her, point out all the things that were in place to help protect her. Cite statistics, how unlikely it was. But fuck, maybe she *knew*. Somehow, she knew.

Gina Ross: I remember one weekend that spring, me and Lillian walked across the Williamsburg Bridge. The tulips on the Manhattan side were in full bloom, Technicolor pinks and purples and yellows. Such a bizarre juxtaposition, I remember, to my disgusting hangover from the night before. But Lillian had called earlier, said she wanted to talk, walk a bit, if I was up for it. And I jumped on it, because Bobby was keeping her on such a tight leash by then, and she was perpetually worried about all sorts of shit, like those stupid letters. Felt like I barely saw her anymore, not even in our shared office—she'd become a full-on squatter in Bobby's room.

Anyway, we get our coffee from the bodega right near the bridge and we take our stroll and the sun is beaming, nice warm breeze off the East River. One of those perfect New York mornings that makes you think maybe this place isn't such a postapocalyptic hellscape. But I can tell she's off. Consumed with something, you know, and I'm prying. "Hey, you okay? Anything in particular you want to talk about?"

She's dodging me, so our conversation eventually meanders into this abstract consideration of the show's status, the season. We start brainstorming people Aaron should think about bringing in, but I can tell her heart's not in it . . . and when we're at the peak of the bridge, right over the deepest water, she stops and slowly spins around.

"We're nowhere right now," she'd said. "Right on this spot. It's so nice to be nowhere for once."

I mean, I got the callback, I'm not an idiot. I knew about Lillian's weird obsession with liminal spaces, how she clung to the magic of unclaimed territory. We were exactly between Manhattan and Brooklyn, yeah, the in-between—but hell, it was odd, her delivery. Tired. Defeated. I think about that moment a lot.

At the time, I shook it off, lightened it up. "Okay, creep!" That sort of thing. God, if I could go back. So many moments I'd change, but that one right there? It stings.

Bobby Everett: I only found out much later that they'd taken regular walks together. Lillian didn't say anything to me about that. She'd just say she was popping out for coffee with Gina, told me where they'd go, safe places, nothing for me to worry about. But I did worry. She was not street smart, even after a year or more of living there. It was that Manhattaphobia, right? Her self-imposed exposure therapy. She took unnecessary risks trying to feel comfortable in the city, and Gina only fueled her recklessness. Look at what happened in LA, the two of them together. I'm not surprised that Gina talked her into walking across bridges, for Christ's sake, at all hours. I just wonder if she talked her into walking *off* one.

[*He pauses. Drinks water.*]

I don't really think that. I shouldn't say that. We'll never know, but I truly don't think that. That's my anger talking, wearing the mask of blame, as my shaman says. Still, the fact is, the night she died, Lillian was on a bridge. And then she wasn't anymore. So who knows. If she hadn't gotten in the habit of strolling over the Williamsburg Bridge with Gina Ross, who on earth knows.

Stevie Doyle: I pointed it out to people. First as a friend, to Kent and Sam, concerned for Lillian—I'm not a total asshole, you know—but then, yeah, professionally. Because it was affecting the show, our livelihoods. Lillian wasn't as good, creatively, as she'd started out. You look at the last few episodes of season two? Lillian's a wax figure of herself. Glassy-eyed. I don't know if it was drugs or lack of sleep from partying or worrying or what, but she wasn't delivering. And nobody wanted to hear it. Not from me, anyway. They wouldn't contemplate replacing her. She was still so damn beloved.

Gina Ross: The finale was garbage. Hot garbage. Just, whatever chemistry we'd had, our synchronicity, was gone. It feels messed up to blame the dead, but Lillian was gone too, a pale shell of herself. Kent and I did okay on the desk, but Sam was our fake correspondent that week—a film critic for *Narcolepsy Weekly*—and the whole bit bombed. Audience fell asleep along with him. Honestly, nothing landed that episode. Season two ended like a three-legged marathon, all of us stumbling and crawling across the finish line. I took comfort in my summer plans. A lot of us had LA to look forward to.

If I had only known how ridiculously pear-shaped things were gonna go from there, I would have delighted in that shitty episode.

FROM LILLIAN MARTIN'S NOTEBOOK

Girlfriend prodding, aggravating, making boyfriend nervous, angry. Tapping into all his phobias, her fault.

NY vs. LA sketch—therapeutic sunshine, mirror image, everything reversed like through the looking-glass

Or: Alice rabbit hole to LA, commenting on (whatever it's like)

Picturing striped letters piling up, taunting me, but I'm not there. If they follow me to California, I'll really worry.

Long flight Thursday. Bobby needs to study his script. Bringing The Hotel New Hampshire. Up in the air, nowhere at all.

X.
SUMMER IN LA

Fatigued

[Summer 1982]

COMPILED TRANSCRIPTS

Bobby Everett: That summer. So many regrets. *Kaukritya* is what it's called in Sanskrit. The first step in healing, I've learned, is to simply acknowledge that mistakes were made and that there's no coming back from them. I have touched peace now, but back then, I was in a muddle. Having an identity crisis. I was a New Yorker, had always been a New Yorker, but now I wanted to see if I could do something else, live in California and make art. Real films, with real character work.

It was exciting and scary and Lillian got caught up in the whitewater-rapids ride of it all. Not in a good way, not like I'd hoped when we got there. Those first few days were idyllic, I'll say that, moving into our little furnished rental bungalow in the Hollywood Hills. Playing house instead of playing apartment. I'd taken her shopping for new sundresses, big glasses, that kind of Southern California aesthetic. Brought along my guitar. It was great. And then filming started on *The Blackboard*. And Gina and Kent's circus rolled into town.

Kent Romero: I was the vanguard of the western migration that summer. Needed to fly out and work on the script for *Fatigues* a little bit before the cameras rolled. It was close, but it wasn't there. And then—I'll be embarrassingly honest with you here—I was in Malibu and I met this girl. This model. I'm not going to name names, but you've heard of her, and she was married at the time. Is that enough information?

Madeline: I mean, I'd—

Kent Romero: Great. I got distracted, needed help punching up this screenplay, so I tapped Gina. Uncredited, out of my own pocket. That's how we were working together in season two of the show anyway, back-and-forth writing. And she had that cute cadet role to shoot, too, thanks to me. Not too many days on set, but with the script work, I thought it would be worth her while to come out for the whole summer. Hang out and assist, as it were. And then when it didn't work out with said model . . . [*He grins.*] We wound up having a fine time together, me and Gina. Very fine. The first half of the summer, I'm talking about now. It was a lovely beach bonfire, while the second half was a trash can filled with lit kerosene.

Gina Ross: Would love to say LA in the summer of '82 felt like going home, but it was more like circling back to a very depressed version of *This Is Your Life*. Like touring a museum exhibit about me and actually reading the placard for the first time. *Gina Ross, 1979. Natural Habitat: State of Insatiable Angst and Restlessness.*

Visiting Holly's was particularly surreal. I saw everything I must've ignored during those years I'd spent hustling out there—the penicillin-pink wallpaper, the holes in the carpet. I'm not trying to be an asshole, but it turned out the Round was a dump. Holly had an eye for talent, sure, but her domestic touch was severely lacking. The club was heading into its twilight hour by that point. It was sadly apparent. In the two years since I'd left, the regular crew had shifted, too.

Madeline: How so?

Gina Ross: It just didn't feel half as sparkly. Dominic Demoggio, my old Round entry point, was now just an occasional guest—he'd given up, sold out for a nine-to-five job, some sales gig, had a kid on the way. And unfortunately, Jake, the most talented one of all of us, was struggling in every sense. He was skin and bones that summer. Going out there, I'd had half a mind to maybe tap him professionally, get him an audition or something, pay it forward, but once I laid eyes on him, it became instantly obvious he was now a professional junkie. And I know I'm being "pot-kettle." I was snorting or popping or smoking nearly everything I could get my hands on in New York at that time, but there was one thing I stayed light-years away from: heroin.

That stuff, man, it was game over in those days. Still is. Takes hold of a person, flies them to heaven and back, then leaves them in the gutter begging for another ride. And Jake, he looked like the model for an anti-heroin PSA. Irritated veins rippling down his gaunt arms, needle marks barely hidden under his T-shirt . . . I mean, still adorable, with those big blue eyes, high cheekbones, but there was this ragged, haunted shade about him now that looked like it was going to stick. He was only twenty-five.

The Round's whole scene made me uneasy in a nameless dread kinda way, and I was ready to go from the moment I got there. But before I could slip out of the place, after my respectable and obligatory two-drink minimum, before the main act goes up, Holly finds me saddled on my old barstool and flings her arms open like I'm the prodigal daughter returned. "Gina! My star girl's come home!" Sure, Holly. I mean, it was common knowledge that she despised me—guess fame really does change everything.

Dominic Demoggio: I remember that night. I remember all the guys due up went into comic lockdown mode as soon as Gina walked in the door. Started scrambling to adjust their sets, to use only old material. That's what you do when a big name drops by; you don't use your best stuff, lest it get stolen. And by that summer, Gina Ross was a big name.

Gina Ross: Holly asks how long I'm in town for and when she finds out I'm working at Paramount with Kent on *Fatigues,* straightaway offers me Saturday nights for the rest of the summer, the prime ten P.M. slot. I stammer a yes—Holly will never not be an authority figure in my book, and I will never not be fueled by Catholic guilt—and so suddenly, in the course of one five-minute conversation, I'm back at the Round, working every summer weekend in addition to spending all week on set. The guys start eyeing me up as the new Round alpha, although naturally, they're still dismissing my stuff; the whole "women aren't funny" bullshit. Asking if my whole set's gonna be about tampons and yeast infections.

MADELINE: That was what I most struggled with when I was trying to break in. How female comics are always "female" first, as . . . almost an apology to the men in the audience for being onstage.

GINA ROSS: Lots of women lean into that—I once saw a stand-up comic spend twenty-five minutes talking about the mechanics of the perfect blow job. I mean, sure, my acts were self-deprecating—that's comedy, to a certain extent, exposing yourself for the sake of laughs—but for me, gender and, you know, genitalia are only part of that story. But hey, everybody's got their own taste.

MADELINE: But that's what I mean. Are women really allowed to have the full range of taste in comedy? Or is it ultimately narrowed down to material about being female, versus just being human?

[*Gina stays silent, considering.*]

MADELINE: Let's get back to *Fatigues*. Your character, Katie, really did feel like an exception. Was that your influence or was it already in the script when you signed on?

GINA ROSS: It was me, but it took some time. I was so green, remember. I'd never worked on a film production before, and there I was pulling up to the old Apex Pictures lot in Burbank each morning, meeting with John Landis, trying to turn my role, "Girl Cadet," into a flesh-and-blood character with jokes of her own. The original screenwriter, Kurt Miller, had set up her dialogue as all feed, no punchline. She was a cardboard cutout. That's what needed to change. And you know who had my back? Kent Romero. He doesn't get much credit as a feminist ally these days, probably because if you called him that to his face, he'd laugh you out of the room, but for my money, he's the real deal.

MADELINE: I actually wanted to ask you about Kent. He told me you did punch-ups throughout the *Fatigues* script, but you went uncredited. How is that feminist?

Gina Ross: I guess I'm having trouble understanding the question, if there is one. Leaving aside, you know, union regulations, let me hit you with a hypothetical. Let's say you, Madeline Cohen, get a call from . . . Glen Powell's people. He likes your culture articles, whatever, wants to hire you to punch up a comedy script he's attached to star in. He's gonna pay you, but you're not getting your name in the credits, hell no, except maybe, *maybe,* as a "special thanks." You're gonna, what? Walk? Or are you going to say yes please, do the work, build that relationship, and open the door to the possibility of Glen helping you get your own script produced down the line?

Madeline: I mean—

Gina Ross: Listen, you've made your point. The system can be shitty and demoralizing. But this is the real world, Cohen. Not everything is a feminist crucible.

I didn't get WGA membership through that gig, but I did get credibility, confidence, new leads on new opportunities. If you get off your high horse long enough to walk around on the ground, you may actually experience this for yourself one day. Complex power dynamics have always existed through time immemorial and *will* always exist—the people who succeed are those who figure out the rules of the game and play it, rather than throwing down their gloves and going home.

Anyway. What the fuck were we talking about? Right. Kent. Speaking of complex dynamics, he had this famous secret girlfriend for about two weeks when I first arrived, but when that imploded, he and I became something. Something-ish. We had this delicious push and pull. When one of us was interested, the other played hard to get. We'd go out, get wasted with the cast and crew, walk around the Roxy or Whisky, lock lips, end the night in bed together. Monday morning on set, we'd be Professional Work Buddies again. Made out in the props room once, I'm remembering now. Also shagged in a classroom set for *Extracurriculars*—that was filming that summer on the Warner lot across the street. Can't even remember why we were over there.

MADELINE: So where was Lillian during all this? I'd thought you'd spent a lot of time together that summer . . .

GINA ROSS: Depends when you mean. Our respective routines in June versus July, Cohen . . . worlds apart. Those *first* few weeks out there, yeah, Lillian and I were inseparable, freaking giddy over these new opportunities—and Bobby, thank Jesus H., was mercifully tied up with his saintly teacher masterpiece.

Lillian came to set my entire first week, brought Randy's donuts for everyone—and by set, I mean *our* set, *Fatigues,* not Bobby's. I'm not sure she was welcome while he was shooting *The Blackboard,* too distracting or some BS, so she hung with us. She took me out for surf and turf at Spago that week as well. Ha, you know, I'd forgotten that until now. Ordered a bottle of Dom for the two of us and told our Austrian waiter, "You know my best friend, Gina Ross? Gina is short for genius." The waiter just gave her a blank stare. Clearly not a late-night comedy fan! To which Lillian followed up with this dramatic, "Well, get *ready,* fine sir, because you *will* know her. Your future daughters are going to idolize her." She poured him a drink from the Dom, forced him to toast us. *And* she made me sign an autograph for her on a cocktail napkin, as if I didn't see her every day. But that was her, you know? True ride or die.

[*Gina blinks, as if fighting back tears.*]

By the way, my first *actual* script credit, *College Crush,* did come out of *Fatigues.* That's where I met Ella Caro, and how we got Landis to eventually hear the pitch and later produce. But from *Crush*'s inception, the main sorority girl, Sarah, was always going to be Lillian. I had written her *as* Lillian.

[*Her smile turns sour.*]

Like I said, June versus July. Big difference.

BOBBY EVERETT: A lot of things were changing for me very quickly that summer. And I was too young and stupid to know how to integrate them all into a life that made sense for me. Here's one example: I had it in my head that I needed to somehow, I don't know, sever my

Midnight Show life from my "serious actor" life—and please do put "serious actor" in quotes when you print this. So I told Lillian to hang out at home while I went to set, keep separate spaces. It was silly of me to think that she'd have impacted my performance, silly to think she'd be happy to stay home and play housewife, and especially silly to think she wouldn't, in fact, go out and about and have a life of her own as a young woman in LA for the first time.

The result of me trying to distance myself was that . . . well, I distanced *myself*. I'd invited her to join me out there because I loved her desperately, couldn't bear to spend months away from her, but then I put up a defensive emotional wall between us as soon as we arrived. When I think of what that summer could have been like if I had been more enlightened, the time we could have spent together . . .

[*Bobby goes silent for a long moment, before I hear a sniff.*]

I was very focused on the film. I do think it wound up showing in my performance, although Dustin should have won that year, not me, and you can quote me on that, too.

I was not as focused on Lillian as I should have been. I missed the warning signs. Going out with Kent and Gina, trolling the Sunset Strip. Hanging out on their set during the day, getting pulled back into their toxic orbit at night. I had some late shoots, but even when I didn't, I'd get home and Lillian wasn't there. It felt like we'd broken up before we'd broken up.

Now, as to the *actual* breakup . . . it was Fourth of July weekend. I remember because I had a few days off and I'd booked us a suite at the Holiday House in Malibu. It's Geoffrey's now, the restaurant—you should check that out, too, while you're here; make sure to tell them you're a friend of mine. Our plan had been to watch the fireworks from the beach there. But it was on that Friday, the night before we were meant to leave, that I had what I guess you'd call a panic attack. Not physical, purely emotional. My spirit was pulling me, and my ego was resisting. The crux of it was that I'd decided not to go back to *The Midnight Show*. I loved filmmaking, the rhythm, the intense, deep work, versus the sort of shallow, frantic, adrenaline-fueled ephemera of live TV—which I *do* miss now, by the way. I have a profound respect for the ephemeral at this point in my journey. But I'd given notice to Aaron, and now it was time to tell Lillian. I was going to stay in LA. Sell the New York apartment, buy a place out west, and . . . where did that leave us?

I'd opened a bottle of wine. Ordered in dinner from Ah Fong's, served it up, lit candles. She was probably expecting a proposal. My God, another huge mistake. And instead I laid it out. I was staying here. I was leaving the show. What was she going to do? If we were going to stay together, I was obviously hoping she would do what I was doing. I mean, she had as much promise as I did on the movie front. There was some interest, it was only a matter of finding the right project, but . . . it was too much, all at once, and she did not take it well.

She picked New York, *The Midnight Show,* right away, and was so upset by what she considered, I don't know, an ultimatum on my part, that she wanted to break up right then and there. She packed her bags and went. And I sat in our bungalow with the candles burning down, staring at our uneaten Chinese banquet, and thought, "Bobby Everett, you *fucking* idiot."

GINA ROSS: I'm curious. What did Bobby say, exactly, about their breakup?

[*I tell her. More or less.*]

GINA ROSS: Fascinating. So I would most certainly call that "bullshit." Wait, crap, this is on the record, so let's say "fiction," to be kind. That doesn't square with Lillian's account of what happened *at all.*

It was Fourth of July weekend, that Friday. I remember distinctly because Rainbow had just thrown this "Red, White, and Mötley Crüe" bash out on Sunset. Kent had gotten trashed and gone home early, but I stayed out, got back to my rental around four, ready to render myself comatose, when I hear this knocking at the door. Real tempered—especially given the hour—like the knock of a Jehovah's Witness. *Tap, tap, tap.* "Hi there, ma'am. Please pardon the crack-of-dawn interruption." So I wasn't that inclined to open up.

I was in studio temporary housing in West Hollywood, nothing super memorable, you know. Let's call it Corporate Rental Chic. Bear in mind geography, Cohen—West Hollywood is on the other side of the range of hills from where Lillian is staying. Anyway, I finally stumble bleary-eyed to the door to find my friend standing there.

She's a wreck: mascara raccoon eyes, bobbed hair wild and tangled, like a witch who'd just ridden across the 405 on a broom, which didn't make sense. Lillian had gone home before I had that night—she'd been biding her time at Rainbow, eager to run home to Bobby. They had some romantic dinner planned.

Bobby had been such a purposeful buzzkill all summer long. Not sure you know this, but "very serious" actors must remain serious at all times—eat egg whites for breakfast, be in bed before the ten o'clock news—and so that night as she's on my doorstep, I made some dumb joke, asking if she'd awkwardly caught Bobby "meditating."

She bursts into tears. He'd thrown her out. *Physically,* she tells me. Locked the dead bolt so she couldn't get back in, said he'd have the locks changed the next morning. Lillian's got no money on her, no way to check into a hotel, not even a quarter to ring anyone, so she walked down the entirety of Mulholland Drive, through the canyon, to my place in WeHo. Being the sweetheart that she was, she worked in an apology about not *calling* first.

Apparently, as she was struggling to get back inside, Bobby opened a window of their house in the freaking *hills,* with coyotes and rattlesnakes roaming, and told her she could come back and collect her bags when she came to her senses.

MADELINE: What was that supposed to mean?

GINA ROSS: He wanted her to quit the business. Completely. Give up work. Her career was complicating things, he said. He was ready to make a go of being a dramatic actor, and her pathetic continual latching on to the *Midnight Show* teat was keeping him from living his best life. She wasn't prioritizing him. She couldn't possibly love him if she was willfully choosing her career over his. Couldn't she see that?

I was fucking *stunned.* Not shocked enough not to believe her, though. I'd always felt there was something a bit off about Bobby, and the way he'd left at the end of the previous season, coming to blows with Kent, had only underscored my, shall we say, unease. He had always treated Lillian like a dependent or a pet. He was jealous, possessive, and definitely not one of us.

KENT ROMERO: I saw it all along, just not the extent of it. If your sister's in love with an asshole, you need to grin and bear it. It's not until it gets to the level of *abusive* asshole that you intervene. So I was alert to it all along, just, obviously, not alert enough. I'm fallible. On the odd occasion. What can I say.

GINA ROSS: Bobby can charm the Oscar vote out of anyone, but the longer you know him, the more you realize those sparkly eyes are like a sheen on a window. You peer through and . . . nothing. Empty inside. He can write all the philanthropic checks he likes, turn up to backyard spiritual retreats like your favorite wacky uncle, pose for the cover of *Zen Monthly*—it doesn't change the truth, which is that Bobby Everett is a sociopath. Strong word, right, Cohen? Yeah. That's why I chose it.

Suffice it to say that by the time Lillian finished her sob story that night, I was incensed. I told her I was gonna go over there. I was gonna murder him. And she knew I'd do it, too. She physically blocked me from the door. No, no, no, they're done. They need time apart. Don't go over there, Gina. And I got that, I did, but I wanted to clue in Kent. Kent had never trusted that motherfucker, and I wanted that vicarious validation. Plus, once we told Kent, I knew he'd never let Lillian crawl back to Bobby.

Lillian didn't want to talk to Kent just yet. I think she was embarrassed. She considered him family. So I told her, okay, fine, you take the bed, I'll take the couch—which of course she insisted on swapping—we'll sleep in, wake up tomorrow, get a late breakfast at Mel's, and lose ourselves in cheesy TV, and then after my show, I'll come back and we can go watch fireworks and figure things out.

I know that sounds stupidly PG, but that really was the way of Lillian and me—despite how hard we'd party, when it was just the two of us, as you know by now, Cohen, there was something refreshingly Punky Brewster about it.

Lillian sleeps until maybe eleven or twelve that Saturday, and I stay in my room, not wanting to disturb her. By the time she comes to, she says that she does not want to stay in and watch *The Love Boat,* given that her own love life has just capsized. She needs to get out—out of her own head—go nowhere at all. Do I know of anyone who can, you know, help with that? Someone we can call? Can we go out for a while?

I wasn't a moron; I knew damn well what she was asking. So I say, sure, okay, fine, yeah. I had my set that night, so I took her early to the Round, the only place I knew where you could score grass in LA in under thirty seconds, though I warn her it's basically like hanging in a dingy sports bar without the sports.

So we show up around seven or eight o'clock, before the first show. The place is empty but for Hal, Holly, some of the guys—slim crowd, you know, holiday weekend—and right away, I know something's wrong. Obviously there was a shit ton wrong, Cohen; what I really mean is *different.*

Lillian was the type of person who when you were with her, you could feel her focus. She was dialed into you, locked in, like everything you were about to say quite possibly might change the world. You felt . . . important. And that night? Her energy was Central Park pigeon. Barely looked at Dom and Pete when I introduced them. Couldn't sit still, flapping around the stage, the bar. Manic and depressive at the same time. I understood, fine, she needed something to calm down—but before I could politely inquire how we might score some toke, Jake walked in.

I swear, Lillian could feel the danger arrive—*dun, dun, dun,* warning: bad idea—but that's exactly what she wanted. The two of them sidle up to the bar together, immediately. She and Jake walk off at some point, and I get this nagging urge to follow them, but Pete seizes the moment and corners me, starts milking me for career advice. By that point everyone and their mother wanted to audition for *The Midnight Show*. Pete talks so long that patrons start filing in. When I finally break free of his clutches, it's ten o'clock. I'm up.

Worst set of my life. Fine, second worst—nothing will ever top Carson. It's just a monotone monologue. I am half onstage, half panic-scanning the crowd, the booths, the bar. I'm automaton Gina Ross on the outside, while inside, I'm a mother who's lost her kid on the street. That whole time onstage, I know, in my core, mistakes are being made. Huge mistakes. My mind's pinballing through the past twenty-four hours as I dial in my Catholic nun impression—"Lillian's just lost the love of her life." "She might think her career is over." "She was already broken, and my genius solution is to introduce her to a fucking junkie Romeo?!"

Finally, set's done, there's tepid applause, and I round up a full comic search and rescue party. We finally find them out back, in the parking lot near the dumpsters, laughing their asses off. I can tell, straightaway, with gut-punch certainty: Lillian shot up. Her eyes are half-rolled back in her head, and she keeps cradling her arm like an afterthought.

Cohen, I turn red. Hot. I want to throw Jake into the goddamn dumpster. I think I actually grabbed him by the collar, called him a derelict piece of shit.

Dominic Demoggio: Gina scratched the shit out of Jake's face. Drew blood.

Gina Ross: Whatever I do, I only make Jake laugh harder. Strung-out POS motherfucker. God rest his soul, but still. He says, "Calm down, Ross. She's a big girl; she can do what she wants!" *All* those assholes are saying as much. Lillian was too! What was I going to do, grab her by the hair, like she was my actual wayward child, and drag her home?

What to do but ride this ill-advised tide? It's about eleven by then, I'd say, the night still young. The guys pile into Pete's car, Jake and Lillian flopping into the hatchback, the pair of them all loose laughter and delighted sighs. I take shotgun and can't shake my mom vibe.

They're calling me Cadet Buzzkill—thanks, *Fatigues*. We went to the Roxy first, I think. Lillian and Jake do some shots, splay out on one of the place's long couches, staring at the ceiling like it's just opened, portal-style, to another dimension, floating together on their own little hazy cloud. I'd love to say they were a spectacle, but they fit right in.

It wasn't Lillian. None of it was. She was running away from herself faster than I'd ever seen her run before.

DOMINIC DEMOGGIO: That was a weird night. Weird summer, actually. I couldn't tell if Gina was jealous of Lillian or of Jake for *stealing* Lillian. I tried to distance myself from the Round crew after that. I was becoming a father, you know? I shouldn't be, like, partying with junkies.

GINA ROSS: I wanted to shake her. Scream at her: "Seriously?! Are you an idiot?" One time using H, and you're in the Needle Cult. That shit is so defeatist. "Take me, Oh God of the Veins. Send me to ecstasy." I judged Lillian for it, sure I did.

Looking back, I understand how an experience like that might have held real appeal for her, but my dominant emotion that night—the rest of that summer, quite frankly—was fury.

We crawled along the Strip until dawn that night. I was finally the party pooper who insisted on calling it quits. I had a job—I needed to be shiny and chipper on set, day after day. So as soon as we're back at my place, when I can tell that Lillian's coming down, I suggest again, "I know you've just been through a lot, but maybe we should talk about all this with Kent." To hell with talking to Bobby; as far as I was concerned, she was never speaking to him again. But Lillian starts sobbing, stammering like a small-time crook in a mob movie. "Nonononono, come on, Gina. Kent'll kill me. He'll kill Bobby. It was one time, I swear, I don't know what came over me, I just needed something different. Never again."

MADELINE: And was that the last time? Did she keep her word?

GINA ROSS: What the hell do you think, Cohen? It's *heroin*.

Madeline: Right.

Gina Ross: The rest of the summer was lather, rinse, repeat. I'd wake up during the week, scramble to set, spend all day reworking dialogue with Kent and Landis, run scenes. Production days are *long*. I'd hang around after we'd wrap each day, because Ella Caro had asked if we could start hammering out a loose beat sheet of *College Crush* after hours, just since we had easy access to John [Landis] all summer. Then every night, I'd drive back to West Hollywood dreading what I might find.

Some nights, I'd come home to Lillian passed out. On furniture. On the rug. Other times, she and Jake would both be splayed out on the floor of my bedroom, mumbling gibberish mantras to invisible gods. Some nights, Lillian would be throwing open my front door before I even crossed the threshold—"You ready, babe?"—bobbed hair wild and punky, makeup fully done, sequins and combat boots, ready to hit the town. And those eyes, those vacant, nowhere eyes.

One night, there were, like, eight dudes hanging at my place, some of them huddled in the bathroom, one rifling through my underwear drawer. Never met any of them besides Jake, and they're all smashed out of their minds. It was like she was building an annex to Skid Row right through my living room.

Still, I'd go out with these motherfuckers! I felt like I had to protect her. If I left her alone with Jake, she could end up tossed into an alley somewhere. I got the sense that they were sleeping together, if—*big if*—he could even get it up, but who knows. I barely had a moment alone with her to even ask. Partying became my second job. Scratch that, *third* job—I was still working Holly's stage on Saturdays, too. Those sets are some of my most bitter material to date. It was basically just me ranting, like one of those "my shtick is bitch" comics I'm sure you could write a thesis on, Cohen. Oh, and on top of everything else, I couldn't even explain why I was such a zombie on the *Fatigues* set, since Lillian had begged me to keep Kent in the dark! Man, I was disgustingly pissed at her. And super ornery from lack of sleep.

MADELINE: Did you have any idea what was going on with Gina and Lillian that summer?

KENT ROMERO: I massively misinterpreted the situation. Naturally, I assumed it was all about me. As this is not in fact a therapy session, we will not dig deeper into that assumption. You couldn't say two words around Gina without getting a cutting remark in reply. Okay, wait, you've met her. *More cutting than usual.* I thought it was because I was going out less, that Gina'd taken umbrage with that, or she'd assumed I was dating someone. I wasn't, actually. I was just exhausted from shooting. I was growing up, is what I was doing, and it irritated me that Gina wasn't. It was just antics with her, nonstop—or so I thought. Lillian was visiting set less and less, and of course I thought that was down to Bobby, that she was spending more time at home with him. They'd all shut me out. Which was good for *Fatigues,* in the end. Really fucking terrible for Lillian.

GINA ROSS: Then comes the Friday night when I arrive home to find Lillian in a heap on my bathroom floor, head bleeding. I mean, it was . . . terrifying. Somehow I kept it together, woke her up, cleaned her up, put her to bed. No stitches, per Doctor Gina's expertise, just vodka over the cut, but I was finally, like, fuck this.

I drove straight to Kent's.

I leveled with him, told him everything, and that I'd only kept things from him because Lillian was ashamed. Because I felt this vague obligation not to bother him, thanks to his help on *Fatigues*. But I was at my wit's end. I needed help—and no way were we calling Bobby, with which he vehemently agreed. I didn't even know where to begin. Were we going to try to find her family in Canada? The conversation basically went, in no particular order: What the fuck is going on? How can we handle this? How can we manage her?

MADELINE: What did you do when Gina came to you about Lillian?

KENT ROMERO: My initial calm thought, first plan of all the plans, was that I was going to drive up into the Hollywood Hills and take a fucking baseball bat and beat Bobby Everett to death with it. To which Gina replied, "This! This is why I didn't tell you sooner!" and yes, fine, I could see that.

Second thought, an obvious one to anyone in this day and age but maybe not to us at the time: *rehab*. This wasn't an alcohol addiction. This wasn't even a coke habit. This was something that scared me.

But it was different back then. These days, you have these spa hospitals that are practically run by the Illuminati, they're so good at keeping secrets. In 1982, not so much. Just the thought of getting Lillian into a car and driving her all the way to the Betty Ford Center was daunting. And wrangling her inside without being noticed? Her name would have been all over the tabloids before she'd even come down, let alone checked out. It would have meant the end of her career, and neither of us was willing to do that to her.

There was also a certain amount of arrogance involved. Shocking, I know. Gina and I felt like the anointed pantheon of comedy that summer, which translated into an all-around overestimation of our own intelligence and capability. In other words, we really thought we could manage her detox ourselves. With all our medical training.

What can I say? We were young.

MADELINE: When you say you "managed" her detox . . .

GINA ROSS: I hear that high horse neighing again, Cohen—*again*, it was a different time. Not a stock excuse, just a fact. Understand where we were coming from: Kent and I were, what, twenty-five? Lillian said she'd die if we involved her parents, so we believed her. And Lillian's manager? Forget it. Mandy Druthers was a snake and a half. Her favoritism toward Bobby was criminal. I *knew* that Bobby had been trying to sabotage Lillian's career. Turn her into his Stepford housewife. If I told Druthers anything, she'd use it to Bobby's advantage. Of course she would! And we sure as shit couldn't tell Aaron. Or Sally. Not at that point. So yes, Kent and I *managed* it.

Madeline: Okay. So what did that entail?

Gina Ross: You ever see *The Exorcist,* Cohen? Linda Blair had nothing on Lillian. Jesus Christ. Sweating. Sobbing. Chills. Nausea. Vomiting. She'd go back and forth between apologizing profusely for being such a bother and screaming at us to get out of her way, she had to find Jake, she couldn't take it anymore.

We were killing her, that's what she'd say. She broke Kent's heart about three times a day. I coped by locking myself in the bathroom and unleashing a fucking torrent at myself in the mirror. I caught Kent crying a couple times, though he won't admit that to you. And don't put it in the article—I mean it.

That first night of our ill-advised "vigil," I insisted that Lillian take my room. I never slept in that disgusting bed again. I think Kent ran to Sears twice a week for new sheets. He and I could barely keep her hydrated. Between the retching and the cold sweats and the crying and . . .

[*Gina goes very still.*]

It was fucking insane to think we could handle it. Longest two weeks of my life.

Kent Romero: I spent those first two weeks keeping vigil with Gina at her place whenever I wasn't working. Gina was wrapped by then, script locked, so she stayed home with our de facto daughter, then I'd come home and help. Cleaning up the place to make it halfway livable again, ordering in meals for us, cooking other ones Lillian could keep down, scaring away the hangers-on who kept turning up looking for Lillian, seeking partners in their depraved misery. I liked that "scaring away" part. Got to use my baseball bat.

Madeline: Do you remember if Jake ever came by?

Gina Ross: Once. Kent got him in the ribs with the bat and I thought, fantastic, now we'll have a police report on top of everything else, but

Jake never piped up about it. Just left, tail between his legs. That was the last time I ever saw him. He died a month after Lillian did, so whatever grief I'd have felt for him got completely blotted out, if I'm honest.

Kent Romero: When Lillian finally got out of bed, I thought, phew, I can go home now, she's fixed at last, but she looked like a sock puppet without a hand in it. Sucked dry, weak and sad and scared. And deeply, deeply humiliated. I couldn't leave her.

We all stayed there at Gina's. We could have moved to my place at that point, but I don't know. I was wary. Needed an escape hatch, which I did use from time to time, when Lillian was more herself and less of a demonic entity. I kept going to work, did my damndest not to drag the stress of my real life onto the screen.

And then filming on *Fatigues* ended and it was time to go home. I was desperate to get back to One Astor. Back to normal. Or so I hoped.

Gina Ross: We'd all reached a turning point that summer. Career-wise, a positive one: I was going to have my first film to point to, and was working on my own script with John Landis attached. Kent was poised to be a comedic leading man. Lillian, Sam, Sally, the rest of the gang—we were all going back to a hit TV show.

Personally? That summer broke me and Lillian. Quickly ended the fun and games between Kent and me, too. It had all gotten too real. The two of us had managed to co-parent Lillian through August, get her out of Los Angeles alive—no mean feat—but things still felt dicey enough that I'd made damn sure to fly with her back to New York in early September. After seven weeks of living in that West Hollywood drug house together, I wasn't going to let her out of my sight.

I still remember my juddering wave of relief as I took my seat on our TWA flight, stared out the window at a sheath of cheery blue, all those clouds. Escape from LA complete. I thought, "We made it. There's Sam in New York, Stevie. Aaron, Sally. Kent and I can step back. Maybe we can all share the load." I get myself a drink in celebration. And then another. About an hour of blissful silence into the flight, Lillian says, "Gina?" in that songbird voice of hers.

I summon my razor-thin thread of remaining patience—almost there, almost done—and turn, smiling, three tequila-sodas in by this point. Lillian's looking at me with these watery doe eyes and whispers, "I'm not sure what to do. I have no place to go. I have to move out of Bobby's apartment, and my money's tangled up with his. Maybe could I, possibly, perhaps, if you find it in your heart to let me . . . could I live with you for a while? Until I sort all this out?"

It was like bugs started crawling over my skin. I'm just, like, *blahhhhhhk.* [*Gina's neck tenses; she begins manically waving her hands in demonstration.*] I think my exact words were "Oh, hell no. You're getting your own place. We're done with that."

[*Gina turns quiet as she studies me.*]

Don't be like that.

MADELINE: I haven't said anything.

GINA ROSS: And yet I can feel you auditing. Yes, Cohen. If I could go back in time, of course I would. Of course I feel motherfucking guilty about it. Of course I wish my tolerance for epic levels of stress was higher. But it wasn't. I was in the moment. I was living with this noose around my neck, and in order to survive, I thought, hey, maybe I needed to pull a *Bobby*. Cast her off.

BOBBY EVERETT: There's so much I only found out after Lillian died, and I am willing to accept my share of responsibility for that. I'm the one who caused our estrangement by pushing her to move to LA. That much I did do. But what I *didn't* do was introduce Lillian to heroin, encourage her to use it, and then abandon her once she went clean. Maybe I've got the wrong end of the stick with that story, but that's what I've been told happened between Lillian and Gina and, to some extent, Kent, not that he would ever deign to admit fault. I'm not saying the two of them pushed Lillian off the bridge that night. But like I said before, they certainly helped push her onto it.

Gina Ross: Speaking of Bobby, you ever find that marriage certificate? Ever talk to the wife?

Madeline: Yeah, I'm working on tracking her down. Although I'm not sure how Yuna Claasen's going to fit into my feature.

Gina Ross: Cohen, the wife was in the mix, or wanted to be. She came to One Astor during the early days. Sally met her. Ask her about it.

Sally Schumacher: Yes, I did meet Bobby's wife. Pretty sure I was the only one who ever did, apart from Aaron. Pure happenstance—she turned up at One Astor sometime in those first few weeks to surprise Bobby with a homemade lunch. I happened to be passing through the lobby and saw Bobby intercepting her, shooing her straight out of the building. I found an excuse to walk to the subway with her. I guess I felt a little sorry for her, even then. And I was curious. She was Dutch, I think. Noticeable accent. She said she was a poet, that she'd known Aaron for a while. That was the extent of my interactions with her, and no, I didn't tell anybody about it until years later. Part of my job was keeping the cast's secrets intact, making sure no boats got rocked. And it was pretty darn obvious that Bobby wanted his private life kept private.

Gina Ross: Wife plus Lillian plus Bobby equals trouble. In other words, kid, do your job.

In many ways, *The Midnight Show* began as a love story. Throughout decades of irreverence and hilarity, one can sense the palpable underpinning of what started it all—a romance for the ages.

"She was my first love," Everett says, speaking to me beside Martin's gravestone on her birthday, tears in his eyes. "My first, biggest, most innocent love. I'd spent my life wandering the world alone and didn't think anything of it until Lillie came along and I said, oh. This is what it feels like. It was fate. Pure and simple."

—Philip Horton,
It Started at Midnight: A TMS History

NOTES

July 1

Name	Details	Correspondence Status
Yuna Everett	SAT tutor, Tucson Too young	
Yuna Claasen	In Utrecht	Replied; not her
Yuna Claasen Bakker	Living in Berlin	No reply yet
Yuna Fay	Singer; in Turkey; looks a little young	No reply yet
Yuna Adebayo	National Poetry Foundation COO; no photo; not sure	No reply yet
Yuna R. Byrne	At Oxford; right age	No reply yet

UPDATE, JULY 6: Yuna Adebayo wrote back. It's her, and she's here in the city. Coffee set for next Monday.

TRANSCRIPT OF INTERVIEW WITH YUNA ADEBAYO

July 10, 2023

At Gregorys in the Financial District, I meet Bobby's ex-wife, a tall, thin blond woman in large sunglasses hovering near a bartop by the window. The whole vibe is very Hitchcock.

Sally's memory has served me well—Yuna is indeed Dutch, accent still heavy despite many years of living in the States.

MADELINE: Thank you so much for meeting with me. I know this might seem odd after all this time.

YUNA ADEBAYO: I was surprised, but only for a moment, if that makes sense. There's a strange feeling of inevitability to this conversation. I think part of me has been waiting a very long time for an email like yours and a conversation like this. And I think it might provide some catharsis for me to talk about Bobby more openly. So thank *you,* I suppose?

MADELINE: How long were you and Bobby together?

YUNA ADEBAYO: Five years and a bit. I was in graduate school at NYU, studying for an MFA, working as a personal assistant–slash–companion to an elderly society woman who lived on the Upper East Side. Bobby was her upstairs neighbor. I rode the elevator with him a few times and made small talk before we were properly introduced, but I'd already noticed he was endearing, good-looking but not in an ostentatious way. A safe sort of handsome, or so I thought. And then Emeline doted on him so much, almost like a nephew.

MADELINE: This was your employer?

Yuna Adebayo: Yes, Emeline Loughlin. She was a kind woman at her core. Her wealth rendered her ridiculous—she had this stream of young boyfriends, for one thing—but I never held that against her. The fact that she doted on Bobby was the first checkmark that he was a good person, to me. And she was desperate to get us together. I don't know, in hindsight, if he put her up to it, but she used to hold these little salons and started inviting both me and Bobby. That was where I met Aaron Adler, actually.

Madeline: I saw his name on your marriage certificate and wondered.

Yuna Adebayo: Yes, he was Emeline's, I guess you'd say, boy toy at the time. Part of that scene. These New York intellectuals would come and parade their importance and connections and Emeline would have me read from my poetry, very proudly, and Bobby would play the piano and charm everyone. He charmed me. Quickly. I think he proposed to me on our sixth date. It was at the Palace, famously the most expensive restaurant in America. I was very intimidated, and he had a lavish plan in place, with champagne and the waiters in their white tails lined up waiting as he got down on one knee in front of all the other diners. There was no way to say no.

Madeline: Did you want to say no?

Yuna Adebayo: It's complicated. It was too fast, no question, but I was so swept up in all that affection and attention, and I loved him. I really did. It's so hard to know now how much of it was manipulation and how much was genuine, because even now I can tell you there really was so much to love about Bobby. The outer elements, the trimmings, if not the core of him. I'm not actually sure there is a core of Bobby.

[*Yuna looks away, blinking for a moment, before she continues.*]

We were married very soon after that. At the time, I found the rush romantic, but now I know it was a form of control. He wanted me locked down quickly. Full ownership. I'd wanted to have my parents come over from Delft, which is where I was born, and that was the first time Bobby became cold with me. He was very hurt that I was prioritizing them over starting our life together. He told me that if we were going to make marriage work, we would need to be the only family we considered in our decision-making and let everyone else fall by the wayside, which sounded impossibly heartfelt to me at the time, but I was also attuned enough to sense that there was an ultimatum hidden in that overture. He was saying I had to choose, them or him, and the manner in which I'd be choosing was to essentially elope instead of having even a modest wedding to which my own family would be invited.

I chose Bobby. I chose to elope. We were married downtown at a government office, with Emeline and Aaron as witnesses. It was lovely, actually. We went to the Tavern on the Green afterward with a few more friends, and Bobby was so happy, he kept asking for a calendar so he could mark down the day we'd have our "big" wedding, bring my family over at last and celebrate all over again with them. Of course that never happened, but at the time, I believed him.

Then, of course, there were more changes.

MADELINE: What kind of changes?

YUNA ADEBAYO: Well, he said it was too awkward for me to continue working for Emeline, which made sense. We lived in the same building, we were peers now, but surely, I thought, I could pop downstairs from time to time and keep her company. Bobby was not comfortable with that. He wanted to visit her with me, and not very frequently. But it seemed within the bounds of reason, so I didn't push back. Then that reticence grew to affect all my friendships. My MFA program, too. I came home from a meeting with my dissertation advisor one day and found Bobby stone-faced on the balcony, refusing to look at me, staring out at Central Park as if he'd come to some terrible realization. It took an hour of begging to get him to explain himself to me. And he finally said that he knew I was in love with my professor, that I'd lied to him about my academic interests, that our marriage was a sham. I pleaded with him, assured him that wasn't the case, but the only way to prove myself to him in the end was to quit my master's program. So I did.

Eventually, I stopped seeing my old friends. I only went out when he wanted to, where he wanted to. I dressed how he liked me to dress. Changed my hairstyle. He liked shorter hair on women, chin-length, and I wanted him to be happy. He was incredible when he was happy, it was contagious, but when I disappointed him, which was more and more often, the clouds would roll in and it felt like I would never be warm again. I learned to tiptoe.

MADELINE: Meaning you were afraid of him?

YUNA ADEBAYO: Yes. *Yes.* I was *terrified* of Bobby.

[*She stops. Presses her hand to her mouth.*]

Of his emotional swings, the way he would turn on me, find the part of myself I was most ashamed of and mine it for maximum pain. He was very talented at that. He never hit me, a fact that he brought up often as a sort of armor against argument. But he never had to hit me. He controlled me entirely.

[*Yuna shakes her head.*]

When he was cast on *The Midnight Show,* after the initial rush of celebrations and excitement, he accused me of being jealous of him, of his success, of not adequately cheering him on. I lost my composure, told him he was a ridiculous person, and right there, in our bedroom, the rage that rippled through him. You could feel it, across the bed. His lips went white. I really thought he would cross that line, that he would hit me, or worse. I *wanted* him to hurt me physically, to end the ambiguity of it all.

MADELINE: I'm so sorry.

YUNA ADEBAYO: That's how it works, that kind of abuse. I felt like a terrible person when I was with him, like I didn't deserve him, or even deserve to exist at all. Like I was weak. Disgusting. Like I was the problem, even as I *knew* it wasn't me. But he didn't hit me that day or ever. He went to work, cheerful as can be, and I was so hopeful that there would now be something else that would consistently keep him away from home. And then when I went to the set for the first episode, at Aaron's invitation, not Bobby's, and I saw my husband flirting with Lillian Martin just offstage, unaware that I was there—I don't think any of the cast members even knew I existed—my overwhelming reaction was . . . relief. He'd moved on from me. It was petrifying, like being pushed from an airplane, but liberating as well.

[*She laughs. Shrugs.*]

I will say, though, the way he went about it was terrible. I came home one day from buying groceries and there was a moving company rifling through our apartment. They were packing up all my things. He wasn't even home. He'd left me a note, something along the lines of accepting my request to be freed from my "ridiculous husband." I'm happy to tell you I've mostly forgotten the contents of that letter, as it was, in fact, ridiculous. I was devastated then, completely at loose ends, of course, given that the thread had now been cut.

There were moments after the breakup that I wish I could erase. There was an incident with a pretzel cart, my God. It doesn't matter. I breathed so deeply when I left that building for the last time.

[*She inhales with a smile, as if in demonstration.*]

I couldn't stay in the city, couldn't risk seeing him again. I went back to the Netherlands for almost fifteen years. Met my husband, who is originally from Nigeria. He was at The Hague but then was appointed to work at the UN, so when I moved back to New York, it was finally safe. I had a husband with a security detail; Bobby was very famous, living in LA. And I had escaped my worst fear: that he would lose interest in Lillian and hunt me down, that he'd never forget me, never relent. Not only did he relent, but he erased me. Entirely. He never talks about me in interviews. It's as if I never existed. I was utterly struck from the record.

[*She turns to me, eyes opaque.*]

Exactly how I wanted it, but even so. Don't you think it's odd?

NOTES

July 11

I have to admit, I was quite shaken by Yuna's account yesterday.

Maybe that's why it took me far too long to connect the dots.

From Lillian's notebook:

> *Crazy ex grabs you, pretzel cart wrestling match, restraining order, going into courthouse in disguise. Which one of us is the villain?*

Yuna mentioned an incident with a pretzel cart. It stands to reason that Yuna's the "crazy ex" in question.

Does this mean Lillian filed an actual restraining order against her?

XI.
SEASON THREE
Lillian's Last Act
[Fall 1982—Winter 1983]

COMPILED TRANSCRIPTS

Kent Romero: Lillian killed my swagger. Murdered it dead. Coming into season three, I'd planned to lord it over everybody that I was now a movie star and they weren't, but I couldn't. I was so unbelievably drained. Did I resent Lillian for it? A little. I was also smart enough to know that a good chunk of my success was down to her talent, not my own. So I owed her. But it was more than that. She was family to me. I still feel that way.

I got back to New York a few days after Gina and Lil. Assumed Lillian would be staying with Gina, but apparently not. Had to track Gina down at the Mudd Club to find out the address of Lillian's hotel, which pissed me off. Raced uptown to the Carlyle and thank God, Lillian was in her room, working on something in her journal, which I thought was entirely healthy until I saw what she was writing. Not sketches, exactly, or even deep dark thoughts, but this stream-of-consciousness in-between, chronic anxiety dressed up as a brainstorm. Maybe that had been her creative process all along. I'd never peeked at her pages before then. What I saw in that moment, though, was a willful avoidance of real life.

I took the notebook from her and set it aside and said, "Here's what we're going to do." I laid it out: I'd help her find a new place to live, not as expensive as the Carlyle but not seedy or riddled with temptation. I'd get in touch with her manager to sort through the finances amicably, get her a new bank account. Make her an independent human being once again. When I was done with my spiel, she started crying, and I put my arm around her and just let her cry for a good long while.

Then I called Nolan.

Nolan Young, excerpt from "Nolan's Final Bow," *Village Voice*: It was important to me to help other people, because I'd been helped, you know? Back in California, it was Louis Thibodeaux, an elder statesman in the Black community, who took me aside and said, "You're killing yourself, and this has got to stop. You've got too much damn promise for that, and your people need you to keep shining." Now, Lou, he was a trombonist by trade, not an actor, but he'd been where I was. He took me through it; he was there for me. Got me into the program in private. Had to be discreet, right? I was starting on Carol Burnett. But I kicked the junk, and I kicked everything else out with it, and I've been clean since then. It is a fight every single day. Still is. I'm stuck in this bed, and I still think about it: hey, wouldn't it be nice, just one time? It's a demon in your brain and you've gotta be in conversation with it, because it's never gonna go away completely.

That's what I told Lillian Martin when I went to see her. She was right where I'd been, years back. And she was ready—because listen, I was only ready to help people who were ready to accept help. There were plenty of people I knew who were not going to respond well to an intervention or what have you, and I'm going to be real with you, I didn't have the energy for all that. It was not my life's work; my life's work was comedy. But what Lillian needed was a friend who got it, somebody she could come to and say, "Today is bad," and they would understand. Tell her a joke, get her through it, find another way to put one foot in front of the other. That's what I did for my friend. Now, did it work, in the end? That I can't tell you. And that's what still breaks my heart.

Gina Ross: The summer before, heading into season two, we'd returned to One Astor basically riding on chariots, all hail the new kings and queens of comedy! Heading into season three was dead men walking. A slow, dread-filled crawl back to fifteen. At least for me. I had no idea how to act around Lillian. Were we just going to go back to being colleagues, after nights when she went to bed spooning my toilet?

It was awkward with Kent, too. After our fun, flirty little affair in June evolved at warp speed into shared custody of our addict "daughter," I couldn't keep it light with him either. The season before, the desk had been foreplay. Now it felt like we'd been married for thirty years, and not in a good way. The comedy-sex was routine, obligatory. Our punchlines landed like overused safe words.

The movie had also gone to Kent's already-inflated head, and he'd shown up that first Monday launch meeting completely over-the-top. He basically never stopped playing Corporal Sherman from *Fatigues*. I'd been seeing him all summer, but in the aggregate, he'd probably dropped ten pounds, put the same back on in muscle mass. He'd be doing pull-ups in the doorframe of his office, barking in the writers' room like a drill sergeant—he wore that stupid *Fatigues* jacket everywhere. Round the clock. Totally annoying, alienating everybody. So it's not like Lillian was the sole reason for our "split."

Phil Ackerman: After the films started rolling, of course there were some bigger heads. Yes, Kent wore aviator sunglasses for a week straight, morning to night. *Fatigues*-style. You know creatives. Gotta love 'em!

Aaron Adler: Forty-plus years into this business and I've realized that the tenor of every production ebbs and flows. It's natural. But after the highs of the first two years, there was no denying that we'd dropped into a comedic rut in season three. The synergy was off from that first Monday through the rest of the autumn. I'd assumed it was hurt feelings from Bobby leaving, the dynamic of the ensemble shifting. I thought it would pass naturally, without the need for serious intervention on my part.

We'd thought about adding in a new cast member, but there wasn't much time before the season started. I didn't like the prospect of scrambling, so I adopted a "This too shall pass" approach. I do think the fact that you're speaking to me now at One Astor, still on *The Midnight Show* set all these decades later, speaks to the wisdom of that philosophy.

Stevie Doyle: They started auditioning for Bobby's replacement week one. Parading the prospects in front of us. I'm like, *hello*? I said to

Sally, you know, "What are you thinking?! You'd save a ton of money by just bumping me up to regular cast member." I wouldn't even ask for a raise. Not right away. But Sally kept patting me on the shoulder, saying, "Wait for the right time, wait for the right time." Bullshit. Meanwhile, I'm watching a guy with a parrot puppet walk by my office on his way to test. Wasn't sure if I wanted to bash his head into a wall or my own.

Sally Schumacher: Stevie was persistent. Of course we were going to bump him up at some point just so he'd stop begging. I was merely trying to delay the inevitable and ensure that Stevie could stay gainfully employed for as long as possible. Ultimately, we put the brakes on replacing Bobby at all in the early season. We weren't finding what we needed, still stuck in trying to catch that lightning in a bottle of the first class, instead of letting the show become something new, which is how it ultimately thrived.

Gina Ross: It was good that *TMS* wasn't my entire world anymore. Ella [Caro] and I had talked to John [Landis] in August. He loved the *College Crush* pitch, called it *Animal House* meets *Obsession,* which is still one of my all-time favorite elevator pitches. A stalker comedy—I don't know if you could get away with that these days. John wanted to see a draft, so Ella and I were scheduling frequent bicoastal phone calls and dividing up the writing. Quite a feat in the pre-internet era, let me tell you, Cohen.

Madeline: I'm struggling to even picture the logistics of that.

Gina Ross: It wasn't pretty. When we were getting close, maybe October, Ella asked if I'd clued in Lillian yet, shown her any pages. She still assumed Lillian would headline. I told her Lillian probably wouldn't be interested, she was writing so much that season with *TMS.* We never broached the subject again, and by the time I was ready to reconsider Lillian for the part, Ella had already put an offer out to Jamie Lee Curtis, who wound up being fantastic in the role. But that created a certain secretive vibe around the office. I have no idea if Lillian knew my movie was on its way to being greenlit.

Brooke Balsinger: Of course Lillian and I knew what Gina was working on! I could recite beats from that stupid movie, that's how loud Gina would be on those "top secret" [*uses air quotes*] Hollywood calls. Gina was punishing Lillian. It was obvious. *That's* why Lillian started working with Nolan. She was smart, and she knew Gina wasn't stable.

Nolan Young, excerpt from "Nolan's Final Bow," *Village Voice*: The side effect of spending all that time with my little pixie princess friend Lillian was that we started teaming up on writing sketches. Not just pitching concepts, which I'd done before, but putting pen to paper, the actual grind. I considered myself a comic actor before that point, nothing else, but Lillian thought I was selling myself short. I didn't expect to love the act of writing as much as I did. It felt like going back to my childhood, writing little stories for my grandmother up in Harlem. So even though so much was falling down around me, so much sadness out there, so much fear, that was still a pretty special time in my life. Work became my lighthouse, and that was down to Lillie. Without that girl's encouragement, my one-man Broadway show, my Tony, none of that would've happened.

Gina Ross: Obviously, I was thrilled to see Lillian and Nolan team up: He was a fantastic dude, just an all-around blast of a person, a steady force. Lillian needed some stability in her life, and Nolan was a good influence, having been clean for eight years himself. There were rumors later that his image was a sham, that he'd been high for most of *TMS,* or that he relapsed after Lillian died, while he was doing Broadway. *All* of that was bullshit.

We know now what he was struggling with after Lillian's death. He'd get sick for long bouts but was committed to not telling anyone, so people made assumptions, and those assumptions were fucking unfair.

MADELINE: What about you and Lillian? Did you ever make amends that season?

GINA ROSS: I'd cooled off by the fall, and I missed her. Hard. I was . . . well, what the hell is Eeyore without Tigger, right? Just a sad fucking donkey.

By the time I was ready to move past the summer, though, she was long gone. She and Nolan were thick as thieves by then. Lillian had this new assured energy about her. More mature in Monday meetings, outspoken with feedback during table reads. I wouldn't say she had her sparkle back. She had a different glimmer.

And listen, yay sobriety. Obviously, I'm a fan. I've gone through my own twelve-step trip through self-betterment over the years. I get it. You've got to surround yourself with people who support what you're trying to do. I have no idea how Nolan was able to be on the scene as much as he was. I was still partying hard at that point, and . . . *TMS* was musical chairs. The music had stopped, and now Lillian and I were on opposite sides of the room.

BROOKE BALSINGER: I obviously don't know much about addicts, but one thing I've learned from *TMS* and, like, the movies is they cannot *stand* it when other people go clean. Ruins the party. Gina thought she hid it well, but I could see plain as day how resentful she was of Lillian all of a sudden.

SAM PETROSIAN: It was very difficult to see someone I cared about so wrung out, and tough for me to know what kind of support I could offer that wouldn't rock the boat even more. Throughout our friendship, I was always careful not to . . . I'm not sure this is quite the right word, but . . . *infantilize* Lillian. She may have been petite and adorable, yes, but she was an adult. An independent person, an incredible one, going through a difficult period. I stayed at arm's length, watchful, ready to jump in if she needed me to. Lil was always straight with me; if she wanted my help, she would ask. Plus, she was so close with Nolan during those days. Boy, I was glad for that. He was a stand-up guy.

SALLY SCHUMACHER: It's so strange to look back on that time, knowing what the media narrative became about it all. How contradictory it all is.

For example, the press likes to pretend the first sign of trouble for Lillian's mental health was her disappearing from the club scene. She wasn't going out, wasn't getting photographed—bad sign, right? But that was a *good* thing. That was her getting better. And you know, there were times I'd look around me at three in the morning and think, "Why am I still doing this? I could be in bed right now." And I was only twenty-nine!

It was starting to age me. The revolving door of people, of substances. The specific scene would shift from venue to venue, but it was still the scene, and it was souring. But I guess my point is, the less I saw Lillian outside of office hours, the less I worried about her. Even at the obligatory post-show Aaron parties, Lillian would say a quick hello, then take the network limo back home. She had a nice doorman place, Park and 60-ish, was thinking of getting a cat. It was all going well. And creatively, she seemed to be coming back, which was a godsend for the rest of us.

GINA ROSS: I sound like a broken record by now, but comedy . . . it's personal. If you aren't jibing with someone on a human level, you sure as hell are going to struggle to make a sketch baby together. I had all these ideas I didn't know what to do with. The spring before, Lillian and I would have pushed them to the limits, been giggling through table reads—and in season three, it was tumbleweeds. I was still writing fake news for the desk, mind you, but that hustle was always left to Fridays, last-minute, breaking headlines stuff. So most of the week? Lone cowboy Gina.

MADELINE: But obviously not for long, given . . . well. You know. When did you and Sally team up?

GINA ROSS: Took you long enough to ask about that. So linear, Cohen. Lucky for you, it was right around that time. After my work on *College*

Crush, I was more interested in writing about women. And that's a lot easier to do when you're writing *with* women.

MADELINE: Interesting.

GINA ROSS: I'm not necessarily talking about a unique feminine mystique here, Cohen. I'm a pragmatist. It's useful not to waste valuable writing hours trying to convince your collaborators that women are also human. Or can play whatever the hell they want. The whole "A *female* potato president, my *God,* are you insane?" conundrum, like we've talked about.

I'd done a Jane Fonda impression at the end of our first season when Bowie had been on, and I'd been wanting to return to it. Turn it into a series where Fonda is a cult leader, and her devotees are housewives converted into Jazzercise assassins. I thought we could play around with an arc through the season, where by the final sketch, Fonda's like this Aerobics Empire crime boss wanted by Interpol.

Sally had phenomenal notes. If you've seen it, there's this choreographed routine as they're robbing American Savings Bank . . .

MADELINE: Yeah, it's a meme now. People still post it all the time.

GINA ROSS: Due credit, all her. Sally has this sixth sense when it comes to funny. She's always known exactly how far to push a sketch's absurdity without falling off the edge. She's self-effacing about it; she'll tell you [*launches into a Southern accent*], "Lawd's sake, I'm not the funny one. I'm just a lil' old shepherd, herding the funny flock into their field."

MADELINE: That sounded more like Morgan Freeman.

GINA ROSS: [*A rare smile.*] Yeah, well, impressions were Lillian's thing. Anyway, Sally's plenty talented in her own right. You know that; you've seen her stuff. And it was natural after that. Wonderfully, headbuzzingly natural. A progression from professional to . . . something even more interesting.

Our relationship developed easily. Quickly, I'd say. The most surprising thing about it all was me. I knew Sally was gay, obviously, but I didn't know that I was? I knew I looked at people differently, maybe. Both male and female. Always considering and calibrating my brand of attraction to them, because sometimes it was unexpected and complicated. We were not the generation to shout, "I'm bi! Pan! Both!" loud and proud—but I tell you what, Cohen, for all the shit I give you and your cadre of critics, you zoomers have really created that forum, a space for people to figure themselves out.

Like, looking back, I think about girls I knew over the years who I'd thought I was *envious* of. I'd stare at them and think, "She's got something I wish I had." Then I'd keep on staring, and now it's pretty obvious that what I was really feeling was infatuation. A spark. That's how it was with Sally, when I first met her. Envy, rivalry, whatever you want to call it. But the truth was, I thought she was pretty fucking special. All along.

KENT ROMERO: I want to make one thing clear, Madeline, while I'm speaking to you on the record. Yes, there was a love triangle. No, it was not all three of us at the same time. But you might let them know I'm still open to the possibility.

GINA ROSS: I remember the night when I finally—when *we* finally—acted on that spark. It had gotten to a point, working together, where I was starting to get nervous, butterflies and everything, when Sally and I were alone together. I'd fixate like a teenager that I was going to say something stupid, fuck it up. But I was starting to think about her all the time, making excuses to stop by her office with ideas for new sketches that I wasn't in love with, necessarily, but that I knew she'd dig and want to work on, just so I could spend more time with her. I'd shown her the pages for *College Crush,* too. She made so many improvements, she ended up with a byline when the script was finally greenlit, which helped launch her own screenwriting career. That was the Writers Guild's call, by the way, as much as I'd like to take credit.

Anyway, one night, the week that the Rolling Stones were the musical act, Sally and I were alone in the studio, running Jane Fonda choreography into the wee hours, and—

Wait. Sally, you wanna tell the story, honey? Come in!

SALLY SCHUMACHER: Is it my turn again? Madeline, you sure you don't want some lunch? I've got leftovers in the fridge—

GINA ROSS: She'll survive for a few minutes, Sal, just . . . tell her our grand inspiring love story. How we got together.

SALLY SCHUMACHER: [*Flops beside Gina on the couch.*] You mean the Rolling Stones week? You kissed my neck.

GINA ROSS: That's how you want to tell this story? Mick Jagger was in town and Gina went full vampire?

SALLY SCHUMACHER: You did, though! We were doing this sort of ridiculous pas de deux, trying out all these poses, and she was behind me holding my waist and she leaned over and kissed the nape of my neck.

And I turned and looked at her for a second and I think what I said was "Oh good, we're doing this?" And we, um . . .

GINA ROSS: We made out. Basically.

SALLY SCHUMACHER: And that was pretty much that. Didn't hurt that we happened to live in the same apartment building either. You were, how shall we say, geographically desirable?

GINA ROSS: Ha, you were on six, right, and I was two floors below? Those hot elevator rides definitely helped fast-track the relationship.

SALLY SCHUMACHER: And I was so done with the casual sex thing.

GINA ROSS: I didn't know that I was until we got together, and then I thought . . . holy shit. Is *this* how real relationships are? Easy and healthy and like, actually good for me? And once that sort of clicked into my masochistic brain, I guess I realized, why would I ever want anybody else?

MADELINE: How long have you been married now?

SALLY SCHUMACHER: Legally?

GINA ROSS: No, screw that, we had a real ceremony. Decades ago. God, Sal, how long has it actually been? How old is Atticus? Our first son's thirty-one, so as far as I'm concerned, yeah, we've been married thirty-two years! Long time.

SALLY SCHUMACHER: Doesn't feel like all that long.

[*They smile at each other.*]

KENT ROMERO: Can I just tell you how delighted I was when I finally found out? I like to think that once they'd both sampled Kent Romero, they knew no other man could possibly compare, and so where else was there to turn but to each other? But they really are an excellent match. I'm glad they've stuck it out over the years. They've got two kids, you know that, right? I'm not the father. I feel it's imperative to make that clear.

SAM PETROSIAN: I had no idea Gina and Sally were together back then. But apart from that oversight, season three was when I got my head screwed back on straight. We weren't riding adrenaline and ego anymore. We knew we'd hit a lull, but for me that was a good thing! I needed to calm the partying down, get back to why I'd gone into comedy in the first place.

And Lillian was back. The one I knew. She was shaky . . . I want to say September through November, I was still worried. Didn't know if she'd wind up staying in New York, let alone on the show. But she wasn't hiding herself away like she used to. Started growing out her hair again. Smiling more and more.

And there were some baby steps being taken back toward the friendship we used to have. One day, without preamble, she got to the table read and silently passed me a black-and-white cookie from the commissary. I broke off the black side, handed it to her. That became a weekly thing all over again. Here's Sam's half of the cookie. Here's Lillian's. [*He connects his rounded hands into a full circle.*] I can't even tell you how happy that made me.

Kent Romero: I'll say one thing about season three: It was nice not having Bobby Everett there. Like a relaxing spa holiday, all that fresh air he wasn't breathing. Definitely enjoyed that.

Phil Ackerman: I really missed having Bobby around the building! He'd become an office buddy of mine. His musical numbers were my favorite part of every week. Remember that *Paper Moon* parody? *Say it's only a cut-rate set, say we're only a two-bit cast . . .*

[*Phil keeps singing for at least another stanza before Aaron, avoiding eye contact, finally waves for him to stop.*]

Phil Ackerman: Anyhoo. What a special guy.

Sam Petrosian: I was excited to go to work again. The show had started to feel like a means to an end. What end, I didn't even know. I think we'd started to buy into our hype. We'd looked to Kent and Bobby as directions we wanted to head in—toward movie stardom or what have you. We'd started to think of the show as the day job, almost resentfully. But that cookie, I don't know. It rebooted everything for me. And I think that's what helped me tap back into those improv roots, the unexpected, the buzz, the joy. I think it does show in some of those episodes before we lost Lillian. And then, of course, after that, it all died with her.

KENT ROMERO: I was on my way out. I think that was obvious to everybody. But to me, that made the show more fun. I knew I'd never do anything else like it again once I walked away. But it did create tension with some of the people I was quote-unquote leaving behind. Stevie in particular got weird.

STEVIE DOYLE: Season three was when Kent went from charmingly arrogant to absolute fuckface. I was working my ass off trying to keep the show funny. While the cast was checked out, in, like, heroin recovery, taking calls from LA at all hours, there's me, the sap, doing the goddamn job I was paid not very much to do for absolutely zero credit. So yeah, I had an issue with Kent. With all of them.

MADELINE: Including Lillian?

STEVIE DOYLE: When she showed up to rehearsal a half hour late and nobody said anything? When she spouted an idea I'd pitched the day before and everybody acted like she was the second coming? Of course I took issue! It wasn't anything new. But it did start to feel especially old at that point. I was ready for a smidge more respect from everyone, and yes, Lillian was included in that list. You bet she was.

AARON ADLER: There were the usual tensions, I would say, coming into December, but things were improving. We had a fairly solid last episode of 1982, and after the early season we'd just weathered, "fairly solid" was something to celebrate. So I invited everybody to my apartment for a sort of family Christmas party. First time I had attempted that. I dressed as Santa and handed out toys to the network executives' children.

PHIL ACKERMAN: Man, that was the best *Midnight Show* party we ever threw. My kids still talk about it, and they're all grown up now.

SAM PETROSIAN: Definitely the most wholesome of all our get-togethers. I sheepishly gave Lillian a set of Moleskine notebooks, sort of lobbed them at her and ran, but then she flagged me down because she had a gift for me, too. A snow globe of Boston, the exact spot where Beacon Bar was, where we used to do Townies shows. It was perfect.

BROOKE BALSINGER: Yeah, I went to that lame-o holiday party. I brought my fiancé—my first fiancé, Richard—to introduce around. Everyone ignored us all night, big surprise!

GINA ROSS: I remember Lillian was dressed as an elf, helping Aaron hand out gifts to the kids. Perfect job for her, and she clearly loved it. I remember the pillow coming out of Aaron's Santa suit belly and all of us taking turns wearing the beard. I remember playing footsie with Sally under the table, sorta hoping we'd get found out. The sing-along at the piano with the bandleader at the time, leading us in cheesy carols—very last ten minutes of *It's a Wonderful Life*. Kent saying, "Thank Christ Bobby isn't here. He'd play every song in a key only he could sing!" And shit, I don't know if that triggered Aaron's little announcement, but that was it. The bomb got dropped, and there went the party.

AARON ADLER: I thought of it as the final gift of the evening, acknowledging that we had one person in our *TMS* family who was missing, the prodigal son, as it were, and I was spreading good cheer by letting them all know he'd be returning. Not to the cast, of course, but as host.

I must say, I was extremely taken aback by their reaction.

SALLY SCHUMACHER: It was as if Aaron had been asleep for the past six months and had woken up at that Christmas party. I honestly don't know what he was thinking.

SAM PETROSIAN: Aaron stood up and said, "One last treat: I've booked Bobby to come back and host our Valentine's Day episode." A *ripple* went round the room, like the wave at a ball game, except nauseated.

And Brooke, gotta love her, broke the silence by going, "Bobby *Everett*?" No, Brooke, Bobby De Niro, who do you think? That got me laughing, so I didn't see Lillian run to the bathroom.

Gina Ross: I get that Aaron's perennially obtuse. I understand that he likes to keep himself removed, untouched in his ivory tower, by design. But he *had* to know what had happened with Lillian and Bobby; he was friends with Bobby! Still is, from what I've heard. So Aaron's either (a) completely tone-deaf in this situation, (b) slightly sadistic, (c) apathetic to the bounds of human decency, or (d) all of the above. Guess which way I'm voting, Cohen? And anyway, who the fuck was Bobby Everett at that time, without *TMS*? His movie hadn't even been released.

Madeline: Had you considered that Lillian in particular might be upset by the prospect of having to work with her ex-boyfriend again?

Aaron Adler: I . . . assumed we were all adults and professionals and that personal considerations would not impact our enthusiasm for our work product.

Madeline: So that's a no.

Aaron Adler: Bobby told me he was looking forward to seeing her. I was frankly surprised the feeling wasn't mutual.

Gina Ross: When Aaron made his announcement, Lillian crumbled like an open sack of flour. Her panic devoured the room. She bolted to the bathroom, shaking. Sally and I followed. By the time we got there, Lillian had locked herself in. We're trying to talk her down—"It's not that bad, it's going to be okay!"—but like, what could we actually do? Bobby was coming, the offer was out, he'd accepted. Aaron had put down the gavel, and all we could do was wait for the verdict.

But I could tell, right then and there in Aaron's Upper West Side apartment, the next eight weeks of waiting were going to be hell.

Sally Schumacher: I don't care what you've heard about that night. Lillian was not on drugs. She was not drunk. She was not experiencing a psychotic break. She was having a massive panic attack. I could hear her in there wheezing, so the first thing I did was make myself heard through the crack at the bottom of the door, telling her to inhale slowly, exhale longer. I didn't hear anything for a good five minutes and really started to get scared, but then she unlatched the door and let me and Gina in. Just us, nobody else, and I tried to shoo everyone back. The last thing Lillian wanted was an audience. Sam in particular had a hard time stepping away. But Gina and I snuck inside and sat on the floor while Lillian crouched in a ball inside the bathtub, and she finally said, "I can't do it. I quit. I can't do this anymore." I was completely ready to say, "You're right. That's okay. You can walk away, we understand."

But Gina said, "You can do it. Fuck him. We'll help you." That got Lillian out of the room. Got her in a taxi with us and back home to her place.

But it wasn't enough to get her through the next eight weeks. Not sane, and ultimately, not alive.

Kent Romero: As far as I was concerned, from Aaron's Christmas announcement up to the Valentine's show, Lillian was on suicide watch. That's how serious a setback this was for her. So that's what we did. We all took turns, all of us who cared about her. Gina, Sally, Nolan, Sam, even Stevie. We watched her like a police detail. And we waited for whatever the hell was going to happen when Bobby turned up.

FROM LILLIAN MARTIN'S NOTEBOOK

Jan 17, 1983

Horror movie of people trying to help, standing outside window in rain, pressing on window HOW ARE YOU DOING?

Kent's soap actress, with the wig—too mean?

W/ Sam communication through cookies "I speak cookie"

Stevie begging me to quit, "supportive" co-worker sketch

Make John Wayne do a saloon showgirl act in my place, sprained ankle

Feb 11, 1983

Snowed in. Maybe school will be canceled for me, too.

I hope he's petty. Maybe he'll bring a date. Co-host? Could suggest.

Fix Mountie sketch, very long town names, fake animals, American idea of Canada (do I even remember Canada?)

Shadows move on the walls, grow fingers and hair, become more solid. They want to wrap themselves around girl, make her like them. How to make funny?

Doorman with too many keys, ridiculous requests, yes to everything

Yes to everything, yes, I can't do it, but I have to

[**NOTE:** This is Lillian's last entry.]

XII.
THE NIGHT OF

The Valentine's Day Episode
(February 18, 1983)

To: Madeline Cohen
From: medicalexaminer@ocme.nyc.gov
Date: July 21, 2023 4:34 PM
Re: FW: Re: Request for Autopsy Report

Dear Madeline,

Thank you for your emails.

Per OCME policy, and without exception, autopsy records may only be requested by immediate family or next of kin, or otherwise by a government agency or organization. Both forms are available on our website, along with answers to frequently asked questions.

I suggest that you reach out to a family member of the deceased or speak to an organization, depending on the nature of your project and its subject matter.

Please be advised that all requests can take approximately 3 to 6 months to fulfill.

Sincerely,

Office of Chief Medical Examiner
Jacob K. Grayson, MD

NOTES

July 22

The facts of Lillian's final night, February 19, 1983, per police reports, prior accounts, testimony, and interviews:

Lillian performs on *The Midnight Show* from Friday the 18th at midnight to Saturday the 19th at 1:30 A.M.

Lillian's last seen arguing with episode host/on-again, off-again boyfriend Bobby Everett at 2:00 A.M. outside Winthrop's (Kent Romero is there as well; police report calls it "an altercation").

Fans spot Lillian stumbling down 6th Avenue, talking to herself, possibly on drugs.

Lillian is seen getting out of a taxi at Tompkins Square Park in lower Manhattan, heading in the direction of the Williamsburg Bridge.

Gina leaves the *Midnight Show* after-party around 2:30 A.M. and trails Lillian south; eyewitnesses see Gina searching for her around the Williamsburg Bridge.

Gina goes to Lillian's apartment to look for her at 4:00 A.M.; Lillian isn't there, so a "distraught" Gina goes home and calls the police with her doorman around 5:00 A.M.

Vasil Tkachenko is arrested at 11:42 A.M. on Thursday, February 24, for disturbing the peace. In his possession: Lillian's wallet. Her handbag is later found at the Henry Street Settlement.

However: Tkachenko has multiple credible alibis for the night of Lillian's disappearance. He was asleep at the Henry Street

Settlement homeless shelter, which is kept locked between the hours of midnight and 7:00 A.M. Other witnesses report seeing Tkachenko find Lillian's bag in Hamilton Fish Park and ask passersby if it belonged to them.

No charges relating to Lillian's disappearance are ultimately filed.

Theories as to what ultimately happened:

Suicide (although per Gina and Kent, Lillian was afraid of dying)

Drugs/unintentional overdose

Accident—there was a big blizzard the week before and it was still icy

Robbery gone wrong

Murder—Bobby, stalker, Stevie, Yuna, Gina, others?

The autopsy details feel crucial; note to follow up for another interview with Lillian's brother, Glenn Martin.

COMPILED TRANSCRIPTS

Gina Ross: After Aaron's announcement, Lillian devolved entirely. I swore she was using again. I'd seen Lillian on H up close and personal, courtesy of LA that summer, so I knew the signs. That first Monday-morning pitch meeting after the announcement, she shows up strung out, pale, her bob messy and uncombed, like she hadn't slept all weekend. I started catching her hanging around the musical stage at odd hours, whispering with the drummer, Stan. I tried to talk to her about it, but it was easy for her to blow me off, given that our relationship was, at that point, pretty threadbare.

Phil Ackerman: No one bothered to clue me in on the drama between Lillian and Bobby. Given how much bed-hopping there was during those first few years, how much it seemed to impact the ratings, CliffsNotes would've been helpful, I tell ya.

Gina Ross: I'd told Sally the whole LA saga by that point. Of course she was worried; anyone paying attention would have been. We were watching a slow-motion train wreck in the weeks leading up to Bobby's arrival. Kent had us keeping tabs on Lillian's comings and goings. She was not doing well, that was for sure, but she was alive, awake, turning up to work. I went to see her a few times, but I had Sally with me. As a buffer. It hurt too much to face Lillian alone.

And then, at last, that Monday, *he* arrived . . . my God, the awkwardness. The tension. He'd been sending flowers to Lillian. That was the first portent of doom, those roses piling up. Even so, there had been a massive snowstorm the weekend before, and a big part of me was hoping we'd get an announcement that all flights from LA had been canceled, and dagnabbit, we'd have to wrangle a local host instead. No such luck. Bobby turned up right on time, all smiles walking the fifteenth-floor halls, doting and huggy and "so grateful to be back" to the point of obsequiousness—he was always an overactor, especially in his serious roles—but Sally and I saw him for what he was. An enemy who was infiltrating Lillian's safe space yet again.

SALLY SCHUMACHER: There was a certain relief involved in his arrival. It was the thing we'd all dreaded and now we could get on with it, get through it, and then clear away whatever wreckage there was. So what I was expecting to navigate were the hurt feelings and raw emotions of a recent nasty breakup. I felt like I could handle that. I mean, we all could, but, you know, *I* was everybody's emotional battery. That was my job. I was also supporting Gina to some extent. She felt real guilty about what had happened back in LA, and I knew she was at a loss about how to help, so I stepped up. I'd been babysitting Lillian, or trying to and failing, since the Christmas party.

When I saw Bobby in the hall during lunch break that Monday, gripping both of Lillian's hands in his, his forehead pressed against hers, I broke out in goose bumps. I peeked into her office. It was covered in bouquets. That Monday was Valentine's Day, but he'd been sending them for days, leading up to coming back. Now, this may seem like none of my business, but it was, literally, my *business*. My work lay in getting ahead of potential bombs so they wouldn't explode. So I looked at one of the notes. "Can we start again? I miss you desperately. Will you forgive me for being an idiot and be my Valentine?" And when I came out of her office again, fuming, I saw her walking back into the writers' room with Bobby. Holding his hand. Back together, just like that.

And . . . I will admit it. I thought, "I get it, why Gina gave up. I've got to wash my hands of this, too."

MADELINE: That's interesting. You previously described your job, or part of it, as "standing sentinel."

SALLY SCHUMACHER: I'm not sure what you mean.

MADELINE: I mean that it was your business. Like you said. In a lot of ways, in terms of an actual active physical presence, and given how conflict averse Aaron clearly is, you were the head of *The Midnight Show* during that time. But I'm getting this sense from you that simultaneously your hands were always tied and that your hands touched everything. So which was it?

SALLY SCHUMACHER: It was both. That's the reality of having too much to do and having a boss. In terms of caretaking the cast's personal life, which I'm assuming is what you're talking about here, I did have to start setting professional boundaries. I resented being everybody's babysitter, and it was around then that I started, rightfully, pulling back from that. Is that—?

MADELINE: I'm actually not just talking about Lillian but about the whole culture there. The cutthroat pitching, the dismissive attitude toward women. For instance, you know that classic still of Brooke Balsinger in the milkmaid costume? The image is very funny, but also quite exploitative.

[*Sally sits up, her eyes sharpening.*]

SALLY SCHUMACHER: Okay, so you're talking about the Von Trapp sketch. Late season two. Gina was Maria, Lillian was Liesl. Brooke, the milkmaid. Host Jeff Bridges, musical act the Clash. Joe Strummer and Mick Jones were at each other's throats to the extent that I wasn't sure there would *be* a Clash by Friday night, so I had calls out to other acts asking them to hold the date right up to airtime. The stagehand union was angry we were using contractors; I had to keep them from walking. Last-minute script changes changed not only dialogue but sets, wigs, lighting, props, extras, costumes, all of which needed my sign-off in the two hours before dress. So, to finally answer your implied question, no, I don't beat myself up that Brooke showed too much cleavage in her milkmaid dress. And no, I did not have time to beg

Lillian to make better life choices in the days leading up to yet another fraught live production.

My hands weren't tied, no. But they sure were tied up.

BROOKE BALSINGER: Bobby leaving the show had been great—we could all stretch out and fill the space he'd gobbled up with his silly little piano songs. And then, surprise! He's back, connected at the hip with Lillian again, even better. And now armed with a host trump card to dominate the lineup. Triple vomit.

SAM PETROSIAN: It kills me to remember this, but . . . there was a form of closure between me and Lillian. Of me saying goodbye. Bobby had won her back—that was undeniable—and I was ready to move on from, you know, *hoping* so damn much. The whiplash of that week leading up to the Valentine's Day episode pummeled me. Seeing them together, staying chummy enough with Bobby to make our sketches work . . . I wasn't going to get through the actual performance without first saying what I needed to say.

There was no screaming this time. I found Lillian down on the evening news floor, alone in the lounge, asked to speak to her. I told her I wanted her to be happy. That I loved her and always would. That I was like our cookie, breaking in half over and over again, and I needed it to stop, so this was me letting her go. I'd thought I would have to explain more about our friendship and boundaries and whatnot, but she nodded, said she understood. She cried, completely silently, I remember. Just streaks.

MADELINE: Do you think that conversation had any impact on what happened to her that night?

SAM PETROSIAN: I believe that everything has an impact on everything. But I do think it was a robbery, not self-harm. I firmly believe it was a situation of wrong place, wrong time, but boy, maybe that's my guilt talking.

[*He pauses. Collects himself.*]

At the end of the day, though, I really don't think I mattered enough to Lillian to tip the scales one way or the other.

Gina Ross: Lillian was barely in our office that week, took up permanent residence in the host office with Bobby. As if the summer hadn't happened. As if it had all been one long hallucination. This man had thrown her out on her ass, tried to sabotage her career, and now it was all love and overblown roses.

But it's funny. I wasn't *mad* at her. Because that's when I truly realized what a vindictive son of a bitch Bobby really was. He was good. Too fucking good. Lillian didn't stand a chance, not without reinforcements. I tried so hard that week to get her alone, to get through to her. But he was Velcro, Cohen. I literally don't think I saw Lillian without Bobby all week.

Stevie Doyle: Everybody was done with Lillian. Silent treatment. She was a broken record, and everyone was sick of listening to it. Only one who kept watching her, and I mean *constantly* watching her, was Gina. There was an element of horrified fascination, I think, more than frustration. For her, I mean. I'd written Lillian off a long time before then.

Madeline: You visited her at home, though, didn't you, in the weeks leading up to Bobby's return? Kent said there was a rotating patrol.

Stevie Doyle: Yeah, I got roped into that. I mean, she was like my little sister, so it was . . . What I'm saying here is I didn't trust her. And I knew the world would always revolve around her and her stupid decisions.

When she coupled back up with Bobby, I took the high road. Of course I did. I worked on a couple of sketches with Lil, two of which survived to the dress rehearsal. I was such a team player that I finally got Aaron to agree to give me an on-screen appearance. Everybody thinks I started in the season four cast, but no, it was going to be a soft launch that episode. It made it past dress. Didn't get cut for time. I called my family, told them to watch, said there would be a big surprise after the opening monologue.

And I wasn't wrong, was I? I think everybody but Bobby Everett was pretty fucking surprised!

Aaron Adler: I didn't know what the monologue was going to be. Bobby told me he wanted to keep it fresh. I assumed he was being cheeky, that it would be some sort of farcical tease of his film career, perhaps a nod to *The Blackboard*. So, yes, I was as blindsided as anyone.

[**NOTE:** Bobby Everett's monologue is notorious. It's not the kind of thing they're going to feature on the *Midnight Show* website, but it's become a morbid cult classic of its own, a source of obsession among fans.]

TRANSCRIPT OF BOBBY EVERETT'S EPISODE OPENER

2/18/83

MONOLOGUE

BOBBY EVERETT: Hello, everybody! Hello, New Yorkers, you beautiful, beautiful reprobates. And [*to camera*] hello, America. I've missed you. You don't have to say it back, it's fine. As you may know, I've been lured away by the sunshine and . . . actually, pretty much just the sunshine of the West Coast. Been filming a little movie I hope you'll go and see called *The Blackboard*. But I'll tell you, there's been something missing in my life. I'm being sincere right now; don't snicker. This show, yes, of course, but *The Midnight Show* will always be my home away from home, I hope—that's why I was so thrilled when they called me up to host tonight. No, there's something else I've missed desperately. Some*one* else, and I know you all love her too. Lillian Martin, would you come on out here, please?

[*Audience applause as Bobby waits, looking to the wings. Lillian leaps onto the host stage, still in her Rogue Soprano costume from the cold open. She pulls her wig off and makes a gag of fixing her hair.*]

LILLIAN MARTIN: Hi, Bobby.

BOBBY EVERETT: Hello, Lillian.

LILLIAN MARTIN: Is your monologue not going well? Did you need a little help?

BOBBY EVERETT: Always. No, it's just that I couldn't let this moment pass without making a grand gesture. You deserve no less, and so . . .

[*He signals to the band. They start playing an orchestral version of "Reunited." Lillian looks confused but plays it off, laughing.*]

LILLIAN MARTIN: Are we going to . . . are we singing this? Am I Peaches or Herb here?

BOBBY EVERETT: Neither, it's a backdrop. For this.

[*He gets down on one knee. The audience whoops. He produces a ring.*]

BOBBY EVERETT: Lillian Martin, I don't deserve you, but will you have me as your husband?

LILLIAN MARTIN: Haha! Well. Wow. Um, gosh, what can I say but . . . yes?

[*To applause, Bobby stands, picks Lillian up, and twirls her around, kissing her. She lands awkwardly, plays the same fixing-hair gag, to laughter.*]

BOBBY EVERETT: You know what, ladies and gentlemen? Life's too short. Let's just do it now. Father? Would you come out, please?

[*From offstage, someone tosses Bobby a veil and a clip-on bow tie. He affixes the veil in Lillian's hair, then the bow tie on himself, crooked. He shrugs. Lillian shakes her head, then adjusts the bow tie, turning. A "reverend"—not a cast member—takes the stage.*]

REVEREND: I've been told this show only runs until one-thirty in the morning, so we'll keep this brief. Robert Everett, do you take this woman as your lawful wedded wife?

BOBBY EVERETT: I do.

Reverend: Lillian Martin, do you take this man as your lawful wedded husband?

Lillian Martin: I do. Is this—?

Reverend: By the powers vested in me, I pronounce you man and wife. You may kiss the bride.

Bobby Everett: Oh, I will. But first—what are we doing? Let's get on with *The Midnight Show*!

[*Lights dim as he kisses her. Cut to band, then next sketch.*]

COMPILED TRANSCRIPTS

Bobby Everett: I came back to New York certain of two things, Madeline. One, I'd made the biggest mistake of my life letting Lillian go. And two, I wanted to marry her. And I knew she felt the same way. About both of those things. When she took me back earlier that week, when she *forgave* me, I was . . . I was finally whole, in bliss, just so damn happy. I got swept up in it. Changed my whole monologue at the last minute. I asked one of the deacons from Grace Church to come up—he'd presided there when I was a boy and was an early spiritual guide for me—wonderful man, very open-minded. Somehow I managed to keep it under wraps from the entire cast and crew, except for one entry-level PA whose name is escaping me right now. It was a CIA-level operation, let me tell you.

Madeline: Was it a real ceremony? A lot of people have wondered over the years whether you and Lillian actually got married.

Bobby Everett: Legally? Of course not, no. And I remember that Reverend Miller was pretty adamant about us coming round the church for an actual liturgical ceremony at some point or other, one condition of his appearing on live TV for the first time. But in my heart? Yes. We were married that night. And thank *God,* you know. Who'd have known that was my last chance? One final beautiful moment. Of course I wish we'd had so many more, but at least . . . at least we had that.

Brooke Balsinger: Desperate ratings grab. Did Aaron put him up to it? I wouldn't put it past him! Knowing Aaron, we'll never get a straight answer.

Kent Romero: I . . . [*He exhales slowly.*] Honestly, I still feel rage cascade through my body when I think about that night. Lillian, holding on to that smile for dear life while she was on camera, and then the second the cameras moved off her, the way she had to *slide*-duck to evade Bobby's grip, still smiling; wouldn't want to anger him. She used her costume change as an excuse to run for the greenroom. She was in the sketch after the one that was on-air, had about twenty seconds to change into a Catholic school uniform, big red clock flashing a count-down, and while hair and makeup people were braiding her hair, I came up and just, what could I say? I got down low. "You okay?"

She let out this desperate laugh. She was shaking. Teeth clacking together like a wind-up toy. And before I could say anything else, help her breathe, whatever, she had to go onstage again. People like to talk about how wooden she was for the rest of that episode, but if you really look, what's going on with her is that she's trying to stop her teeth from chattering.

SAM PETROSIAN: There are so many things I'm sad about. Sometimes it hits me in the morning when I wake up, completely fresh, as if it happened yesterday, and I have to hang on and wait for the world to stop rocking. But yeah, one of the things that really gets me is that *that* episode was Lillian's last performance. It was not what she would have wanted to leave behind. It wasn't representative of who she was as a performer.

STEVIE DOYLE: So yeah, my sketch got cut for time! Didn't get to go on after Bobby went rogue and overran his slot. Does anybody put an arm around me, say, *Sorry, man. We'll put it in next week*? Give just the merest nod to my contributions to the show and its success? Nada. Everybody was all over Bobby like flies, shaking his hand, offering congratulations as if he'd really gotten married instead of, what, shat all over my episode? Well . . . at least I had the other sketches I'd worked on with Lil, right? Franchise potential for those. But she tanked.

So, yeah, I was pissed. Also worried for her. But mostly pissed. Listen, how was I supposed to know what was going to happen? I left One Astor early, in a sulk, yeah, but can you blame me? Went straight to Winthrop's to drown my sorrows, so I was pretty fucking drunk by the time the rest of them turned up.

Lillian came straight to me, trying to apologize for my appearance being cut, the only person to do so, but at the time, I didn't take note of that. I walked away, blanked her, gave her the silent treatment. I'm an asshole, in case you hadn't noticed. But in my own defense? [*He shrugs wildly.*] Fuck! I couldn't have known!

Sally Schumacher: So we had Aaron fielding network calls congratulating him for the stunt, Bobby parading around between sketches shaking everybody's hand like he was at an actual wedding reception, Lillian reduced to a collection of nervous tics, Kent looking like he was going to kick all the sets over, Sam smiling big trying not to cry, Stevie storming off set—honestly, that one was a relief—my own girlfriend manic with shock, to the extent that if I hadn't known her so well, I would have thought she'd snorted something right before joining Kent at the desk. And who do you think managed all that, Madeline? One guess.

Gina Ross: *What did it mean?* That was the panicked mantra playing through my head all night. Also: Who the hell was that reverend? Was Lillian going to leave the show? Become Bobby's housewife?

I remembered quite clearly the terms he had laid out for her in LA. So was her "yes" an acceptance of all that, too? The death of her career, her future, destiny? I couldn't let that happen, let her do that. I had to talk some sense into her. She was so far gone, Cohen. Bobby had handed her a bomb on live television, and she'd *accepted* demolition.

As for the episode, we got through it. Made it to one-thirty. That's about all I can say for it.

Aaron Adler: After the episode, I had network people calling, but I headed straight to Winthrop's, which had, over the course of the show, become a wedding reception venue versus an after-party spot. I needed a moment alone. It isn't my habit to micromanage my stars, not now, not then, but yes, I was surprised by the cavalier way Bobby had reorchestrated my show for his own agenda. I cooled off, as I always do, and greeted everyone with a smile on my face. I've found over the years that the only way to ensure continuity is to become the constant yourself. If that means pulling myself out of the emotional fray, so be it.

Sally Schumacher: Aaron has this industry reputation as the calm within the storm, when I suspect the truth is he's a highly anxious individual whose go-to coping mechanism is dissociation. I've seen him in countless stressful situations over the years, and it's always the same. That night was classic Aaron—his eyes went wide, his face didn't move. You could have said anything to him at that point. He wasn't hearing it.

Bobby Everett: I'd taken liberties with the show, but it was a calculated risk, not recklessness. I knew I could afford to spring a surprise on Aaron because I could draw on the currency I held in our very deep and authentic friendship. We're still like brothers, you know, to this day. I think I might be his oldest friend, and the reverse is also true. So I went into the after-party knowing Aaron would understand, but Lillian . . .

In hindsight, I should have factored in that she was still on the payroll there. This was her place of work. She was rightfully worried about rocking the boat. My heart was in the right place. I walked her over to Aaron's booth, ready with an apology, not groveling, just due respect, and God, was Lillian squirming. Every second was fraught.

At a certain point, she wanted to get some air, practically ran out of there, and I followed behind. Concerned, obviously. She was off-balance; it was palpable. I wanted to talk her back from the edge. I usually could, but a lot of time had passed since the last time we were together, and things had changed for her mentally while I wasn't there to keep my hand on the rudder.

Kent Romero: I witnessed the fight. I'd debated coming to the party at all. By the time I did decide to suck it up and make an appearance,

I was about a half hour late. Got out of my limo and Bobby and Lillian are standing on the sidewalk, pinned between shoveled gray piles of snow, practically spitting at each other.

No. That's not accurate. Bobby was spitting at Lillian. She was trying to keep him from cornering her. She seemed afraid of him. Backed up into the snow, slipped a little. I heard only a snippet of what they were saying, but I jumped in, put my hands up, got between them, and Lillian bolted in my direction.

I had the impulse to grab her, but that was the last thing she needed, that's what fuckers like Bobby would do, so I just kind of trailed her as she walked away and asked her where she was going, like we were off to some fun after-party or other, trying to lighten the mood. She said, "Nowhere."

I thought it was the name of a club I wasn't hip enough to have heard of yet. I was about to ask for the address when she added, "I can't be anywhere right now. I need to be nowhere. Just nowhere." Concerning, right? I asked if I could come along, and that stopped her. We were over on 6th Ave by this point. She turned and hugged me and said, "I'm sorry." "For what?" "All of it. Everything."

MADELINE: So she wasn't talking to herself, like the police report said?

KENT ROMERO: No. Well, not at that point. She was talking to me. And then she ran into the road to flag a taxi and that was that. I went back to the party. And of course Bobby demanded to know what I'd done with Lillian, but I blithely ignored him, went straight to Gina, told her everything Lillian had said.

GINA ROSS: As soon as Kent said those words, I knew. "Nowhere." The bridge, *our* bridge.

KENT ROMERO: Gina starts going on about the Williamsburg Bridge, trying to rally a search party, but . . . God help me, I thought she was being irrational. I tried to calm her down. Not sure whether I was being a sexist prick, Madeline, accusing my female friend of hysteria, or just trying to assure myself that everything was going to be okay when I felt in my gut it wasn't.

Meanwhile, Bobby—who, by the way, had been lurking, little *güevón,* listening to every word coming out of Gina's mouth—gives this grandiose speech thanking everyone, apologizing for needing to leave the party so early, so by the time Bobby was out the door, Gina had lost the attention of her potential posse, scant as it was.

She wound up bolting downtown on her own. I didn't go with her. I have no idea what happened after that.

Aaron Adler: It's always been fairly clear to me what happened from that point. Lillian Martin was a queen when it came to comedy, lightness and laughter incarnate on the stage, but there had always been a current of darkness running through her in the day-to-day. Anyone who spent real time with her could sense that. And unfortunately, that night, it overwhelmed her.

Sam Petrosian: I wish she'd stayed at the party. Or gone home with Bobby. Or let Kent leave with her that night, wherever she was heading, even just to walk the bridge. He's a big guy, you know. Odds would have been a lot slimmer that any mugger would have approached the two of them together. But maybe I'm kidding myself. Maybe they'd both be dead if that had happened.

Madeline: You're certain it was a mugging, then.

Sam Petrosian: The person they pegged at first? No. We know it wasn't him. But a robbery gone wrong, at that time of night, in that part of town? It's not unlikely. There wasn't any cash left in her wallet that was found. And I can't believe it was something intentional on her part. She was *life* to me. She was the one who would come to the rest of us and calmly remind us that there was always a solution, that everything was temporary. To get over ourselves, in other words! She wouldn't. I know that's the common narrative now, but I simply cannot go there, not knowing her like I did.

STEVIE DOYLE: As I said, I was shitfaced. Sally finally put me out of my misery, dragged me back to her place that night to sleep it off. Everything else I know is pieced together from news reports.

MADELINE: Sally really did hold down the fort, didn't she?

STEVIE DOYLE: Well, she'd clock out from time to time. She went out again that night, actually—I heard her front door shut at some point, before I woke up the next afternoon on her sofa with a raging hangover and made my way home. We all had the next week off. Nothing seemed wrong until the *following* Monday morning, when Lillian doesn't turn up. Aaron comes in, grave as an undertaker, says Gina called the police and Bobby's confirmed that . . . yeah. Lillian's missing.

So we get on with the show, but in the background, we're trying to figure it all out ourselves, like we're detectives. Like you're doing now. We know Lillian headed toward the Williamsburg Bridge because we have eyewitnesses who saw her all along that route. Nobody on the bridge, though. Nobody witnessed her jump.

MADELINE: That's what you think happened?

STEVIE DOYLE: At the time? No, of course not. We thought she'd *gotten* jumped. They'd arrested some poor schmuck, but he was cleared within days. She'd left her bag behind in a snowdrift in some park downtown and he found it. He didn't kill her; he had an alibi. And who mugs somebody, murders them, tosses the body in the water, and then leaves the bag behind on *dry land* for somebody else to find? So what alternatives are left, given that they found her at the bottom of the East River? I mean, maybe she slipped, but—

MADELINE: There have been other theories, though. People who knew her. Fans. She'd received threatening letters over the years, always from the same person.

STEVIE DOYLE: That was . . . yeah, that got investigated, I think. It didn't turn out to be anything. Or they didn't find the person, I'm not sure.

MADELINE: But what do you think?

STEVIE DOYLE: I don't think it's worth digging into, if that's what you're asking. If you're looking for some crazy stalker, I think you're going to come up empty-handed. Unless, hey, maybe it's Gina. Maybe she sent those letters. Wouldn't put it past her. She barely talks to the press, right? Maybe there's a reason.

Listen, I'm running short on time, so if there's anything else, maybe you could hit me up via email.

[*Stevie closes our Zoom call.*]

GINA ROSS: Wait, he hung up on you? What the hell did you say?

MADELINE: Nothing that shocking. I was pressing him, I guess, asking for his take on what happened—I brought up those letters that Lillian got with the same stationery, the ones you mentioned. The envelopes with the stripes. Actually, he suggested you might have sent them, Gina.

GINA ROSS: *The fuck?*

[*Sally and Gina exchange a very long look. Gina gives the teeniest shrug.*]

SALLY SCHUMACHER: Okay. Madeline, I'm going to tell you something, but please just be responsible with this piece of information. I.e., do not quote me specifically. I didn't tell the police about it during the investigation, and I really don't want to have to answer for that, so anonymous source, okay?

[**NOTE:** Flagging this section for confidentiality: redact for the final feature.]

SALLY SCHUMACHER: Stevie sent those letters. He came to me in a panic after Lillian was declared missing and confessed everything.

MADELINE: I . . . sorry, what?

GINA ROSS: You heard her, Cohen.

MADELINE: I don't understand. Was he stalking her? Brooke had mentioned the letters but kept implying there was something she wasn't allowed to tell me. I sort of assumed that was just, you know, her attempt at a persona.

SALLY SCHUMACHER: Safe assumption, but in this case, there really is something she's not allowed to tell you. Stevie paid her off, and she can't say a word about it; she's got a rock-solid NDA in place. But we don't.

Here's what happened: Brooke found his stationery one day, rifling through his desk for a pen or something. She put two and two together, connected the dots that Lillian was getting those striped envelopes. Could easily have been a coincidence, but she had an instinct for trouble. If anything, at that point, she became the stalker. Stevie had decided to drop his partnership with her. As retribution, she confronted him. Stayed in the office later than usual and caught him with a letter, ready to send it. From there, she blackmailed him into resuming their alliance.

MADELINE: Not for money? Just—

GINA ROSS: Just airtime! Ridiculous, the lengths she went to, but I guess she was desperate. I told you her shit wasn't good.

SALLY SCHUMACHER: Anyway, Stevie worked with Brooke, eventually stopped sending those letters. Everything was normalizing, and then, in season three, Lillian vanished. And all those letters were entered into evidence.

MADELINE: And you never told the police it was him?

SALLY SCHUMACHER: One, it wasn't him. He sent the letters, yes, but he didn't lay a hand on Lillian. He got so wasted at that after-party that I had to drag him back to my place and let him sleep it off on the sofa. He was there until I kicked him out at dinnertime the next day.

MADELINE: And you were home that whole time? You didn't go out again?

SALLY SCHUMACHER: Absolutely not. I wasn't catatonic like Stevie, but I was tired enough to call it a night, that was for darn sure.

[*I notice she fidgets when she says it, though, and breaks eye contact.*]

MADELINE: That's his alibi, I suppose, but it still seems like there was motive—

SALLY SCHUMACHER: Not really. This wasn't a psycho stalker situation. That was just a role he was playing. Trying to scare her off the show. That's what he told me, and it tracks. He used to come to me over the years, and say, "Have you seen Lillian? She looks shaken up. Maybe she could use a week off from the show. This isn't good for her."

MADELINE: Why would Stevie have wanted that? Clearly, he was frustrated with her and with the show for not having him as a cast member, but—

SALLY SCHUMACHER: That I don't know. I think you'll have to go to the source to find out exactly why. Please do send him my mildest apology for telling the truth after all this time and maybe remind him gently that I did not sign an NDA.

MADELINE: I'm curious. Why share this now? Why me?

Gina Ross: This is called "looking a gift horse in the mouth," Cohen.

Sally Schumacher: No, it's an interesting question. [*She pauses, starts to talk, then pauses again. Finally, she starts.*] I guess the older I get, the less tolerance I have for lying. For bullshit. Especially when it comes to slander against my wife. I am tired of continually covering up other people's messes. I was a caretaker back then, and look at me. Decades later, still standing sentinel. I'm . . . just done.

[*Gina reaches out to squeeze Sally's hand.*]

Stevie Doyle (via email): I think a phone call might be best. Let me know some times that work for you.

Then:

Stevie Doyle (via telephone): This has embarrassed me for a really long time, so I'm going to keep this quick and direct, if you don't mind. And off the record, yeah?

Madeline: All right.

[**NOTE:** Flagging this section: again, redact for confidentiality.]

Stevie Doyle: Yeah, fine. It was me. I sent, I want to say, fifteen letters to Lillian purporting to be a fanatical admirer between the middle of season one and the middle of season two.

I'm left-handed, but I wrote them with my right hand so they would look more unhinged. It was a horrible thing to do and I regret it every day, but before you ask if I was some psycho, in love with or obsessed with Lillian, that is not true, and it also isn't true that I hated her. I didn't. As I told you, she was like my little sister. And, like in many families, she annoyed the crap out of me. I think I've been honest about that in our conversations, don't you? But it went a little deeper than that, and the reason I haven't brought it up directly before now is because I've been trying to protect Lillian's reputation. Not my own. That's the truth.

Here's the reality, though: Lillian wasn't an angel! And she wasn't a consistently creative genius, some bottomless well of comedy, like everybody likes to pretend either. She had dry periods. And from time to time, she flagrantly stole material. Mainly from me, because she knew nobody would listen if I complained about it. And she was right, they didn't.

MADELINE: You've alluded to this before. I have to say, I'm pretty shocked she stole material. Could you give me an example?

STEVIE DOYLE: Mole people summer vacation. All those sketches. Everybody thinks I worked on them but Lillian came up with them, and it's bullshit. I ran it past her, just shooting the shit, when we were having lunch together—family of subterranean people who come up through a manhole to visit the normal people as a vacation. And then lo and behold, she pipes up in the next pitch meeting, "I've got kind of a crazy idea." I was shocked too. Like you, I didn't think she was that kind of person. Still, it took a long time for me to realize I had to keep my mouth completely shut around her. She still had ways. She'd steal roles from Brooke, very sweetly, and Brooke would blame me for it, of course, because Lillian would sit there and say, "Stevie and I have partnered on an idea this week," and it would be the one I was working on with Brooke. Lillian was a snake, as I said. A very cute one.

But here's the thing: she also *wasn't*. Not the Lillian I knew from back in Boston. The show was changing her, and we all hated it. Watching her get polluted. Ask any of her old friends whether they thought being on *The Midnight Show* was healthy for Lillian. Ask Kent. Ask Sammy! Fuck her legacy to comedy, was fame *good* for her? Hell no. So I did what I did, selfishly and also unselfishly. I wanted her to make the right decision, which would have been to step away, but she didn't. And you see what happened in the end.

MADELINE: But don't you think your letters might have contributed to that end?

Stevie Doyle: You know what? Lillian would love for me to think that's what did it. My prank, yeah, that's it, those letters are the reason she's gone. I don't fucking know. Maybe.

[*Stevie pauses. I'm unsure if he's hung up. Then:*]

I hold a lot of anger toward Lillian. Obviously. And talking to you, you know, I wonder if part of that is . . . I always thought we'd make up. After the show, someday, we'd get past it all and be family again. I'd have a chance to apologize and vice versa. And she took that option away from me.

[*Again there's silence over the line. I hear a hard sniff, like he's trying not to cry.*]

I'm angry that she died and left me with all this guilt for all these years. It's never gonna go away now. No shot.

And I know my resentment makes me look like a schmuck at best, a suspect at worse, but I was never a threat to Lillian. It never went any further than what I told you just now.

Madeline: I just want to get complete clarity about this . . .

Stevie Doyle: Sure, fire away. What else do I have to lose? My career's been dead for decades. Probably died with her, if I'm being honest.

Madeline: There *was* no stalker. No obsessive fan. Not you, not anybody. Not Gina, as you seemed to want to suggest—

Stevie Doyle: Gina's far from innocent. She was pretty damn obsessed with Lillian. And then, of course . . . [*He laughs dryly.*] There was Bobby.

Bobby Everett: As the Buddha says, patience is the highest Nibbana. It's taken a long time for me to come to terms with the fact that we'll likely never know who did it. Unless there's some deathbed confession, which does happen. But the one thing I do know, absolutely, is that this was not something Lillian did to herself. She was happy. *We* were happy. We had the rest of our lives to look forward to.

Kent Romero: The suicide angle is bullshit. No, never bought it. Lillian was too afraid of dying. Now, as for other theories . . . Bobby left the party conspicuously soon after Lillian did. The timing works for him to have caught up with her. He has an alibi, supposedly, but I will always suspect him, the fucker. And he knows full well what I think. Why hide it? I don't play nice, not with stakes like these.

Madeline: Do you have a sense of what his motive would have been?

Kent Romero: I think, in his mind, she'd humiliated him. He'd made this grand gesture in front of the entire country, and he expected gratitude. Submission. By leaving that night, Lillian was on some level rejecting him, and it sent him over the edge.

Bobby Everett: I was exhausted. It had been a whirlwind week. Lillian had been staying with me over at the Plaza—I'd sold my apartment back in January and bought a place in Brentwood—so I figured she'd make her way to the hotel once she'd walked around a bit, burned off some stress. I headed to my suite and turned in, basically. There was a bellhop there who saw me come in, quoted one of my old sketches to me, which was sweet. He said as much to the police.

Kent Romero: You know one of the fun things about bellhops? They're right up there with drivers and doormen as the easiest people to bribe.

Madeline: What about Yuna? Did you suspect her at all?

Gina Ross: Bobby's ex? Not really, no.

Madeline: Did Lillian have a restraining order taken out on her? There was something in her journal . . .

Gina Ross: I can't remember if it went as far as a restraining order, but yeah. Yuna confronted Lillian on the street a few times, called her a whore, grabbed her. It got ugly. By '83, though, Yuna had moved on with her life, as far as I know. I don't even think she was in the country.

MADELINE: We haven't ever discussed Sam as a possibility either.

GINA ROSS: For what, her murderer? Sam as in Sam Petrosian or the Son of Sam? Sam *Petrosian*? A human teddy bear turned psycho killer? That's some Five Nights at Freddy's shit right there. To set your mind at ease . . . actually, Sally can better speak to this. She was at the party a little longer than I was.

SALLY SCHUMACHER: Honestly, Sam was the voice of reason that night. Probably the most calm of all of us, partly because he had his girlfriend with him.

MADELINE: I didn't realize he had a girlfriend at that point.

SALLY SCHUMACHER: I think they'd just started dating, but yeah, it was Susan.

GINA ROSS: As in his future wife. How's that for an alibi? So what do you think? Have we exhausted the list of "everyone Lillian ever met"? I told you, I've said everything I have to say on this subject. Decades ago. It wasn't foul play. That never crossed my mind. Not given the state that Lillian was in that night. So it had to be drugs, much as it guts me to once again say it.

MADELINE: Can we go back a bit, to when Kent told you that Lillian said she was going "nowhere"? What exactly did you do?

GINA ROSS: This is all in my statement, but okay. Let's get into it. I chased her to the Williamsburg Bridge. It took me for-fucking-ever to hail a cab to get near enough to the bridge, then from that point, it was a footrace. And I'm not an athletic person—doing some of those Jane Fonda videos for sketch research was the extent of my exercise regimen back then. My muscles were screaming, and it was frigid, below zero, the city still covered in piss-riddled snow. I was crying with worry; I remember that feeling of crystallized tears on my face. And just thinking over and over again, "I need to find her. I need to talk to her before something happens. I hope I'm not too late."

All these horrible scenarios were flooding my mind, of her scoring easily, then passing out on the Lower East Side somewhere, never having made it to the bridge, or God, losing her step, her control, and . . . people had seen her, people I asked on the street, heading to the bridge, and then I got there. To the middle. To the other side. And she wasn't walking across it. She wasn't anywhere. Not anymore.

Brooke Balsinger: Broken record, but I'll say it again: Lillian's blood is on Gina's hands. There was real jealousy there, Millie, a need to own or possess her. Hand to God, it was more than just a crush. It was *dangerous*. Gina was fixated, and when Bobby proposed or married Lillian or whatever the hell happened in that episode, Gina snapped, went on the hunt for Lillian.

I'm not saying it was cold-blooded murder, but maybe the opposite? You know? I mean, Gina Ross has an uncontrollable and well-documented temper. Maybe things got physical. Heck, maybe *Gina* was on drugs and pushed her off that bridge, ever think of that? All I know is that the last thing I heard Gina say before she bolted out of Winthrop's that night was "I know where she's going." Everybody heard her say it, but no one will ever speak out about it except me.

There are so many lies, so much hypocrisy—that's the word, *hypocrisy*—in that group of people. That's why I don't do reunions. I have too low a tolerance for the smell of bullcrap. Bobby Everett agrees with me, by the way. He won't do reunions either, so why should I?

Anyway. If you're looking for a suspect who knew Lillian well, my money has always been on Gina Ross.

Madeline: So you don't think it was suicide?

Gina Ross: Even after all this time, I don't. I think it was a mistake, a tragic, infuriating, and likely avoidable accident. I was there with Lillian in LA, during the hazy days. It was never about checking out of life entirely, it was about sanctuary. Going to "nowhere," a place she couldn't be found. In-between places are scary for most, but for Lillian, they were where she could hide.

That said, heroin is a game of roulette. It's a very, very dangerous drug. Never touched it, never will. I think she was riding high in terrible weather and lost control, fell off. It's still devastating.

Madeline: But you went to her apartment after that? The report said—

Gina Ross: Of course I did. I mean, at the time, I was hopeful I had it wrong. A thousand thoughts were flying through my head when I searched that whole damn bridge and Lillian was nowhere to be found. I thought . . . I don't know, maybe I'd just missed her, or misunderstood, jumped to the wrong conclusion, and she was snug in bed watching late-night *Laverne & Shirley* reruns or scribbling in her journal.

Madeline: So you searched the bridge area for around an hour? In the freezing cold?

Gina Ross: Yep. Searched both sides.

Madeline: Then you headed uptown, went to Lillian's apartment, at 680 Park Avenue, around four. The doorman let you up, but Lillian, obviously, wasn't there.

Gina Ross: Jesus, you really do love a timeline.

Madeline: And then you headed back to your own apartment. At 23 East 63rd, a building one avenue and three streets away. Around five A.M., the report says, you speak to another doorman—your own doorman—and you call the police together.

GINA ROSS: Correct. I was a mess. And Carlos was a class act. I knew he would help. Really not sure what you're doing here, kid.

MADELINE: Bear with me. I'm a little hung up on why that took another hour. Did you knock on Lillian's door, get no reply, and then stay there, in her building? Or take a long detour home?

GINA ROSS: Well. If you must know, I sat down in her hallway. The way the mind works during trauma isn't linear or rational. I was on the edge myself that night, about to have a nervous breakdown. So I sat for a while, who knows how long, and I cried.

MADELINE: But we do know how long—for over forty-five minutes.

GINA ROSS: What the hell are you trying to get at here?

MADELINE: The truth.

GINA ROSS: Ambush-style. You know, for someone so critical of archetypes, you're Cliché Hack Journalist Incarnate right now—

MADELINE: I'm getting the sense that no one else has given this a second thought. And I know it might be hard to talk about, but it's within my rights to ask—

GINA ROSS: "Within my rights." What rights? This is painful shit, and you're in my home, choosing to rub my face in it. Asking why I didn't, what, jog home from my best friend's apartment and hit the hay once I realized she could really be dead?

MADELINE: I think there are many people hiding—

GINA ROSS: Are you implying I'm hiding something?

MADELINE: I'm not trying to upset you. I'm trying to do my job.

GINA ROSS: Christ, Cohen.
I think you've got what you need. That's all for today.

[*Sally sees me out.*]

XIII.
FINAL NOTES

NOTES

July 26

That was pretty rough.

I do need to do my job, though. Consider this from all angles. I'm not sure she intended to, but one thing Gina reminded me of was Lillian's journals.

Maybe it's time for another read.

Observations:

> Kent was right about Lillian's "in-between" creative process. There are several places where she took whatever was happening in her real life and channeled her stress straight into sketch concepts, like the restraining order about the "crazy ex." Who was clearly Yuna.
>
> There's also the "keeper" sketch, boyfriends locked in the basement—this was right after her altercation with Sam, him describing her as a "collector."
>
> "'NY vs. LA' and 'Alice rabbit hole to LA' sketches" were right before she headed out to California.
>
> The Yuna excerpt leads into "secret society of doorman superheroes." And later, "Doorman with too many keys." She was very attuned to doormen, for some reason.

There was something else Kent said: "You know one of the fun things about bellhops? They're right up there with drivers and doormen as the easiest people to bribe." In the police report, we have a reference to the bellhop Bobby mentioned, but also the names of Lillian's doorman and Gina's.

NOTES

July 27

Looks like Lillian's doorman Robert Wiseman passed away twenty years ago (if I've got the right guy), but Gina's old superintendent/doorman, Carlos Ortega, is in an assisted living facility outside of Albany.

That's a hike. But if I want to fill in that gap between Gina leaving Lillian's apartment building and arriving at her own, maybe he's the man to talk to.

I also text Gina asking for a follow-up tomorrow afternoon. It takes her all day to respond, but around eleven P.M., I get:

GINA
Sure.

COMPILED TRANSCRIPTS

MADELINE: I'd love to talk about the aftermath. The memorial service, in April of '84. You had left the show by then, correct?

KENT ROMERO: A lot of us had. Me, Sam, Gina. Bobby, obviously. The memorial felt a little like a high school reunion.

MADELINE: There's some gossip surrounding you and Bobby—

KENT ROMERO: It's not gossip, it's the truth. I punched him in the face. Twice. The old one-two. Is that what you're getting at? He got up and gave the most meandering, self-centered, martyr-drenched eulogy I'd ever heard in my life. Lillian was nowhere in it. Just Bobby. Which wasn't surprising. I was prepared to let that go. I'd gone into the whole thing mentally ready, wanting to be respectful to Lillian, and also show up for Gina, who'd put a shitload of work into the event.

Gina Ross, among the greatest friends I've ever had, has many laudable qualities, but self-effacement is not one of them. That afternoon in Sheep Meadow was a massive exception. The understated way she went about organizing the day, opening it up to the public, offering space for loved ones, and even fans, to speak about Lillian, without ever seeking credit, it said a lot about how much this meant to her. So when Bobby comes down from that stage, sidles up to Gina, and says, I shit you not, in this *undertone* he obviously thought I couldn't hear, "How you feeling today, Gina? Is all this making the guilt go away?" Well. I reacted how I reacted and won't apologize for that. And the major upside of the altercation, as we like to call it, is that Bobby doesn't come to reunions anymore, which means I can show up and not worry about seeing his lying face in person ever again.

BOBBY EVERETT: It's quite unfortunate that Kent chose to turn a day that was supposed to be all about Lillian into one focused on him and his jealousy of me. But even he couldn't fully ruin such a beautiful afternoon for such a beautiful soul. I walked away feeling healed to some extent. And gosh, the other things that have helped to heal me over the years have been one: the unfaltering dedication of my spiritual guide, Robin Westing, who deserves a world of recognition and without whom I would be lost. Two: my work, going on character journeys and processing my own trauma through those experiences. And three: the *incredible* amount of public support I've received. Even now, all these decades later, I'll be out to dinner and someone will come up and say how much they loved Lillian. It means so much. It really does. You know, I go to her grave every year on her birthday. Doesn't matter if I'm filming abroad; everybody on set knows we're going to have to pause for that. I don't miss it. And I see so many fans there, every single year. Some the same, year after year, devoted. That's why there are so many photos out there of these gatherings. The press has picked up on it too. It's very affirming.

Brooke Balsinger: I was surprised when Gina put together this big, like, funeral for someone who hadn't even been legally declared dead? I wondered what was in it for her, but then I realized that the investigation was still ongoing, right? Pretty smart way to throw the cops off the scent of her as a suspect. Who throws a massive memorial service for the person they murdered, am I right?

Madeline: You . . . I mean, are you directly accusing Gina of murder here?

Brooke Balsinger: I'm throwing out hypotheticals, Mabel. Either way, Gina came out looking great, right? Everybody still at *The Midnight Show* was, like, kneeling before her and Kent and Sam, like thank you *so* much for hanging out with us again for a few days. Totally pathetic.

Madeline: I did want to ask about the sudden decision to throw a memorial service before the body was discovered.

Gina Ross: Well, Cohen, seeing as it had been over a year and the case had gone all but cold and it was becoming pretty fucking obvious with each passing week that Lillian wasn't waltzing back into One Astor ever again, I wouldn't necessarily call it a *sudden decision*. Felt inevitable. Mandatory. Everyone needed closure, a time and space to grieve.

I got the idea in my head around the one-year mark. That February. By that time, most of the first class had already left the show. We were on year-to-year contracts, and if any of us had been on the fence about staying, Lillian's death made the decision for us. Kent signaled that he was stepping away first, let everybody know he'd be leaving at the end of season three, which was like a starting gun. I thought, you know what, screw this; the only thing keeping me here at this point is Sally, and most couples don't share a workplace, for a multitude of reasons. We'd pair up professionally again later, but at that point, considering everything, it felt like time for a change. And then Sam put in his notice, for personal reasons: On top of the movie offers he'd started getting, his fiancée was from California and wanted to go back west and be closer to her family.

Sam Petrosian: All those years I was friends with Lillian, I think there was a fraction of my stubborn brain that was holding on to the hope of a romantic future with her. I think that's why I became such a slut, to be honest. I'd earned the worst reputation of all of us by the beginning of 1983, if you can believe it. Kent likes to pretend he's some unfeeling playboy, but the truth is, he's a serial monogamist at heart, and he's stayed friends with almost everyone he's ever slept with. I was the true revolving door. One-night stands only, and I'd pretend not to know them when I saw them out again. I know, I know, what a jerk. [*Hides his face.*] But with Susan I could finally let go of that little voice in my head saying every relationship was a placeholder. I saw her for the gem she was, put my wild single days behind me, moved out west with her, and married her the next year. Almost forty great years—ups and downs, sure, but a life well worth living, two beautiful children, three grandkids who are more hilarious than I could ever hope to be.

Susan and I divorced last year, but we're still good friends, talk all the time. I think Lillian would be pleased. I really do.

Kent Romero: My filmography speaks for itself, I'd say. I'm semiretired now, settled into my ranch here, where I can enjoy a blessed amount of solitude. Ironic, huh? Returning to my roots. I'm thinking of putting it on the market, but that's another story. The show? Well, I've done reunion specials, like I said. But I never hosted. There's always been an open invitation for me to come back. It's just too wrapped up in memories of Lillian for me. My heart hardened toward that place, toward everything, really, after she died. It had to. It was how I kept going. And hey, maybe that's why I have this reputation now as a heartless bastard. I hope, Madeline, that after all our chats, you can see that that's not the whole truth. But if you can't? [*He grins.*] I don't actually give a shit.

Stevie Doyle: I stayed. Got bumped up to cast member that next season, but it only lasted a year. I found I liked staying behind the scenes after all.

Sally Schumacher: Aaron and I finally caved to Stevie's requests, and guess what? My initial impression of Stevie was still accurate. He was dead weight on-screen. I guess it took the experience of flopping live every week for him to finally see it for himself.

Stevie Doyle: I kept writing for the show until '96, when there was a big shake-up and I was basically booted. Sam threw me some work, I did some spec scripts, but my kind of comedy had become passé and my heart wasn't in it anymore. There's been a dry period since, not gonna lie. But, you know, the party can't last forever.

Brooke Balsinger: I moved on to a sitcom where I played the long-suffering wife. Then a couple stepmom and neighbor gigs. I know we're all supposed to be *so* grateful to be working at all in such a tough industry, but . . . let's just say when the best offers I was getting were for bowel-regulating-yogurt commercials, I knew it was finally time to gracefully retire.

MADELINE: But . . . you did do those commercials. They're still airing, right?

BROOKE BALSINGER: I mean, I still need paychecks! Don't get all high-and-mighty with me, Macie. Gotta put those grandkids through private school. Stepgrandkids, but you know what I mean.

SALLY SCHUMACHER: I probably stayed longer than I should have. Gina was begging me to walk away, to go with her to LA. We were writing screenplays the whole time—this was before we sank our teeth into TV. I was selling specs on my own, but the show . . . it felt ungrateful for me to abandon Aaron. I needed to ease my way out. Or so I thought. Truth was, Aaron hired new writers and new cast members, got a new set of yes-men in place, and didn't even notice when I stopped showing up to writers' meetings. Brooke went after season five, and then Nolan left mid-season to develop a one-man show on Broadway, which raked up all the awards—it was fantastic—but then closed abruptly for what we now know were health reasons. He kept his illness a secret until the end, until that *Village Voice* interview, four days before AIDS got him. Even Gina didn't know he was sick. When he left, it felt like the true end of an era, and at that point I was ready to say goodbye.

AARON ADLER: If *The Midnight Show* is about anything, it's about constant reinvention. It's current, it's now, it's ever-evolving. Season three was a crucible, an enormous trial for us all, but we got through it. We brought in new performers who were really exciting, always recalibrating and finding the right mix for this moment. And as you can see—

[*He grandly motions around him at the long studio hallway, lined with photos of four decades of* TMS *stills.*]

We continue to thrive today.

Vera Ivanov (*TMS* cast member, 1995–2005): You can't overstate Lillian Martin's influence on young women growing up in the '80s. *TMS* is why I got into comedy, why I hung on to the show as long as I did. I'd be camped out in front of my family's little box, watching Lillian and Gina week after week, and then later, Amy Shuller, Rosie McNicols, and the like. But Martin was the gold standard. Her comedy style was so sincere, so wacky, fresh, off-the-cuff. I consider her a mentor in the greatest sense, even though we obviously never had a chance to meet.

Amara Johnson (*TMS* cast member, 2019–present): Those '80s women—they had balls! Wait, correction: ovaries of steel. I'm not saying today's funny girls don't face roadblocks, misogyny. Even in fucking 2023, we still hear "Women aren't funny," right? But before those founding mothers of *TMS,* there was no road. They had to pave it, brick by brick. So I salute you, Lady Lillian. Hope you're still laughing somewhere.

Gina Ross: Sometimes I still reflect back on that dinner we had at Spago, summer of '82, when Lillian splurged on that absurdly overpriced champagne. Her words to the waiter still haunt me: "Your future daughters are going to idolize Gina Ross." That waiter's daughters should have grown up watching Lillian. Generations, scores, of daughters.

Lillian had so much more to do. And a helluva lot more to say.

TRANSCRIPT OF FOLLOW-UP INTERVIEW WITH GLENN MARTIN

(Lillian Martin's brother)

July 26, 2023

[**NOTE:** Second phone interview with Lillian's older brother to discuss Lillian's autopsy, as he's the last surviving person with legal access to it outside of OCME.]

MADELINE: Thanks again for speaking with me, Glenn. I realize this may be a bit of a painful subject to discuss, but I was hoping you could tell me about the aftermath of Lillian's death from your perspective. Were you in touch with the police throughout?

GLENN MARTIN: We were. I mean, it was Sam who first called up and let us know she was missing. From that point, we were connected to the folks over at the NYPD, sporadically, but Sam still kept in touch, which I thought was nice. You know, the *Midnight Show* folks had their own memorial service for her in New York after she'd been missing a year and the writing was on the wall. In Central Park, so fans could come. I think it was Gina Ross who put the whole thing together. We didn't opt to go ourselves. It was gonna be too raw and uncomfortable for us. There were bound to be reporters and Hollywood types there, and we just didn't want any part of that. So we stayed home, watched the clips on *Entertainment Tonight*. But it was after that that Mom and Dad had a gravestone made for Lillian in our local churchyard, right next to their plots, so I guess there was a kind of closure. They're buried there now, beside where Lillian would have gone.

MADELINE: Did the police alert you as soon as her body was recovered?

GLENN MARTIN: I mean, they let us know there was a Jane Doe they'd found who fit her description. Same height, build, hair color, that kind of thing. At that time, there wasn't DNA testing to identify her, but they offered that later. I want to say . . . in 1986? Might have been '87.

MADELINE: So she was already buried in Woodlawn Cemetery at that point. You didn't want to ask to have her moved?

GLENN MARTIN: Sorry, I wasn't clear. We opted . . . well, I suppose *I* opted not to exhume the body and do those tests. You've got to understand, my folks were barely hanging on. I could barely say Lillian's name around them, let alone bring up the idea of digging up her durn body. It was our choice, as the family. So I declined on behalf of all of us. Sometimes you've got to make those tough decisions and let the dead lie.

MADELINE: So . . . I'm sorry. To be clear, you're saying that the body under the Lillian Martin gravestone at Woodlawn Cemetery was never formally identified as Lillian Martin?

GLENN MARTIN: I'm not saying it isn't her, I'm just saying nobody knows for absolute sure . . . and I really wasn't comfortable pulling her out. It wasn't gonna change anything. Either way, she was gone.

MADELINE: Have you ever told anyone about this?

GLENN MARTIN: This isn't the kind of thing that comes up in everyday conversation! You know, I've had plenty of interview requests over the years, but I always declined. I wasn't ready to talk about her. Now I'm retired, my kids are grown, and I'm looking back on my life a little bit. But there was a long stretch there where I was very focused on moving on, first for my folks and their well-being, and then for my family. And I suppose for my sister, too. That grave you're talking about . . . I think it was fans who pulled together the money to buy it, which just shows you how much love there is out there for Lillian. And I think that's worth maintaining. Don't you?

INTERVIEW WITH CARLOS ORTEGA

July 27, 2023

Carlos Ortega, Gina Ross and Sally Schumacher's former superintendent, currently resides at the Crossgate Senior Living Facility in Albany. I elect to rent a car and conduct the interview in person.

Ortega has to be at least eighty-five. Assisted by a walker and a nurse, he meets me in the facility's community room.

CARLOS ORTEGA: Ah, let's see . . . haven't thought about those days in a long while. Didn't know Ms. Martin too well, but her friends . . . I'd been the super of Ms. Ross and Ms. Schumacher's building, 23 East 63rd, you know, for over a decade. They didn't live *together,* not back then, but I had the sense early on, just based on their comings and goings and whatnot, that they were a couple. Not that I ever broadcasted their business, not me. I believe they were considering buying the building's penthouse unit, but in the end, they moved on. Maybe too many heavy memories associated with the place. I was sad to see them go. Funny gals, the both of them. Very, very funny.

MADELINE: I'd love to talk about February 19, 1983, the night of Lillian Martin's disappearance. I know it's been a long while, but can you walk me through what you recall from that night?

CARLOS ORTEGA: Oh. Well, everything I recall, I told the police back then. That might be a better record than anything I tell you today. I'm still sharp, but not that sharp, you know?

MADELINE: Totally understand. You do seem sharp, though, so really anything you can share with me would help.

[*He laughs.*]

Carlos Ortega: All right. You're sharp, too, I can see. I, ah, was working the midnight shift that night. I was the superintendent of the building. I did mention that, didn't I? I'll tell you, I worked my way up the ranks, from being handyman to running the place, worked the night shift steady for two years before the promotion. That was how we did things back then, but that next generation, *pfft*. [*He waves his hand.*] One of my doormen, young kid, quit that January, no notice, nothing. As a building super, you've gotta pick up the slack, you know, so there I was, forty-four years old, working the graveyard shift myself until I could hire someone permanent.

Anyway, Ms. Ross and Ms. Schumacher and their crowd . . . they would come in at all hours. That was the way of comedy, they used to tell me, always howling at the moon. They'd come in doing their, you know, their acts, trying out material on me. I figured half the time they were three sheets to the wind, but I'll tell you, it helped pass the time, all those late hours! In fact, that night, Ms. Schumacher had come in with an inebriated fella going on and on about a marriage proposal that had ruined his life. Lost a girlfriend, was my guess, but I couldn't really tell, he was so far gone. He could hardly talk, was leaning on Ms. Schumacher like she was a life buoy. That was the middle of the shift, and then at the end, in comes Ms. Ross with . . . with herself. Alone. She . . . yeah.

[*Carlos starts to cough. I grab him a glass of water.*]

Madeline: You were saying when Ms. Ross came in—?

Carlos Ortega: Ah, she was upset. Very upset. She'd gone to Ms. Martin's apartment and not found her! You know? Ms. Ross was crying, telling me we needed to call the police right away, so that was what she . . . what we did. You know, dear, I'm feeling very tired.

[*He tries to stand, lurching for his walker.*]

Madeline: Hold on, please. I can help.

Carlos Ortega: I'm sorry, I don't remember anything more.

[*He almost falls out of his chair trying to escape. As I leap up to assist, the nurse comes back in.*]

Nurse: I believe that's enough catching up for one day. Thank you, Miss Cohen. Can I see you back to your room, Mr. Ortega?

NOTES

I listened to the recording of the Ortega interview several times on my drive home.

This is it.

This is the cover story.

TRANSCRIPT OF INTERVIEW WITH GINA ROSS

July 28, 2023

GINA ROSS: All right, Cohen. Iced tea to your liking? Room temperature just right? What else can I do to make you more comfortable after my ten-hour day filming the same two-minute scene in the Village?

MADELINE: I'm good.

GINA ROSS: You have your moments. Seriously, though, I'm beat, so can we get to it? What haven't we yet gone over, back, around, and through again fifteen million times already?

MADELINE: Following up on some new information, I'd like to go back to that night. February 19. That hour you spent moving between Lillian's apartment and your own.

GINA ROSS: I have to assume you're referring to my breakdown in Lillian's hall. Yet again. The whole "why I felt compelled to mourn my friend" conundrum? You're really grasping at straws with this, kid. And it's *really* starting to irk me.

MADELINE: I spoke with your old doorman, Carlos Ortega.

[*Gina closes her eyes.*]

MADELINE: And based on that conversation, along with—

GINA ROSS: Did you seriously pester an old man in his nursing home?

MADELINE: Glenn Martin let me know that the Jane Doe they found in the river was never formally identified as Lillian.

GINA ROSS: Jesus, Cohen, what—

MADELINE: I'm fairly certain you know where I'm heading with this, but I'd love to hear it from you.

GINA ROSS: What the hell do you think we've been doing for the past eight weeks? I *am* telling you the truth, just like I *am* fairly certain that you're one hundred percent losing—

MADELINE: Not the whole truth. It's the in-betweens, Gina. I know I have Lillian in my head, using that word, but I do keep thinking about those gaps. You, down at the bridge, all that fuzzy time. The hour between going to Lillian's place and your own, only a quarter of a mile away. According to Stevie, the time Sally was away from her apartment. When I look at it together, it adds—

GINA ROSS: I'm gonna cut you off here before you go full Holmes on me, Cohen. What are you accusing me of? Say it. You think I murdered Lillian.

MADELINE: No, that's just it. I don't. I think you'd prefer me to think that.

I don't think anyone killed Lillian. I don't even think the toxic patriarchal culture of comedy killed Lillian. Not in the literal sense.

[*Gina stares at me for a long beat, silent.*]

MADELINE: I just want the full story, Gina. That's all I was ever after.

GINA ROSS: Okay. Right.

[*She stands.*]

You want the full story? Maybe, maybe, I can make that happen. On one condition: You've gotta press pause before running off to that big-time editor of yours with your cover story. Do we understand each other?

[*I nod. Gina calls into the office.*]

Hey, Sally? Did you book our flights to Nice yet?

SALLY SCHUMACHER: I was going to do it today. Why?

GINA ROSS: Just hold off a sec.

[*She turns to me with a sigh.*]

All right, Cohen. Before we go any further, moment of truth: How's your French?

XIV.
SUMMER TRIP

La Pause

(August 2023)

NOTES

August 6

Sally drives our rental car, Gina's in the passenger seat, I'm sitting in the back like their child. We turn off a paved road outside a town called Vence onto an unmarked dirt track.

"Nearly there, Cohen," Gina murmurs.

"You don't need to be nervous," Sally says.

Not sure if she's talking to me or Gina.

Out the window is a pastoral wonderland: rolling hills, cypress trees, a sunflower field, as if we've driven straight into a Van Gogh painting. We approach a fawn-colored château.

As we get out of the car, a yellow Lab runs out to greet us.

Then a woman emerges from the house. I'm going to have to find a way to keep breathing, because even after Sally and Gina confessed, I still can't believe I'm here, about to meet her. In person.

I can see how she managed to disappear all this time. Her hair is as long as it was during season one but almost pure white with streaks of slate gray and braided loosely down her back. She's wearing a cotton dress with big pockets, tied with a broad sash at the waist. She wears no makeup. And in no way does her dress or presentation say, *Look at me.* Yet I recognize her instantly. There are other signs of time passing—smile lines, mostly, crinkles at the outer corners of her eyes—but it is very much her, alive, here in France.

I am in awe.

Gina steps in front of me to kiss her cheeks in greeting before I can say anything.

Gina: "Madeline Cohen, meet Faye Blanchet."

I nod. "It's an honor to meet you. Faye."

Faye smiles. "Likewise. Gina and Sally have both spoken very highly of you."

I've heard Lillian's voice thousands of times in old *TMS* sketches, but always as a performer, never as herself. It's deeper than I expected.

"Have they? That's reassuring. I half suspected they brought me all the way out here to hide my body in a sunflower field."

Gina smirks. "Don't get complacent. We haven't ruled it out yet."

"Come and sit. There's a table in the sun around this way. *Foufou, assez, non*, leave her alone." Faye brushes away the dog. "Can I get you all something to eat first?"

She disappears and then minutes later brings out a spread of cheese, bread, fruit, and cornichons, a bowl of salad, and beverages. Once everyone's been served, Faye motions to my cell phone. "Do you want to record?"

"Are you sure you're ready?"

"I was ready when Gina called, asking if she could bring you along. So yes. Go ahead. Red button. Great. Where should we start?"

IN-PERSON INTERVIEW— FAYE BLANCHET, GINA ROSS, AND SALLY SCHUMACHER

MADELINE: Let me just prop it here, out of the breeze. This place is gorgeous, by the way.

FAYE: My late husband, Claude, was a banker, but he hated the city. We wanted to retire someplace quiet, so we came out here fourteen years ago.

[*She motions at the landscape, in the direction of a vineyard we passed on the way here.*]

MADELINE: Do you find it tough to be immersed in French culture, which is so centered on wine, given your history?

FAYE: There was an adjustment period, along with everything else. Maybe that made it easier; the upheaval was a fresh start to stop doing the things that were harming me. But there's this concept in recovery circles that you have to treat the central urge or need or hurt or whatever it is, or everything you do to stop habitually drinking or using is going to continue to be a white-knuckle battle.

GINA: "Central hurt," that was Bobby for you. He was the real issue, and everything else stemmed from that. In my opinion.

FAYE: Bobby, but also fame. With both, I was in a difficult position. I couldn't figure out how to escape, and in my youth and my panic, I tried all sorts of things to free myself.

MADELINE: Does it bother you that your legacy is wrapped up in drugs and alcohol? I've always found it reductive, this narrative that it happened in a vacuum. Like it was preordained, instead of a direct result of the environment you were dropped into. They did it to Janis Joplin, too—sold this idea that she was weak, somehow. Tragically flawed. It takes any blame off the industry and the men that surrounded her. I've always seen that in your story too. That was my angle for this piece.

Faye: I think that's interesting from a critical perspective, but in terms of me, looking back on my own legacy? I don't pay any attention to it. Neither good nor bad. I'm being very honest when I say that. The thing about fame is that everybody knows everything about you. I *hated* that. It wasn't the only issue in my life, far from it, but it held a magnifying glass up to everything else.

I felt like a burning ant. I wanted people to know nothing about me. So in a way, if the public has a gross misconception about my life, that's preferable. It means they don't really know me at all, which is what I wanted all along. But I can now understand that there are people out there, like you, Madeline, who are driven by wanting to arrive at real truths. And I respect that.

Sally: It's been a long road, holding on to all this.

Faye: I know it has. For me as well, but you two, still being in the middle of it all in a lot of ways . . . that's part of why I said yes to today. It's too much. Forever is too long.

Gina: Listen, I was prepared to keep going. I was even subtle about Bobby.

Madeline: You were more subtle about Bobby than he himself was.

Faye: Bobby is disarming, though. People trust him implicitly.

Madeline: I mean, he is charming, in a way.

FAYE: I think he probably believes everything he's told you. I don't know what he said, but I'm sure he's convinced himself that this was our past, our love story, that there was no shadow on it besides, you know, my death. Because that's what narcissists do. They rewrite the story the way that best suits them.

MADELINE: Gina said sociopath, but would you say he's a narcissist?

FAYE: I don't say anything about him, and that's the point. I got out. Thanks to this one.

[*Faye reaches out and takes Gina's hand.*]

I will tell you, I *loved* Bobby. For the good parts of him: his earnestness, his brilliance. That's what made it harder to pull myself free. But it was almost textbook, what he did to me. I was *so young*. I didn't know about relationships; I believed everything he told me.

I didn't intend to get so deeply involved with him. I was used to seeing Sam and Kent and Stevie flirting with everything that moved, and I thought, "Well, he's cute. Why not accept his invitation?" Just a date, right? But gosh, Bobby was adorable. We had very different backgrounds, but he acted as if any similarity—not being close with our parents, for example—was an earthshaking synchronicity. And he was so complimentary. I was *brilliant*. I wasn't just beautiful, I was *from another world, an angel*, it hurt his heart to look at me!

He gave me gifts—I would mention my affection for park squirrels, and two days later, I'd find a squirrel brooch wrapped up for me in my office. Generous sexually, too. I wasn't a virgin when I met Bobby. There was a boy in college I'd slept with a few times experimentally, then fled when he wanted to call it a relationship. Now, that poor guy from my undergraduate psychology course was not particularly impressive in bed—I certainly hope he's improved since then—but Bobby was different. Older, more experienced. He'd been married, for goodness' sake.

MADELINE: I did want to ask you about that.

Faye: Did I know Bobby was married when we started dating? Yes and no. He told me they were estranged, finalizing their divorce. She was crazy, it was unhealthy, he was trying to extricate himself as gracefully as possible.

I didn't expect to meet Yuna—she moved out before I ever stayed the night—but then I was walking to One Astor one day, late October, Halloween costumes everywhere, and this woman steps out, walking backward to block my way. At first I thought it was some sort of performance art. Times Square, you never knew. So I'm smiling along, trying not to be rude, and it takes me a while to understand what she's saying through her accent. "You're the new me. He'll get sick of you too and leave you with nothing and nowhere to go. Hope you're happy now, you little slut, because you won't be for long."

By that point I had reached the front doors and security had taken note. I was obviously very rattled, but I felt for her. Her heart was shattered, and I was culpable, clearly. But then a few months later, she stopped me again outside Bobby's place. He wasn't with me—I think she'd have run off if she'd seen him. She grabbed my arm, that's what frightened me, but when I replay it now, I think I overreacted. There was a painting up in the apartment that had been her grandmother's and she wanted it back, but I was too flustered to listen. Believe it or not, it was a street-corner vendor who broke it up. He grabbed her, I ran inside, and the doorman called the police. Later, Bobby encouraged me to file a restraining order. Turns out I filed it on the wrong person.

Madeline: She's doing well, for what it's worth. I spoke with her. She's married to a diplomat and works for a nonprofit.

Faye: Thank you for telling me that. I'm really pleased to hear it. The Yuna situation, the restraining order, it was an entry point for Bobby to become worried about me. Protective. And then in short order, overbearingly controlling. If I pushed back, said I did not need an escort or to report my every movement to him when we weren't together, he accused me of being immature, naïve about the dangers of the city, a country mouse, essentially, that would have already been eaten by a cat if it weren't for him looking out for me.

And this was a smart tack to take, because there was a lot about the city that terrified me. My landlord, for one, who today we would call a stalker, and better yet, one with a key to my apartment. But it wasn't just the city. I was . . . fundamentally unprepared for the changes that success in the public eye would bring. It had happened so quickly, like an amusement park ride, too much of a blur to think, "Where are we going? What does this lead to?" When people started to recognize me, to ask for autographs, write me fan mail and wait outside the studio so they could take a photo, I was thrown completely off-kilter. This was the goal for Sam and Kent; it was what they'd dreamed of. Fame and success. I was happy for them. I felt like they needed me to keep being a Townie so they could climb even higher.

[*She sips her water. Then she laughs. Shakes her head.*]

No, that's bullshit. And also reductive. I got caught up in the game of it, too. As much as I disliked the notoriety, I loved the internal starting gun and sprint from those Monday-morning pitch battles to Friday night, seeing who would come out on top. I used to play league chess in high school. The competitiveness of that writers' room activated the same part of my brain. It took me a few weeks to cotton on to what you needed to do to stay relevant and make it to air, and that if you had a week of not having your ideas make it, you'd have to fight twice as hard the next episode and so on.

I hadn't seen it clearly at first. Kent and Sam and Stevie and me, we came in as a team. But one week, I pitched an idea, and it was sort of . . . gently stolen from me. Pried out of my hands, given to Kent and Sally instead. And I thought, oh. Maybe I do need to fight a little dirty.

Madeline: The potato sketch.

Gina: We talked a lot about that one, actually, for a variety of reasons.

FAYE: I'm still really proud of that one. Obviously, *TMS* has done just fine without my input, but that's the direction I would have taken the show myself, had I been at the helm. More of a *Kids in the Hall* type of comedy. Do you know them? Pure absurdism, less topical satire. It is interesting, though, that the bulk of the surrealist troupes are male only. Women are the feed. Only men are allowed to be ridiculous. Of course there are exceptions, like Miriam Margolyes in *Blackadder* . . . oh, but I'm rambling.

[*She may be rambling, but I can see a glimmer in her eye that wasn't there a moment before. A certain professional authority.*]

All this is to say that after the potato sketch incident, I started writing with Gina.

GINA: You and Kent as my writing partners might be the most fun I've ever had. Until I left to do screenplays with Sal, of course.

[*Sally leans over and gives Gina a kiss.*]

FAYE: It *was* fun, wasn't it? It felt more like what improv had offered me creatively. More immediacy, tossing everything out there, upping the ante. But I actually think the fact that you came from stand-up, which relies on a great deal more preparation, made our writing more interesting and balanced. You could rein me in a little. In a good way.

GINA: Offer's still out, anytime you want to work on anything. Under any pseudonym you want.

MADELINE: From a fan's perspective, that would be amazing.

FAYE: No, that's all behind me. And I'll tell you why: I became *such* an asshole. Even Sally would admit that, wouldn't you?

SALLY: Oh, I have! I love you, but you were never some perfect little princess.

Faye: Nor did I want to be.

Gina: Cohen and I talked a lot about that, too. She made a pretty decent point about archetypes. Looking back at our old crew, we were polarized. The bitch, the Rapunzel, the slut. I'd argue there's actually a wide variety of flavors out there when it comes to female funny, but once the audience has decided what you are, it's next to impossible to break out of that. I don't think that's true for white guys. I mean, look at Bobby's whole career. He gets to play anything he wants.

Faye: That's why I pulled the stunts that I did, to undermine the way everybody saw me. To be flagrant and get called out. But nobody *ever* called me out! Poor Stevie. I lifted ideas from him all the time. Talk about punching down. They weren't even great pitches. I felt this rot growing in me. I used to get ulcers and chug Pepto-Bismol the way you guys drank whiskey. And then, of course, I started drinking whiskey too. One of the gang. From there, it snowballed fast.

Madeline: Was Bobby into the party scene?

Faye: He pretended to be. He would fake being drunk, going toe to toe with everyone, but he'd pour his drink out when no one was looking and observe. File things away for later use. Same with weed, same with coke. He did not like being out of control. He liked *me* to be out of control, so he could be forced to take care of me and then judge me for it. And the more he judged me, the more I wanted to do it, these knee-jerk micro rebellions.

We'd all be out downtown and he'd be watching and I would feel his condemnation like a hair-dryer blast, and then I'd look the other way and total strangers would wave at me, as if we'd met before, and I just felt the strongest desperation to run. But it was coupled with near-total paralysis. Like I was physically trapped by this life, by the choices I'd made, by my love for my boyfriend and my job, and I knew, of course I knew, that I should be grateful for it all. How many people would have killed to be in my position? So I ran in small ways. Sniffing and pill popping and then, God help me, injecting.

Although that, I think, was different. At that point, I did not fully wish to be alive. Bobby had systematically stripped away my confidence, any core sense of who I was underneath all the fame nonsense and the day-to-day frantic scramble to be the most influential cast member of *The Midnight Show*. So when he tossed me an impossible ultimatum—quit acting or we're done—then kicked me out of that house in the hills, I felt like I was already dead. Like . . . I simply no longer existed without him there to tell me who I was.

Classic coercive abuse, I now know. He was very good at it. Whenever he pushed too hard, he backtracked, groveled, debased himself, begged for forgiveness. I'm not sure whether this was something he learned from his mother—I know they had a difficult relationship—but I stopped analyzing him a long time ago. He's a damaged person, and he can only find peace within himself by terrorizing the people he purports to love.

GINA: Or through enlightenment. Don't forget, he's achieved Nirvana.

MADELINE: When did you realize the truth about him? About your relationship?

FAYE: Some part of you knows what's happening while it's happening, but you're too afraid to face up to it, because, first of all, acknowledging the truth means admitting you've been scammed. Dealing with heartbreak is difficult enough, then add to it the logistics of extricating yourself from a life with someone, which was terrifying for a young person with limited knowledge of how to be an adult. But once it was done, and Kent and Gina, these angels on earth, got me through the worst of my addiction recovery and back on a plane to New York, I woke up and realized that I was lucky to be clear of Bobby Everett.

And Nolan, bless his memory, he was a godsend. He kept everything so light, upbeat. I'd want to relapse, I'd tell him, and he'd laugh, say, "Right on schedule, Lillie. You're doing great! So what you do now is just have a cup of coffee with me and get on with the rest of your day instead." The itch to use started to feel like this petulant little imp in my brain that would have a temper tantrum from time to time, and I learned to ignore it. Lovingly. Playfully. That was Nolan's way, and it worked for me.

[*She pauses, emotional.*]

I hope I didn't hurt him too badly, doing what I did.

Sally: I don't think you can draw a line between your death and his, Faye, and I'm being serious when I say that. I've played it out over the years, and I think he was sick for a lot longer than we knew.

Madeline: So what really happened on the night of . . . well, your death?

Faye: I'll start with what almost happened. I very nearly threw myself off the Williamsburg Bridge. Just like everyone thinks.

Gina: Not everyone. You should have heard some of the theories this one came out with—

Sally: Let her *talk,* Gina!

Gina: Yeah yeah yeah, I'm the worst. [*She mimes locking her mouth.*] Old habits die hard.

Faye: Thank God for your big mouth. It's what saved my life. After what Bobby did that night—well, that whole week, really—I was petrified. He'd been back not fifteen minutes before he had me almost completely back under his control. Back in his bed, at a hotel this time, happy, but in a sickened way, hating myself for how much easier it was to just let him take the steering wheel again. And then the stunt on camera. The wedding.

[*She's gripping the arms of her patio chair very tightly.*]

I didn't know if it was real or not. It was a gag, clearly, but I had met that man before, the reverend, and when we both left the stage, he said, "Best wishes to the bride" to me, as if it were real. And Bobby, right before I was about to go on for a news reporter bit, pulled me into him and whispered, "We'll be together forever now."

I went to the bathroom between setups and vomited. I don't know how I got through the rest of that episode. It was a nightmare. And I thought—I *knew*—Bobby would never release me. I wasn't Yuna. We were this beautiful famous couple that America was in love with, and he was never going to let that go.

It coalesced from that point. The Winthrop's after-party. I went outside. He followed. I told him I didn't want to be married, that we needed to get an annulment if the marriage was real, and he laughed at me, called me an idiot, said of course it wasn't real. Then it got nastier. I was ungrateful, unworthy, stupid, a child. Kent broke it up, but only physically. Not in my brain. I ran off with all that scrolling through my head like ticker tape. I was worthless. I needed to escape, forever. From comedy, which was making me monstrous, from fame making me terrified, from him. And what else was there? So a full escape it would be.

Two things saved me. One, it was a beautiful night. Cold but clear. There was a reflection of the moon on the East River, snow on the banks. I stood in the exact middle of the walkway on the Williamsburg Bridge and looked out. I thought, "I'm going to miss this." Not life, as in me making my way through it, but the water. The air. The rippling moon. Everything around me that wasn't me, that had nothing to do with me at all. I stood there for a long time, taking one last look. I wasn't even gathering my courage. I wasn't afraid. Just so . . . sad.

The second thing that saved me was Gina Ross's unparalleled bull-headedness.

GINA: I think Madeline here might have me beat. Here you go, Sergeant Cohen: I *did* find her on the bridge that night. That's what took so long. She was smack in the middle of the arch, shivering against the beams and looking down at the water. Nowhere, as she called it. She looked so fucking lost. When I saw her, that's when I started crying. But I knew that wasn't gonna help matters, so instead, I began to . . . I don't know. Monologue.

FAYE: She jogged up to me, no preamble, no "Don't do it, Lillian." Just, "So I don't have any personal contacts directly, but I think through friends of friends, if you know what I'm saying, I think we could arrange to have Bobby taken out. Permanently."

[*Her Gina impression is un-freaking-canny. Sally turns away to cover her laughter.*]

GINA: I do not sound like that.

FAYE: "We both know you're not the problem, he is. What you're doing here is absurd, and you're smart. I know we can crack this, I swear we can. Let's come up with another solution." I was so tired. I sat down cross-legged on the pavement, and Gina sat facing me. I said, "He's never going to let me go." She said, "I know. He's a fucking psycho." And I laughed. I really needed that. But I was also concerned that she seemed to be serious about murdering Bobby!

GINA: That was my actual plan until we came up with a better one.

MADELINE: Which was to fake your death.

FAYE: We sat for over an hour in the cold there, huddled up, chatting away like we were at a slumber party. We got around to what we would have done if *The Midnight Show* had never happened.

GINA: I'd have been serving drinks at the Round until I inevitably turned into Holly. Low-hanging tits and all.

FAYE: And I said I'd have been studying for my PhD in French literature at Boston University. Gina said, "There. Good. Do that. But not at BU. Let's just get you to France, shall we?" It blurs from there. I think we doubled back to dump my bag in the park, make it look like I'd left it there before jumping, though we took my apartment key.

GINA: Before you ask yet again, yes, it was at that point that we went back to her apartment together. Lillian waited in the alley while I got what she needed. Her doorman knew me, so I went right on up, told him I was looking for her. I had her key, remember, so I let myself in, grabbed her passport, a change of clothes, a hat, et cetera. The stop was easy enough to explain away to the cops, at least—I was bereft, searching for my friend, exploring all possibilities of where she was. No one has ever grilled me on it to the extent that you did.

MADELINE: Well, you picked the perfect cover. Sobbing in Lillian's hallway. I assume most interviewers would be uncomfortable pressing on that. Whereas I'm a failed comedian and therefore extremely comfortable feeling uncomfortable.

GINA: As we've borne witness to repeatedly. Anyway, on the night in question, Lillian and I then went to my apartment, where *yes,* we ran into your new pal Carlos. Had a real heart-to-heart, made an appeal to the guy—he was such a supporter of mine and Sally's, and I told him we'd take care of him for a good long while if he'd cooperate. Corroborate, rather. We cooked up his testimony together: He would say that I came back, *alone, myself,* around five A.M., at which point he and I called the police. But what *really* happened between four and five A.M., that gap in your precious timeline: I knocked for Sally, clued her in, and she stepped out, quietly, so Stevie wouldn't wake up from his sofa stupor. Fast-forward a few hours, and we got Lillian on the next flight out of JFK that morning under the name Faye Martin.

FAYE: I shaved my head, remember?

GINA: How could I forget?

FAYE: I changed clothes, dressed up like a punk. We ripped one of Gina's T-shirts and reattached the sleeve with safety pins. Sally even gave me a guitar to carry on to sell the effect.

SALLY: It was lying around. I never even played the thing.

MADELINE: So you did know, Sally. From the beginning.

SALLY: Who else could have handled the practical side of these arrangements?

MADELINE: And nobody recognized you?

FAYE: Not a soul.

GINA: Now, remember, this is 1983. No passport scans back then, no easy tracing. And we'd lucked out with that "Megapolitan" blizzard the week before—flights were still being rebooked that weekend, with airline workers overwhelmed, the airport chaotic. Perfect backdrop to blend in, glide through. Her guitar case was lined with cash we'd donated to the cause. The rest is history. Lillian Martin, gone.

SALLY: It was stressful, I'll be honest. After she left, we kept waiting for the other shoe to drop, but it was easy enough for the police to believe that it was an accident, drugs. People were shouting about other theories, and it tipped everything into question. Too many possibilities, no answers.

GINA: Meanwhile, Lillian was nowhere. Dead. Memorialized. And that Jane Doe who emerged from the depths of the river a year later, well—she didn't hurt matters either. Poor thing. At least she got a nice gravesite out of it, whoever she was.

MADELINE: So no one knows who she is, even now. Does that bother you?

GINA: Doesn't keep me up at night. What would have been her other fate, sitting in a morgue for all eternity? Burial in a mass grave? At least this gives her a grave that people visit, flowers—she wouldn't have had that otherwise. And a year had passed without anyone identifying her. It wasn't going to happen. How many young women disappear every year, Cohen, without any fanfare? Without so much as a peep? We could at least give one of them a real resting place.

MADELINE: And you gave Bobby an annual photo op, which I'm sure he appreciates.

GINA: So long as he still thinks she's dead, I'm not complaining.

MADELINE: Have you all stayed in touch this whole time?

GINA: No. That didn't seem prudent. But what was it, 1998? Sally and I got a letter from a newly married academic named Faye Blanchet who lived near Nice and wondered whether we might want to come for a visit. Even if I hadn't figured out it was Lillian, I think we would have shown up just for the vacation.

FAYE: It was 1997. You were in *People*, photos of your wedding, and it made it into the papers here. That was the only time I ever felt like I was missing out. I was sad I hadn't been a part of that. So I took a chance, wrote a letter, and . . . we've been meeting up every year since then, haven't we?

SALLY: A lot's changed over those years. We've watched our kids grow up.

FAYE: I've got a grandchild on the way.

GINA: You didn't tell me that!

FAYE: I was waiting to tell you in person!

Madeline: Sorry, just . . . did you ever worry that it would expose you, if anybody saw you with Gina?

Faye: You know, one nice thing about the French is they could not give *deux merdes* about American comedy. Unless you're Jerry Lewis. Nobody recognized me when I moved here, and I mean nobody. I bleached my hair when it started growing in, but still. It was refreshingly humbling to turn up at the Sorbonne and have their only question for me be how I could explain the employment gap following my undergraduate degree. I went by my middle and last names, Faye Martin, like on the flight—and other than that, I just blended right in, settled into a job editing a literary magazine, very low-key but also interesting, and that was it. I improvised my way into a new life.

Madeline: Did your husband know you'd been a public figure back in the US?

Faye: I told him early on, as soon as I realized he was a wonderful human being and I did not want to start an authentic relationship based on a very big lie. He was incredibly empathetic. He had a full life already, and so to him, it was a point of interest, part of what made me, me, not a flaw. I didn't tell my son until after Claude died. Michel was surprised, to say the least! He's watched a few old episodes of *TMS* since then and reports back which sketches he finds funny. It's sweet. But aside from him, yeah, no one knows. Just us here around this table.

Gina: Which leads us to . . . this very moment.

[*Gina and Sally stare at me with a look that could best be described as locked and loaded.*]

Madeline: I am curious why you agreed to this interview, given the inherent . . . you know, repercussions.

FAYE: Well. I would be lying if I said I wasn't acutely aware of a potential fallout. But on the other hand, I've experienced a kind of droning, chronic stress over the years, forever waiting for the axe to fall.

GINA: This article would be a sharp fucking axe, Faye.

FAYE: I recognize that. My assumption is that there would be an immediate impact once your piece was published, Madeline. Even if you leave out the details of my name, address, all that, I expect reporters will jump on the story and try to make their name by tracking me down. Ultimately, I'm sure someone will succeed in doing so. Of course they will. So I expect I'll have to grapple with a lot of public scrutiny over a finite period of time. Potentially some legal issues as well. Actually, we should probably all wrap our heads around that—

SALLY: We will do whatever we need to, if this is what you want, Faye. But I have to say, what you're describing is an undoing of everything you've built over the past four decades. And that's kind of hard to watch as your friend.

FAYE: No, not everything. I still have my family, your support, my circle here. Just not my privacy. But like I said, when you factor in the counterstress of holding on to this secret—

GINA: You're describing a balanced scale where those two have equal weight. I think that's fantasy logic. Madeline, do you have a journalistic opinion here?

MADELINE: Faye, earlier you mentioned a finite period of time. How are you defining that?

FAYE: I'd guess . . . I don't know, three to five years? Before everyone gets bored with the story and it all settles down?

GINA: Longer.

MADELINE: I have to agree. It would almost certainly be longer. And even then, I don't think you could expect your life to revert to what you've become accustomed to. It would quiet down, sure, but there would likely be a ripple effect. I want to be honest about that before . . . yeah.

FAYE: One thing I will mention: I would prefer to reach out to certain people myself prior to publication. I'd rather they hear the full truth from my perspective rather than finding out from a headline pop-up. I don't expect them to forgive me, necessarily, but I still think I owe them that much.

SALLY: You thinkin' about Sam, hon?

FAYE: Kent, too. Maybe Stevie. My parents have passed. My brother . . . he should hear it from me first. But Sam was the first one to pop into my mind. It really would be nice to see him again.

MADELINE: I have to ask . . . did you ever have any romantic feelings for Sam? Or was it really all one-sided, like he says?

FAYE: Oh my gosh, is that what he thinks? I guess I can see why. No, it wasn't one-sided at all. It was just complicated.

Early in our friendship, I thought I would wind up marrying Sam. Trouble was, I met him when I was nineteen years old. I wasn't ready for a rest-of-my-life romance. Still wasn't ready when we moved to New York. And then Bobby happened and derailed us until there was no possible way back to each other.

It's funny. Looking back, I've had such a wonderful, rich life and a healthy, life-affirming love with Claude, and I miss him desperately, but I still feel some ruefulness when it comes to Sam. He's been married for ages, hasn't he? So obviously it all worked out the way it was meant to, just with a period of drama to punctuate it.

GINA: Sam's divorced.

SALLY: A year, it's been, I think.

FAYE: I'm sorry to hear that.

[*Gina smirks. Sally kicks her under the table.*]

Now, in terms of Bobby finding out. That is something I'd like to find a way to buffer myself from. I don't want to talk to him. He's not going to take it well. He'll find it . . . mortifying.

MADELINE: The complete story does not shine a very positive light on him. And he seems to thrive on a tightly controlled personal narrative.

SALLY: This could destroy his reputation.

GINA: Least that's one silver lining.

SALLY: Yes and no. I worry what his response to that might be.

FAYE: I guess that's something I can prepare for but not necessarily prevent. I mean, it's done, right? I've met this lovely reporter. It's up to her now.

MADELINE: I guess it is. But let me ask directly: If you got to choose, would you rather the general public continue to believe you're dead?

FAYE: Yes. But as I said, it's not my call. You figured it out. You would have landed on the correct theory whether you'd met me in person or not, and presumably gone to press with it. So now the ball is in your court.

GINA: I'm gonna interject here—shocking, I know. Madeline, at the beginning of all this, you set out to write a nuanced, incisive article about the toxic patriarchy in comedy. I don't know, color me naïve, but I bought into it. I guess everybody's got to make a living, but what happened to your feminist high horse? Did it run off? I'm starting to miss it.

MADELINE: Didn't you tell me the most feminist thing you can do is what's best for yourself?

[*Gina throws up her hands.*]

FAYE: Hang on a second, Gina. Let me just say something. Madeline, Gina's been calling me throughout your interviews, keeping me apprised in real time. And I did feel compelled by your pitch. It made me examine aspects of my young adulthood that I hadn't looked at for a long time, maybe in a different light. So I've got to ask—what drew you to this story? You mentioned you're a comedian yourself?

MADELINE: A failed one. I guess I've always grappled with what it means to be not just a woman in comedy as a field but simply a funny woman?

When you're talking about humor, that's a form of intelligence, a point of view, personal autonomy, and these are things that women still have to fight to justify. Like, I find that on dates, when the guy says, "You're really funny," it's not a compliment. It's like, "Check, please."

I guess the experience of trying and failing professionally has made me feel all the more in awe of women who've made it, put up with all those obstacles, and managed to break new ground in a field that's still so male-dominated. But I've always wondered what the personal cost of that is.

And in terms of why you? Well . . . you've always been my favorite.

GINA: I'll pretend I didn't hear that.

MADELINE: Do you ever miss it, Faye? Not the competitive aspect of comedy, obviously. The creative side.

FAYE: A little. But not enough to want to do it again. I don't miss academia either, by the way. I'm happily retired.

GINA: We're talking around this and through this. Are you still planning to write this, Madeline?

MADELINE: I'm not tossing out the article, if that's what you're asking. I'm writing something.

GINA: Okay. Can you be more specific?

[*And this is it. Time to choose.*]

GINA: [*Her jaw clenches.*] Cohen?

MADELINE: Listen. My ego is incredibly gratified by the fact that I've correctly solved a mystery. But ultimately—brace yourself, Gina—I agree with you. I don't think anything from the night of Faye's disappearance onward is relevant to the article I set out to write.

GINA: [*She smacks the table.*] Attagirl.

SALLY: Slow down. What are we saying here?

MADELINE: The forty-year-old cold case? I'm not gonna touch that. A story about the toxic culture of comedy isn't going to land me my first cover byline, but . . . I'm okay with that. You've made a beautiful life here. I'm not prepared to blow that up.

[*Faye reaches out across the table to grip my hand and lets out a slow breath.*]

GINA: How 'bout it, Faye? Can you handle the counterstress of holding on to this secret a little while longer?

FAYE: I mean, just talking about it now is helping. Madeline, you've got this look—

[*She mirrors me, wide-eyed, clenching my glass of water like a microphone. Spot-on imitation.*]

As if you have a dozen follow-up questions piling up in your brain.

MADELINE: I do! They all fall under the category of off the record, though. Hang on a sec, I'm just going to turn this—

[*End of transcript*]

POSTSCRIPT

Rolling Stone

WHAT REALLY HAPPENED TO LILLIAN MARTIN

The iconic comedian's untimely death, long attributed to her own fragility and excesses, was fueled by the cutthroat world of late night, a misogynistic comedy culture, and an emotionally abusive romantic relationship

EXCLUSIVE

By Madeline Cohen
October 2023 Issue

Lillian Martin famously disappeared from the Williamsburg Bridge on the night of February 19, 1983. But for those who were paying attention, she began to disappear long before that . . .

DEADLINE

November 1, 2023

Netflix Locks in Showrunner Power Couple

EXCLUSIVE: Deadline can reveal that Netflix has re-upped its exclusive with Astor Wild, the production shingle helmed by writer-showrunner Gina Ross and her wife and writing partner, Sally Schumacher, with the duo's first limited series, 'Young and Funny,' pitched as 'Girls' meets 'The Midnight Show,' expected to commence filming in New York this summer . . .

People

November 13, 2023, Issue

REAL ESTATE

Home

Funnyman Sam Petrosian is moving—and his incredible Malibu mansion is for sale for $15 million. See inside!

To: Madeline Cohen
From: Faye Blanchet
Date: November 18, 2023 11:52 AM
Re: Checking in

Hello Madeline,

Just writing to say hi. I've been thinking of you, picturing you in New York, strolling in Central Park, bustling through Times Square with one of those scalding deli coffees in hand, and I almost miss it all! (Emphasis on the *almost*.)

I also wanted to let you know that I read your piece. Not a cover story, I know, but I hope you're proud of it nonetheless. It made me cry—and not just from relief! I think you captured the truth of what happened to me in a way that will resonate with a lot of women, not just true crime readers. And by ending your story where you did, with that question still unanswered, you've also protected the life I've built here. I cannot tell you how grateful I am for that.

Should you ever find yourself itching for a getaway with a view of acres of vines, you know where to find me. I've got another visitor coming in a few days, if you can believe it—a very welcome blast from the past. Not sure how long Sam's staying, or where things will go after all this time. But feel free to pop by whenever you like. I'll always make room for our erstwhile comedian.

All my gratitude, truly.

With affection,
Faye

To: Madeline Cohen
From: Gina Ross
Date: December 18, 2023 1:55 PM
Re: What are you up to?

So I told you about that Netflix deal, yeah? We're looking to build out our writers' room. Seeking: a resourceful (irritatingly tenacious) comedian with an incisive viewpoint on women in comedy. Preferably with a journalism background (cover story byline not a requirement). Pay: competitive.

Know anybody?

xx Gina

NOTES

February 19, 2024

A text comes in from Gina:

> GINA
> I have to assume your tardiness is the result of a detour to Payard's xoxo

I laugh, text back:

> MADELINE
> Sorry, different detour, but matcha latte incoming.

> GINA
> Clock's ticking.

> MADELINE
> Don't worry. I'll ride my high horse.

> GINA
> 💋

> GINA
> And you call yourself a failed comedian.

I put my phone away, realizing this might be the first time I've ever laughed in a cemetery.

Lillian Martin's gravesite is modest by Woodlawn standards, but there's no mistaking it. Even after all these years, the plot's still covered with fan tributes. Fresh flowers, a teddy bear dressed up like her coked-up Tooth Fairy character, old cast photos, handwritten letters.

I've brought my own bouquet. Sunflowers, like in Faye's field. A little connection between the woman this gravestone honors and the one who's really been laid to rest beneath it. A message passed between them.

We don't know who Jane Doe is. She's voiceless, faceless, tossed aside. We'll likely never learn her story—but odds are, there were plenty of parallels between her life and Lillian's . . . the only difference is that one of them caught the public's eye.

Peering down at the trinkets left by fans to honor Lillian's most memorable roles, I draw a Yukon Gold potato from my coat pocket and place it among them—then I rest the flowers against the stone.

As I leave, two teens with brightly colored hair approach, quoting the Rogue Sopranos before noting the assortment of offerings, and then:

"Wait. Somebody left a potato? That's—"

"Potato president, right?"

"Ohhh. Was that her? I thought it was—"

I turn around. "It was hers. Nobody else could've come up with that."

The girls look at me like I'm insane.

And that's my cue to go.

"Wait." One stops me. Sheepish. "Can you take our picture? She's our idol."

I smile. Take the phone from her. "Yeah. Mine too."

A fine comedienne in her own right, a beauty for the ages, and the beloved wingwoman of the legendary *Midnight Show* funnymen who have forever changed the game. But it's through the unsolvable mystery of her death that Lillian Martin has truly been canonized, a symbol of tragedy more than comedy: forever young, forever alluring . . . and forever an enigma.

—Philip Horton,
It Started at Midnight: A TMS History

LILLIAN MARTIN PROJECT

Computer files archived.

Case closed.

ACKNOWLEDGMENTS

Re-creating a time and a place is no mean feat, and we are indebted to myriad sources for helping us bring to life the world of 1980s comedy and late-night culture:

Live from New York: The Complete, Uncensored History of Saturday Night Live as Told by Its Stars, Writers, and Guests, edited by James Andrew Miller and Tom Shales; *Saturday Night: A Backstage History of Saturday Night Live* by Doug Hill and Jeff Weingrad; *Wild and Crazy Guys: How the Comedy Mavericks of the '80s Changed Hollywood Forever* by Nick de Semlyen; *Johnny Carson* by Henry Bushkin; *Carson the Magnificent* by Bill Zehme and Mike Thomas; *This Time Together: Laughter and Reflection* by Carol Burnett; *The Princess Diarist* by Carrie Fisher; *Say Everything: A Memoir* by Ione Skye; and *Fame: The Hijacking of Reality* by Justine Bateman.

We benefited hugely from the *New York Times* article "What New York Was Like in the Early '80s—Hour by Hour," as told to Caroline Bankoff, Heather Corcoran, Nancy Hass, and M. H. Miller, and the *New York Times* article "Lives of the After-Party" by Paul Brownfield; as well as listening to Dana Carvey and David Spade's *Fly on the Wall* podcast. Finally, we would be remiss in not thanking the groundbreaking fifty-year institution of *Saturday Night Live* and its wealth of episodes, sketches, and recent anniversary specials, as well as the show's creators, writers, producers, and talent for inspiration.

We would like to attribute these sources for our deeper understanding of the female comic experience: *Not Funny: Essays on Life, Comedy, Culture, Et Cetera* by Jena Friedman; *Bossypants* by Tina Fey; *Yes Please* by Amy Poehler; *Hello, Molly!: A Memoir* by Molly Shannon with Sean Wilsey; *Just the Funny Parts* by Nell Scovell; and *You'll Grow Out of It* by Jessi Klein; as well as numerous articles on the pressures of fame and the toxicity of celebrity culture when it comes to famous young women.

This book would not be possible without our own on-the-ground experiences with comedy: Many thanks to the Groundlings for those Intro Track classes, and to the improv theater and training center The Lab, particularly Shyla Hungerford and Andrea Duffy, for their guidance and instruction. A special shout-out to the bright young NBC pages who gave us an excellent tour of 30 Rock. We're grateful to Donna Gordon for her insider look at the '80s nightlife scene, as well as to Tom Perks for the ins and outs of forensics and police procedure during that era.

Enormous thanks to Amy Einhorn, whose vision and enthusiasm have elevated this story beyond measure, and to Austin Parks for her wonderful insights and attention to detail, along with the rest of the Crown team: Chris Tanigawa, Heather Williamson, Liana Faughnan, Sibylle Kazeroid, and more, with special applause for Ben Wiseman, creator of the stunning cover, and Aubrey Khan, who crafted the incredible interior. Undying-devotion-level appreciation, as ever, to our beloved agent Katelyn Detweiler, as well as Sam Farkas, Denise Page, and the whole JGLM family.

LEE: Endless gratitude to my family: Jeff, who believes in me, always. To Penn and Summer, our resident budding comedians. My mom, Linda, my first reader. My dad, Joe, for all the family productions. My best friends and sisters Jill and Bridge. Jon, Mike, and my Kelly family. And of course, to Jenn: Who's Tigger, who's Eeyore? Depends on the day.

JENN: My love and gratitude to my family, especially Rob, Oliver, and Henry for the constant laughs. Jane, Katie, Jo, Lexi, Adrienne, David for early reads and sharing of memes. My mom (and not just for the NYC 1980s party scene confessions). Last but never least, my writing ride-or-die Lee—let's keep one-upping each other, shall we?

ABOUT THE AUTHORS

LEE KELLY and **JENNIFER THORNE** are the coauthors of the novels *The Antiquity Affair, The Starlets, My Fair Frauds,* and *The Midnight Show*. Independently, Kelly is the author of the acclaimed speculative fiction novels *City of Savages, A Criminal Magic,* and *With Regrets*. Thorne is the *USA Today* bestselling author of *Diavola, Lute,* and the forthcoming *Newbourne Park,* as well as several books for younger readers.